A SONG FOR THE DARK TIMES

When his daughter Samantha calls one morning at 5 a.m., John Rebus knows it's not good news. Her partner Keith has been missing for two days. Rebus fears the worst . . . and knows from his lifetime in the police that his daughter will be the prime suspect. Though he wasn't always the best parent — the job always came first — now his child needs him more than ever. But is he going as a father or a detective? As he travels to the windswept coast of a small place with big secrets, he wonders whether this might be the first time in his life when the truth is the one thing he doesn't want to find . . .

IAN RANKIN

A SONG FOR THE DARK TIMES

Complete and Unabridged

CHARNWOOD
Leicester

First published in Great Britain in 2020 by
Orion
an imprint of The Orion Publishing Group Ltd
London

First Charnwood Edition
published 2021
by arrangement with
The Orion Publishing Group Ltd
London

A catalogue record for this book is available
from the British Library.

ISBN 978–1–4448–4744–4

Published by
Ulverscroft Limited
Anstey, Leicestershire

Set by Words & Graphics Ltd.
Anstey, Leicestershire
Printed and bound in Great Britain by
TJ Books Ltd., Padstow, Cornwall

This book is printed on acid-free paper

In the dark times
Will there also be singing?
Yes, there will also be singing.
About the dark times.

Bertolt Brecht

We love making damaged people
our playthings.

Jon Ronson
So You've Been Publicly Shamed

Prologue

i

Siobhan Clarke walked through the emptied flat. Not that it *was* empty; rather the life had been sucked from it. Packing crates sat the length of the hallway. The kitchen cupboards gaped, as did the door to the tenement stairwell. The window in the main bedroom had been opened to air the place. It looked bigger, of course, without the furniture and the restless figure of John Rebus himself. Bare light bulbs dangled from each ceiling. Some curtains had been left, as had most of the carpeting. (She'd run a vacuum cleaner over all the bedrooms the previous day.) In the hall, she studied the boxes. She knew what they held, each one written on in her own hand. Books; music; personal papers; case notes.

Case notes: one bedroom had been filled with them — investigations John Rebus had worked on, solved and unsolved, plus other cases that had held an interest for him, helping keep him busy in his retirement. She heard footsteps on the stairs. One of the movers gave a nod and a smile as he hefted a crate, turning to go. She followed him, squeezing past his colleague.

'Nearly there,' the second man said, puffing out his cheeks. He was perspiring and she hoped he was all right. Probably in his mid fifties and carrying too much weight around his middle.

Edinburgh tenements could be murder. She herself wouldn't be sorry not to have to climb the two storeys again after today.

The main door to the tenement had been wedged open with a folded triangle of thick cardboard — the corner of a packing case, she guessed. The first mover, tattooed arms bared, had reached the pavement and was making a sharp turn, left and left again, passing through a gateway. Beyond the small paved area — probably a neat garden in the distant past — stood another open door, this one leading to the ground-floor flat.

'Living room?' he asked.

'Living room,' Siobhan Clarke confirmed.

John Rebus had his back to them as they entered. He was standing in front of a row of brand-new bookcases, bought at IKEA the previous weekend. That trip — and the clash of wills during the shelves' assembly — had put more strain on the friendship between Rebus and Clarke than any operation they'd worked on during their joint time in CID. Now he turned and frowned at the box.

'More books?'

'More books.'

'Where the hell do they keep coming from? Didn't we make a dozen trips to the charity shop?'

'I'm not sure you factored in how much smaller this flat is than your old one.' Clarke had crouched to give some attention to Rebus's dog Brillo.

'They'll have to go in the spare room,' Rebus muttered.

'I told you to ditch those old case notes.'

4

'They're sensitive documents, Siobhan.'

'Some are so old they're written on vellum.' The mover had made his exit. Clarke tapped one of the books Rebus had shelved. 'Didn't take you for a Reacher fan.'

'I sometimes need a break from all the philosophy and ancient languages.'

Clarke studied the shelves. 'Not going to alphabetise them?'

'Life's too short.'

'What about your music?'

'Same goes.'

'So how will you find anything?'

'I just will.'

She took a couple of steps back and spun around. 'I like it,' she said. Wallpaper had been removed, the walls and ceiling freshly painted, though Rebus had drawn the line at the skirting boards and window frames. The heavy drapes from his old living room's bay window fitted the near-identical window here. His chair, sofa and hi-fi had been placed as he wanted them. The dining table had had to go — too large for the remaining space. In its place stood a modern drop-leaf, courtesy of IKEA again. The kitchen was a narrow galley-style affair. The bathroom, too, was long and narrow but perfectly adequate. Rebus had baulked at the idea of a refit: 'maybe later'. Clarke had grown used to that refrain these past few weeks. She'd had to bully him into decluttering. Thinning out the books and music had taken the best part of a fortnight, and even then she would sometimes catch him lifting an item from one of the boxes or bags destined for the charity shop. It struck her that he didn't have much in the way of family mementoes or what could be termed 'heirlooms' — no bits and pieces that had belonged to his parents; a handful of framed photos of his ex-wife and his daughter. Clarke had suggested he might want to contact his daughter so she could help him move.

'I'll be fine.'

So she had applied for a week's leave and rented a small van, big enough for runs to IKEA, the charity shop and the dump.

'Cornicing's the same as your old place,' she said, studying the ceiling.

'We'll make a detective of you yet,' Rebus said, hefting more books onto a shelf. 'But let's save the next lesson for after we've had that mug of tea you're about to brew . . . '

At the end of the kitchen was a door leading out to the enclosed rear garden, a large expanse of lawn with an ornamental border. Clarke let Brillo out before filling the kettle. Opening cupboards, she noted that Rebus had rearranged her work of the previous day — obviously there was some system he preferred: pots, tins and packets lower down; crockery higher up. He had even swapped around the cutlery in the two drawers. She popped tea bags into two mugs and lifted the milk from the fridge. It was the old fridge from the upstairs flat — same went for the washing machine. Neither fitted quite right, jutting out into the room. If it were her kitchen, she'd always be bruising a knee or stubbing a toe. She'd told him they wouldn't fit, that he should replace them.

'Maybe later,' had come the reply.

The two movers did not require tea — they seemed to work on a supply of fizzy drinks and vaping. Besides which, they were almost done. She heard them fetching more boxes.

'Living room?' one asked.

'If you must,' Rebus answered.

'One more trip, I reckon. You'll want to lock up after us.'

'Just pull the door shut when you're finished.'

'No last wee sentimental look-see?'

'I've got the meter readings, what else do I need?'

The mover seemed to have no answer to this. Clarke watched him retreat as she took the mugs through.

'Forty years of your life, John,' she said, handing him his tea.

'Fresh start, Siobhan. Keys are going to the buyer's solicitor. Post's being redirected.' He seemed to be wondering if he'd forgotten anything. 'Just bloody lucky this place fell vacant when it did. Mrs Mackay had been here almost as long as me. Son living in Australia, so that's her twilight years taken care of.'

'Whereas you couldn't bear to move even fifty yards.'

He fixed her with a look. 'I can still surprise you, though.' He jabbed a finger towards the ceiling. 'You reckoned they'd be carrying me out of there in a box.'

'Is everyone this cheery when they move house?'

'Maybe you're forgetting why I'm moving.'

7

No, she hadn't forgotten. COPD: Chronic Obstructive Pulmonary Disease. He was finding stairs too much of a chore. So when the For Sale sign appeared in the downstairs front garden . . .

'Besides,' he added, 'two flights wasn't fair on Brillo and those poor wee legs of his.' He looked around for the dog.

'Garden,' Clarke explained.

The pair of them headed through the kitchen and out of the door. Brillo was sniffing his way around the lawn, tail wagging.

'Settled in already,' Clarke commented.

'Might not be so easy for his owner.' Rebus peered up at the tenement windows that surrounded them, then gave a sigh, avoiding eye contact with Clarke. 'You should go back to work tomorrow. Tell Sutherland you don't need the full week.'

'We've stuff to unpack.'

'And you've a murder waiting for you. Speaking of which: any news?'

Clarke shook her head. 'Graham's got his team assembled; doubtful I'd make much of a difference.'

'You'd make a difference,' Rebus countered. 'I think I'm just about capable of lifting things from boxes and failing to find anywhere to put them.'

They shared a smile, turning as the movers arrived. The men entered the living room and reappeared a few seconds later.

'Reckon that's us,' the older man said from the kitchen doorway. Rebus approached him, digging banknotes from his pocket. Clarke watched

8

as Brillo came trotting up to her, settling on his haunches, eyes expectant.

'You going to promise me you'll look after him?' Clarke asked.

The dog angled its head, as if considering how best to answer.

ii

Siobhan Clarke's own flat was just off Broughton Street, across the city from Rebus. One storey up in a tenement she'd been considering moving out of for the past several months. DCI Graham Sutherland had gone from being an occasional colleague — albeit several rungs above her — to her lover. Sutherland headed one of the major incident teams. His own home was in Glasgow, and he'd asked her to move in with him.

'I'll have to think about it,' she'd said. She'd visited his place several times, stayed over just the once. Though divorced, signs of his ex-wife lingered, and she doubted he had bothered to buy a new bed.

'Maybe a flat in the city centre would be more your thing,' he had suggested, without managing to sound enthusiastic, since when he'd directed her towards a couple of properties he'd found online, his emails headed FYI. One of them she'd actually quite liked. Without saying anything, she'd driven through to Glasgow and parked outside the building, getting out and walking around, getting a feel for the area. It was fine, she told herself. It wouldn't be bad.

Then she'd driven home.

Rebus had basically dismissed her this evening. She'd suggested takeaway curry from his favourite place, but he had shooed her out.

'Take a break. Go tell your boyfriend you want back on the team.'

She checked her phone. It was nearly eight o'clock and Sutherland hadn't replied to either of her texts, so she put her jacket on, grabbed her keys and headed downstairs. It was a short drive to Leith police station — she could almost have walked it. She paused halfway to dive into a shop, emerging again with a carrier bag. Parking by Leith Links, she made for the police station and was buzzed in. She climbed the imposing marble staircase to the upper floor and entered the MIT room. Two familiar faces looked up from their computers.

'Aren't you on holiday?' DC Christine Esson asked.

'That's why I'm bringing you souvenirs.' Clarke emptied out the bag of shopping: salted peanuts, crisps, chocolate brownies and bottled water.

'Better than a postcard,' DC Ronnie Ogilvie said, just beating Esson in a dash to the treats.

'Boss gone home?' Clarke asked.

'Meeting at the Big House.' Esson retreated to her desk with her share of the swag. Clarke followed her, peering over her shoulder at the computer screen.

'Rest of the team?'

'You're looking at the late shift.'

'How's it shaping up?'

'You're on a break,' Esson reminded her. 'How's the move going?'

'How do you think?' Clarke had turned towards the wall behind Esson — the Murder Wall. It was covered by a large corkboard covered in blue felt. There were photos of the victim and the locus pinned to it, plus maps, some details of the autopsy, and a staffing rota. Her own name had been crossed out. Typical that she'd arranged to take time off during a really quiet spell, only to have a big case pop up on day one. She'd tried telling the DCI that she could postpone her break, but he'd been adamant: 'John needs you — he'd never say it, might not even know it, but it's the truth.'

'We're getting a bit of outside pressure,' Ronnie Ogilvie said through a mouthful of crisps.

'Because he's rich?'

'Rich and connected,' Esson qualified. 'His father, Ahmad, is worth squillions but thought to be under house arrest somewhere in Saudi Arabia.'

'Thought to be?'

'The Saudis aren't exactly being forthcoming. We have a human rights charity to thank for the gen.'

Clarke was scanning the information on the wall. Salman bin Mahmoud had been a handsome young man. Age twenty-three. Drove an Aston Martin. Lived in a four-storey Georgian town house on one of Edinburgh's best New Town streets. Short black hair and a neat beard. Brown eyes. A couple of the photos

11

showed him smiling but not laughing.

'Not every student gets a DB11 for their birthday,' Clarke commented.

'Or lives in a house with five spacious bedrooms.' Esson was standing next to her. 'Best thing is, he wasn't even studying here.' Clarke raised an eyebrow. 'Enrolled at a business school in London, where he happens to have a lease on a penthouse apartment in Bayswater.'

'So where's the Edinburgh connection?' Clarke asked.

Esson and Ogilvie shared a look. 'You tell her,' Ogilvie said, opening one of the bottles of water.

'James Bond,' Esson obliged. 'He was a nut for James Bond, especially the films, and more specifically the early ones.'

'Meaning Sean Connery?'

'Son of Edinburgh,' Esson said with a nod. 'Apparently both homes are filled with memorabilia.'

'Explains the DB11 but doesn't answer the really big question — what was a rich Saudi student with a James Bond fetish doing in the car park of a carpet warehouse on Seafield Road at eleven o'clock of a summer's night?'

'Meeting someone,' Ogilvie suggested.

'Someone who stabbed him and left him bleeding to death,' Esson added.

'But didn't rob him or even bother to drive away in his expensive car.' Clarke folded her arms. 'Any joy from CCTV?'

'Plenty sightings of the car. Heriot Row to Seafield Road with no obvious stops.'

'Salamander Street's just along the way

— used to be popular with sex workers,' Clarke mused.

'We're checking.'

'Is his mother coming to claim the body?'

'Embassy seem to be taking care of things — reading between the lines, I'd say they don't want her travelling.'

Clarke looked at Esson. 'Oh?'

'Maybe afraid she wouldn't go back.' Esson gave a shrug.

'What did the father do that put him in the bad books?'

'Who knows? The family are from the Hejaz region. I've done a bit of reading and he's by no means the only one under house arrest. The usual charge is corruption. Probably just means he's pissed off a member of the ruler's family. Some pay a hefty fine and are released, but it's not happened to Ahmad yet.'

'It's always the money, isn't it?'

'Not always, but often enough.'

There was a sound behind them of a throat being cleared. When they turned, DCI Graham Sutherland was standing in the doorway, feet apart, hands in the trouser pockets of his charcoal suit.

'I must be seeing things,' he said. 'Because I could have sworn you were only halfway through a week's much-needed leave.'

'I come bearing gifts.' Clarke gestured towards the desk.

'There's no place for bribery in Police Scotland. Detective Inspector Clarke. Can I invite you to step into my office for a carpeting?'

He started towards the door at the far end of the room, opening it and gesturing for Clarke to precede him into the cramped, windowless space.

'Look,' she began as soon as the door was closed. But Sutherland held up a hand to silence her, seating himself at his desk so that he was facing her.

'Shocking as this news will be, we're managing fine without you, Siobhan. I've got all the resources I need and a blank cheque should I need more.'

'The flat move's almost done, though.'

'Great news — you can put your feet up for a couple of days.'

'What if I don't want to put my feet up?'

Sutherland's eyes narrowed but he said nothing. Clarke held her hands up in a show of surrender.

'But be honest with me — how's it really going?'

'A clear motive wouldn't go amiss. And what friends we've been able to talk to haven't exactly been forthcoming.'

'They're scared of something?'

Sutherland shrugged and ran a hand down his burgundy tie. He was in his early fifties and not far shy of retirement, but proud that he had kept his figure along with his hair, the latter the subject of unfounded rumours of a weave. 'We're getting help from the Met — they're looking at his London contacts. Seems he wasn't a great one for going to classes. Nightclubs and racecourses were more his thing.' He broke off.

'None of which should be of any interest to you.'
He changed position slightly on his chair. 'How's
John doing?'

'He says he can manage. He'd much rather I
was at work, being useful and productive.'

'Is that so?' Sutherland managed a thin smile.
Clarke felt she was losing this particular battle.

'Will I see you later?' she enquired.

'Relegated to the sofa?'

'I probably couldn't be that cruel.'

'Maybe I'll risk it then.'

'I bought extra provisions on the off-chance.'

He nodded his thanks. 'Give me another hour
or two?'

'Careful you don't burn out, Graham.'

'If I do, they'll need a fresh, fully rested
replacement. Know anyone who'd fit the bill?

'I'll give it some thought, DCI Sutherland . . .'

iii

Rebus had to give a slight tug on Brillo's lead.
Having been for their evening walk to the
Meadows, the dog had made for the tenement's
main door.

'We're both going to have to get used to this,'
Rebus said, pushing open the gate. 'But trust
me, in time you can get used to just about
anything.' He had managed to avoid looking up
at the curtainless window of his old living room.
When he unlocked the door to his new flat, he
caught a slight aroma beneath the smell of fresh
paint: the merest trace of the previous occupant.

It wasn't really perfume; it was a blend of who they'd been and the life they had lived. He had a note of Mrs Mackay's new address in Australia, in case the redirection service failed. He had left something similar in his old flat. He had an inkling it had been bought to be let out to students — no real surprise there. Marchmont had always been student turf, the university just the other side of the Meadows. Rebus had only very occasionally had to complain about a noisy party, and even then not for several years. Were students cut from different cloth these days? Less rowdy; more . . . well, studious?

Walking into the living room, manoeuvring between boxes, he realised his computer had yet to be unpacked. No rush: they weren't doing the broadband for another couple of days. At Siobhan's suggestion he had one night begun composing a list of people he needed to notify of his changed circumstances. It hadn't even covered half a sheet — and come to think of it, when was the last time he'd seen it? He could hear Brillo in the kitchen, feasting on dry food and fresh water. Rebus hadn't bothered with dinner; he never seemed particularly hungry these days. There were a few bottles of beer in the kitchen, and several bottles of spirits sitting on the shelf of the alcove adjacent to the window. A couple of nice malts, but he wasn't really in the mood. Music, though: he should select something special. He remembered moving into the upstairs flat with Rhona half a lifetime ago. He'd had a portable record player then and had put on the second Rolling Stones album, grabbing Rhona and dancing her around the vast-seeming room.

Only later had the walls begun to close in.

When he peered at the spines of his LPs, he saw that they weren't in anything like the same order as upstairs. Not that there had been any real sense of cataloguing — it was more that he'd known pretty much where he'd find whatever he wanted to hear. Instead of the Stones, he decided on Van Morrison.

'Aye, you'll do,' he said to himself.

Having eased the needle onto the vinyl, he stepped back. The record skipped. He looked down at the floor. Loose floorboard. He placed his foot on it again and the same thing happened. He stabbed a finger at the offender.

'You're on my list now, pal,' he warned it, keeping his footsteps soft as he retreated to his chair.

It wasn't long before Brillo curled up on the floor next to his feet. Rebus had promised himself that he'd unpack a few more boxes before bedtime, but he realised there was no urgency. When his phone buzzed, he checked the screen before answering: Deborah Quant. He'd asked her a while back if they were courting. She'd replied that they were friends with benefits — which seemed to suit both of them just fine.

'Hiya, Deb.'

'Settling in?'

'Thought you might have popped round to check.'

'Busy day, mostly thanks to your lot.'

'I'm long retired, Deb.' Rebus paused. 'I'm

17

guessing this is the Saudi student?'

'Police and Procurator Fiscal don't seem to trust me to establish cause of death any more.'

'You reckon pressure's being applied?'

'From all sides — government here and in London, plus our friends in the media. Added to which, Muslim burials usually take place within two to three days — embassy are pushing for that to happen.'

'Handy for whoever killed him, if you can't keep the body for future examination . . .'

'Which I've explained until I'm blue in the face.'

'So it's the full tourniquet, eh?' He paused again. 'I take it you didn't find anything out of the ordinary?'

'Thin-bladed knife, maybe four to six inches long.'

'Did they know what they were doing?'

'They went for his neck rather than chest, abdomen or stomach. I'm not a hundred per cent sure what that tells us, but then that's not my job. Angle of incision suggests someone of similar height and probably right-handed. Can I assume you've been discussing it with Siobhan?'

'She's champing at the bit.'

'But she's a loyal friend, too.'

'I've told her I'll be fine from here in.'

'So where are you right now?'

'Chair in the living room, Brillo at my feet.'

'And you've got the hi-fi set up, so all's well with the world.'

'Will I see you tomorrow?'

'I'll try.'

18

'You work too hard.' He listened to her laughter.

'It was the right move to make — you do know that, don't you?'

'For the sake of my lungs, maybe.'

'Try spending a day without them, John. Give Brillo a scratch behind the ears from me. We'll catch up soon.'

'Night, Deb.'

And then she was gone. She lived less than a mile away, in a modern block where minimalism ruled. Her possessions were few because there was nowhere to keep them — no Edinburgh press or understairs cupboard, no nooks and crannies. Just clean lines that repelled the very notion of clutter. Her office at the mortuary was the same — no files were allowed to linger long on her desk.

Rebus thought again of the books he'd decided he couldn't live without, even if he would never read them; the albums he played maybe once or twice a decade but still clung to; the boxes of case files that seemed a veritable part of him, like an extra limb. Why would he part with them when he had a spare bedroom no overnight guest ever graced? His only family consisted of his daughter and granddaughter, and they never opted to stay. That was why he had ditched the old bed and replaced it with a two-seater sofa, leaving space for more bookshelves, the suitcase he doubted he would ever use, and his second-best record player, the same one he'd had when dancing with Rhona that first night. It no longer worked but he reckoned he could find someone to fix it. He would put it on his list.

When he went into the kitchen to make a mug of tea, he examined the central heating timer. Mrs Mackay had left the instruction manual but it looked straightforward enough.

'Heating bills are quite reasonable,' she'd told him. But then she had always opted for another layer of wool rather than an extra degree on the thermostat. He wondered if her various cardigans, pullovers and shawls had accompanied her to Australia. He wouldn't bet against it.

While the kettle boiled, he walked into the main bedroom. With the double bed, plus his old wardrobe and chest of drawers, floor space was limited. Siobhan had helped him make up the bed, only having to shift Brillo half a dozen times in the process.

'Tell me he doesn't sleep next to you,' she'd said.

'Of course not,' Rebus had lied.

The dog was watching now from the hallway. Rebus checked his watch. 'Soon enough,' he said. 'Just one more mug of tea and maybe another record, eh?'

He wondered how many times he would wake up in the night and not know the new route to the bathroom. Maybe he'd leave the hall light on.

'Or stop drinking bloody tea,' he muttered to himself, heading back into the kitchen.

iv

But it wasn't his need to pee that woke him at 5 a.m. It was a call. He fumbled for both his

20

phone and the bedside lamp, waking Brillo in the process. He couldn't quite focus on the screen but pressed the phone to his ear anyway.

'Dad?' His daughter Samantha's urgent voice.

'What's wrong?' he asked, sitting up, growing more awake by the second.

'Your landline — it's been cut off.'

'I meant to tell you about that . . . '

'About what?'

'My landline's not the reason you're calling at this hour. Is it Carrie?'

'She's fine.'

'What then? Are you all right?'

'It's Keith.'

Her partner; Carrie's father. Rebus swallowed. 'What's happened?' He listened as Samantha began to sob quietly. Her voice cracked when she spoke.

'He's gone.'

'The bastard . . . '

'Not like that . . . I don't think so anyway.' She sniffed. 'I mean, I don't really know. He's disappeared. It's been two days.'

'And things were all right at home?'

'No worse than usual.'

'But you don't think he's just — I don't know — maybe gone on a bender somewhere?'

'He's not like that.'

'You've reported him missing?'

'They're sending someone to talk to me.'

'They probably told you two days isn't long?'

'Yes. But his phone just goes to voicemail.'

'And he didn't pack a bag or anything?'

'No. We've got a joint bank account — I

21

looked online and he's not bought anything or taken money out. His car was left in the lay-by near the church.'

Rebus knew where she meant — a five-minute walk from their home. He had parked there himself once to take in the view. Samantha lived on the edge of the village of Naver, on the wild north coast eight miles east of Tongue. The wind had rocked Rebus's car as he'd sat in it.

'Problems at work?' he asked. 'Money troubles?'

'He knew I'd been seeing someone,' she blurted out.

'Right,' Rebus said.

'But that's over and done with. It's not why he left — I'm sure it's not. He'd have taken his things. The key was still in the ignition . . . Parked so close to the house . . . it doesn't make any sense. Does it make sense to you? I'm just . . . I've been awake all night going over it again and again, and I'm scared the police will think I had something to do with it.'

Rebus was quiet for a moment. 'Why would they think that, Samantha?'

'Because everyone here knows we were going through a rough patch. And they know about me and Jess.'

'He's the guy you were seeing? Did Keith ever square up to him?'

'I don't know. But this can't have anything to do with Jess. It really can't.'

'Most likely outcome is that Keith will turn up — I'm speaking from experience here.'

'I've got such a bad feeling, Dad.'

22

'I can be there before lunchtime. What time are they coming to talk to you?'

'They didn't say.' She took a deep breath. 'I've got to get Carrie to school, I told them that.'

'It's going to be okay, Sammy, I promise.' Sammy: his name for her until she'd decided she was too grown-up for it. For once, she didn't correct him.

'Thank you,' she said instead, so quietly he almost didn't catch it.

Day One

Day One

1

Siobhan Clarke woke to a text from Rebus. She decided it could wait until she'd made coffee. It was just gone seven and Graham Sutherland had already gone. She wondered if she should be unnerved by his ninja-like ability to dress and depart without her noticing.

'Could have made me a drink, though . . .'

She tramped back to her bedroom, still in her pyjamas, mug cupped in both hands. Placed it on the bedside table and lifted her phone, swiping it awake.

Big favour. Look after Brillo today. Key under half-brick next to front door. Talk later.

'The hell?' Clarke seated herself on the edge of the still-warm bed and made the call.

'I'm driving,' Rebus warned her. 'Don't want to get a ticket.' His old Saab had no hands-free option. She could hear the engine churning.

'Where's the fire?'

'Samantha. Her partner's gone AWOL.'

'You're driving to Tongue?'

'Not quite — they moved to the next village along a couple of years back.'

'And you reckon your rust bucket's up to the job?'

'I almost asked to borrow yours.'

'Why didn't you?'

'It was five o'clock. I wasn't sure you'd have thanked me.'

'I'd also have held you back with a few questions.'

'That too. Brillo doesn't need much looking after — a bit of a walk and you can leave him to his own devices while you go beg for a place on the MIT.'

'You don't want me unpacking for you?'

'It's all done.'

'Liar.'

'Don't you go rummaging through my stuff without my say-so.'

'You reckon you'll only be away for the day?'

'Mispers, Shiv — they almost always turn up eventually.'

'Where are you now?'

'Just south of Pitlochry.'

'On the dreaded A9?' She paused. 'Is Samantha all right?'

'Would you be?'

'How long's he been gone?'

'Two days, one night.'

'Suicide risk?'

'Not overly.'

'Oh?' Clarke tipped the mug to her mouth.

'Samantha says she was seeing someone else.'

'Ah.'

'He didn't pack a bag; car left near the house; hasn't used his debit card.'

'Maybe trying to give her a fright?'

'In which case he'll be getting a slap.'

'From her or from you?'

'Let's catch up later. You know where Brillo's stuff is.'

'I did until you rearranged the kitchen.'

'Always good to have a challenge, Shiv.'

In the time she took to shape her reply, Rebus had ended the call.

★　★　★

It was just after ten by the time she reached the MIT office. The room was buzzing with activity, Graham Sutherland leaning over Christine Esson's desk as she explained to him whatever was on her computer screen. When he spotted Clarke, Sutherland broke off the conversation and sauntered in her direction.

'Can't seem to keep you away, DI Clarke,' he said, folding his arms as he planted himself in front of her.

She gave a shrug and what she hoped was an endearing smile. 'John's headed out of town. I've literally got nothing else to do.'

'But like I said, I've a full complement here.' He gestured to the desks. Clarke recognised everyone: Esson and Ogilvie; DSs Tess Leighton and George Gamble, another DC called Phil Yeats. She'd worked with them before as part of Sutherland's team. They all knew about her and the boss. Only Gamble ever gave her any stick.

'No DI that I can see,' she commented.

'That would be me.'

She turned towards the doorway. Malcolm Fox had just entered, carrying a sheaf of paperwork.

'You get around, Malcolm,' Clarke said.

'Major Crime Division are taking an interest,' Sutherland explained, not sounding exactly

29

thrilled about it. 'They've loaned us DI Fox for the duration.'

'Making daily reports to our elders and betters, I dare say.'

'Above all else, I'm a team player, Siobhan — you know that.'

Clarke couldn't help glancing in Tess Leighton's direction. The look Leighton gave her signalled that the relationship she'd had with Fox hadn't lasted.

'I can be useful, sir,' Clarke said, turning her attention back to Sutherland. 'You know I can.'

Sutherland took his time considering. 'It would mean sharing a desk with Malcolm.'

'As long as he promises not to copy my classwork.' Clarke knew what Sutherland was thinking — just as Fox would be keeping an eye on them and reporting back to his bosses, so she'd have an eye on him, keeping Sutherland in the loop.

Fox seemed ready to remonstrate, but decided on a resigned shrug instead. 'Fine by me,' he said. 'Catching the killer is the priority.'

'Well said. I'll leave the two of you to find a spare chair from somewhere and then get reacquainted.'

They watched Sutherland retreat to his office. Fox held out a hand.

'Welcome aboard.'

Clarke stared at the hand. 'My town, my ship. You're the passenger here.' She heard Tess Leighton stifle a laugh. Fox's face began to redden.

'Same old Siobhan,' he eventually said. 'Light on charm, heavy on offensive. Almost like you

30

learned from the master. Speaking of whom . . . '

'House move's done and dusted.'

'But his health's okay? I mean, no worse than it was?'

'Phone him sometime and ask.'

'I gave up trying.'

Clarke was looking around, in search of a free chair.

'Maybe the support office.' Fox gestured towards the corridor. 'I'll do it if you like.'

Clarke nodded her agreement.

'While you make us some tea.' He made his exit quickly, before she could respond.

Clarke marched over to the kettle, checked it for water and switched it on.

'There's a kitty,' George Gamble growled from behind his desk. 'Five quid in the tin.'

'And hello to you too, George.' Gamble seemed to be wearing the same suit as ever — three-piece in too loud a check. His hair was still unruly, face blotchy, stomach straining against his waistcoat. Seated opposite him, Tess Leighton seemed a ghost by comparison — slender, pale-skinned, hollow-eyed. Both were good enough detectives in their different ways, even if Gamble seemed to be counting the days and hours until retirement. Clarke had only worked with them once before, and was better acquainted with Esson and Ogilvie, both of whom came from her team at Gayfield Square. Phil Yeats was another of Sutherland's regulars, a fair-haired twenty-something who specialised in doing what he was ordered to do, no more and no less.

31

Esson had brought a mug to the kettle, ready for a refill.

'What's the story?' she asked quietly.

'John's off north to see his daughter.'

'Leaving you in the lurch.'

'We'd pretty well finished the move. Just a few boxes left.'

'Find anything interesting tucked away in his flat?'

'No porn or dead bodies. Turns out he likes a Jack Reacher book, though.'

'I'm more of a Karin Slaughter girl. They're both coming to Edinburgh if you — '

'Christine,' Clarke broke in, 'when exactly were you planning to tell me about Fox?'

'What's to tell? Far as I knew, you were on leave.'

'So when I dropped by yesterday . . . ?'

'I thought it might annoy you ever so slightly.'

'I'm not annoyed — I just like to be apprised.'

Esson puckered her mouth for a moment. 'See anything of DCI Sutherland last night?'

Clarke glared at her. 'What if I did?'

'He didn't spill the beans either — same reasoning, I'm guessing. We just wanted you to unwind. DI Fox tends to have the opposite effect.'

The kettle had finished boiling. Clarke lifted it too high as she poured, scalding liquid slopping from the first mug. She cursed under her breath.

'Break's obviously done you a power of good,' Esson teased, watching Fox carry what looked like an interview-room chair into the office.

Clarke ignored her, finished making the tea

and carried both mugs to Fox's desk. He was moving his things to one side — laptop, stationery, phone charger — with all the delicacy a man of his proportions could muster. Clarke tried to get comfortable on the chair. Fox hefted his mug in what looked like a toast before taking a sip.

'So where are we?' Clarke asked.

'To start with, we're treating it as homicide,' Fox obliged. 'No weapon recovered as yet, and nothing substantive from CCTV — though we're still looking. Victim was an overseas student and there have been a few attacks recently.'

'Oh?'

'Mostly in St Andrews actually — rich kids hounded by local idiots. But there have been a couple of incidents around the Meadows. Students have organised themselves so no one needs to be out there at night on their own. Then there's the race angle — Brexit has led to a rise in attacks, mostly verbal but occasionally physical.'

'In Edinburgh?'

'Again, just a few reports. But one of the victim's close friends was beaten up a few weeks back.'

'That's interesting.'

'Not far from the deceased's home. We're not seeing an obvious connection as yet, but it's on our radar.'

'What about Salman's lifestyle? I know he liked James Bond, but that's about it.'

'The guy seems to have lived like James Bond,

too.' Fox put a series of photographs up on his screen. 'These are from his social media. Nightclubs and champagne. The Aston he drives in Edinburgh is a new model, but in London he has a classic DB5.'

'Isn't drinking frowned on? I assume he's a practising Muslim . . . '

'Different rules seem to apply.' Clarke watched shot after shot of Salman bin Mahmoud, in immaculate tailoring, embracing a succession of glamorous young women in clubs and at sporting events.

'You'll notice he favours a martini,' Fox commented.

'What about drugs?' she asked as another page of photos appeared, courtesy of Fox's finger on the trackpad.

'Not as far as we know.' Fox began to tap at the faces. 'That one's the daughter of a Conservative MP. And this one is Scottish gentry — Lady Isabella Meiklejohn. Her dad owns a goodish chunk of the Flow Country.'

'The what?'

'Caithness and Sutherland. Peat bog mostly.'

'They all look like supermodels.'

'Wonder what attracted them to the exotic playboy millionaire.'

Fox was rewarded with a twitch of the mouth from Clarke that almost constituted a smile.

'How rich was he?'

'We don't really know. His father's been under house arrest for a while, but there's obviously still money — only so far you can run a lifestyle like that on credit. We've added photos of his

Edinburgh abode to the Murder Wall.' Fox gestured in its general direction. 'And the Met have sent us some of his London pad — not too shabby in either case.'

'And he wasn't known to us before this happened — neighbours complaining of wild parties, speeding tickets on the streets of the New Town?'

'A fistful of parking fines that went unpaid. He wasn't keen on walking any distance to his front door, which meant leaving the Aston on the occasional yellow line.'

'Catnip to the wardens.'

Fox nodded his agreement. He had come to the end of the photographs. Clarke sat back in her chair. It wasn't exactly built for comfort — she was going to have to bring in a cushion from her living room. 'So what do you think happened?'

'It comes down to the locus. Seafield Road that time of night — he was either at the start of a long drive south or else he was meeting someone.'

Clarke nodded her agreement. 'None of his friends live out that way?'

'Not that we've found.'

'Maybe he was looking for a hot hatch to race. Not unknown of an Edinburgh night, especially in the suburbs. If I had a car like his, I'd be tempted.'

'Carjacking gone wrong is certainly something we're looking at. Aston's been examined; only its owner's prints. Plenty fuel and no obvious mechanical issues.'

'So he didn't pull off the road for a breakdown.' Clarke nodded again. 'Mobile phone records?'

'Have been requested in full. So far it looks like his last call was to a male friend — actually the same one who was mugged. He says they were just chatting about this and that, plans for the weekend and such.'

'How long before he was killed?'

'A couple of hours.'

'Have you talked to his friend?'

'Me personally?' Fox shook his head. 'I've not long arrived.'

Clarke made eye contact and held it. 'Why *did* they send you, Malcolm?'

He offered a slow shrug. 'It qualifies as Major Crimes, Siobhan.'

'Why, though?'

'Because certain people insist.'

'Our political masters, you mean?'

'There are international ramifications. With us leaving Europe . . .'

'We need all the trading friends we can get — including regimes?' Clarke guessed. 'But the Saudi rulers don't exactly see the deceased's father as a bosom buddy, so why the pressure?'

'I really can't say.'

'Which is a diplomatic way of telling me not to push it?' Clarke cocked her head. 'Are we going to hit brick walls along the way, Malcolm? People we won't be allowed to question, information that's not going to be forthcoming?'

'I honestly have no idea.' Fox lifted the mug to his lips again. 'But something tells me you're

36

going to clamber over any walls you find
— almost like you learned from — '

Clarke stopped him with a wagged finger.
'Anything John Rebus taught me is long gone,
and so is he.'

She hoped the words sounded more confident
than she herself felt.

2

Rebus had forgotten how long the drive took. A distance of around 250 miles and he could swear he'd done it in under four hours in the past. Today, however, it was more than five, with just the one stop to refuel car and driver both, giving the Saab's bonnet a reassuring pat to let it know he appreciated the effort. The A9 itself hadn't been too bad considering — some lorries and caravans and a couple of sets of roadworks. The process of dualling was ongoing and would continue to be ongoing long after Rebus had headed to the traffic-free highway in the sky. He hadn't thought to bring anything. There was just the one CD in the car — a compilation Siobhan had burned for him. She'd written the words 'Songs for Dark Times' on the disc in black felt pen. He'd asked her to explain the title.

'Some to make you think,' she'd said, 'some to calm you down or get you dancing.'

'Dancing?'

'Okay, nodding your head then.'

It was indeed a mixed bag. One track might be funk that sounded beamed down from the 1970s, the next a piece of Brian Eno minimalism. Leonard Cohen sang about love and loss, and another band about post-Brexit England. Then there was Black Sabbath with 'Changes'.

'Nice touch, Siobhan . . . '

At the petrol station, adding a toothbrush and toothpaste to his purchases, he'd asked the woman at the till if they sold CDs.

'All Bluetooth these days,' she'd explained.

'Hopefully not after brushing,' Rebus had replied.

The rain had arrived well before Tain, accompanying him to Altnaharra and beyond, thirty-odd miles of single-track road, but mercifully free of other vehicles. His eyes felt gritty and his spine, shoulders and backside ached. When he paused in a passing place to relieve his bladder, he took deep breaths in an effort to appreciate his wilderness surroundings. Steep peaks, glassy lochs, bracken and birdsong. Not that he had taken in much of the scenery, being too preoccupied with thoughts of Samantha. Her mother, Rhona, had died a few years back. There had been a sparsely attended funeral in a commuter town outside London. Samantha had grown up in the flat in Arden Street, eventually moving with her mother to London. Then back to Edinburgh for work, before finally settling in Tongue with Keith. Carrie had arrived thanks to IVF — a final throw of the dice, in Samantha's words. They'd moved a few further miles east from Tongue to a modern bungalow that kept the heating bills down. Rebus had met Keith only a handful of times, preferring to visit during working hours. Likewise, Keith seldom accompanied Samantha and Carrie on their rare trips to Edinburgh.

Did Rebus even know his surname? Samantha must have told him. In one ear and out the other probably. Seemed to work hard enough though, provided for his family. Last job Rebus knew of was helping decommission the old nuclear power plant at Dounreay. There'd been a leak the previous year and Rebus had phoned to check Keith was all right. Samantha had assured him that all the tests had come back negative.

'You'll still need a bedside light then?' her father had joked.

Dounreay wasn't exactly next door to Naver. About a forty-five-minute drive each way. He'd once asked Samantha why they didn't move closer to Keith's work. The answer was Carrie. She had friends and was in a good school. Put those on the scales and the commute weighed nothing.

Good old Keith. So why had Samantha been seeing another man?

As he passed by Tongue, Rebus switched off the wipers. The sun had broken from behind a bank of cloud. The sea, when he caught sight of it, was gleaming and calm. The wind had died down. Past Tongue was another stretch of single-track road, winding inland so that he lost sight of the sea again for a bit. Eventually he reached Naver, driving through the village. As he passed Samantha's bungalow, he checked for a patrol car, seeing no sign of one. The church was a few hundred metres further along, the lay-by just in front of it. Keith's dark blue Volvo XC90 sat there.

Rebus drew to a stop behind it and got out, rolling his shoulders to loosen them. The key had been removed from the Volvo's ignition and the doors were locked. Rebus peered inside without noting anything unusual. He estimated the distance back to the bungalow — a walk of a few minutes? He doubted public transport was plentiful, though there was a bus stop on the other side of the road. Maybe Keith had hitched a ride or organised a taxi or something. Maybe mates from Dounreay had taken him drinking in Thurso and he'd woken up ashamed at something he'd done, lying low in a hotel or a spare room until he could summon the courage to confess.

After all, hadn't Samantha confessed?

Or had she? Had she told Keith, or had she been found out? Rebus watched as a car approached. It was a Mondeo rather than a marked vehicle, but he somehow knew it was the police. Unmarked meant CID, so it was no surprise when the car pulled up next to Rebus's Saab, blocking half the carriageway. The driver put the flashers on and got out, leaving his door ajar, engine running.

'Can I help you with anything, sir?' he asked, in a tone that suggested something needed explaining. He was in his late twenties, short black hair already going silver at the temples. Clean-shaven, square-jawed, ruddy-cheeked, broad-shouldered. In other circumstances, Rebus might have taken him for a farmer.

'You're here to question my daughter,' he said. 'And that's why *I'm* here.'

The man arched his back a little, as if for a more appraising look. 'You'll be John Rebus then?' He saw Rebus attempt to disguise his surprise. 'Internet makes it easy these days. I ran your daughter's name and there you were.'

'It's her partner you should be interested in.'

'Everybody interests me, sir.' A hand was shoved towards Rebus. 'I'm a detective sergeant, all the way from Inverness.'

'Long way to come.'

'Not nearly as far as some.'

Rebus shook the proffered hand. 'Does the detective have a name?'

'Robin Creasey.'

'And you know I'm ex-CID?'

'Strictly civvy street now, though.'

'Is that you telling me not to get involved?'

'Of course you're involved — you're her family. But if this *does* turn out to be police business . . .'

'It'll be none of *my* business?' Rebus guessed.

'We understand one another.' Creasey looked at Rebus's car. 'You've just arrived, eh? I can feel the heat coming off the engine.'

'I might need to get that seen to.'

Creasey offered a broad smile. 'Let's go see your daughter then.' But he paused halfway to his Mondeo, scanning his surroundings. 'Odd place to leave the car, isn't it? I wonder if he was much of a churchgoer . . .'

★ ★ ★

Samantha kept biting off bits of her fingernails throughout the interview. The living room was messy, most of the damage done by Carrie. Rebus doubted Samantha had even noticed. The

42

same was true in the kitchen — the previous day's dishes piled in the sink; breakfast leftovers on the table. Rebus had made them mugs of tea. Samantha was on a chair, Creasey the sofa. Rebus took the spare chair, moving toys and books from it. Creasey kept his questions short but incisive. Problems at work? At home? Was this sort of behaviour out of character? Could she give him Keith's phone number, and those of his friends and family? Rebus learned that Keith's surname was Grant and his parents were deceased. He had a sister in Canada but they weren't close. Did he ever go for a swim — there was a beach nearby, after all? No, because he'd never learned.

'He didn't drown himself,' Samantha stated.

She'd tried his phone, of course, but had he maybe used his bank card? He had not. Why did she think he'd left the car in the lay-by? She shook her head in response, choosing a fresh fingernail to gnaw on. Rebus noticed how many framed photographs there were in the room, mostly posed shots of Carrie, taken at her school — but family holidays too, everyone smiling for the camera. In the flesh, Samantha looked tired, hair long and straggly with an increasing amount of grey in it. Rebus reckoned she'd lost some weight, her face gaunt, skin loose at the neck.

'You should tell him,' he announced, just as the interview was winding down. His daughter gave him a hard stare. 'He'll find out anyway, if he's as thorough as I think he is.'

Creasey looked from daughter to father and

back again, content to bide his time. Samantha focused her eyes on the wooden floor at her feet.

'There was a guy I was seeing for a while. It's finished now, but Keith found out. Hard to keep secrets in a place this size.'

'How long ago was this?'

'A couple of months.'

'This other man — a friend of his?'

She shook her head. 'He runs a commune. That's what you'd probably call it. Keith and me were curious, so we visited one day. Keith didn't go back, but I did.'

'So Keith does know the man?'

'His name's Jess Hawkins. Far as I know they just met the once, and only really for a quick handshake.'

'When Keith found out, he didn't go looking for Mr Hawkins?'

'I told him not to. Whatever it was, it had ended by then.'

'How did he find out?' Rebus asked. 'Did you tell him?'

She shook her head again. 'A note — anonymous, of course.'

'Someone in the village, then?' Samantha shrugged. 'Do you still have it?'

'No.'

'Have you seen Mr Hawkins since?' Creasey enquired.

An eventual slow nod of the head. 'In social situations, yes.'

'I appreciate you sharing this with me, and I have to ask if you think it could have anything at all to do with Keith's disappearance.'

'I don't think so.'

'There must have been an impact on your relationship, though?'

She glared at the detective. 'I don't remember booking to see a counsellor.'

Creasey held up a hand in appeasement. 'It's just that it might explain Keith's actions — he needs to go somewhere to clear his head, think things through.'

'He's had a couple of months to do that,' Rebus reasoned.

'Time for things to fester,' Creasey countered. Rebus noticed that he hadn't touched his tea. It sat on the floor on a ceramic coaster. 'I'd imagine things were difficult, Samantha. Did he retreat into himself, or is he more the type who lashes out?'

Samantha gave a snort. 'Keith's never ever raised a hand to me.'

'You talked? Tried to work things out?'

'When he was around.'

'He started staying out more than usual?'

'He had his hobby people. They probably saw more of him than Carrie and me did.'

'What's the hobby?'

'Local history. There's an old POW camp back towards Tongue. They're looking at its history, doing some excavating. There's a half-baked plan to open it to tourists.'

'Maybe not so half-baked — you're on the North Coast 500 after all. Plenty new visitors.'

'Mostly speeding past in their sports cars,' Samantha said dismissively. Creasey turned towards Rebus.

'It's a circuit that's become popular with drivers.'

'I know,' Rebus replied. 'I might live in the far-off lands to the south, but news sometimes travels.'

Creasey decided to ignore Rebus's tone and turned his attention back to Samantha. 'What do you think's happened to Keith, Samantha?'

'Something.'

'Could you be more specific?'

'An accident maybe.' She offered a shrug and checked her phone. 'I need to fetch Carrie soon.'

A glance at his watch told Rebus his daughter was exaggerating — school wouldn't finish for another hour or two. He saw Creasey come to the same conclusion, yet nod all the same.

'One last question then — when did you last see or speak to Keith?'

'That same evening. After dinner, he said he was going out.'

'He didn't say where?'

'No.'

'And he seemed all right?'

Samantha nodded slowly.

'Then let's leave things for now.' Creasey got up from the sofa and handed her a business card. 'I'll file a missing person report, but if he does turn up or anything changes . . .' Samantha gave another nod. 'Are the keys to the Volvo here? I wouldn't mind checking the interior. I'll pop them through your letter box when I'm finished.'

'On the table by the front door.'

Creasey stretched out his hand to take hers.

'People almost always come back,' he said. She returned the handshake without looking in the least bit convinced.

Rebus got up and said he would see the detective out. Creasey lifted the car keys while Rebus opened the door. Both men stepped outside, Rebus closing the door after them, making sure it wasn't locked.

'You reckon it's nothing to worry about?' he enquired.

'Early days. If she'd not mentioned the affair and I'd found out after, I might have wondered what else she wasn't telling me.' He paused, studying Rebus's face. 'I know she's not always had it easy. She was twelve, wasn't she, when that nutcase got hold of her? Held a fearsome grudge against you.'

'Thirty-odd years back.'

'Then a hit-and-run in her twenties. She was in a wheelchair for a time. Still has a trace of a limp when she walks.'

'Is this us playing detective Top Trumps?'

'Aren't Top Trumps a bit after your time?'

'You're forgetting I've got a granddaughter — plus a daughter who's turned out perfectly well adjusted, despite your insinuations.'

'I've not met too many folk who're 'perfectly' well adjusted, Mr Rebus.'

'Go look at the car, head home, file your report.'

'Leaving you here to do what exactly?'

'Help my daughter as best I can.' Rebus opened the door and disappeared back inside.

3

They got the living room and kitchen tidy, Samantha checking her phone every few minutes in case she'd missed a text from Keith.

'So nothing at all out of the ordinary that day?' Rebus asked.

'No.'

'Keith came home from work, had dinner, then went out?'

'Weren't you listening when I told the detective?'

'Just getting it clear in my mind. What time did you start to worry?'

'Bedtime, I suppose.'

'You suppose?'

'I texted him.' She waved her phone in front of her father's face. 'Take a look if you don't believe me.'

'Of course I believe you.'

'Doesn't sound like it to me.' She checked the time again. 'Anyway, I really do have to go fetch Carrie.'

'Creasey knows, you know.'

She scowled at him. 'Knows what?'

'That you lied to get rid of him.'

'I couldn't stand it another minute.' She lifted her coat from the back of a chair and started putting it on. 'You coming?'

'Does Keith keep anything about the POW camp here?'

'In the garage.'

'I might stick around then.'

'Suit yourself. It's not locked. And you can leave the door unlocked here, too.'

'Everywhere used to be like that,' Rebus commented.

'A nice safe place to bring up kids,' Samantha said, mostly to herself, wrapping a long scarf around her neck and making for the door.

When she was gone, he wandered through the house. There were no bedside drawers in the main bedroom, just identical small tables. Her side: a half-empty blister pack of ibuprofen; nail scissors; phone charger; clock radio. His: a football biography; iPad; headphones. The iPad required a password. The screen saver was one of the framed photos from the living room — a beach holiday, father and daughter presumably with Samantha on the other end of the camera. He considered opening the clothes drawers and the fitted wardrobe but managed to stop himself.

Carrie's room was a riot of colour and toys, including one he remembered buying her for her eighth birthday. There wasn't much else apart from the small bathroom and a box room being used for storage, so he donned his coat and headed to the garage. Shelves filled with DIY stuff, tools and lengths of wire and cable. And in the centre, where a vehicle might sit, a large trestle table with a folding wooden chair. Rebus sat down and started examining the reams of paper, books, notebooks, plans and photocopied photographs.

Camp 1033 was also known as Borgie Camp,

named after the river that ran past it. Rebus got the sense that it had housed different sets of people at different times during the Second World War, from 'aliens' long resident in the UK to captured German soldiers. Keith had been diligent. There were books about the history of concentration camps and about specific camps in Scotland and elsewhere. He'd picked them up from dealers, the cardboard packaging tossed on the floor nearby. To Rebus's mind, that spoke of an urgency, a hunger — maybe a way to stop thinking about what had happened with Samantha? Immersing himself. Losing himself. There was a long handwritten list of official documents and books that he had yet to get his hands on. The words 'National Library?' had been double-underscored.

Rebus knew he could spend hours here without necessarily learning much that would help. All the same, he was curious. If Borgie was Camp 1033, presumably that meant there were at least another 1,032 camps like it scattered throughout the British Isles. Why hadn't he known? One of the books was dedicated to another Scottish camp called Watten, near Wick. Not so far away in the scheme of things. There was also a flyer for a camp called Cultybraggen, near Comrie, which, practically intact, already operated as a tourist destination. Rebus saw that Keith — or someone — had made scribbled calculations about how much it would cost to do something similar with Camp 1033. The answer was several hundred thousand pounds. Whoever had written the figures had added a frowning face to the final underlined sum.

He listened as a car drew up, engine idling for half a minute, before driving off again. He made his way from the garage to the bungalow, unsurprised to find the Volvo key fob on the floor of the hallway. Picking it up, he closed the door again and decided to walk to the lay-by. The wind whipped around him, making him wish he had a hat while also aware that he'd have had trouble stopping it flying away. He unlocked the car and climbed into the driver's side, closing the door on the elements. He turned the ignition and the engine sprang into life. When he tried the hi-fi, the radio was tuned to Radio Scotland, but there was no signal.

The navigation system offered few clues, no destination having been set. Around here, it paid to know your routes rather than depending on technology to know them for you. As if to reinforce this, there was a road atlas in the passenger-side pocket. Rebus couldn't quite reach it, so, leaving the engine idling, he got out and rounded the car, settling in the passenger seat. Quickly he realised it was damp. He got out again and pressed his palm to the seat. Definitely damp. He grabbed the road atlas and flicked through it, concentrating on the pages showing the local area. Nothing had been marked or circled. Leaning back into the car, he lifted the central armrest. The storage space below was empty save for a few chocolate wrappers and sticks of chewing gum. Keith wasn't a smoker, though Samantha had admitted to Creasey that he liked the occasional night at the pub with his cronies, these mostly being people he worked beside. The pubs ranged from the local in Naver to as far afield as Thurso. No driving while inebriated, though — always a cab or a willing teetotal friend.

The glove box held nothing other than the car's log book and various garage bills. Rebus closed the passenger-side door and checked the back seats, then the boot, which contained a muddy cagoule, a pair of thick knitted socks, and hiking boots that had seen good use. Rebus imagined this would be Keith's kit for trips to Camp 1033.

Retreating to the driver's seat once more, he stared out through the windscreen at a view of rising hills. The land here was greener than in nearby Tongue, less scraped and craggy. He knew from previous visits that dunes lay to the other side of the churchyard and led to a long, curving stretch of sandy beach. He thought he remembered Samantha saying Keith had grown up in Dundee, but that there were family ties to the local area — summer holidays with relatives; fond memories. He wondered if he should leave the key in the ignition, for when Keith returned. But Samantha had made the decision to take it home with her, so he turned off the ignition, locked the car and put the key in his pocket.

When he reached the bungalow, there was no sign of Samantha, so he climbed into his own car and set off for the village proper. Its only real shopping street lay just off the main road. There was a bar called The Glen, a shop that doubled as post office and café, and a pottery. When he parked outside The Glen, the first person he saw was Creasey. He was in conversation with a couple of locals outside the shop. Rebus knew what he was doing: same thing Rebus himself intended to do. Namely: dig. He entered the pub and walked up to the bar. The place was dead, apart from a barmaid rearranging glasses on a shelf. She glanced in his direction.

'Your friend's just been in,' she said.

'What gave the game away?'

'I know a copper when I see one. I'll tell you what I told him.' She faced Rebus, her hands pressing against the bar top. 'Keith keeps his nose clean; knows when he's had enough.'

'He's a regular, then?'

'Sits over there with his history group.' She gestured towards a corner table. 'Couple of pints apiece and that's them done.'

'This is the same group that's been researching Borgie Camp?'

The barmaid studied him. 'Your friend didn't know its name.'

'You told him, though?'

'But now I'm wondering how come you know and he didn't. Makes me think I might have jumped to conclusions a bit soon.'

'I'm John Rebus. Samantha's my daughter.'

'You used to be police,' she said with a slow nod.

'So you weren't far out in your assessment.'

'Good to know I've not lost the touch. The other man was asking about Samantha — did she come in with Keith, did they seem to be getting along as a couple.'

53

'Mind if I ask how you answered?'

'A kid can put a strain on a relationship. Keith's commute means he's away long stretches of the day.'

'And when he's not busy at work, he's got Camp 1033.'

'Have you been there?' Rebus shook his head. 'Can't have been much fun for the prisoners — freezing in the winter and a gale constantly howling. And yet some of them stayed put when the war finished, settled down with local lassies.'

'I get the feeling you speak from experience.'

'My dad.'

'You don't seem old enough.'

She rolled her eyes but didn't look unflattered. 'Second marriage for him when his first wife died. He was nearly fifty when I came along. He'd changed his name from Kolln to Collins. Christened me May after the month I was born — lack of imagination if you ask me.'

'Is he still with us?'

'In his nineties but wearing well enough.'

'Nice to meet you, May.' Rebus shook her hand across the bar. He'd had to revise her age upwards by around a decade — the climate hadn't managed to leave its mark on her features. Dark shoulder-length hair, a face that needed little or no make-up. She held herself with the no-nonsense confidence of bar staff everywhere. 'What else was DS Creasey asking?'

Instead of answering, she offered Rebus a drink. 'Just to keep me company.' When he shook his head, she poured herself lemonade from the mixer gun, adding a slice of lemon.

54

'We're sophisticated up here,' she said as she dropped it into the glass.

'So I've noticed.'

She was thoughtful as she sipped; Rebus got the idea she was trying to decide what to tell him.

'He asked me if I knew Samantha's history,' she eventually confided. 'That surprised me. I mean, she's not the one who's done a runner. Whereas Keith's biography didn't seem to interest him at all.'

'Almost as if he suspects her of something?' Rebus offered.

'I refused to play along. Rumours are quick enough to spread without anyone aiding and abetting.'

'Did he ask what you think might have happened to Keith?'

She gave a slow nod, eyes fixed on her drink. 'People leave all the time for any number of reasons. I've thought of it myself more than once.'

'So what keeps you here? Your dad, I guess.'

'Maybe — or maybe the same reason people move here in the first place: to turn their backs on all the shit happening elsewhere. That's why I hardly ever switch that thing on unless a customer demands it.' She gestured towards the TV that sat high up on the wall above the door. Rebus noticed the framed pictures alongside. They showed John Lennon and Yoko Ono.

'Just been listening to him in the car,' he commented.

'We get a few fans in now and again.'

'Why's that?'

'He used to come here. Well, Durness really. Holidays when he was a boy. Then there was the accident.'

Rebus walked towards the TV. One of the photos showed a car, its front severely dented.

'He was bringing Yoko north to show her his childhood haunts,' May Collins explained. 'They went off the road, ended up in hospital in Golspie.'

'I don't think I knew that.'

'That's my kind of local history.'

Rebus turned back towards her. 'Did Keith's group ever quiz you about your dad?'

'They're nothing if not thorough.' She fixed him with a look. 'You're pretty thorough too, for a pensioner.'

'That's not what I am, though, as well you know.'

She nodded her understanding. 'You're a parent. Means you've a personal stake in the game.'

'So if you happen to think of anything that might help me . . . ' Rebus wrote his mobile number on the beer mat in front of him and slid it in her direction. 'I'd be really grateful. And maybe next time I'm in, I can buy us both a drink.'

She waved the mat at him. 'Size of this place, I won't need to phone you — a loud enough shout will do the job just as well.'

★ ★ ★

Outside, there was no sign of Creasey. In fact, the street was empty. Rebus walked its length and then retraced his steps back to the Saab. But when he turned the key in the ignition, nothing happened. He tried again, pumping the accelerator. A single click was all he received for his troubles. He got out and opened the bonnet, staring at the engine.

'Who are you kidding?' he muttered to himself, slamming it shut and heading into The Glen.

'So soon?' May Collins said.

'Car won't start. Is there a garage I can phone?'

'In Tongue there is, but we usually rely on Jess Hawkins.' She saw the look on Rebus's face. 'Ah, you know about Jess. I wasn't sure.'

'He's the guy from the commune?'

'All manner of skills out there. There's usually someone who knows about engines. Want me to phone them?'

'They have phones, then?'

She smiled. 'They're not exactly the Amish.'

'So what are they?'

'Remember what I said about what brings people here?'

'Shit happening elsewhere?'

'Fresh start's what they aspire to. That and saving the planet. So should I phone?'

Rebus considered his options and gave a nod. But when she tried, there was no answer.

'Maybe leave it an hour and try again,' she suggested. 'You can always park yourself with a drink and the paper.'

Rebus shook his head. 'But I'll leave the car key with you if that's okay. When you need me, I'll be at Samantha's.'

'I could give you a lift.'

'And shut the bar?' Rebus shook his head. 'Despite appearances, I've still got the use of my legs.'

'So I might see you out jogging later?'

'That's always been more of a morning thing with me.' Rebus gave a wave as he made his exit, grabbing the toothbrush and toothpaste from the unlocked Saab and stuffing them into his pocket.

★   ★   ★

He was half lying on the sofa in the living room — and probably three quarters asleep — when Carrie came careering through the front door, leaving duffel coat, backpack and shoes in her wake. She drew up short at the sight of him. He met Samantha's eyes.

'I wasn't sure you'd still be here,' she said, explaining why his appearance was coming as a surprise to his granddaughter.

'Hiya, Carrie,' he said, opening his arms. Carrie marched forward as if into battle, resting her head against his shoulder as he embraced her and kissed the top of her head. Her hair was fair, cut short, her face round, eyes inquisitive. 'You look more like your mum every day,' he said.

'Mum's got grey hair,' Carrie countered.

'I mean when she was your age.'

Carrie studied him. 'Can I see a photo?'

'Of your mum?' He made show of patting his

pockets. 'I don't have one on me.'

'You've got a phone.'

'Grandad doesn't keep photos on his phone,' Samantha said, coming forward to rub her daughter's hair.

'Why not?'

'Let's get you some milk and a biscuit.' Samantha started ushering Carrie towards the kitchen, head half turned towards her father. 'Do you want anything? Are you staying for dinner?'

'My car's died on me.'

'Wondered where it was.'

'They said in the village Jess Hawkins was my best bet.'

Samantha didn't answer. Rebus got to his feet and followed her into the kitchen.

'It's probably true,' she said as she poured out the milk. Carrie had settled at the table and was busying herself with what looked like her own personal iPad. 'I mean, there'll be someone there who can help.'

'Where does he live?'

'Towards Tongue.'

'So near Camp 1033, then?'

'Practically next door.'

'I took a look at all the stuff in the garage.'

'So you'll appreciate it's become a bit of an obsession with Keith.' Samantha glanced at her own phone before slipping it back into her pocket — still no message.

'Where's Daddy?' Carrie asked.

'Working,' Samantha said.

'He's *always* working,' Carrie complained. 'When I grow up I'm not going to do *any* work.'

'That's the spirit,' Rebus said. Then, to his daughter: 'Where's the nearest B and B?'

'You can stay here,' she said, placing a plate of biscuits on the table.

'You've not got room.'

'We've got a sofa. You'd like Grandad to stay with us, wouldn't you, Carrie?'

Carrie glanced up, but whatever was on the screen was the focus of her attention now, and Rebus failed to catch her mumbled response.

'Once Carrie's in bed, we can do some catching up,' Samantha continued. 'And you can tell me why you no longer have a landline. I did a bit of thinking and my guess is you've moved.' She stared him out until he nodded. 'Moved and not told me,' she said. Her voice was emotionless but her eyes weren't.

'It literally happened yesterday,' Rebus argued. 'I was going to phone you today.'

'It's the stairs, isn't it? You can't manage the stairs any more.'

Carrie looked up. 'Why not?'

'I'm getting a bit creaky,' Rebus explained.

'Are you going to die?' She sounded curious rather than fearful.

'Not for a while yet.'

'Daddy spends all his time with dead people.'

Samantha tried to laugh. 'That's not true, Carrie.'

'In the garage.' She flapped an arm towards the outside world. 'All the photos and the names — hardly any of them are still alive.'

Samantha jumped as her phone sounded, her face falling as she saw the name of the caller on the screen. 'Jenny's mum,' she said, answering. Carrie gave a little wave, as if Jenny could see her. Samantha walked into the hallway. Arrangements for a play meet seemed to be the subject under discussion.

'I need to make a call too,' Rebus informed his granddaughter, checking for a signal — one bar; good enough. Samantha was in the living room, so he stood in the hallway and tapped in the number, wondering how Siobhan Clarke was going to react to the news he was about to give her.

4

'So when will you be back?' Siobhan Clarke, phone pressed to her ear, watched Brillo sniffing the grass thirty-odd feet away. The dog suddenly squatted, and Clarke gestured for Fox to take the small black polythene bag from her outstretched hand. His face registered an objection, quickly countered by her glare.

The Meadows was relatively busy: a few barbecues they'd had to coax Brillo away from; an improvised game of football; joggers and cyclists; toddlers connected to their wary parents by reins; prone students readying to rouse themselves for an evening elsewhere.

'Can't you just rent another one?' Clarke asked, watching Fox as he crouched to complete his task. He looked for the nearest bin and strode towards it, while Brillo returned to tracking some invisible spoor.

'Christ, John . . . ' Clarke gave a loud sigh. By the time Fox reached her, the call had ended.

'He's staying put?' Fox guessed.

'Car trouble.'

'Is his daughter okay?'

'Her other half's gone AWOL. I think she's pretty much on her own up there apart from her daughter.'

'So what do we do with the dog?'

Clarke managed a thin smile, grateful for that 'we'.

'I should probably take him home with me.'

'After we've spoken to the deceased's friend?'

Clarke nodded. 'I'll come pick Brillo up after.' She clapped her hands against her thighs and Brillo bounded up to her. Clarke clipped the lead onto the dog's collar and all three walked back to Melville Drive, crossing it and heading up Marchmont Road. When they turned into Arden Street, Brillo hesitated at the entrance to the stairwell but seemed resigned to the gate leading to the small garden. Clarke unlocked the door. While she checked the food and water bowls in the kitchen, Fox paced the living room, reaching into a box and pulling out a handful of seven-inch singles.

'Archaeology, most of these,' he said when Clarke found him.

'John says he wants it put on his gravestone: 'He listened to the B-sides'.'

Fox smiled and scanned the room. 'Feels weird — same stuff, different setting. He talked to me about buying a bungalow . . . '

'Like the one you live in?'

'Said that was the main reason he couldn't bring himself to do it.'

'What did he mean by that?'

Fox put the records back in their box. 'It was just a general dig, I think. You know what he's like.' He brushed his hands together as if to rid them of dust. Clarke was checking her phone. 'Almost time? The dog'll be okay here on its own?'

'I said I'll come back after — unless you're offering.'

'I'm not good with animals.'

'Me neither.'

There was a snorting sound from the doorway. Brillo sat there, head cocked.

'He knows a bar when he sees one,' Fox said with a grin. 'Come on then, let's go see what a trust fund looks like nowadays.'

★ ★ ★

Circus Lane was one of the most picturesque and therefore photographed streets in Edinburgh. At one time it would have provided stabling and staff accommodation for grand houses nearby. These days its mews homes were highly sought-after and immaculately maintained, with floral displays gracing some of the frontages. Clarke would once have described the road surface as cobbled, but she knew better now — the stones underfoot were setts, being more brick-like than pebble-shaped.

Giovanni Morelli lived halfway along the street. Clarke and Fox had been expecting to meet him inside, but he was on his doorstep. He wore no jacket, but had tied a fashionable-looking scarf around his neck above a yellow woollen V-neck and white T-shirt.

'Mr Morelli?' Clarke felt it necessary to ask. The young man nodded. He was clean-shaven, albeit with a five o'clock shadow, and tanned, with thick dark hair that he ran a hand through before nodding. There was a woman with him, dressed in a short suede jacket, jeans and knee-high boots. She stood several inches taller than the Italian, with broader shoulders. Her hair was thick and straw-blonde, swept back over one ear. As she concentrated on her cigarette, Clarke had a view of varnished nails, expertly manicured.

'Issy was visiting,' Morelli explained. 'I don't like the smell of smoke, so . . . '

'Thanks for agreeing to see us,' Fox said, introducing himself and Clarke.

'So here we are, on the street like a couple of tramps,' the woman called Issy snapped. 'Will this take long? We're heading to a drinks party.'

'Lady Isabella Meiklejohn?' Clarke deduced. Meiklejohn seemed only momentarily thrown by the identification. She was in her mid twenties, with flawless skin and pearly teeth.

'We should start by saying we're sorry for your loss,' Fox stated. 'As you know, it's our priority to get to the bottom of whatever happened.'

'By trying to put Giovanni in the frame?' Meiklejohn muttered, grinding her cigarette stub under her heel.

'Issy, please,' Morelli said, placing his fingers lightly on her arm. She wrapped them in her own hand for a moment.

'One theory,' Fox went on, 'is that the two attacks could be linked. Someone with a grudge against Salman and yourself, Mr Morelli.' He ignored the roll of the eyes from Meiklejohn. 'The mugging took place here, didn't it?'

Morelli nodded, pointing to a spot only a few feet away. 'I was coming home.'

'Where had you been?'

'Salman's.'

'He lived — what? — five or so minutes' walk away?'

Morelli nodded again. 'Midnight or maybe just after. One attacker, I think. From behind. A blow to the head.' He placed his hand on his crown. 'I fell over. One more blow, I think.'

'A fist, or . . . ?'

'The hospital thought maybe an object of some kind.'

'Were you dressed much like tonight?'

'A jacket. It was later, which means cooler.'

'A hooded jacket?'

'Yes, you're correct — they said the hood softened the blows.'

Meiklejohn was making show of checking and sending texts on her phone.

'I think you went to the hospital with Mr Morelli?' Clarke asked her.

'We've been through this more than once,' Meiklejohn said. 'Which means it's on record, which means you know damned well I did.'

'You're just a friend?'

Finally the woman looked up, her eyes meeting Clarke's.

'Yes.'

'And with Mr bin Mahmoud?'

'Again, yes.' Her eyes went back to her screen. 'Look, we all know it's down to Brexit. Attacks on foreigners have rocketed.'

'Not too many fans of Brexit in these parts,' Fox commented.

'Is that so? My family's full of them.'

'They live locally?'

'London and Sutherland.' She looked at

66

Morelli. 'We're going to be late.'

'There's a bar around the corner if you're desperate,' Clarke suggested.

'We're meeting people in the Cowgate.'

Clarke's brow furrowed slightly. 'The Devil's Dram?'

Meiklejohn shook her head. 'The Jenever Club.'

'We won't keep you too much longer,' Fox said.

Morelli touched his friend's arm again. 'Take a taxi. I'll follow you.'

Her face twisted. 'And leave you alone with a couple of cops? No chance.' Then, to Fox: 'You seriously think Gio's tap on the head is linked to someone murdering Salman in cold blood?'

'What do you think?'

'I think I hear the faint rustle of straws being clutched at by a police force that couldn't find its own backside on a dimly lit bidet.'

'You'd probably have more experience of bidets than we would,' Clarke commented, her demeanour hardening alongside her tone. Fox motioned to Morelli that he had a further question.

'The person who attacked you — you got no sense of their height, age, sex?'

Morelli offered a shrug.

'They didn't say anything or take anything?'

Another shrug.

'Ergo a hate crime,' Meiklejohn interrupted.

'With race crimes, the attacker most often vents verbally as well as physically,' Fox countered. 'They want the victim to know why

67

it's happening to them.'

Meiklejohn dismissed this with a twitch of one shoulder.

'How did the three of you meet?' Clarke asked into the silence.

'At a party,' Morelli said.

'One of Mr bin Mahmoud's?'

A shake of the head. 'A mutual friend in St Andrews.'

'You're both students here?' Clarke watched them nod their agreement. 'English literature?' Another nod.

'Whereas Mr bin Mahmoud was attending a business course in London . . . '

'But part of our circle nonetheless,' Meiklejohn said.

'Sort of like networking?' Clarke offered.

'A social network,' Meiklejohn said, smiling as if pleased with the line.

'I remember that film,' Morelli said.

'Me too.' Clarke nodded. 'A bunch of entitled rich kids stabbing each other in the back.'

Morelli frowned. 'I don't remember it like that at all . . .'

★ ★ ★

Clarke had parked her Vauxhall Astra on St Stephen Street. As they passed the Bailie pub, Fox asked her if she fancied a pit stop.

'Not here,' she replied. 'Besides, I'm on dog-sitting duties, remember? I'll drop you back at your car.'

'Did we learn much from the two of them?'

68

'What do you think?'

'I'm asking you.'

'So I notice.' She paused as she unlocked the car and got in, doing up her seat belt while Fox did the same. 'They didn't seem shocked or grieving or any of that.'

'Evidence of the stiff upper-class lip?'

'Or theirs is a world where you know people without ever becoming really close. Salman had money, good looks and pedigree. I'm sure Lady Isabella seems every bit as exotic to the likes of him and Gio as all of them seem to you and me.'

'It certainly feels like a different world.' Fox was silent for a moment. 'Morelli has much the same build as the deceased, similar skin tone . . .'

'Bin Mahmoud had a beard, though.'

'But say someone followed him from the deceased's. They were behind him and he had his hood up.'

'A case of mistaken identity?'

'The lane is a nice quiet spot for an assault.'

Clarke seemed to ponder this as she started the engine and eased the car out of the tight parking spot.

'I didn't think you were entirely fair about that film, though,' Fox added.

'Me neither,' Clarke admitted with a smile. 'But it was all I had to work with at the time.'

'Well, that and a bidet,' Fox said, returning the smile.

5

Having collected Brillo and all his paraphernalia, Clarke sat in her tenement flat while the dog explored his new surroundings. He seemed both puzzled and a little bit sad, clearly missing his owner and maybe wondering if this nomad's existence was to be his life from now on. Having eaten some leftovers from the fridge and half finished a mug of peppermint tea, Clarke put her coat back on and made for the door, Brillo trying to accompany her. Out on the landing, she listened to the barking from within before unlocking the door again.

'If you insist,' she said, scooping the dog up into her arms.

Brillo was well behaved in the car, tail wagging, paws pressed to the passenger-side window as he watched the passing parade of shops, bars, restaurants and pedestrians. Clarke's destination wasn't far. She left the window down an inch when she climbed out, telling him to 'Stay, good boy.' Brillo seemed contented enough with this arrangement.

They were just off the Cowgate, towards its eastern end. Late-night weekends, the street could get messy with drunken fights and related idiocy, but it was neither the weekend nor late. Nevertheless, most venues boasted one or two heavy-set doormen, ready to deter or deal with trouble. Clarke had googled the Jenever Club and had been proved right. Until a few months back it had been a nightspot called the Devil's Dram. Back then, it had specialised in expensive whiskies and overpriced food, along with nightly DJ sets and dancing. It seemed whisky had given way to gin, without the exterior having been given much of a makeover.

Clarke couldn't help glancing to her left as she crossed the street, towards where the mortuary sat in faint anonymity. Those who worked there referred to it as the city's 'dead centre', yet around it life continued in its thrumming heat and intensity — at least judging from the blast from the club's interior as a suited doorman opened the door for her. But before she could enter, a hand rested on her shoulder.

'Fancy meeting like this.' She spun towards the beaming face of Malcolm Fox. 'I was about ready to give up on you.'

Rather than entering, the pair of them stepped to one side. 'Okay, I'm impressed,' Clarke said, managing to sound anything but.

'I think it was when I suggested a drink and you said 'not here'. That told me you had somewhere else in mind — and as the Devil's Dram had already been mentioned . . . '

'You're in danger of getting good at this.'

'But there's more, isn't there?'

Clarke considered for a moment before answering. 'Meiklejohn wasn't what you'd call high, but she'd taken something — my guess would be cocaine.'

'I hadn't actually noticed that.' Fox looked annoyed with himself.

71

'Maybe I've seen more coke-heads than you.'

'It's true I've led a sheltered life. But putting two and two together, you're not here to keep an eye on Gio and Issy — who've not turned up yet, by the way.'

Clarke stared at him. 'You've been here all this time?'

'Didn't have any other plans. I'm right, though, aren't I? The Dram used to be owned by a certain Morris Gerald Cafferty; no reason to suspect he's not still in charge just because drinking trends have changed.'

'And the other thing we know about Cafferty is . . . ?'

'He probably still controls a good portion of the local trade in illicit substances.'

'And now you know as much as I do. Odd that they haven't turned up yet, though — they seemed keen enough earlier.'

'Almost as if they just wanted rid of us. So what's the plan, DI Clarke?'

'A quick drink at the end of a long day,' Clarke answered with a shrug.

'Yeah, Cafferty'll definitely believe that.' Fox held out a hand. Clarke looked at it. 'Good working with you again, Siobhan.'

'Likewise,' she answered eventually, shaking it. But when Fox loosened his grip, hers intensified. 'And now that we're getting chummy, time for you to tell me why Gartcosh are so interested.'

She watched intently as Fox debated with himself. Eventually he nodded and drew her back a few more steps along the pavement.

'A request from Special Branch in London,' he

72

explained in an undertone. 'They're wondering if there could have been state involvement. The Saudis, I mean. Though it's not especially their style.'

'In that he wasn't chopped up and taken away in a suitcase?' Clarke released the pressure on his hand. 'What's your feeling?'

'Too early to tell.'

'Some sort of message to the father?'

Fox just shrugged. 'You're all caught up.'

'Do the rest of the team know?'

'Special Branch's feeling is best keep it quiet.'

'Why?'

'If I were being generous, I'd say it's because they want us to have an open mind.'

'And on those odd days when your mood's less generous?'

'They don't want the Saudis thinking we suspect them. Might jeopardise those precious trade relations.'

'The fewer people who know, the less chance of a leak.' Clarke nodded her understanding. 'No more keeping stuff from me, Malcolm,' she warned.

'Can I assume you'll be telling the DCI?'

'Any reason I shouldn't?'

'Your call, Siobhan.'

'My call,' she confirmed, heading for the figures flanking the doorway.

★　★　★

They decided their first task would be to check the toilets, see if anyone was doing a line. The main room was noisy. There was a dance floor, its multicoloured squares illuminated from below. The DJ stood swaying gently behind a couple of laptops while people danced. The place was maybe half full, the evening young, but plenty of sweat and noise was being generated. The bar was doing brisk business with cocktails, the staff putting on a show. There was a balcony reached by a transparent staircase, and a basement that would almost certainly be quieter.

Clarke wasn't a stranger to the place, though she hadn't been here since it changed its name. The cheesy occult decor of the Devil's Dram had been replaced by mock-Victorian — heavy drapes; nickering wall lights mimicking gas lamps; dark wood panelling. She pushed open the door to the ladies' loo and pretended to be checking her appearance in the long mirror above the row of sinks. Only one cubicle door was closed. When its occupant emerged, she stood next to Clarke while she fixed her hair with one hand, phone glued to the other.

'Dead in here tonight,' Clarke offered.

'I've seen it livelier.'

The door to the bar opened and another young woman clattered in on three-inch heels. She gave Clarke a quizzical look, taking in the sensible clothes — and probably their wearer's age, too. It struck Clarke that yes, she was old enough to be the mother of either of these young women.

'Gary's being a right prick,' the new arrival stated into her phone, eyes on its screen as she headed to a cubicle.

'Gary?' Clarke asked the woman next to her, receiving a shrugged reply. A quick tug on the short sparkly dress, another check in the mirror and then she was gone.

The voice behind the cubicle door was echoey, Gary's shortcomings entailing a lengthy list. Clarke took a final look around for any traces of white powder, then pulled open the door. A large, unsmiling figure stood there. When she looked past him towards the gents', she saw that Fox, too, had been paired with a new companion.

'He wants a word,' she was told.

'Of course he does,' she replied. She looked across towards Fox and saw him give a shrug. She nodded and allowed herself to be led past the dance floor, following Fox and his minder up the staircase to where the bulky, shaven-headed form of Morris Gerald Cafferty sat alone at a corner banquette.

'Thought it was you,' Cafferty said with a grin, gesturing for them both to sit. There was just enough room, though Clarke was conscious of Fox's thigh pressing against hers. 'Fetch you a drink?'

'We're fine,' Fox said.

Another gesture from Cafferty sent the two doormen on their way. He focused on his visitors. 'You walk into a club but you're not after a drink. Still on duty, I presume?'

'You've changed the place,' Clarke said, keeping her tone conversational.

Cafferty waved a hand across the balloon-shaped glass in front of him. 'Gin's the thing nowadays. Cheap and quick to distil. Add a mixer — and everybody does — and it's hard not to turn a profit.'

'Refit probably wasn't expensive either,' Clarke commented, enjoying watching Cafferty try his best not to look irritated.

'You're working the murder of that Arab student?' Cafferty posited.

'Good guess,' Fox said.

'Had to be high-profile enough to bring you scurrying from Gartcosh. Still Major Crimes, DI Fox?' Fox nodded. 'Probably still a bit of a thorn in DI Clarke's side that you got the promotion she deserved.'

'Salman and his friends were regulars here?' Clarke asked, not about to be deflected.

'They came a few times,' Cafferty allowed. 'I've turned the cellars into a VIP area. If I like the look of you, you get a little black card that allows you in.'

'You didn't have a falling-out, by any chance?'

'With the prince?' Cafferty smiled at the absurdity of Clarke's question.

'I don't think he was a prince,' Fox commented.

'He liked it when I called him that, though.' Cafferty shifted position. 'I looked his history up online, saw the stuff about his dad. Politics, eh? Root of all evil.' There was a gleam in his eye as he spoke. Clarke wondered what game he was playing. 'I hear you've turned house mover, DI Clarke. Remember — always bend at the knees. How's Rebus enjoying his retirement flat?'

'Do Salman and his entourage ever buy

76

anything from you?' she enquired.

Cafferty's eyes widened in mock horror. 'Is this you accusing me of peddling drugs? Next thing I know, I'm cutting open a young Arab student over a deal gone wrong?' He made a dismissive noise. 'I see those CID brains are the usual blunted tools. And speaking of tools, you still keeping your bed warm for your boss, Siobhan? Office romances seldom end well. Just look at Malcolm here and . . . ' He clicked his fingers, brow furrowed. 'Her name's on the tip of my tongue.'

'We didn't come here for this,' Clarke said, sliding out of the banquette. 'We were told that a couple of the victim's friends could be found here. Just had some follow-up questions for them. Okay if we check out this so-called VIP area of yours?'

'Be my guest. In fact, I insist on it. You'll find the razor blades and the rolled-up fifties on a gold-leaf table next to the bar. Maybe something even more exotic if you guess the secret password . . . ' Cafferty was chuckling as he watched them leave.

Fox couldn't help glancing back as they started their descent.

'He's getting old,' he said to Clarke. 'That sheen on his face doesn't look exactly healthy.'

'Or else he's been sampling the goods.'

'He wouldn't, though, would he?'

'No,' Clarke admitted.

'Who do you think's passing him all the news about us?'

'Could be anyone. Show me a cop shop that

couldn't double as a colander.'

'Fair point.'

They had reached the next set of stairs down. It was protected by a better class of doorman, who stood, hands clasped in front of him, next to a black velvet rope. He unhooked it at their approach.

'Thought we had to show a card,' Clarke said.

'Not for officers of the law,' the man said in a voice like the bottom of a quarry.

Clarke and Fox headed down. The light was different, a little brighter, and the piped music was softer. There was a small bar staffed by a glamorous woman who looked underworked. The tables all around were empty.

'Not so much as a rolled-up fiver,' Fox said under his breath.

An arched doorway led down an unreconstructed brick-lined passageway. Clarke picked up the faint smell of damp. She knew that the Old Town boasted dozens of these underground passages and storage cellars. There were intimate spaces off to both sides, and these were where the possessors of the black card had chosen to set up their lairs. Each room was lined with purple crushed velvet. Real candles replaced the electric lighting of the upper floors. Champagne in ice buckets was the tipple of preference. Though the smoking ban seemed to be holding firm, a few people were vaping. Passing one of the rooms, Clarke caught sight of Meiklejohn and Morelli. They had obviously just arrived and were shedding their outerwear while greeting the three drinkers already gathered. Neither of them bothered to look up as Clarke and Fox passed. Clarke signalled to Fox to retrace their steps. Even when they passed the arched doorway for a second time, the group paid them no heed.

Back in the bar area, they stopped for a moment.

'Know who that was?' Clarke asked.

'I've not gone senile.'

'I don't mean Posh Spice and the Italian Stallion — I mean the guy with the two fashion models.'

'I didn't really get a chance to — '

'His name's Stewart Scoular. He was an MSP till the SNP kicked him into touch. Some racist comments he posted online. Tiptoed away for a bit and reinvented himself as a property developer.'

'Okay.'

The hostess was asking them if they wanted something to drink. 'Compliments of Mr Cafferty,' she added.

'Not while we're on duty,' Fox said, watching as her fixed smile began to dissolve.

Clarke was already climbing the stairs. Fox followed her out of the Jenever Club and onto the Cowgate.

'That's why he had that glint in his eye,' Clarke was saying.

'Cafferty?'

She nodded, deep in thought. 'When he said that thing about politics — he knew damned well we were going to find Stewart Scoular downstairs. It's like he was setting the coordinates for us on his GPS.'

'Hence the insistence we go exploring?'

Clarke nodded again. 'What are you up to, Cafferty?' she muttered.

'Not so unusual that a wealthy developer would know the likes of Meiklejohn and Morelli, is it?'

Clarke considered this. 'He's probably fifteen years older than them, but no, I don't suppose it is.'

'Well then . . .' Fox broke off, straightening his shoulders when he saw the look Clarke was giving him. 'Is this where you tell me your intuition's sharper than mine? Maybe that's why you deserved the promotion they handed to me?'

'You know Cafferty — if he can hammer a wedge between us, he will. That's what that cheap shot was all about.'

'But you do think he was telling you something with that line about politics?'

'I'm fairly sure.'

'Though you're not sure what?' He watched her shake her head slowly. 'So where does that leave us?'

'It leaves us heading home. I just hope no one's stolen Brillo.'

'You left him in the car? I'm not sure John would approve.'

'Then he should get his arse back here, shouldn't he?'

'I'm sure he's working on it.'

Clarke stared at him. 'Are you?' she asked.

'Not really,' Fox admitted, holding up his hands in defeat.

★ ★ ★

A waiter had arrived, swapping Cafferty's empty glass for a full one. It was lemonade, but no one needed to know. Cafferty liked to fool his customers into thinking he was a fan of the product. Back when he'd sold whisky, apple juice had provided a passable imitation. He busied himself on his iPad, running back the CCTV footage and replaying it. He couldn't be sure Clarke had clocked Scoular, but he reckoned it was a safe bet. If it had just been Fox, that lumbering bear of a guy, things might have been different.

'Interesting, though,' he said to himself, zooming in and out of the footage, then checking angles from different cameras. There was the fragrant Lady Isabella and her olive-skinned companion, larger than life and not eight feet from Clarke and Fox. Yet the detectives hadn't confronted them — meaning Clarke had been lying about wanting to question them. Meaning the visit had been a fishing expedition. Yes, of course. Both of them needing the facilities at the self-same time? They'd been on a hunt for drugs.

Cafferty gave the thinnest of smiles. 'Should have hung around for that free drink, Shiv.' He reckoned that in the next few minutes Lady Isabella would be reaching into her clutch for a smallish bag, happy to share its contents with her chums. Scoular would buy another bottle of champagne, so the club was still making some money. They wouldn't all partake — Scoular liked to keep his nose clean, as it were. But Cafferty had footage aplenty of the others, including the ill-fated Salman bin Mahmoud. Maybe none of it would ever prove useful, but you could never tell, could you? And meantime, he should go and offer his condolences. Hadn't they just lost their friend, after all, and wasn't tonight by way of a wake? He might even manage to slip in the question uppermost in his mind: what had the boy prince been doing in such a grim part of town, so far from his Georgian town house and all its trappings? Was there something Cafferty had missed in those hours and hours of video?

Next time he upgraded the system, he'd be sure to add sound to his list of requirements; but meantime, with all the solemnity he could muster, he rose to his feet and scooped up his refilled glass.

Day Two

Day Two

6

Rebus had awoken on the sofa to find a pair of eyes watching him intently.

'Where's my daddy?' Carrie asked softly.

He sat up and checked his watch. It was just gone seven. His granddaughter was still in her pyjamas.

'I heard Mummy crying,' she continued. 'Did Daddy leave because Mummy was shouting?'

'Shouting?'

'They both were. But Daddy was trying not to.' She pushed her bottom lip out.

Rebus blinked the sleep from his eyes. 'They were having an argument? The night Daddy left?'

'Because I told Daddy we'd been to see the chickens.' She was on the verge of tears.

'It's not your fault, Carrie, none of it.' Rebus paused. Then: 'Whose chickens?'

'Jess's,' his granddaughter sniffled.

'You should get dressed,' Rebus said. 'I'll see you at breakfast. Don't worry about anything, okay?'

Without saying another word, she padded off to her room. Rebus got into his clothes quickly and folded the duvet as best he could, then opened the window to air the room. It had rained in the night but the sky was clearing. He could hear the wind, though. It caught the curtains and shook them. Samantha had poured them both a few whiskies the previous night as they'd sat and talked — safe topics mostly; desperate not to fall out. Now she was tapping at the living room door, fetching him a mug of coffee.

'Sleep okay?'

'Like a baby.'

'You all right with cereal? We've not got much else.'

'Coffee usually does me.'

She nodded, mind elsewhere.

'No news.' It was statement rather than question.

She shook her head. 'I'll get started on breakfast,' she said, turning to leave.

'Something I forgot to ask yesterday, Samantha — the Volvo's passenger seat was damp.'

'The window was down.'

'When you found it?'

She gave another nod. 'Rain got in.'

'Any idea *why* it was down?'

'I'll get started on breakfast,' she repeated.

'Hang on — there's something else. The night Keith walked out, you'd had an argument, hadn't you? About visiting Jess Hawkins?'

Samantha's face darkened. 'That little madam.'

'You can't go blaming her — she's already doing enough of that for herself. But you didn't think to tell Creasey?'

'So?'

'So if he goes asking and someone else tells him instead . . .'

'It was nothing, Dad, really. Keith wasn't happy I still visited, but I like the people there. They're on my wavelength.'

86

'More on your wavelength than Keith?'

'I don't know . . . in some ways . . . ' She stared at her father. 'Are *you* going to tell him?'

'I'd much rather it came from you.'

'And I'd much rather you kept the hell out of it.' She left the room, slamming the door after her.

Rebus waited until he could hear the hubbub from the kitchen — mother and daughter discussing some school project — before making for the bathroom and a hot shower. By the time he reached the kitchen, they had almost finished eating. He glanced at the remaining bowl and spoon, conscious that both were placed in front of what would be Keith's chair. He stayed standing, trying not to get in the way. Samantha was reeling off a checklist as she placed things in the dishwasher.

'Got it' or 'done it' Carrie would say in reply to each item.

'Just coat and bag then,' Samantha eventually said, closing the dishwasher door.

'Okay if I walk with you?' Rebus asked. Carrie looked wary at this breach of the normal routine.

'I don't know if that's really necessary,' Samantha said coldly.

'I'd like to, though.' Rebus's eyes were on his granddaughter. 'Would that be all right with you?' he asked. Eventually Carrie nodded.

'Thank you,' Rebus said.

They walked in silence for a minute or two, Carrie casting glances back over her shoulder towards the house, Samantha with her phone held in her free hand like a talisman. Naver, despite its size, boasted both a primary and a high school, both with rolls in the tens rather than hundreds. Samantha had always been enthusiastic about the quality of teaching, and when asked, Carrie reeled off her current teacher's good points.

'It's keeping the teachers that's the problem,' Samantha added.

Entering the village proper, Rebus saw that the bonnet of his Saab was open, a man in blue overalls and a padded cotton jacket leaning down into the engine.

'I'll leave you here,' Rebus said to his daughter and granddaughter. 'Have a good day at school, Carrie.'

She managed a non-committal sound and skipped away ahead of her mother. Rebus watched them leave, hoping Samantha might turn towards him so he could wave. But she didn't. May Collins was emerging from The Glen with a mug of tea. The mechanic paused in his work to take it from her. She gave Rebus a welcoming smile.

'This is John,' she informed the mechanic. 'He's Samantha's father.'

'Mick Sanderson,' the man said, waving oily fingers to excuse the lack of a handshake. He was in his mid twenties, with curly red hair and a heavily freckled face.

'Thanks for doing this,' Rebus said. 'Any joy?'

'Just getting started,' Sanderson explained. 'Might be something or nothing. Older a car gets, the more TLC it needs.'

'I might have been lax in that regard.'

88

'Believe me, I can tell.'

'If it's fixable,' May Collins broke in, 'Mick's your man. There's a tractor on the commune that should be in a museum by rights — Mick seems to get it going year after year.'

'Is that what it is, Mick?' Rebus asked. 'A commune?'

The mechanic shrugged. 'Good a term as any. We live communally, share the workload — you're welcome to visit.'

'I might do that.' Rebus paused. 'It won't be news to you why I'm here?'

'Heard about Keith, if that's what you're asking.'

'You know him, then?'

'He visited one time with Samantha.'

'He didn't take to the place the way Samantha did?' Rebus watched Sanderson shrug. 'Or maybe it was the people he didn't take to?'

'People and place are much the same thing in my experience.'

'He works at a nuclear power station — not much of a New Age angle there.'

'He's dismantling it, though, isn't he? Making it safe. No quarrel with that. Whereas this gas-guzzler . . . ' Sanderson rapped his knuckles against the Saab.

'In my defence, I bought it in the days before global warming.'

May Collins laughed and even Sanderson managed the beginnings of a smile.

'I'm forgetting my manners,' May said. 'Can I make you a tea, John?'

'I'm okay, thanks.' Then, to Sanderson: 'Has

May given you my number?'

'When there's news, I'll let you know. I'm assuming you'd be happy if it'll drive as far as a garage?'

'If that's what's on offer.'

'I'll see what I can do.'

Rebus nodded. 'Thanks again. By the way, does your commune have a name?'

'Not really.'

'And opening hours for visitors?'

'Day and night, you'll find someone there.' Sanderson had placed his mug on the tarmac and was leaning down into the engine again.

'The day Keith disappeared, Samantha and Carrie had been to visit.'

'Oh aye?'

'To see the chickens.'

'I might've been busy elsewhere.'

Rebus watched the man work for a few more seconds. 'I'll leave you to it then.'

May Collins squeezed his arm. 'We open at noon,' she said. 'Bring Samantha in for lunch. It's only soup and sandwiches, but it might be good for her.'

'I'll ask,' Rebus said.

Her grip on his forearm tightened. 'See that you do.'

Rebus walked back to the bungalow with hands in pockets, jacket buttoned to the neck. It was probably only three or four degrees colder than Edinburgh, but the wind was from the north and not about to be tamed, it seemed, even in summer. The door to the house had been left unlocked. He went inside but felt restless. He found the keys to the Volvo. It had been brought back from the lay-by and stood outside. He scribbled a note and left it on the kitchen table — didn't want Samantha thinking Keith had returned and taken the car. But she was approaching the house as he made his exit.

'Just going for a drive,' he said.

'My company's not good enough for you?'

'It's not that. But I work best when left to my own devices.'

'So you're not *just* going for a drive?'

'I probably am, though. And while I'm doing that, you can be phoning Keith's workmates and pals — see if there's any news; maybe there's someone you missed when you rang round before.'

She studied the phone in her hand. 'That detective called.'

'Creasey?'

'After I'd dropped Carrie off. More questions about me and Jess.' She gave Rebus an accusing look.

'I've not said a word. Did you mention the argument?'

'It wasn't an argument.'

'Even so.' Rebus paused. 'I'll be back for lunch — May Collins said we should go eat at the pub.'

'Maybe,' Samantha eventually conceded.

Rebus leaned forward to peck her on the cheek, but she drew away. Nothing for it but to head to the car.

He drove away from the village, west on the A836. He had the coastline — albeit largely hidden from view — to one side of him, and hillside with the occasional grazing sheep to the other. Eventually he noticed a makeshift sign alerting him to a backpacker hostel and café. This comprised a fair-sized solid-looking house with a modern single-storey extension. He pulled in to the unpaved car park and walked towards a wooden door that boasted another handwritten sign proclaiming 'Yes, we really are open — try the handle!' He did, and entered a room big enough for four tables and a serving counter. A man around his own age stood behind the counter and greeted him with a wave.

'How can I help?'

'Just a coffee,' Rebus said, taking a look around. One wall was covered in photographs and postcards. The cards were from hill-walkers grateful for the welcome they'd received along with the hot drinks, scones and cakes. The photos showed visitors posing with the café as backdrop, or else pausing on a hillside, laden with rucksacks and wrapped in as many layers as manageable. The man turned from the coffee machine.

'I'm guessing you're not a walker — not today, at any rate.'

'The clothes give it away?'

'The lack of boots primarily.'

'I'm into history more than geography.'

'Camp 1033?'

Rebus approached the counter. 'That's right. Local history group told me about this place.'

'They come in,' the man acknowledged with a slow nod.

'You've heard one of their number's gone missing?'

'Keith Grant, yes.' The man fixed Rebus with a look. 'And you're Samantha's father, pretending to be a casual tourist. News travels, you know.' He gestured towards the window. 'And that's Keith's car you're driving.'

'My daughter's up to high doh,' Rebus confessed. 'I'm just asking around in the hope of finding some answers.'

'I don't really know your daughter, but Keith was — is — a regular. They'd almost have to drag him away from the camp at dusk. Then they'd pull two tables together so they could sit round and pore over their maps and notes and photographs. Doubtful I'll ever retire on the proceeds, though.' He broke off and held up the coffee he'd just finished pouring. 'You still want this, or was it merely a pretext?'

'I definitely want it.' The mug was placed on the counter and Rebus picked it up. 'When you talk about retirement,' he said, 'I can't help thinking . . .'

'That at my age I should already be retired?' The man ran his fingernails down one ruddy cheek. His eyes sparkled beneath bushy silver brows. 'Well, you're not wrong. Wife and I moved up here after we sold our business. We're Lancaster originally. She passed away last year.' He looked at his surroundings. 'This was her idea — she liked being around folk. Not in the sense of living in a city, but visitors, you know? She'd cajole the life stories from most of them, then write a few lines about them in one of her

93

notebooks — a sort of hobby, you might say.'

'Sounds like a local history group might have been her thing.'

'Oh, it was. That's one reason they started coming here — my Rosemary even suggested Camp 1033 as their pet project.'

'I'm sorry she's no longer with us.'

'Me too.' The man stuck out a hand for Rebus to shake. 'I'm Ron Travis, by the way.'

'John Rebus. So you'll know Keith fairly well, Ron?'

'Which is why I'm as in the dark as you are. Completely out of character, if you ask me.'

'An accident then, maybe?'

Travis considered this, rubbing at his cheek again. 'Is that what your daughter thinks?'

Rebus studied the man. 'I'm realising this is a hard place to keep secrets.'

'Keith had Camp 1033, she had Jess Hawkins and his lot.'

'The commune's not far from here?'

'Five more minutes along the road.'

'Close to the camp?'

Travis nodded. 'All sorts wash ashore here, John. People like me and Rosemary, looking for a change, and people like Hawkins and company, after much the same thing. Doesn't always go down well with the locals, the ones who've been here for decades, scratching a living.'

'Samantha and Keith are incomers, too.'

'But they've got a kid — that helps get you accepted. Half the folk in the local history group came here from elsewhere. Funny that they're

94

the ones who show a passion for keeping the stories alive.'

'Keith certainly seems to have been doing that for Camp 1033. He's turned his garage into a museum.'

'Well, it's an interesting story — and practically forgotten. Have you seen the camp?'

'I'm heading there next.'

'You know it housed all sorts? When war broke out, scare stories weren't far behind. Italians and Germans who'd been in the country for generations found themselves locked up. Later on, it was proper war criminals — Nazi hard-liners and the like. The Poles even locked up their own countrymen if they didn't like the look of them. Half this coastline was patrolled by Polish infantrymen.' He saw the look Rebus was giving him. 'Can't help listening in sometimes when the group gets talking. They have this dream of a community buyout for the camp, turn it into a tourist attraction. That was Keith's idea, as I recall. Won't happen, though.'

'I saw the sums.'

'Even if they could raise the cash, I doubt the owner would sell.' Travis chuckled. 'He had plans to turn this whole area into a spaceport.'

'A what?'

'Launching satellites. Fell through, though. After that, it was to be a dark-sky park — to attract stargazers. Big new hotel and lots of guest lodges. Still on the drawing board as far as I know, though now with a golf course and country club attached.'

'You own this place, though?'

95

Travis nodded. 'But I'm pretty well hemmed in by thousands of acres belonging to Lord Strathy — who of course lives in London rather than up here.'

'Lord Strathy owns the land the commune's on too?'

'But he reckoned without Jess Hawkins. Hawkins had the tenancy agreement structured in such a way that it'll be hellish pricey to shift him if he's not for shifting. I hear Strathy has a bunch of expensive lawyers trying to find loopholes. So far, no joy.'

'I've never heard of this Lord Strathy.'

'Surname's actually Meiklejohn — one of probably dozens of landowners you've never heard of. Doesn't stop them owning a decent chunk of the country you and I call home. You know the theatre company 7:84?' Rebus shook his head. 'Called themselves that because of the statistic — seven per cent of the population owned eighty-four per cent of the wealth. That was a while back, mind.'

'You don't sound as though you think those figures will have changed for the better.'

'I sometimes think I ended up here so I could stop having to live with it. Rosemary and me, we used to be active — go on marches, sign petitions and all that. CND, anti-apartheid, Friends of the Earth. We were drunk for two days when Tony Blair got elected.' He smiled at the memory. 'Made not a jot of difference really.'

'Yet I don't sense you have much time for the commune.'

'To my thinking, they've turned their backs on

the world. As long as they're all right in their little bubble, the rest of us can go burn. And Hawkins . . . well, he's obviously got something, or they wouldn't stick around, but I'm damned if I can see what it is.' His eyes met Rebus's. 'Samantha saw it, though. I'm assuming you've heard about that?'

'I've heard. But it didn't last long and she patched things up with Keith.'

'A patch is a patch, though — reminds you there's damage beneath.'

Two motorcyclists pulled up outside, their bikes laden with camping gear. The riders dismounted and began peeling away layers of leather and tugging off their crash helmets. Both were silver-haired.

'First of the day,' Travis commented.

'NC 500?' Rebus watched Travis nod. 'How much do I owe for the coffee?'

'Two seventy-five. Toilet's to the left when you head outside — you won't find much at Camp 1033.'

'Thanks.'

'Good luck, John. Tell your daughter I'm thinking of her.'

'I will.'

The bikers said hello to Rebus as he passed them. He got the feeling they were Scandinavian. They looked ruddy-faced and wholesome and comfortable with their place in the world. He felt his heart pounding after the injection of caffeine. His knees and back still ached from the previous day's long drive and his head was slightly thick from the whisky he'd imbibed with Samantha.

He sat in the Volvo and composed a text to Siobhan Clarke, updating her on the Saab and hoping Brillo wasn't pining too much. He tried to imagine being out on a bike all day and then setting up a tent and crawling inside, sheltering from the elements; doing it all again the following day.

'Different strokes,' he muttered to himself, wishing he hadn't had to give up the cigarettes.

His phone announced that it had a signal by ringing suddenly. An Edinburgh number, but not one he recognised. He answered anyway.

'Hello?'

'John? It's John Neilson. I heard you'd moved.'

Ex-cop, a decade older than Rebus. Stationed at Gayfield Square and the high street when Rebus had known him. They used to share the occasional drink and story.

'Who grassed me up?' Rebus asked.

'Kirsty.'

Owner of the Oxford Bar. One of a select few Rebus had confided in.

'She didn't think you'd mind me knowing.'

'As it happens, she's right.'

'Is it the COPD?'

'I suppose so.'

'Neither of us is getting any younger. Just calling to check you're managing.'

Rebus thought of something. 'You still keeping your nose in a few books, John? Maybe you could help me. I've taken a sudden interest in Second World War prison camps.'

'A cheery subject.'

'There's a list of documents and books I'm

trying to track down.'

'It's not a library you need, it's the internet.'

Rebus had forgotten that since his retirement Neilson had developed an interest in computers. He'd boasted once of recovering a wiped hard drive. 'How would I find out what sites are useful?' he enquired.

'Camps in Germany?'

'The UK,' Rebus corrected him. 'Internment rather than POW, and specifically Camp 1033.' He sensed Neilson picking up a pen and beginning to write.

'I'll send you some links. What's your email?'

Rebus spelled it out for him.

'AOL, John?' Neilson chuckled. 'You really are a dinosaur. Leave it with me.' He paused. 'So the move's gone okay? I know it can all be a bit traumatic. When do I get to see the place?'

'Let me finish unpacking first. You'll get that gen to me?'

'Wee bit of police work — I miss it every bit as much as you do.'

Rebus ended the call, started the Volvo and got back on the road.

7

He managed to drive past Camp 1033 without really noticing, mistaking it for tumbledown farm buildings. Realising his error, he doubled back, parking on the grass verge and trudging to a broken-down metre-high fence. He recalled from the photos in Keith's garage that back in the 1940s a high fence topped with barbed wire had formed the camp's perimeter, along with a tall gate. None of that remained. The replacement gate came up to just past Rebus's knees and could be stepped over by those younger and nimbler than him. There was no lock as such, the height of the grass serving to keep it closed.

A forceful push and he was inside the compound. Overgrown paths were laid out between the shells of elongated Nissen huts, their roofs mostly gone, windows shattered. There was a bit of graffiti, but not much. A large blue tarpaulin, weighted with rubble, showed where the history group's archaeological dig was taking place.

As Rebus moved further into the camp, he became aware that it was larger than he'd thought. He remembered the plans in the garage. They had shown not just accommodation blocks but a water plant, cookhouse, surgery, guard-rooms and more. It was a bleak spot, which made it perfect. If anyone absconded into the hills, they might be lost for days, growing weaker and weaker without ever reaching civilisation. If they headed for the road, they would easily be spotted in their inmates' garb. He peered through the gaping doorway of one of the accommodation huts. It would have contained bunk beds and a stove and probably not much else. There would almost certainly have been no insulation to speak of, just thin breeze-block walls and a corrugated roof.

He took out his phone and noted that the single bar denoting already minimal signal had disappeared altogether. Rain was blowing in again. No cars passed him and there were no signs of livestock. No birds in the sky either. He had seldom felt further from the comforts of home. Having not heeded Travis's advice, he felt his bladder make sudden complaint, so found a section of wall out of view of the road and unzipped his fly. When he was done, he trudged further into the camp, trying to visualise it filled with men — internees and guards both. Hundreds of the former; presumably dozens of the latter, armed with rifles and pistols.

There was yet another accommodation block to his left, and in a slightly better state of preservation, in that both its roof and door were intact, though again what windows Rebus could see lacked the glass they would once have had. The door still possessed a handle, which he turned. Walking in, he noticed the skeletal remains of a couple of bunk beds. Blackened embers and grey ash showed where a makeshift fire had been lit a long time back, possibly by the party-goers who had left a couple of rusted beer cans nearby. There was something at his feet. A brown leather satchel. He picked it up, but it was empty. Then he saw the boots protruding from behind one of the bed frames. He sucked in a slow lungful of air and composed himself before taking a few steps forward.

The face was turned away from him, the body twisted and stiff. Rebus knew a corpse when he saw one — and knew a likely crime scene, too.

'Christ's sake, Keith,' he said in a low voice. He crouched and tried the throat and wrist for signs of a pulse, knowing it would be a miracle if he found one. Knowing too that this was not a time of miracles. A few flies were busy in the gaping wound visible at the back of the dead man's skull. He tried waving them away, but then remembered that their larvae could be useful for establishing a rough time of death — Deborah Quant had told him often enough. He stood up again and checked his phone — no signal. How was he going to break it to Samantha? What was he going to tell her? Keith hadn't run away, hadn't committed suicide or been the victim of an accident.

He studied the floor, seeking the weapon. He lifted his phone and photographed the empty satchel. Then, with a final silent apology to Keith, he walked out of the hut, taking a few steadying deep breaths as he headed to the Volvo.

He was within sight of Travis's hostel before he tried his phone again. Still no signal. Nothing for it but to pull up outside the café and go in. The bikers were finishing their scones and coffees. Travis was busy at the sink.

102

'Can I use your landline?' Rebus asked.

'You look like you've seen a ghost,' Travis joked, before quickly realising the import of both Rebus's demeanour and his voice. He led him behind the counter into a cramped office and then retreated. Rebus tapped in the number the detective had given him.

'DS Creasey,' the voice eventually answered.

'It's John Rebus. I've just found Keith Grant's body.'

'Where?'

'Accommodation block at Camp 1033.'

'The internment camp?'

'The very same.'

'Did he fall or something?'

'Hit from behind. His skull's cracked open.'

'Who else knows?'

'Right now, just you and me.'

'It'll take me a couple of hours to get a scene-of-crime team there. I'll call Thurso. I'm sure they can spare a uniform or two until then, secure the locus if nothing else.' Creasey paused. 'What took you there, John?'

'Questions later,' Rebus said firmly. 'For now, get the ball rolling.' He ended the call, staring at the handset while squeezing the bridge of his nose, trying to organise his thoughts. After a few moments, he walked back into the café. Travis was clearing the visitors' table. Rebus watched their bikes roar off in the direction of Tongue.

'Don't worry,' Travis said, reading his mind. 'They've no plans to stop at the camp.' Then: 'Sweetened tea's supposed to be the thing for shock . . .'

103

Rebus shook his head. 'But I need to do a spot of guard duty — maybe a couple of filled rolls to take away?'

'I can do you a flask of something hot to go with them?'

'Great, aye, thanks.'

'Am I allowed to ask what's happened?'

'Afraid not.'

'The poor lad. I did warn him about sleeping there.'

Rebus stared at Travis. 'You did?'

'He had a sleeping bag, mind, but you can still catch hypothermia, even in summer.'

'When was this?'

'A month or so back. After the trouble at home. I was driving past one night and saw his car parked by the fence. He was in one of the huts. I told him I had a bed for him here, but he said no.'

Rebus opened his phone and found the photo of the satchel. 'Recognise this?' he asked, turning the screen towards Travis.

'Looks like his bag. Kept his history stuff in it.' Travis paused. 'And his laptop, of course.' He seemed to realise the import of the photograph. 'It wasn't the cold that killed him?' he guessed.

Rebus shook his head, saying nothing.

'Oh.' Some of the blood left Travis's cheeks. 'I'll fetch you that flask,' he said distractedly, shuffling off towards the kitchen area. 'Ham or cheese for the rolls?'

'Maybe one of each.'

'Yes, of course.'

Five minutes later, Rebus was back on the

road, having warned Travis not to say anything to anyone. He parked in the same spot as before but stayed in the car this time, one window lowered until the rain started blowing in. The radio was failing to find stations on any of its wavelengths. The flask was filled with lentil soup, which poured like sludge into the cup and was saltier than Rebus liked. Not that he really tasted it; same went for the rolls. Travis had added lettuce and tomato, Rebus tossing both onto the verge.

It was the best part of an hour before he heard the approaching engine. The patrol car's blue lights were flashing as it pulled to a skidding stop alongside the Volvo, effectively blocking the road. Rebus got out and watched four uniformed officers — three men, one woman — decant from the vehicle.

'Blues and twos all the way from Thurso, eh?' he enquired.

'We were told to hurry.'

'Well, you've successfully alerted every living thing within forty miles that something's happened. Rumour mill will be grinding as we speak.'

'Who are you anyway?' the driver asked, reckoning attack a better tactic than defence.

'I'm the one who alerted CID. How long till the SOCOs get here?'

'So you found the body?' All four officers turned to look towards the camp. One reached into the back seat of the patrol car and brought out a roll of blue-and-white tape with the word POLICE printed on it.

'Whole camp is a crime scene until we know otherwise,' Rebus said. 'With you four guarding the perimeter, meaning the fence.' He nodded towards the tape. 'I'd say you're probably a few hundred metres short if that's all you brought.'

'Who *are* you?' the driver asked again, with a quizzical look on his face.

'I'm a man who's dealt with more than a few homicides in his time. If you don't want a bollocking from the murder team when they get here, you'll take instructions from me — understood?'

'You're not our boss,' the driver stated, taking a step towards Rebus and sizing him up. 'Far as I can see, you're nobody's boss. So do us all a favour and point us in the direction of the body. Then — and I say this with all due respect — piss off back to wherever you came from.'

Two of his colleagues weren't going to wait. They had already started climbing over the low gate. Seconds later they were tramping towards the nearest line of buildings. Rebus gave a shrug of resignation and retreated to the Volvo, watching as all four uniforms headed into the camp and out of sight. He knew he was going to stay put; partly because Creasey and his team would be on their way, but mostly to defer playing the role waiting for him back in Naver. He remembered Carrie watching him as he slept on the sofa.

Where's my daddy?

I heard Mummy crying.

Many more tears, he knew, would be shed before the day was finished.

8

There had been another attack overnight, a Chinese student shoved from behind, then kicked several times as she lay on the pavement. She had been checked at A&E and then released. Tess Leighton and George Gamble had been sent to interview her at her flat.

'Her English wasn't exactly fluent,' Gamble said, his eyes on his notepad. 'A friend did the translating.'

'Didn't help that she was in a state of shock,' Leighton interrupted, arms folded tightly across her chest. They were in the MIT office, the rest of the team listening intently. DCI Sutherland had checked the crime scene on the wall map, circling it in pencil. Argyle Place in Marchmont.

'It's mostly shops at ground level,' Leighton told him. 'Pub on the corner. No real witnesses as yet. Another student on their way home heard her groaning. Helped her to her feet. Reckoned she'd tripped and fallen.'

'Let's do door-to-door,' Sutherland said. 'And check if there's any CCTV. No description of the assailant?'

'She had her eyes on her phone, earbuds in and music playing. First she knew about it was when she was sent flying.'

'Universities and colleges are going to reinforce the safety message,' Christine Esson added. 'And the local media websites are leading with it.'

'Did the assailant take anything?'

'Just her phone,' Leighton said. 'Which makes me think it's a straightforward mugging. Despite which, the media are already yelling race crime.'

'Students and rich kids have always been seen as fair game,' Fox cautioned. 'No obvious reason to connect it to Salman bin Mahmoud.'

'Which won't stop social media doing exactly that,' Sutherland growled. 'So give me some good news.' He looked around the room, his eyes fixing on Clarke and Fox. 'Siobhan?'

'We spoke to Isabella Meiklejohn and Giovanni Morelli last night — mostly about the attack on Mr Morelli. They seem to be bearing the loss of their friend pretty well.'

'Meaning?'

'Let's say they weren't exactly in mourning. Had a night out planned at the Jenever Club. They also didn't look jittery, but that may be down to breeding. I'd say they've led pretty insulated lives.'

'I think what Siobhan's saying,' Fox interjected, 'is that if they knew why their friend had been targeted, they were pretty good at hiding it, and they seemed relaxed that they're not about to share his fate.'

'Nice bit of mansplaining,' Esson said, pretending to clap.

'I was just trying to —'

'Enough.' Sutherland held up a hand. 'Last night's attack will be investigated, but our focus

108

remains the homicide. I still don't know nearly enough about Mr bin Mahmoud. The Met are being their usual slow selves, and we're getting precious little joy from either his bank or his phone and internet providers. More effort needed, people.'

'Can we ask the government to apply some pressure?' Esson asked.

'That's gone a bit quiet,' Sutherland admitted. 'If you ask me, the Saudis have shrugged their shoulders. If they wanted a result, they'd be letting ministers and diplomats know, and we'd be getting a regular boot up the arse.'

'This is because the victim's family isn't flavour of the month?' Clarke asked.

'So no trade deals are in danger of being compromised, whatever the outcome.'

'Unless it turns out he was bumped off by Saudi agents,' Leighton said. When Gamble snorted, she turned towards him. 'Stranger things have happened, George.'

Fox, trying to avoid Clarke's eyes, was relieved when his phone began vibrating. He lifted it and studied the screen. Number withheld. He looked to Sutherland for guidance. Sutherland gave a jerk of the head in response. Fox answered the call as he made his exit.

'DI Fox,' he said, closing the door after him.

'Malcolm.'

That steady drawl, slightly nasal. 'Cafferty,' he said. 'How did you get this number?'

'Good to see you last night. I hope you got what you came for.'

'We came to see if you were shifting any

cocaine.' Fox listened to the momentary silence and the barked laugh that followed.

'I wasn't expecting that.'

'What?'

'The unvarnished truth.'

'What is it you want, Cafferty?'

'I hear there's been another mugging. Anything taken?'

'Victim's phone — why?'

'I was going to offer my services. Now that cops like Rebus are history, you lot have lost a valuable resource.'

'Meaning?'

'Snitches, grasses, eyes and ears on the street.'

'Human intelligence is the term these days. You're offering to put the word out — mind if I ask why?'

'Call me a concerned citizen. Not going to be in anyone's interests if people are scared to go out at night.'

'Night being when you do most of your business.'

'Guilty as charged.' There was silence on the line for a moment. 'Now that I've got you, though . . .'

'Finally he gets to the point.'

'Know what? That tone of voice is making me change my mind. Might be better taking it direct to your boss.'

'I can give you his number.'

'I don't mean Sutherland.'

Fox's brow furrowed. 'Who then?'

'Your boss at Major Crime, Assistant Chief Constable Jennifer Lyon.'

'And what exactly is it you think she needs to know?'

'Best done face to face, Malcolm. You know the address?'

'I was there last night.'

'I mean my home address. Half an hour — probably best make some excuse to Siobhan. Your boss would want it that way, trust me . . .'

★ ★ ★

Cafferty's flat comprised the top three storeys of a contemporary glass-and-steel construction in what for a long time had been the grounds of the city's main hospital, now rebranded as Quartermile. Fox was there within twenty minutes, having exited the police station without bothering to give a reason. He pressed the bell and was buzzed into the building, taking the lift to the penthouse. The door off the landing was open, Cafferty himself standing there, a tomato juice in his hand.

'Come in, come in,' he said by way of welcome, leading the way.

The hallway led to a vast open space with a mezzanine above. Floor-to-ceiling windows gave uninterrupted views across the Meadows towards Marchmont and the Pentland Hills beyond. To the east could be seen Arthur's Seat and Salisbury Crags, the outlines of hardy tourists visible on the peak.

'Not bad, eh?'

'Crime pays, as the saying goes.'

Cafferty laughed, gesturing towards the

kitchen area. 'Coffee or anything?' Fox shook his head.

'Let's get this over with,' he said.

'All brisk and businesslike — good man.' Cafferty settled himself in a leather armchair, unsurprised that Fox stayed standing. 'So here's the thing . . . ' He broke off. 'Sure I can't get you a drink?'

'Spit it out.'

Cafferty raised the glass he was holding. 'I would, but it's one of my five a day. Doctor says I've to take care of myself. Don't want to end up like poor old Rebus, can't even manage a flight of stairs.' He gave a sigh when Fox remained mute and as still as a statue. 'Here's the thing then — your boss, ACC Lyon. Way I hear it, her career progression's ongoing. Chief Constable will be put out to pasture in a year, maybe two at most. He'd be gone by now if he had his way, but they won't let him. Poor bugger's knackered, though, put body and soul into getting the organisation back on an even keel. Budget still needs sorting out, but I doubt that'll ever change.' He fixed Fox with a look, gave a wide smile. 'As you can tell, Police Scotland has become a bit of a hobby.'

'I'm still not hearing why I'm here.'

'You're here because Jennifer Lyon's friction-less upward trajectory might be about to go into free fall.' Cafferty's free hand made a downward corkscrew motion. 'Which would be a shame for her. And the irony is, it's not even her fault, not exactly. It's all because of her husband.' He took a sip of his drink, eyes apparently on the view outside his window.

Fox slid his hands into his pockets; not much of a reaction, but a reaction nonetheless.

'So here's what you need to do, Malcolm . . . ' Cafferty broke off again. 'Sure you don't want a seat, by the way? You've gone a bit pale.'

'Just tell me.'

He took another sip of his drink first, seeming to savour it. Then, when he was good and ready: 'I can make it all go away — the photos and the video. Now, she may not want to hear that, so if you like, what you tell her is that *you* can make it all go away. My name doesn't have to feature, if that's the way you want to play it. What matters is that this is your fast track to promotion once she's installed in the top job.'

Fox's jaw tightened. He wasn't going to give Cafferty the satisfaction of asking the obvious question. Cafferty smiled into his near-empty glass. The juice had left red stains around his mouth.

'I still haven't heard what it is *you* want,' Fox said quietly.

'The answer is: not much. And nothing illegal.'

'So tell me.'

Cafferty made show of rising to his feet. 'Maybe a wee top-up first . . . '

'*Fucking tell me!*'

Cafferty eased himself back to sitting, a contented look on his face. Then he started to speak.

★ ★ ★

The Scottish Crime Campus was based at Gartcosh in Lanarkshire, purpose-built on the site of an old steelworks, the land around it still largely undeveloped. Nominally, Police Scotland's HQ was at Tulliallan, but everyone knew Gartcosh was where the serious business got done.

ACC Jennifer Lyon always strode the corridors and open areas of Gartcosh with a sense of purpose. Fox had deduced long ago that this was more to do with deterring people from collaring her with a request than because she had anywhere she needed urgently to be. He'd been weighing up his opening gambits ever since starting the hour-long drive from Edinburgh. Even so, the sight of her walking towards him, multiple lanyards swinging from her neck, almost caused his mind to go blank. He was about to be the bearer of bad tidings, and recipients never forgot.

'Malcolm,' she said, by way of stony-faced greeting. 'I take it there's news?'

'News?'

'The murder case.'

'Not as such, ma'am.'

She tilted her head slightly. Her hair was straw-blonde, no slivers of grey allowed, and cut to resemble a protective helmet cupping her skull.

'Well then,' she prompted.

Fox cleared his throat. 'Best done in private, ma'am.'

She looked around at the huge open atrium. Staff shuffled past quietly, some whispering into

114

phones, others glancing in the direction of the feared and powerful ACC.

'Please tell me I'm not going to have to cover your arse for something.' Fox shook his head. 'Well, that's a blessing.' She started walking again, Fox maintaining a slight distance.

No one was waiting in the reception area attached to her office. Her assistant glanced up from her computer, recognised Fox and gave the thinnest of smiles in acknowledgement. Lyon was behind her uncluttered desk by the time Fox had closed the door. He stood for a moment, but her glare told him to sit. The chair was tubular, solid, and not built for comfort. Fox's throat felt a little dry. He cleared it again.

'It's a message of sorts,' he began. 'Not from someone we'd classify as friendly. I'll tell you who if you like, but ignorance might work in your favour.'

'Maybe give me the message first.' She leaned her elbows on the desk, angling her body forward a little to signal that he had her undivided attention.

'Something about your husband, ma'am. Photos and video — I'm guessing involving him — that could prove an embarrassment to you and maybe even affect your career.'

He watched as Jennifer Lyon digested the information. Her eyes lost their focus momentarily. She eventually lifted her elbows, leaning back in her chair, her shoulders stiffened.

'All right,' she said in a toneless voice. 'Who was it told you?'

'You're sure you want to know?'

'Just tell me, for Christ's sake.'

'Morris Gerald Cafferty.'

'Aka Big Ger.' She nodded almost imperceptibly. 'Photos and video?'

It was Fox's turn to nod. 'Not that he showed me any.'

'Unlikely to be a bluff, though?'

'He sounded fairly confident.' Fox paused. 'You've always managed to keep your personal life private . . .'

'You know who my husband is, though?'

Yes, Fox knew. His name was Dennis Jones; he was vice chancellor of one of the newer west-coast universities. 'I'm guessing it's not financial impropriety,' he posited. 'Not sure that would yield much in the way of interesting footage.'

Lyon's mouth twitched. 'An affair,' she said, her eyes fixed on the desktop. 'Not a student, before you ask — a member of staff, also married. Brief, stupid and finished.'

'Speaking of stupid . . . Could the two of them have enjoyed a night out in Edinburgh? Maybe at a club on the Cowgate?'

'Cafferty owns one, does he? Covered by plenty of cameras, I assume.' She picked up a pen, studied it and tossed it back onto the desk. 'Why are men such bloody idiots?'

'You said it's over — is that because you found out?'

'And made the usual ultimatum.'

'Recently?'

She gave him a hard stare. 'Does it matter?' But then she relented. 'A couple of months back.' She sprang to her feet, walking behind her chair, gripping its frame with both hands. 'So what now?' she asked.

'He says he can make it all go away if we do him a favour.'

Lyon shook her head determinedly. 'You know we can't do that.'

'If it helps, it's nothing illegal. He just wants us to mount an operation, do some digging, maybe a spot of surveillance . . .'

'Against a competitor?'

Fox shrugged. 'I'd assume so. We might have a better idea afterwards.'

'What does he expect us to find?'

'I'm not sure he knows.'

'And who's the target?'

'A developer called Stewart Scoular.'

'I know the name.'

'He was an MSP for the shortest time. I happened to see him yesterday evening.'

'Oh?'

'Drinking in Cafferty's club. He was with a couple of friends of Salman bin Mahmoud.'

'He's part of your investigation?'

Fox shook his head. 'He's not been nagged up as yet.'

'Well, I'd say he's been flagged up now, wouldn't you agree?'

'Yes, ma'am.'

'Nothing as yet to suggest Saudi state involvement?'

'No.'

'I'll keep Special Branch posted.' Lyon considered for a moment before sitting down again. 'I should meet with Cafferty.'

'With respect, that would be reckless. I'm happy to act as intermediary.'

'Do we have anything at all on this man Scoular? He's not come onto our radar at any point?'

'Is there any harm in looking?'

'You tell me, Malcolm. How far would you trust your chum Cafferty?'

'No distance at all. But he wants something and he thinks we're his best chance of getting it. And I *am* intrigued by his interest in Scoular . . . '

'So we humour him until we have an answer?'

'Or until he hands over the photos and video.'

Lyon pointed a finger at Fox. 'You need to be shown what he's got, Malcolm. I don't want to see it, but you should. Just so we know we're not dealing with a bullshitter.'

'Understood.'

'And any digging that happens, the quieter it's done the better.' Her eyes brightened. 'In fact, the case you're attached to is perfect — just lasso Scoular and make him part of it. Can you do that without attracting undue attention?'

'I doubt I could raise a surveillance operation.'

'Depends what you dig up, doesn't it?' There was the merest edge of need to her voice and her demeanour.

'I'll do everything in my power, ma'am,' Malcolm Fox said.

9

When Rebus answered the knock at the door, May Collins was standing there, solemn-faced and holding out two large carrier bags.

'They're yours if you want them,' she said. 'Belonged to my late husband. You're about the same size. I mean, I'm assuming you'll be staying put, and you won't find many clothes shops around here . . . ' She broke off.

Rebus accepted both bags and peered into one of them. 'You've heard, then?' he said.

'Oh John, isn't it terrible?' Her voice cracked. 'How's Samantha doing?'

'She's taken Carrie to a friend's.'

'Were you the one who broke the news?'

Rebus sucked in some air, nodding while exhaling.

'That must have been terrible.'

Terrible? Rebus wasn't sure the word was strong enough. Samantha had backed away from him, lashing out when he tried to touch her, wailing and roaring and inconsolable. Shock soon replaced the look of horror: what would she say to Carrie? What words would lessen the blow? She had looked at her phone, checking the time. She would have to go to the school. Where was her coat?

Her father: you need to sit down first. Just take five minutes.

'*Haven't you done enough?!*' A yell of

accusation, a howling at the only thing in the world at that moment close enough to deserve it. And when Rebus tried reaching out again, she slapped at his hands. 'I've managed fine without you all these years . . . '

Despite Rebus having given no answer, May Collins was nodding as if he had — a nod of sympathy and understanding. 'I could make you a cup of tea, but I'm not sure that would help. A belt of whisky maybe?'

Rebus shook his head, watching as Collins remembered something. 'Mick got your car started. He's not saying it'll get you home, but I've got the key.'

Rebus took it from her. 'What do I owe him?'

'I doubt he'd accept anything- especially now.' She gave another sigh. 'If you need me, you know where I am.'

They both turned at the sound of vehicles speeding past. Two cars, one van, no markings. Professionals who were about to be busy at Camp 1033.

'I'm not sure I should be asking,' May Collins said quietly, 'but did he do away with himself?' Rebus's face remained impassive. 'An accident then?'

'No accident,' he said.

Her mouth formed a large O, her eyes widening at the realisation.

'Well,' she said, 'I suppose I'd better . . . ' She was twisting the top half of her body, motioning to leave while hoping he would invite her to stay.

'Thanks for the clothes,' Rebus said, going back into the bungalow and closing the door.

In the bathroom he selected a few items and changed into them, then went into the kitchen and stuffed his own clothes into the machine, selecting the quickest wash available. A car was drawing up outside. He beat Creasey to the door and was waiting for him.

'Mind if I come in?' the young detective sergeant enquired, as solicitously as any funeral director. Rebus led the way to the living room.

'Samantha's at a friend's.'

'How's she doing?' Rebus could only shrug. 'And the little one?'

Another shrug. 'I wasn't there when Samantha told her — *if* she's told her.'

Creasey settled on the edge of the sofa. 'It's bloody awful news, of course, and it'll take time to sink in . . .'

'But you need to interview her all the same?'

'You know we do. And Forensics are going to want to inspect the Volvo.'

'They'll find my prints.'

'And mine,' Creasey said. 'So we'll need yours and Samantha's for purposes of elimination.'

'You've been to the camp; you've seen him?' Creasey gave a slow nod. 'The empty satchel — he used to keep his notes and laptop in it, according to the guy who runs the café along the road.'

'We're in the process of getting a statement from Mr Travis.'

Rebus realised he had lowered himself onto the arm of one of the chairs — he wasn't about to get comfortable.

'Keith slept there a few nights after he found

out about Samantha and Jess Hawkins.'

'We'll be talking to *everyone*, John, trust me.' Creasey paused. 'You are going to trust me?'

'Why do you ask?'

'Because of everything I've learned about you; because you've worked your whole life in the central belt and you might think those of us based up here are a bit . . . rustic. I'm here to tell you that we know the job, and we'll be every bit as thorough as you'd want and expect.'

Rebus was staring at the floor. 'It has to be something to do with that camp,' he stated.

'Why?'

'The missing laptop.'

'The one thing any opportunist would take with them — portable and easy to sell on. His phone is missing too.' Rebus was shaking his head, and Creasey gave him a disappointed look. 'So what was it about the camp that was so important to Mr Grant?'

'I don't know, but the garage here is full of research. You need to talk to the local history group. They might have some answers.'

'We'll get round to it.'

'I suppose the autopsy comes first? Cause of death as starting point? Fingertip search of the camp?'

Creasey was nodding along.

'With my daughter as a suspect, maybe even the main suspect?'

'You've been in my shoes; you know how this plays out. It doesn't mean we won't show discretion. And Victim Support will be here for your daughter and granddaughter as and when they need it.' Creasey rose to his feet. 'Volvo keys on the hall table?' Rebus nodded. 'I'll take them with me then. Samantha may have a spare set, but she'd be wise to leave the car untouched until we're finished with it.'

'I'll make sure she knows.'

Creasey reached out his hand and clasped Rebus's. 'You need to be a father now, leave everything else to us.'

Rebus met Creasey's eyes as he nodded. 'Tell me,' he said. 'Did they take his cash and credit cards?'

'His wallet was in his pocket, untouched by the look of it.'

'And you still think robbery's a possible motive?'

'Everything's a motive at this point.'

'Try not to forget that, son. Don't get lazy.'

He saw the detective to the door, watched through the living room window as he got into his car and drove off, heading in the direction of the crime scene. When the engine noise had faded, he put his coat on and headed out to the garage. Settling himself on the fold-down chair in front of the trestle table, he began to read more thoroughly about Camp 1033.

10

Fox was halfway back to Edinburgh when he decided to answer Siobhan Clarke's latest attempt at calling him.

'What's with the Houdini act?' she enquired.

'I was summoned to Gartcosh — boss there needed me.'

'Must be nice to feel wanted. But meantime I've had a text from John.'

'On his way back?'

'The exact opposite — a body's turned up. His daughter's partner.'

'Bloody hell. Suicide?'

'Text didn't say and I can't get him to answer his phone — it's almost like he's taking lessons from you.'

'I was in a meeting.'

'But you're on your way back now?'

'Another half-hour or so — where will we meet?'

'I'm taking Brillo to the Meadows. Need to pick up a couple of things from John's flat.'

'I'll see you there.' Fox ended the call, checked his mirror, signalled, and pulled out to overtake. Almost thirty years he'd been driving, and never a ticket or a scratch or a dent. Because he was cautious. He stuck to the rules. He knew what he was doing.

He wondered whether he would cross the line — and how far — for Assistant Chief Constable

Jennifer Lyon. And for his own prospect of promotion.

* * *

'He's going to have to go into kennels,' Clarke said, watching as Brillo tracked yet another of the Meadows' innumerable scents.

'You might be right,' Fox agreed. 'Still heard nothing more from John?'

She shook her head. 'I can't keep him shut up in my flat all day — or his owner's, come to that.'

'Is there maybe a neighbour?' Clarke's eyes bored into his. Fox lifted both hands. 'No, no, no. I told you, I'm not an animal person. Besides which, I'm working the same insane hours as you.'

'And neither of us with much to show for it.'

'What about someone else in the office — Christine or Ronnie? You could pull rank on either of them.'

'It's crossed my mind.' Clarke dug her phone out of her pocket and checked the screen. 'Speak of the devil,' she said, answering. 'What can I do for you, Christine?'

'We've just had the most colossal break in the case.'

'Very funny.'

'Time was you might have fallen for that.'

Clarke could hear the soft clatter of computer keyboards in the background.

'Getting a bit bored in the office, are we?'

'Obviously, but I'm phoning to see if you think John Rebus might be up for a night at the theatre.'

'The theatre?'

'Remember I told you Lee Child and Karin Slaughter are coming to Edinburgh? Well, it's tonight and my date's dropped out, meaning I've got a spare.'

'John's still up north.'

'In which case, this is your lucky day.'

'Have you asked Ronnie?'

'He only reads comics.'

'Graphic novels.' Clarke heard Ronnie Ogilvie correcting Esson from across the desk.

'I'll let you know,' she said. 'Has my absence been noted yet?'

'The DCI's had another summons from our lords and masters. Ronnie and me are about to bask in front of several hours' worth of CCTV.'

'I won't keep you then. Bye, Christine.' Clarke ended the call and then whistled for Brillo to come to her, readying his leash. She glanced in Fox's direction. 'It was nothing earth-shaking then, your trip to Gartcosh?'

'No,' he said with a shake of the head.

'No updates from London about Middle Eastern hit squads jetting in and out again?'

'Passenger lists have been scoured. Special Branch are nothing if not thorough.'

'You stressed that we're all working ourselves to death here?'

'Absolutely.'

'That's fine then.' Clarke had taken a couple of steps in the direction of Melville Drive, but stopped when she saw that Fox wasn't about to accompany her.

'I'm parked that way,' he said, gesturing in the

vague direction of the university buildings beyond the Meadows.

'That's miles away,' Clarke said. He offered a slight wrinkling of his mouth.

'Catch you back at base,' he said, turning away from her.

She watched him go. He half turned his head as if to check on her, then quickened his pace. Clarke started walking in the opposite direction, Brillo looking up at her, wondering if she might morph back into his owner. He seemed happy enough when she scooped him up into her arms, turning to follow Fox. There was no good reason that she could think of for him to have parked so far away. He had his phone out, looking at it as he walked. Clarke made a slight detour off the path and onto the grass. There were plenty of pedestrians about, plenty of dog-walkers and students playing with frisbees and footballs. An observant eye might still spot her, but there were no further backward glances from Fox as he headed up Middle Meadow Walk. He took a left at the first café, heading into the Quartermile complex. There was an underground car park there, but it was pricey. Too pricey, she reckoned, for the frugal Malcolm Fox. Reaching the narrow footpath that led down the side of the café, she saw no sign of him. The street ahead was clear. So either he *had* descended into the car park or . . .

She tiptoed through the nearest gateway and glanced around a corner towards the entrance to the first of the modern apartment blocks. Its glass door was just rattling closed. She waited a moment, then moved towards the door, still cautious. Looking through the glass, she watched as the quartz display panel above the lift ticked over a series of numbers, pausing on a letter rather than a number.

P for penthouse.

Clarke met Brillo's questioning eyes. 'We know who lives there, don't we, boy?' she said in a whisper. Then, staring upwards, her neck arched: 'I hope you know what you're doing, Malcolm. I really do . . .'

★　★　★

As soon as he left Cafferty's block, Fox got on the phone to Jennifer Lyon.

'It's tame stuff,' he informed her. 'They're in the Jenever Club. Upstairs at first, till a flunkey hands them a card. It confers VIP status, so they head to that area of the club.'

'Go on.'

'There's a bit of dancing . . . kisses and cuddles.' He cleared his throat.

'Yes?'

'That's about the sum of it. They're intimate, but there's no actual . . .'

'I get the picture.'

'Cafferty says it wasn't their only visit to the place, but my guess is, if he had anything more incriminating he'd have shown it to me.'

'Okay, thanks.'

'It really is fairly tame.'

'Nevertheless, he *was* sleeping with her. If Cafferty releases the footage, Dennis would have some explaining to do.'

'He could always deny it went any further.'

Fox heard her sigh. 'I've looked up this man Scoular online. He seems perfectly legit. Did Cafferty give you any more of a clue why he's interested or what he thinks we might find?'

'None.'

'Then let's go ahead and buy ourselves some time.'

'By digging a bit deeper into Scoular's life?'

'As a salient part of the bin Mahmoud inquiry.'

'Whatever you say, ma'am.'

'I appreciate this, Malcolm. Don't think I'll forget it.'

'Thank you.'

When the call ended, Fox found he had a bit of extra spring in his step as he headed towards his car. One thing he didn't think Lyon needed to know about — the brief foray by her husband and his lady friend into the alcove occupied by Scoular and his associates. The line of cocaine offered and accepted. Followed by champagne and laughter and the sheer look of relaxed pleasure on Dennis Jones's face . . .

★ ★ ★

'See when I phone you, Benny,' Cafferty snarled into his mobile as he stood by his apartment window, staring out across the city, 'I expect you to pick up on the first fucking ring. Do you understand? I don't care if you're in the middle of a shit or a shag, nothing's more important than my time.'

129

'Sorry, boss. Need me to bring the car round?'

'What I need you to do is get off your fat arse and go talk to a few people. Chinese student was mugged last night and her phone taken. If it's some wee fud from the schemes, he'll be blabbing about it. You need to go to those schemes and find out who he is.'

'What for?'

'Because I'm telling you to!'

'Sure, boss, absolutely.'

'Attack happened in Marchmont, so maybe start in the south — Moredun, Gracemount . . . psycho country, in other words. You got any contacts there?'

'Some, aye.'

'Fuck are you waiting for then? News or no news, phone me in two hours.'

Cafferty stabbed at his mobile, ending the call. He waited for his breathing to return to normal. Maybe sixty or seventy per cent of his job was act and attitude. He wasn't like some of these younger thugs who needed to be tooled up to get what they wanted. A look and a word was usually enough — or it had been in the past. It was getting harder, the world was changing. The younger model of gangster tended to have no boundaries and no off-switch. They were creeping north from places like Manchester and Liverpool, muscling in on cities like Dundee where the last thing the resident population needed was a cheaper but altogether more venal and threatening source of drugs. So far Cafferty's reputation had protected much of his Edinburgh operation, but he wasn't sure that would last much longer. Even so, he still had his club, the boutique hotel in the New Town, the car wash and the betting shop.

And then there were the flats he rented out, many of the classier ones to overseas students. Predominantly these days those students were Chinese. One of their number got attacked with no comebacks, they might begin to wonder if Edinburgh was the place for them. Wouldn't matter so much if there were other nationalities to replace them, but with the uncertainty of Brexit . . . A large part of his income was clean these days and he wanted to keep it that way. Property had proven a solid investment, and he was considering moving into commercial land development — Stewart Scoular's domain, to be precise. It was a world he hoped would bring him closer to people of quality, people like Lady Isabella and the bin Mahmoud family. People like Giovanni Morelli.

And further all the time from Benny and his ilk.

Cafferty cast his eyes around the room he was standing in.

'Never enough,' he said to himself.

No matter how much and how far, it was never anything like enough.

11

The main street of Naver was busier than Rebus had seen it. Knots of locals deep in conversation, cars cruising up and down, their occupants drinking in every moment and interaction. Rebus knew that the media would be on their way, too, ready to swell the ranks of gawpers. He unlocked his Saab and turned the ignition. The engine started first time but didn't sound one hundred per cent. When he pushed down hard on the accelerator, eyes turned to look at him. He turned the engine off and got out again.

He kept his head down as he walked, ignoring the couple of questioning voices, people who obviously knew who he was. The house he wanted was towards the end of the street. He rang the doorbell and waited. A woman in her seventies, slightly stooped, opened the door and gestured him inside as if welcoming a refugee. She gripped both his hands in her own.

'A terrible, terrible shock to all of us.'

'Thanks for seeing me at such short notice, Mrs McKechnie.'

'Not at all, not at all. Please, this way. And call me Joyce.'

The sitting room was small and cluttered, china ornaments everywhere, framed family photos covering the walls. The fire was lit and seemed to be sucking all the oxygen from the confined space. There was a metal tray on the coffee table, cups, best china, and biscuits laid out. A man a few years younger than Mrs McKechnie had risen to his feet.

'Edward Taylor,' he said, shaking Rebus's hand.

'Sit down, the pair of you,' Joyce McKechnie commanded. 'Let me sort this out.' She lifted the teapot. 'Edward takes his black.'

'Spot of milk, thanks,' Rebus told her, sloughing off his jacket. Taylor was offering the plate of shortbread but Rebus shook his head.

'Dreadful news about Keith,' Taylor said. 'My condolences.'

'Thank you.' There was silence until McKechnie had settled herself. 'And I want to thank you again for agreeing to speak to me.'

'The very least we can do,' McKechnie said. Her accent was local, but Rebus got the feeling Taylor was from further south.

'Even from my short time here, it's obvious to me that Keith loved the history group.'

'He was our hope for the future,' Taylor said. 'The rest of us are in what some would call our twilight years.'

'The other members?' Rebus nudged.

'I phoned Anna, but no answer,' Joyce McKechnie said. 'I don't think they're back from their holiday.'

Anna and Jim Breakspear: the two other names Rebus had found in Keith Grant's notes.

'A select gathering,' he commented.

'On paper, we've well over a dozen members, but not everyone can spare as much time as they'd like.'

133

'On the other hand,' Taylor added, 'Keith held down a full-time job and still played his part.' He began to fiddle with one of the buttons on his dun-coloured cardigan.

'You're all fairly spry, though,' Rebus reasoned. 'I saw the digging you'd been doing.'

McKechnie gave a chuckle. 'We twisted a few arms and managed to rally volunteers from the youth club.'

Rebus nodded his understanding and switched on his phone, finding the photo he needed. He rose to his feet, turning the screen away from him and holding it out. 'Keith's satchel has been found, but it was empty. What would you expect to be in it?'

Taylor peered at the photo. 'Maybe his latest notebook — he filled dozens of them.'

'And his laptop,' McKechnie added.

'Any idea what he'd keep on the laptop?'

'They're not even called that these days, are they?' Taylor interrupted before taking a sip from his cup. 'Something to do with burnt knees and a lawsuit.'

McKechnie had been pondering. 'Notes about the camp, of course. And photos, maps, that sort of thing.'

Rebus's phone buzzed and he checked the screen, noting that he'd missed a few other calls. Two were from Laura Smith, crime reporter on the *Scotsman* newspaper. He switched the phone off and pocketed it.

'Would you say the camp had become an obsession?' he asked.

'Probably,' Taylor said, while McKechnie

nodded her agreement.

'Though I did wonder . . . ' McKechnie broke off, mouth tightening.

'Anything you say could be helpful,' Rebus prompted.

'Well, the camp is practically next door to Stalag Hawkins . . . '

'Stalag Hawkins?'

She gave a thin smile. 'Keith's name for it — we all found ourselves using it in time.'

'You mean the commune?'

Taylor brushed a few crumbs from the legs of his trousers. 'You know Samantha had become quite friendly with them?'

'She told me about her and Hawkins, if that's what you're asking. But that was over and done with.'

'Of course.'

Rebus focused on McKechnie. 'The camp was a way for Keith to spy on the commune? It's not even visible from there, is it?'

'But cars coming and going are.'

'He told you this?'

She shook her head. 'We just wondered, that's all.'

'It hardly explains the amount of work he put in — all the costings to turn the camp into a visitor attraction.'

'You're right, of course,' Taylor said, placing his cup back on the tray and refusing the offer of a refill. 'The place got its talons into him.'

'Ghosts don't have talons, Edward,' McKechnie said with a thin smile.

'Ghosts?' Rebus looked from McKechnie to

135

Taylor and back again.

'Plenty of people perished in and around Camp 1033 during its short existence. Some from illness and natural causes, others by firing squad or other means.'

'Other means?' Rebus echoed.

'Murder; poisonings . . . '

'And Keith was interested in all that?'

'Quite interested,' Taylor agreed.

Rebus rubbed a hand along his jaw. 'I've been through all his notes I can find. I think I saw mention in at least one of the books he'd bought of deaths at other camps. But nothing about Camp 1033.'

'He even recorded some interviews, didn't he?' McKechnie looked to Taylor, who nodded his agreement. 'With those who remember the camp — and before you ask, Mr Rebus, it was *slightly* before my time.'

Rebus managed the smile she seemed to be expecting. 'Just so I'm clear, you mean interviews with people living right here?'

'He also wrote to a few survivors overseas — internees who'd returned to Germany or Poland after the war.'

'Or England or the States,' Taylor added.

'Filmed interviews?' Rebus enquired.

'Audio, I think.' Taylor looked to McKechnie, who offered a shrug. 'Kept on a memory stick.'

Rebus tried to remember if he'd seen any in the garage. 'We can't be talking about many people,' he said.

'And fewer all the time,' Taylor acknowledged.

'I know he spoke to May Collins, but he

interviewed her father too?'

'Joe Collins, yes. And Frank Hess, Stefan Novack, Helen Carter . . . ' Taylor's eyes were on Joyce McKechnie again.

'I'm pretty sure those are all that remain,' she agreed.

'It would be a huge help to me,' Rebus said, leaning forward, elbows on knees, 'if you could maybe put your heads together and write down anything you can remember about those interviews and the deaths at Camp 1033. Would that be possible?'

'The ghosts didn't kill him, Mr Rebus,' McKechnie said, not unkindly.

'I'm just trying to get a sense of who he was. I really wish I'd taken the chance while he was alive.'

'We quite understand,' Taylor said. 'And we'll do whatever we can.'

'I appreciate that,' Rebus said, getting to his feet.

★ ★ ★

Samantha was in Carrie's bedroom, packing a bag. Her eyes were red-rimmed when she looked at him.

'Your stuff will be dry soon. Where did the clothes come from?'

'May Collins.'

'Her husband's?'

'Aye.'

'She kept her dead husband's clothes?'

'What are you doing?'

137

'Carrie's going to stay with Jenny.'

'You've told her?'

She puffed out her cheeks and expelled air. 'Where have you been anyway?'

'Talking to the local history group.'

She gave him another look. 'Any particular reason?'

'He was found at the camp, Sammy.'

'Please — it's Samantha.' She zipped shut the bag, considered for a moment. 'Toothbrush,' she said, squeezing past him. He followed her the few steps to the bathroom.

'Can we talk?'

'What about?'

'Keith's satchel was at the camp. Looks like whatever was in it was taken.'

'So?'

'You never mentioned a satchel. Or his laptop — that's missing, too, unless you know better.'

She froze, eventually turning to face him. 'Who the fuck am I talking to right now? I really need to know it's my dad standing there and not just another cop who's pulled me in for questioning.'

'Sammy — '

'*Samanth!*' She was choking back tears as she barged past him. By the time he caught up with her, she was circling the kitchen table, looking around her wildly as if trying to locate something irretrievably lost.

'They all think I had something to do with it,' she blurted out. 'Eyes on me as I walk past. Facebook and the rest ready to burn me at the stake. Your lot need fingerprints, a hair sample

138

for DNA; they need a statement, a formal identification. And they're just getting started.' The fire inside her began to die back a little. 'We'd had a row that night. Not much of one in the grand scheme of things, but your pal Creasey won't see it like that. I'm so tired and I'm at my wits' end and Keith's dead and I have to keep Carrie from seeing me falling apart.' She blinked the world back into some kind of focus. 'Any words of wisdom, Detective Inspector?'

'I'm here for you, Samantha.'

'Same as you ever were, eh? Phone call twice a year if Mum and me were lucky.' She sucked in some air and gestured towards the washer-dryer. 'When that's done, I want you to leave.'

'Christ's sake, Samantha . . .'

'I mean it. I can manage. I'm going to have to.' She wouldn't meet his eyes. 'I heard they fixed your car, so there's really no excuse.'

'There's every excuse — you're the only family I've got, you and Carrie. I want to help.'

'Then answer me this.' Her eyes were boring into his as she approached, until their faces were inches apart. 'Am I a suspect?'

'The police need to be able to rule you out.'

'And until then I'm ruled *in*, is that it? By you and them both?' She shook her head slowly. Her voice when she spoke again had lost all its force. 'Just go, Dad. Don't be here when I get back.' She hoisted the bag over one shoulder, paused at the door to the outside world.

'A dead man's clothes,' she said, more to herself than for his benefit. And then she was gone.

139

He considered following her, tailing her all the way back into the village. Didn't Carrie deserve to see him? Couldn't Samantha be made to see sense? But instead he slumped onto one of the kitchen chairs and waited for the machine to finish its cycle.

★ ★ ★

Thirty minutes later, he walked into The Glen. The place was busy. Conversation quietened as he entered. One local was being interviewed by a journalist, a phone held up to record whatever story was being told. Rebus marched up to the bar. May Collins' attention was on the two bags of clothes he was carrying rather than on Rebus himself. Eventually she lifted her eyes to meet his.

'Don't suppose this place has rooms?' he asked.

12

A bar five minutes' walk from the MIT base at Leith police station had become the team's haunt of an evening. Graham Sutherland would sense that motivation was flagging or fatigue setting in and would announce that 'The downing of tools will be replaced by the downing of beverages'. As ever, it was his debit card that paid for the first two rounds — boss's rules. There was a corner table that seemed always to be available, supplemented by stools dragged from elsewhere in the bar. Sutherland had admitted to Siobhan Clarke that he phoned ahead and requested 'the usual spot'.

'Meaning a favour owed,' Clarke had responded. 'Careful, Graham, that's a slippery slope.'

'It's not like in Rebus's day. No trips to the back room for a bung or a bottle of Grouse.' Not even a discount — Sutherland had checked that wasn't happening, regardless of whose round it was.

There were six of them around the table this evening. Ronnie Ogilvie's attention was on a TV quiz show, calling out the answers before any of the contestants. Esson and Leighton were busy on their phones, their drinks almost untouched. Fox was focused on the two bags of ridge-cut crisps that lay splayed on the table, licking his fingers after each mouthful.

'Cheers,' Sutherland said, hoisting his half-pint before taking a sip. Clarke had a gin and tonic with an extra bottle of tonic on the side. She thought again of Rebus's generation, doubted many of them would have worried about being breathalysed. It wasn't just that these were different times; it was more that Clarke and her colleagues were cut from very different cloth. There was still the occasional big night out, a release of pressure, but mostly they tended to treat the job as just that — a job. Gamble and Yeats had gone home, one to dinner cooked by his partner and the other to a regular five-a-side game. They were damned if police work was going to consume their every waking hour. Clarke looked across the table to Sutherland and wondered if that was why neither of them had managed to commit to the other, fearing their relationship would become swamped by the job and vice versa. A bit of breathing space was necessary.

Which was why she'd convinced herself to go to the author talk with Esson. They'd grab a quick bite somewhere near the venue, then switch off for a couple of hours. Turning her attention to Malcolm Fox as he washed more crisps down with a mouthful of Appletiser, she saw that his mind was elsewhere. He was pretending to be interested in the same quiz show as Ronnie Ogilvie, but only so he wouldn't have to engage with anyone else. He was deep in thought, working things through, not perturbed exactly but filled with a nervous energy she doubted any of the others could see. He'd said nothing about his visit to Cafferty; had just got to work on his computer, going through the details of Salman bin Mahmoud's friends and acquaintances, even phoning the Met to give them a further nudge. Walking past and pausing to listen, Sutherland had given him a pat on the shoulder by way of encouragement.

Fox shifted his eyes from the TV only when he realised his scrabbling fingers were failing to find any more crisps. Both packs were bare, save a few powdery crumbs. He saw that Clarke was watching and gave a shrug.

'So how much was the parking at Quarter-mile?' she asked. 'Is it as dear as people say?'

'I was in George Square,' he told her. 'That's as much as my wallet will stand.'

'Remember, all of you,' Sutherland interrupted, 'try to keep receipts for any and all legitimate expenses and be sure to put in a claim. We've not gone over budget yet and I doubt we will.'

'I could always go check out the Middle Eastern side of things if that would help,' Esson said with a smile, without looking up from her screen.

'The way Malcolm was pestering our friends in the Met,' Sutherland replied, 'I'm half expecting him to request a London trip.'

'Probably not necessary,' Fox stated. 'The deceased spent most of his time down there. If someone from that part of his life had wanted him dead, he wouldn't have met his end here.'

'Unless they wanted to throw us off the scent,' Ogilvie said, turning his attention from the game show's closing titles.

'I keep coming back to the locus,' Fox added. 'Why that godforsaken spot? Whose choice for a rendezvous — the victim's or his killer's?'

'One thing we've learned — it's been a popular stopping place in the past for drug deals and the dogging community.'

'The dogging community?' Esson laughed at Sutherland's phrase.

'Circles the victim moved in, I wouldn't have thought he had need of either. If he wanted drugs, plenty VIP clubs and friends' drawing rooms. And as for sex . . . '

'Was he sleeping with Issy Meiklejohn, do we think?' Esson asked her question of the table at large. 'Only she seems tight with this Italian guy, and as they say in detective training, *cherchez la femme*.'

Sutherland smiled and held his hands up. 'This was supposed to be a bit of R&R, in case you've forgotten. Somebody change the subject, *s'il vous plaît*.'

There was silence around the table. They lifted their glasses, toyed with their drinks. Tess Leighton was the first to give a sigh. 'I've got nothing.'

'Ditto,' Ogilvie added.

After they'd all stopped grinning, Sutherland suggested another round, but Esson shook her head.

'Me and Siobhan better get going.' She reached down to the floor to lift her bag. 'See you all in the office tomorrow?'

'I might stay for one more,' Ogilvie was telling

144

his boss. Fox looked sceptical, and Leighton, while nodding at the offer, had gone back to texting.

Clarke followed Esson out of the bar. It was still light, and would be for a few more hours. They were halfway to the car when her phone pinged. It was a message from Graham Sutherland.

Later tonight?

She hesitated. Decided not to reply straight away. She'd have to think about it.

★ ★ ★

The talk was being held at the Usher Hall. They'd parked on Grindlay Street and managed a main course at Dine.

'Who knew?' Clarke said, watching the crowd of people making their way into the talk.

'It's a sell-out,' Esson informed her, rummaging in her bag for their tickets.

Clarke had another message from Sutherland.

Heading back to Glasgow soon if you don't need me for anything.

He had a key to her flat, but she knew he would never presume.

If you're okay on your own, head to mine. Don't know what time I'll be back though. She was about to press send when she had a thought. *Anyone sticking around the pub? Malcolm gone home?*

A moment later, two texts arrived in tandem.

Thanks. I'll wait up.

He sloped off just after you.

145

Clarke stared at the screen. She knew exactly where Fox had sloped off to.

'What's up?' Esson asked. Clarke realised she had been studying her.

'Ach, it's nothing.'

'No, it's definitely something. Somewhere else you need to be?'

'I can't seem to switch off.'

'Don't think I hadn't noticed. At dinner it was like talking to a wall.'

Clarke gave a tired smile. 'I wasn't that bad, was I?'

Esson made a shooing gesture with one hand. 'Go. Do what you feel you need to.'

'You sure? I'll pay you for the ticket.'

Esson checked the time. 'Box office will probably take it if I hurry. I think I saw a returns queue.'

'Thanks, Christine. I really am sorry.'

Esson made the shooing gesture again and headed in the direction of the box office. With a final smile of apology, Clarke turned towards Grindlay Street, then remembered they'd come in Esson's car. Her own was still in Leith. She looked across Lothian Road to the taxi rank outside the Sheraton. Three cabs waited there. She dodged the traffic and climbed into the back of the one at the head of the queue.

'Where are we off to tonight?' the driver enquired.

'Queen Charlotte Street — the police station.'

'Turning yourself in, eh? Hard to live with a guilty conscience.' The driver started the engine and switched on his meter.

'I don't know about that,' Clarke answered, too softly for the man to hear.

★ ★ ★

'Evening, Malcolm,' she said, walking into the MIT office. Fox flinched slightly.

'Made me jump,' he said.

Clarke had stopped by his shoulder and was reading the screen of his monitor.

'Friends and associates,' he explained.

Clarke nodded. 'Nothing that couldn't wait till morning.' She looked around the empty office.

'Not much waiting for me at home,' he explained. 'Besides, I like having this place to myself.'

'Means nobody interferes,' Clarke seemed to agree, easing herself onto a chair so that they were facing one another.

'You okay?' he asked. 'What happened to the talk?'

'Found I wasn't in the mood. You had anything to eat?'

'Shouldn't have had those crisps.' He patted his stomach, then watched as Clarke reached over to lift the pad he'd been scribbling on. She flipped its pages.

'Busy boy,' she commented. 'You're almost a one-man Stewart Scoular fan club.'

'We saw him with Meiklejohn and Morelli; stands to reason he knew the deceased too. And word on the street is he's been known to sell a bit of coke to his pals.'

Clarke gave a thin smile. 'And who is it exactly

147

that you know on the street, Malcolm? Always thought of you as more of a desk jockey. You're not even Edinburgh these days.'

Fox's face reddened. 'Doesn't mean I don't have sources, Siobhan. I'm Major Crime — we rely on intel.'

'Give me a name then.' But Clarke held up a hand. 'No, let me guess first. How about Morris Gerald Cafferty? Is there any chance he could have turned snitch for Major Crime and DI Malcolm Fox?'

'Okay, you've had your fun.' Fox folded his arms. 'I assume you tailed me earlier?'

'Did you go to him or did he come to you?'

'A bit of both.'

'And he handed you Stewart Scoular, just like that?'

'More or less.'

Clarke was shaking her head. 'Things are never that simple where Cafferty's concerned. What's going on, Malcolm?'

'I really can't tell you, Siobhan — not yet.'

'Does it have anything to do with that trip you took to Gartcosh?'

'Just stop.' He held up a hand, his palm towards her.

'Does Cafferty know something about Scoular and Salman bin Mahmoud?'

'I don't know.'

'So all he gave you was Scoular and a bit of coke-dealing? How does that tie in to the case we're supposed to be working?'

A smile began to form on Malcolm Fox's face. 'I'm glad you asked me that.'

He signalled to the space next to him, so she sat down facing his computer screen, while he got busy with the mouse and a few keystrokes.

'Who'd have thought the business pages of newspapers could be so enlightening,' Fox began. 'I was about to print out all this stuff, but in the meantime, take a look.' He dabbed a finger against the screen. 'Scoular's company is involved in projects worldwide. Some years back, that included expensive apartment blocks in the Middle East. A lesson was learned along the way.'

Clarke watched as more stories appeared, this time to do with schemes in London, Toronto, Vancouver.

'Not all of these got past the planners, but some did,' Fox was saying.

'The lesson being?'

'People with money want that money to make them more money, but they also want it to be safe, and the Middle East has its risks. Salman's father acted as a facilitator, not only sinking his own money into some of these projects but also sourcing other investors, investors who often-times stayed anonymous, sheltering behind company names, mostly registered offshore.' Fox turned his head towards Clarke. 'But with Salman's father out of the picture . . .'

'You think Salman took over the business? I don't recall any of our searches flagging his name up.'

'Agreed, but take a gander at this.' A few more clicks, another story from the business pages; a single paragraph, easy to overlook. While Clarke

149

read, Fox provided commentary.

'Scoular's firm, with an injection of Saudi money, is pitching to build a golf resort up north, on land owned by Lord Strathy.'

'Lord Strathy being . . . ?'

Another click, and Lord Strathy's biography appeared, along with a photo of him in his ermine robes, roseate with privilege.

'His name's Ramsay Meiklejohn,' Fox said. 'He's Issy Meiklejohn's father.' One further click produced a map of the north of Scotland. 'The area in blue is everything he owns.'

'That's a lot of land.' Clarke pointed to one coastal dot and then another. 'Doesn't quite cover Tongue and Thurso . . . '

'Not too far off either, though. The ancestral home is halfway between the two, just along the road from Dounreay.'

The next photo was of a castle.

'It's not actually that old,' Fox commented. 'Mid nineteenth century. The style is Scots Baronial revived, hence the Disneyland turrets.'

'Christ, Malcolm, when you dig, you dig deep.' Clarke glanced at him. 'Doesn't require you to look so smug, though.'

'But you have to admit, it's starting to connect: Scoular in bed with Lord Strathy; funding from the Middle East; the victim and Isabella Meiklejohn . . . '

'Getting us no closer to why someone might want Salman dead.'

'Except,' Fox said, 'for this . . . ' A fresh page opened on the screen. 'The same consortium had wanted to build a spaceport near Tongue.

150

That fell through, partly from local concerns, but mostly because the money didn't come together. Same problems seem to be besetting the golf resort plan. And it's not like there haven't been costs. With Ahmad bin Mahmoud under house arrest, his financial dealings limited, his son would be the one under pressure to cough up. Pressure in all likelihood applied by the likes of Stewart Scoular and Ramsay Meiklejohn.'

'Any actual evidence of that happening?'

Fox's face fell slightly. 'I've contacted a couple of business journalists but not heard back yet.'

'You've been talking to the press?' Clarke was giving him a hard stare.

'Only by email, carefully worded.'

'Nevertheless, probably not the wisest move.' Clarke scratched her forehead.

'I don't see anyone else around here pushing the case forward, Siobhan.'

'You're doing Cafferty's bidding, Malcolm. He's the one who kick-started this. Don't you think that should give us pause?'

Fox was shaking his head. 'If you ask me, Cafferty thought all we'd find was maybe Scoular giving or selling the odd bit of white powder to his mates. Probably doesn't like that because it's robbing him of prospective customers.' He gestured towards the screen. 'This goes way beyond that, and I'm the one who joined the dots. At the very least, it's worth taking to the boss, no?'

'Sure. But you sound like you're thinking beyond 'very least'.' She studied him. 'A wee chat with Stewart Scoular maybe?'

'Maybe.'

'Before taking it upstairs?'

Fox shrugged. 'No time like the present, that's what they say.' He wasn't quite smirking.

'You've already arranged it?' Clarke guessed.

He checked his watch. 'Want to tag along?'

'Now?'

'Pretty much.'

'At his office?'

He shook his head. 'His home. This being a murder inquiry, I told him time was of the essence.'

'What else did you say?'

'That we were interviewing anyone who might have known the deceased, and his name had cropped up.'

'He admitted knowing Salman?'

Fox was nodding while manoeuvring his arms into his jacket. 'I might be a desk jockey, Siobhan,' he said, patting a corner of the table, 'but sometimes I ride a winner.'

Clarke wasn't entirely convinced of that, but she followed him out of the office in any case.

What else was she going to do?

13

Stewart Scoular's home was part of a Georgian terrace overlooking the Water of Leith in Stockbridge. There were two buzzers next to the front door, one marked 'Office' and the other left blank. Fox pressed the blank button. A few moments later, a voice crackled through the intercom. 'In you come then.'

They pushed open the door and entered a cramped vestibule with two doors off, one of which swung open. Scoular wore an open-necked pale pink shirt, the sleeves rolled up. His feet were bare, Clarke noticed. No rings on either of his hands, no wristwatch or other jewellery. His hair was sandy-coloured and recently barbered, his face lightly freckled, teeth gleaming.

'I see you brought backup,' he said with a chuckle.

'This is my colleague DI Clarke,' Fox stated. 'We appreciate you seeing us at this time of night.'

Scoular waved the formalities aside and led them into a large drawing room with high ceiling, ornate cornicing and sanded wooden floor.

'Lovely place,' Fox said, sounding as if he meant it. The furnishings looked expensive, but the room had an under-used feel to it. Clarke got the notion there would be a version of the man-cave elsewhere, boasting a big TV and all the accoutrements. The drawing room had no shelves and precious few knick-knacks. No books, magazines or family photos.

'You live here on your own?' she asked.

'Not every night,' Scoular said with another chuckle. 'Can I offer either of you a drink?'

'That's kind of you, but no thanks.' Fox had lowered himself onto the leather sofa. It had chrome fittings that would attract fingerprints, not that Clarke could see any. It was either brand new or its owner employed a meticulous cleaner. 'We won't keep you,' Fox was saying, shifting a little to make room for Clarke. 'Just a few questions to clarify how well you knew Salman bin Mahmoud.'

Scoular sat down on the sofa's matching chair and crossed his legs so that his right foot rested on his left knee. Clarke felt he was trying just a bit too hard to appear relaxed and unconcerned. He angled his head upwards as if to aid his thinking.

'I honestly doubt I'd met him more than ten or twelve times. At parties mostly.'

'Including ones he hosted?'

'Once, certainly.'

'He lived a five- or ten-minute walk from here?'

'Something like that.'

'And Giovanni Morelli is even closer?'

'Five tops. I'd say I know Gio slightly better than I knew Sal.'

'People called him Sal?'

'Some of us did.' Scoular had gripped his

154

exposed toes in one hand and seemed to be massaging them.

'Hurt your foot?' Clarke interrupted.

'No.' He seemed to realise what he'd been doing. 'Sorry.' He placed the foot back on the floor. 'Touch of cramp earlier, after my run.'

It didn't surprise Clarke that he ran. Probably had a home gym, too. He was lean and lightly tanned, almost certainly attractive to a certain type of woman. She imagined him pitching one of his projects to a room filled with people who envied his looks and self-confidence. They would see him as a maverick, too, expelled from his political party for being just a bit too edgy.

'I should have asked,' he was saying, 'whether you're making progress with your investigation.'

'We're moving forward,' Fox assured him — a meaningless phrase, but one Scoular was happy to accept.

'When I was an MSP, I had a strong interest in crime and justice. Struck me Police Scotland was underfunded and still doing a hell of a job.'

'We try not to complain,' Clarke said.

'Turning back to Mr bin Mahmoud,' Fox interrupted, 'you met him socially a few times, but was that the extent of your relationship?'

'Pretty much.'

'Ever visit him in London?'

'No.'

'But business takes you there?'

'Sometimes.'

'Your business being . . . ?'

'Property developing — commercial mostly. Hotels and the like. Plenty of land in Edinburgh we could be doing more with.'

'To maximise profit, you mean?'

'To maximise *potential*. It's not always about the money.'

'Added amenities, quality of life?'

Scoular's eyes were probing, wondering if Clarke was being sarcastic. 'Correct,' he said tonelessly.

'We've established that you knew Mr bin Mahmoud and you know Mr Morelli,' Fox said, 'so you probably also know Lady Isabella Meiklejohn?'

'Yes, I know Issy.'

'Is there anyone else in Mr bin Mahmoud's circle we should be talking to?'

Scoular thought for a moment. 'Issy and Gio are the ones to ask. As I say, I was hardly Sal's closest confidant . . .'

'So in your opinion, who was?'

'Issy probably.'

'They were an item?'

'You'd have to ask her. I never got the impression sex was Sal's thing.'

'So what was his 'thing', do you think?'

'He liked clubbing. He liked wearing good clothes, driving nice cars, travelling . . .'

'All paid for by his father?'

'Unless he was doing bar work on the sly.'

Fox just about managed to return Scoular's smile. 'Ever had any dealings with Salman's father?'

'None whatsoever.'

'But you *have* done business in the Middle East?'

'Not for some time and never with him.'

156

Scoular slapped his palms against his thighs as if readying to get to his feet. 'That's us pretty much done, don't you think?'

'Did Mr bin Mahmoud have any enemies, any sign of trouble in his life?'

'No.'

'And the last time you saw him . . . ?'

'At some club or other, I'd guess.'

'The Jenever perhaps?' Scoular stared at Clarke without answering. 'We were told it's one of your haunts.'

'I'd hardly call it that. I might drop by a couple of times a month.'

'You'll know of its proprietor, though — man called Cafferty?'

'Remember me saying I took an interest in crime and justice?'

'So you do know Cafferty?'

'Only by reputation.'

'But despite that reputation, you're happy to add to his profits?'

Scoular looked from Clarke to Fox and back again. 'I'm not sure where this is heading.'

It was Fox who answered. 'We're just trying to paint as complete a picture as we can of Mr bin Mahmoud, his history, his lifestyle.'

'He was fun to be around, the classic playboy, I suppose. There might be jealousy of that in some quarters, but to know him was to like him.' This time Scoular did get to his feet, making show of stretching his calf muscles.

'One last thing,' Fox said, rising from the sofa. 'Any idea what he was doing out by Seafield?'

'I did wonder about that.'

157

'And?'

'Only connection I can think of is that we played golf out that way once.'

'He was a golfer?'

'Not much of one, no, but Sean Connery is. Sal always wanted to emulate his hero.'

'Just the two of you, was it?'

'Gio was there too. Not much better a player, though he definitely dressed the part. You know that scene in the film *MASH?* The pros from Dover — that's who they reminded me of.'

'You probably don't laugh at them to their face, though?' Clarke enquired. 'Not when you need them opening their chequebooks for one of your projects.'

Scoular gave her a scornful look. 'No chequebooks these days, Inspector. Strictly electronic. And I pride myself on never losing a single cent for any of my investors.'

'The golf course up north?' Fox added. 'The one on land owned by Issy Meiklejohn's father?'

'What of it?'

'With Mr bin Mahmoud dead, won't funding be rather more problematic? Or had he already decided not to add any more to the pot?'

'I think I've said all I'm going to.' Scoular walked to the door and held it open. Clarke took her time getting to her feet, her eyes meeting his all the way to the threshold.

'Thanks again for your time,' she commented. Then, gesturing towards his bare feet: 'Watch you don't get chilblains . . .'

★ ★ ★

'Interesting, no?' Fox said once they were back on the pavement.

'We certainly got him rattled.'

'You reckon he's holding back?'

Clarke nodded. 'Same as you do. Question is: what do we do about it?'

'There are forensic accountants at Gartcosh. I might offer it to them.'

Clarke was thoughtful for a moment. 'For someone accused of racism, he has a demonstrably international taste in friends.'

'As long as they're rich and not Jewish.'

'What about the golf course angle? The one near where bin Mahmoud was killed?'

'You reckon there's anything there?'

'I've no idea, Malcolm.' She checked the time on her phone.

'Walkies for Brillo?'

'Poor wee sod's been waiting long enough. You coming along, or do you need to report back to Cafferty?' She watched him start to scowl. 'I'm just teasing,' she said.

'I don't think you are,' he answered, stuffing his hands into his pockets and turning away.

'You've nothing to apologise for,' Clarke told herself in an undertone. 'You're not the one caught between a gangster and Special Branch . . .'

★   ★   ★

Cafferty was at his usual banquette on the mezzanine level at the Jenever Club, nursing his usual lemonade, when Benny called with news.

'Might have something, boss. Good shout on

159

Moredun. This guy lives just off Moredunvale Road, runs the local gang there. Not unknown to the cops.'

Cafferty took a sip of his drink. 'A name would be nice, Benjamin.'

'Cole Burnett.'

'Like the stuff we used to mine?'

Benny spelled it for him.

'Never heard of him,' Cafferty admitted, more to himself than to his employee.

'Want me to haul him in?'

'You've seen him?'

'Not yet. Got his address, though.'

'And what makes you so sure he's our guy?'

'He has a taste for nicking phones. A shove and a kick and he's off.'

'Who does he sell them to?' Cafferty listened to the silence as Benny tried to work out how best to tell him he had no idea. 'Doesn't matter. But yes, I want him hauled in. Maybe to the club, though let's wait till it's shut. Not much noise escapes the cellars — you could have the Hulk wired up to the mains and no one on the street outside would know.'

'Car battery does the job just as well,' Benny commented.

'You'd know more about that than I would,' Cafferty said, though both of them knew that wasn't strictly true.

14

It was gone midnight by the time May Collins ushered the final customers out. She had been joined for the evening shift by a barman called Cameron. He was in his twenties and lived in a caravan behind the pub, which he shared with his tattoos and facial piercings.

'The room you're in is his by rights,' Collins had explained to Rebus, 'but he'd rather be where he is.'

Rebus helped clear the tables of glasses and other detritus, while Collins stacked stools and chairs and Cameron loaded the glass-washer.

'Leave the floor till morning,' Collins suggested.

'Busiest we've been in a while.' Cameron didn't sound displeased. There had been no hassle, no rowdiness. The pub had become a community hub, inquisitive journalists given short shrift. Two of the journalists had been around the last drinkers to leave — one from Inverness, one from Aberdeen. The one from Inverness had approached Rebus at one point to tell him: 'Laura Smith says hello and that you should call her back.' To which Rebus had responded with a few choice words of his own, causing the reporter to retreat, spending the rest of the evening in a huddle with his fellow news-hound.

There had been toasts to Keith's memory and

reminiscences from those who'd known him, but behind it all lay the vast whispered question: did they have a murderer in their midst? Rebus had eavesdropped on a few suggestions. It was travellers, strangers, immigrants. Hadn't there been a murder in Thurso a couple of years back, the culprit never caught? And hadn't that been caused by a blow to the skull too? Necessary stories, he knew — an attempt to deflect rather than explain the reality of the situation. One wilder theory saw a poltergeist placed squarely in the frame.

'I've seen strange things out that way,' the proposer had told his rapt audience. 'Lights, sounds, shadows moving behind the main fence . . .'

Catching Rebus's eye, Collins had shaken her head slowly.

He'd spent the evening nursing a single pint, which, once flat, he'd switched for a whisky, adding plenty of water.

'Sorry not to be putting more into the coffers,' he'd apologised, handing a five-pound note across the bar.

'We're doing grand without you,' Collins had replied.

She opened the till now and scooped notes and coins into a bag. 'Just going to put this in the safe,' she told Cameron, disappearing through a doorway.

Cameron was behind the bar again, pouring himself a cider, everything done that needed doing. Rebus studied the gantry. Among the bottles sat a coat of arms, a few faded postcards from overseas, a fake twenty-pound note, examples of various foreign currencies, and a few snaps taken in the bar down the years.

'That's May's dad,' Cameron said, tapping one of the photos. 'Used to run this place until it got too much for him. Long before my time, mind.'

'Does he still come in?'

The barman shook his head. 'I think the place holds too many memories. Good ones, I mean, but he's a shadow of himself these days.'

'I know the feeling.'

Cameron managed a wry smile. 'You're staying the night here, eh?'

'Samantha needs a bit of space.'

'Understandable, I suppose.' He had finished the cider in a few hefty gulps. 'That's me then.' He lifted his denim jacket from a hook.

'Did you have much to do with Keith?'

'Served him a few drinks now and then.'

Rebus's eyes were on the gantry again. 'What used to be there?' He nodded towards a triangular arrangement of thin nails.

'Believe it or not, a revolver.' Cameron pointed to each nail in turn. 'Barrel rested on that, trigger guard on that, grip on that. Think it belonged to Mr Collins, but I'm not sure. Rusted all to hell.'

'What happened to it?'

The barman gave a shrug. 'May tossed it, I guess. Not every drinker wants a gun staring at them while they try to cheer themselves up.'

'And it just sat there?'

'May might've got it down a few times — just

163

for a joke at chucking-out time. Seemed to do the trick.'

'I'm sure it did,' Rebus said.

Cameron was giving the bar a final look-over. 'Probably see you in the morning, then. May does us bacon rolls before we get the place ready for opening. Wonder if we'll be as busy.'

'The media circus will move on,' Rebus stated.

'Hopefully not for a day or two, though.' Cameron gave a wave as he disappeared through the doorway, just as May Collins came back. She tucked a loose strand of hair back behind one ear.

'A nightcap, I think,' she said, placing a glass under one of the whisky optics. 'I'm hoping you'll join me.'

'I shouldn't.'

'Not planning on driving anywhere, are you?'

'It's a health thing. I've got COPD.'

'Sorry to hear that.'

'Ach, go on then.'

They sat side by side on two of the high stools, clinked glasses before sipping. The silence settled around them, broken only by the hum of the glasswasher and the occasional voice outside.

'She'll come round, you know,' Collins said eventually. 'Samantha, I mean.'

'Maybe.'

'You're her dad — I doubt she can stay mad at you. But right now she needs someone to blame, and you're it.'

'Should I be lying on a couch or something?' Rebus said, remembering that Samantha had had a similar question for Robin Creasey.

'Doesn't take a psychologist, just someone who's had plenty fallings-out with their own dad.'

'Cameron told me your dad used to run this place.'

'In later years, yes. His first wife died and he married my mum — Betsy, her name was. He found it harder and harder after Mum died.'

'So you stepped in?'

'With my husband Billy. Then *he* got the cancer and that was that.' She took in her surroundings. 'Not sure this was ever what I really wanted, but it was here and Dad needed me.'

'Pretty sure *I'm* not what Samantha needs.'

'Maybe not now, but . . . '

'Thing is, May, I always enjoyed my job too much. My wife used to say it was like I was having an affair — staying out late, not home most weekends. And even when I did go home, the cases would still be in here.' He tapped his forehead. 'And it wasn't as if I could share any of it. No way I was going to introduce Rhona and Sammy to *that* world.'

'Maybe that was your mistake then — they didn't need a knight protecting them; Rhona needed a husband and Samantha a father, end of.' She drained her glass and went for a refill, Rebus declining the offer. He watched her at her chosen optic.

'Cameron was telling me about the gun,' Rebus said.

'Oh aye?'

'You got rid of it?'

165

'Not quite.' She settled on her stool again. 'It went walkies.'

'Someone stole it?'

Collins shrugged. 'At first I thought Dad must have it, but he didn't. It's rusted to buggery, though, so there's nothing to worry about.'

'But you reported it?'

'It'll turn up. Soon as one of the kids starts waving it about, I'll know.'

'How long ago was this?'

'Month or so.'

'What does your dad think?'

She took a sip before answering. 'He's surprised I hung onto it as long as I did.'

'It dates back to the war?'

'As far as I know.'

'But your dad was a POW, right.'

'He was an internee, yes.'

'So he wouldn't have had a gun.'

'He found it washed ashore sometime in the fifties, so the story goes.' She put her glass down. 'What's this about, John?'

'Keith was passionate about Camp 1033. He'd even slept there a few nights. Whoever killed him probably took the contents of his satchel — meaning his research. I'm told he interviewed your father as well as you and a few other survivors, but there's no sign of any of that among the stuff in his garage.'

Collins considered this. 'You want to talk to Dad?'

'And the others, if possible.'

'I could invite them round.' She glanced up at the clock. 'Phone them in the morning, see if it

166

can happen before opening time. What do you say?'

'I say thank you.'

'You really think it'll help?'

'I've no idea.'

'Will the police want to talk to them too?'

'If they're being thorough.'

'You don't sound convinced.'

'Creasey seems competent enough, but I know how these things work — they won't all be like him.'

'Well, we'll see what happens tomorrow. For tonight, I'm just glad I've got a knight staying under my roof.'

'Despite his creaking armour?'

'Not forgetting his clapped-out steed.' Collins couldn't hide the fatigue as she slid off the stool. 'Let's put the lights out and head up.'

'You probably knew Keith a lot better than I did. In truth, I hardly knew him at all. What was he like?'

'He was quiet, but he had personality. Everyone loved him, and you could see he doted on Carrie.'

'When Samantha started seeing Jess Hawkins, that must have hurt. Do you really think they patched things up? Properly, I mean?'

'They seemed all right.' Collins considered for a moment. 'I suppose we all tiptoed around it.'

'There was never any reckoning between Keith and Hawkins?'

'Maybe some words, but not blows as far as I know.'

'Samantha told me they only met the once.

Sounded like that was well before the falling-out.'

'Maybe I'm wrong then.'

'You know he found out about Hawkins from an anonymous note — any thoughts on who would do something like that?'

'I don't like the idea that *anybody* would do that.' She made eye contact with Rebus. 'If you're asking me whether Keith might have bottled his feelings up — it's entirely possible. I'm sure it rankled that the whole village knew. Must have gnawed away at him, wondering why none of them had said anything. He was definitely a bit more withdrawn afterwards.'

'And putting all his efforts into Camp 1033 . . . ' Rebus's phone alerted him to an incoming text.

'Samantha?' Collins enquired.

'Edinburgh,' Rebus corrected her. 'I might just phone back before I head upstairs.' He thought of something. 'Actually, can I use the computer in the office?' John Neilson had come good a couple of hours back, mailing various links to internet sites. Rebus had checked his emails on his phone and found Neilson's message there. But if he was going to read screeds, he wanted a decent-sized screen.

Collins was nodding her agreement. 'I'm setting the alarm, though, so don't go wandering too far. See you in the morning.'

'Bacon rolls, I hear.'

'Night, John.'

Rebus walked over to one of the windows. The glass was frosted, so he couldn't see anything. It

168

wasn't completely dark out, despite the hour. He knew they would pay for it come the short winter days, though. No more voices, just a solitary car cruising past. He texted Clarke — *Okay to speak?* — and when she answered in the affirmative, he made the call.

'We're a couple of night owls,' he said. 'Everything okay with Brillo?'

'He's here in the flat with me.'

'Your flat?'

'My flat. How's it all going?'

'Keith was killed.'

'I saw online, but the story was vague.'

'Whacked with a blunt object, not yet identified. The forces of law and order are grinding into action. Samantha's in a state, as you can imagine. Carrie's gone to stay at a friend's.'

'Did he have any family?'

'A sister in Canada — I wonder if Sammy will remember to let her know.'

'No obvious suspects as yet?'

'No,' Rebus admitted.

'So you're rolling up your sleeves?'

'In a manner of speaking.'

'You've a pretty full schedule then?'

Rebus paused, taking in her tone of voice. 'What is it, Siobhan?'

'A tenuous connection between my victim and where you are right now.'

He listened as she explained about Stewart Scoular, the bin Mahmoud family, the golf course scheme, Isabella Meiklejohn and Lord Strathy.

169

'Not the first time I've heard his name,' he commented when Strathy was mentioned. 'Want me to do a bit of digging?'

'Not especially . . . '

He couldn't help smiling. 'Yet here you are calling me in the middle of the night to tell me all about it. I can see through you like a freshly cleaned window, DI Clarke.'

'It would have to be kept off the books, John.'

'Naturally.'

'And if you find anything the least bit relevant . . . '

'I bring it to you straight away.'

'You're sure you've got time for this? I know Samantha's need is a lot greater than mine.'

'Leave it with me, Siobhan, I'll see what I can do. Now get yourself tucked into bed and tell Brillo I'm missing him.'

'Will do, John. And thanks.'

'Speak soon.'

Rebus ended the call and tapped his phone against his chin as he walked through the open bar flap. The light switches were next to where the missing gun had been displayed. He stared at the nails for a moment before plunging the bar into darkness and heading for the office.

★ ★ ★

Three hours later he lay in bed, unable to sleep, staring towards the ceiling. It would be light again in a couple of hours. He reckoned he knew now why Keith had been so interested in Camp 1033. It was to do with how people were treated

170

during the Second World War. Neighbours were locked up just because they had been born outside the UK. People began to distrust their bakers, grocers and restaurant owners. The Isle of Man had for a time become one huge internment camp, as had the Isle of Bute. 'Collar the lot,' Churchill had said, after which it became a free-for-all, everyone of foreign extraction considered a potential fifth columnist, the situation exacerbated when Sikorski, who led the thousands of Polish troops stationed in the UK, began locking up people who disagreed with his politics. Keith had written several long pieces, which Rebus had found filed in the garage along with various rejection letters from magazines and newspapers. His anger at the injustice shone through — perhaps too baldly. In one article, he compared the attitude then to what he saw happening in the here and now. The piece had been called 'The Never-Ending Witch Hunt'.

'Looks like you were one of the good guys,' Rebus whispered to the night.

So why had he been fated to die at someone else's hands?

Day Three

15

At 7.30 a.m., Rebus stood outside the bungalow, the wind stinging his face. The door was locked, no sign of life within. Samantha must already have left; she'd be picking up Carrie from her friend's house. He realised he didn't know where that was. As he was heading back to the Saab, a marked patrol car drew up, blocking him in. The sole occupant got out. He was in uniform and knew better than to bother with headwear of any kind — he wasn't about to let the swirling gusts have their fun.

'You John Rebus?'

'Depends.'

'It's just that you look more like a tramp than an ex-cop. DS Creasey sent me to get your prints.'

'Right.'

'So if you'll step into my office . . . '

By which he meant the patrol car's passenger seat. The fingerprint kit was in the back. The uniform fetched it and got to work.

'You're taking my daughter's, too?' Rebus asked.

'It's all in hand, sir.' The man smiled at what he probably thought of as his little joke.

Job done, the prints sealed in a clear polythene bag tagged with Rebus's name and date of birth, the officer dismissed him with a gesture and got busy on his official-issue radio.

'Nice doing business with you,' Rebus muttered, crouching to wipe his fingertips on the grass and watching as the patrol car reversed out onto the main road, heading to its next destination.

The Saab still didn't sound too healthy, but it started and its wheels turned when Rebus asked them to. Slowly he drove to the primary school. Parents were arriving with their offspring, heads angled into the unceasing wind. Rebus got out of the car and stood by the gates. Many of the parents seemed to know who he was, gave him a wary greeting or just stared at him as they passed. Eventually he saw Carrie. She was holding hands with a girl the same age as her. He couldn't think what to say, so said nothing. The woman with them ushered the girls through the gates, a peck on the top of the head for each, before turning to face him, folding her arms.

'I'm Samantha's dad,' he said.

'I know.'

'How's Carrie?'

'The girl's not daft — she knows something's happened.'

'Samantha hasn't told her?'

'She's tried.' The woman watched the two girls skip across the playground, backpacks swinging. 'And before you ask, I offered to keep Carrie off school today, but Sam wants things as normal as possible. She knows she's asking the impossible, but who am I to deny her?'

'You call her Sam?' Rebus commented with the beginnings of a smile. 'I'm only allowed to use 'Samantha'. I was hoping to talk to her . . . '

'Police have taken her to Thurso. They need her to identify the body, though you wouldn't have thought that was necessary. I said if she waited I'd go with her, but she was adamant.'

'How long ago was this?' The fingerprint cop had almost certainly known, but hadn't said anything. Samantha would have her prints taken either before or after the identification. Christ . . .

'They were at the door first thing.' The woman paused. 'I can see from your face you think you should be there. Trust me, I told her the same.'

'She was adamant?' Rebus guessed.

The woman held out her hand. 'I'm Julie Harris, by the way.' Rebus gripped it. 'Jenny's mum.' Her accent sounded local.

'Thanks for all the help you're giving Sam and Carrie. And if you could keep putting a word in on my behalf . . . '

'She's got a lot to process, you need to understand that. Right now, you're collateral damage.' Harris saw the look he was giving her. 'I'm a nurse. Used to work in A&E before Jenny came along and I decided to be a full-time mother instead.' She paused again. 'You're going to go haring off to Thurso now, aren't you, try and get her to let you help?'

'I'm that transparent?'

'No, you're just a lot like your daughter, Mr Rebus. It's worth bearing that in mind.'

* * *

Leaving Naver, heading east, the road widened to two lanes. Rebus caught glimpses of distant

177

inland wind farms and, to his left, occasional apparently inaccessible bays and beaches, hemmed by steep cliffs. Eventually he spotted the bulbous form of Dounreay's reactor, the same reactor Keith had been busy helping decommission. The large car park was filling with workers' vehicles. He realised he didn't know what specific role Keith had played. He wasn't management, but that didn't mean he wasn't skilled. Quite the opposite, in Rebus's experience.

He had the compilation CD playing softly; recognised The Clash and Jethro Tull but not the three songs that followed. As he hit the outskirts of Thurso, he saw land beyond the water to the north. Orkney, he guessed. The signpost to the ferry at Scrabster hadn't been too far back along the road. Samantha and Keith had taken Carrie there a few times, Samantha rhapsodising about the place in phone calls afterwards.

'You didn't even let her know you were moving,' he muttered to himself. 'Your own bloody daughter . . .'

There was a road sign pointing in the direction of the hospital, which was where he assumed the mortuary would be. He'd considered calling Deborah Quant to see if she could pass word on to whichever pathologist was going to be in attendance, make sure Rebus was allowed past the door. But that would have entailed a bit of explaining — and probably a warning about not overtaxing himself. So instead he planned to wing it. Why break the habit of a lifetime?

Having stopped behind a line of kerbside cars

to allow traffic past in the opposite direction, he decided to wind down the window and get some air. That was when he noticed that one of the parade of vehicles was a patrol car. A patrol car with Samantha in the back, looking pale and shaken. He called out, but to no effect. Cursing, he waited until the traffic had cleared, an eager local motorist so close behind that his front grille was almost kissing the Saab's boot. Having passed the stationary vehicles, Rebus signalled and pulled over, waiting for the road to clear so he could do a three-point turn. Nothing for it but to follow Samantha back to Naver.

But then he remembered passing the village of Strathy, probably halfway between Naver and Thurso. He dug his phone out of his pocket and looked up Lord Strathy, aka Ramsay Augustus Ranald Meiklejohn. The range of photos he found showed a man every bit as fleshed-out as his name. Hair almost non-existent; face the colour of a poppy field in bloom. In one picture he was in full hunting gear, atop his horse and surrounded by eager-looking hounds. Another had been taken in front of Strathy Castle. The building was the full bagpipe-baronial, with turrets and a plethora of crowstep gables. Rebus's phone was soon showing him a map of the castle's whereabouts, a couple of miles inland from the village.

'Don't say I'm not good to you, Siobhan,' he said to himself as he drove, turning up the volume on the CD player.

The patrol car must have been doing a lick, because he had failed to catch up with it by the time he reached Strathy. There was no sign in the village directing him towards the castle, but then again, there was just the one narrow road off to the left, heading away from the coast. He took it, the lane narrowing, fields to either side. Potholes filled with rainwater added to the fun, Rebus slowing to steer the Saab past as many of them as he could, while the engine whined and wheezed. An imposing gateway came into view, stone posts topped by statues, the ornate wrought-iron gates closed. A weathered wooden sign at ground level warned that what lay beyond was PRIVATE.

Rebus got out of the Saab and approached the gates. Looking up, he saw that the statues represented a lion and a unicorn, holding shields in front of them. Both had been eroded by the elements down the years.

'You and me both, guys,' he said, pushing at the gates, feeling them give. When they stood gaping, he got back into the Saab and continued up the drive.

The castle appeared around a long curve. There was a gravelled parking area between the front door and a lawn with an out-of-commission fountain as its centrepiece. Not another dwelling for miles, the views expansive, but precious little protection from the prevailing weather. No trees, no hedges.

As Rebus parked, the heavy wooden door opened. A woman stood there, hands pressed together, almost as if in prayer. He studied her as he approached. Mid fifties, hair tied back in a bun, plain grey skirt with matching cardigan and blouse. Though he'd not met many, he was reminded of a type of nun.

'Can I help you?' she was asking.

'I hope so. I was looking to speak to Lord Strathy if he's about.'

Any trace of affability her face had carried now evaporated. 'He's not.'

'That's a pity. I've come all the way from Edinburgh . . .'

'Without an appointment?' She sounded incredulous at such a course of action.

'We don't often need them.' Rebus slipped his hands into his pockets. 'You've heard about the murder of the Saudi student?'

He got the impression that if she'd been wearing pearls, she might have clutched at them. As it was, she merely squeezed one hand beneath the other, as though wringing a dishcloth.

'You're with the police?' Rebus said nothing, content to let her think what she would. 'Has something happened to . . . ?' She broke off. 'You better come in, please.'

'Thank you.'

The hallway was everything he'd assumed it would be: stags' heads on the walls; Barbour jackets on a row of pegs, below which sat an array of green rubber boots; a preponderance of dark wood and a brown, fibrous floor covering.

'Tea?' she was asking.

'Lovely,' Rebus said.

'Would you like to wait in the morning room?'

'The kitchen will be fine. I'm sorry, I didn't catch your name . . .'

'I'm Mrs Belkin. Jean Belkin.'

181

'My name's Fox,' Rebus told her.

He'd been expecting the kitchen to be below stairs and he was not disappointed. They left the entrance hall behind and entered a narrow unadorned corridor, then down a flight of winding stone stairs to another corridor. The large kitchen had last been modernised in the 1960s, he guessed, and the Aga looked even older. He warmed his hands next to it while Belkin filled the electric kettle. She guessed what he was thinking.

'Hob takes forever,' she said, flipping the switch.

'You're here on your own, Mrs Belkin?'

'If I had been, I'd not have let you over the threshold, not without seeing some ID.'

Rebus made show of patting his jacket pocket. 'In the car,' he apologised.

'No matter, my husband Colin's not far away. He's gardener, handyman and whatever else the place needs.' She was fetching mugs and teapot, milk and sugar. 'A biscuit?'

'Not for me.'

'You've really come all the way from Edinburgh?'

'Yes.'

'And have you heard about *our* murder? It's getting so nowhere is safe.'

'Young man along by Naver?' Rebus nodded. 'A bad business.'

'This world of ours is coming apart at the seams.' She shook her head in bewilderment.

'Hard to disagree.'

He watched her as she took her time deciding

how to frame her next question.

'Is it because of Lady Isabella, Inspector?'

'What makes you say that?'

'She knew the Saudi gentleman — brought him here on a couple of occasions.'

'Is that so?'

'But she doesn't come home very often, prefers the bright lights and what have you.'

'This is more to do with Lady Isabella's father. We've information that he might have been conducting some business with the deceased.'

'What sort of business?' She poured water from the kettle into the teapot. Her hand was steady as she concentrated on the task.

'Does Lord Strathy have an office — a PA or secretary?'

'In London, yes. Most of his business dealings are focused there.'

'Is that where he is just now?'

A sudden flush came into Belkin's cheeks. 'We're not quite sure where he is, that's the truth of it.'

There was a sound behind them. The door to the outside world rattled open and a heavy-set, unshaven man stood there, eyes wary as they landed on Rebus.

'Colin, this is Mr Fox, a detective from Edinburgh,' Belkin began to explain.

'Oh aye?' He didn't sound entirely convinced. 'Bit long in the tooth, aren't you?'

'I'm younger than I look.'

'Bloody well have to be.' The gardener went to the sink, rinsing his hands and drying them on a towel his wife handed him. 'What's this all about?'

183

'The young Saudi,' his wife informed him, as she filled another mug, 'the one who came here . . . '

'What of him?'

Rebus took a step forward. 'We're looking into any business dealings he might have had, and your employer's name came up.'

Colin Belkin took a slurp of tea. 'And how the hell would we know anything about that?'

'It was Lord Strathy I came to see — your wife's just been telling me he seems to have disappeared.'

'Christ's sake, just because a man takes a bit of time to himself,' the gardener growled.

'Is that what he's done?'

'Stands to reason.' Belkin thumped the mug down onto the large wooden table. Then, to his wife: 'Remember that business two years back? The reporter who said he wasn't a reporter?'

'What business?' Rebus asked.

But the gardener had stretched a hand out towards him, palm up. 'Let me see some ID.'

'He told me he left it in the car,' Jean Belkin said.

'Then we'll go to the car and check it out. Against the law to tell people you're the police when you're not.'

'I can give you a number to call,' Rebus countered. 'You can ask for DI Malcolm Fox.'

Belkin dug a phone from his back pocket. 'Let's do that then.'

Rebus turned his attention to Jean Belkin. 'What business?' he asked her again, but she wasn't about to answer.

184

'Door's there,' her husband said with a gesture, 'unless you want to give me that number . . . '

Rebus debated for a moment. 'You'll be hearing from us again,' he said.

Colin Belkin was turning the door handle, still with his phone in his other hand. With a final glare at husband and wife, Rebus made his exit, rounding the property and climbing a sloping path back to where his Saab stood waiting.

At the end of the driveway, he left the gates gaping — it wasn't much by way of payback, but what else did he have? — and pulled into a passing place. He switched on his phone, but found he had no signal. Had the gardener been bluffing then? It was entirely possible. He heard running footsteps, but too late to do anything about them. The driver's-side door was hauled open and Colin Belkin grabbed a fistful of his lapel, teeth bared.

'You're no bloody copper, so who the hell are you?'

Rebus was trying to undo his seat belt with one hand while he wrestled Belkin's vice-like grip with the other. The man was shaking him like a rag doll.

'You keep your nose out of honest people's business!' Belkin barked. 'Or you get this.' He brandished a clenched fist an inch from Rebus's face.

'Which jail were you in?' Rebus asked. The man's eyes widened, his grip faltering slightly. 'I can smell an ex-con at fifty yards. Does your employer know?'

Belkin drew his fist back as if readying to throw a punch, but then froze at the sound of his wife's voice. She was standing in the gateway, pleading for him to stop. Belkin brought his face so close to Rebus's that Rebus could feel his oniony breath.

'Come bothering us again, you'll be getting a doing.' He released his grip on the lapel and reared back, turning and walking in the direction of his waiting wife.

Rebus's heart was pounding and he felt light-headed. He pressed a hand against the outline of the inhaler in his pocket but didn't think it would help. Instead he sat for a moment, watching in the rear-view mirror as Belkin closed the gates with an almighty clang, his wife steering him back towards the castle. When they disappeared from view, he pushed down on the accelerator, feeling a slight tremble in the arch of his right foot. The perfect time for the CD to decide he merited John Martyn's 'I'd Rather Be the Devil'.

Back on the A836, he checked his phone again and found he had one bar of signal, so he pulled over and called Siobhan Clarke.

'How's it going?' she asked.

'Lord Strathy's not been seen by his staff for a while.'

'Must be in London then.'

'That's not the impression I get. I'd say they've been trying to rouse him without success.'

'What do you make of it?'

'That's your job rather than mine.'

'I'll check with his London office. Maybe ask his daughter, too.'

'One other thing — the staff mentioned some press interest a couple of years back. Any idea what that's about?'

'Hang on.' He could hear her sifting paperwork, and a muttering from Malcolm Fox as she asked him about it.

'Strathy's fourth wife,' Clarke eventually said. 'Seems he collects them like hunting trophies. She walked out on him.'

'Is that all?'

'Renounced the high life for the pleasures of hippiedom.'

Rebus's eyes narrowed. 'Meaning?'

'According to reports, she joined some New Age cult.'

'Based between Naver and Tongue, by any chance?'

'Why ask if you already know?'

'It was more of an educated guess. Do you have a name for her?'

'Angharad Oates. Cue tabloid headlines about wild oats being sown.'

'Can you send me what you've got on her?'

'Or you could google it, same as Malcolm did.'

'He's keeping you busy then?'

'Just a bit.'

'Funny that, when he's just been up here asking questions at Strathy Castle . . . '

'Keeping your usual low profile?'

'Just remember who's doing all your dirty work.'

'How's everything else? With Samantha, I mean?'

'She's hanging in.'

'And you?'

'Do me one last favour, will you? Run a check on a Colin Belkin. He's the groundsman and general factotum at Strathy Castle.'

'And?'

'I'm betting a pound to a penny he's got previous.'

'I'll see what I can do.'

16

'Tell me what you see,' Malcolm Fox said, turning his head towards Siobhan Clarke. He had driven them to Craigentinny golf course, passing the scene of Salman bin Mahmoud's murder on the way.

Clarke saw some parked cars, most of them the makes and models preferred by middle-management types — indeed, the sort of car Malcolm Fox himself drove these days. A couple of silver-haired gents were exiting the clubhouse at the end of their morning round, bags of clubs slung heavily over their shoulders.

'Your future?' she pretended to guess. Then: 'Maybe just spit it out, eh?'

'Watch and learn.' Fox killed the engine and undid his seat belt before opening the driver's-side door. Clarke hated him when he was like this. He could never just share a finding or what he thought might be an inspired inkling — there always had to be a song-and-dance. He was walking towards the barrier they'd just driven through. It was a weighted white pole, which could be lowered as necessary. The car park was unmanned, though signs warned of penalties and restrictions. Once Clarke had caught up with him, Fox slapped a hand against the barrier.

'They close it at night — I called and checked.'

'Okay,' Clarke agreed.

189

'Closed *and* locked — you see what that means?' He waited, but she didn't respond. 'Salman bin Mahmoud has been here in daylight, played golf here. The car park is a good place for a meeting, he thinks.' He made a circle in the air with a finger. 'No CCTV, no security guard.'

'He doesn't know it's not usable at night?' Clarke concluded.

'Thwarted, he drives to the first car park he finds.'

'The warehouse.' She was nodding now. 'All of which assumes the meeting was his idea, yet we've found nothing on his phone.'

'Maybe there's another phone we don't know about; or the meeting was planned some other way. Could even have been arranged face to face. All I'm saying is, this gives us the reason he ended up being killed where he did. Added to which, maybe the meeting was to be about the golf course.'

Clarke saw the excited look on Fox's face.

'Any time you're ready,' she said, folding her arms.

'I got talking to my business reporter contact. Craigentinny's a public course, meaning the city owns it, but it's no secret Edinburgh Council's strapped for cash and desperate to save and make money. A consortium made an approach.'

'To buy the golf course?'

'Apparently not just this one — and not just in Edinburgh.'

'This is connected to Stewart Scoular's plan for the golf resort up north?'

190

'Same names keep popping up.'

'Including the bin Mahmoud family and Lord Strathy?'

Fox nodded like a bright kid whose teacher had just taken note. Clarke kept her face emotionless as she thought it through.

'John says Lord Strathy's done a vanishing act. I tried his London office but they've all got degrees in evasion.'

'His daughter?'

'Not answering her phone. I left a message.' Clarke gnawed at her bottom lip. 'How often did Salman bin Mahmoud play here?' Fox shrugged. 'The game with Scoular was how long ago?'

'You know as much as I do, Siobhan.'

'We need to talk to Scoular again, don't we?' The shrug became a slow nod. 'And how much of this do you report back to Big Ger Cafferty?'

'That's probably best kept between me and him, wouldn't you say? Last thing I want is for you to be dragged into this.'

'In case it becomes messy?'

'I've got a certain level of body armour.'

'Better hope whoever comes for you doesn't aim for the head then.' Clarke unfolded her arms and placed her hands on her hips. 'Okay,' she said, 'let's go and see if we can get under the skin of a certain reptilian property developer . . .'

★　★　★

He didn't exactly look pleased to see them.

They had tracked him down to a restaurant just off George Street, where he was hosting a business lunch. He was still chewing as he left his guests and entered the foyer.

'Just a couple of questions,' Clarke said, this being as much of an apology as she was willing to offer. 'You played golf with Salman bin Mahmoud how many times?'

'Three, I think.'

'How many of those at Craigentinny?'

'Just the one.'

'And this,' Fox interrupted, stepping closer as a waiter squeezed past, 'was because of your consortium's interest in taking Craigentinny into private ownership?'

Scoular swallowed whatever was in his mouth. His eyes moved between the two detectives.

'What's this got to do with Salman's murder?'

'That's what we're attempting to ascertain.'

Before Scoular could add anything, Clarke lofted another question in his direction. 'How long ago was your final game with the deceased?'

'Maybe three weeks.'

'Three weeks before he died?'

'I'd have to check my diary, but thereabouts.'

'And this was at Craigentinny?'

'Yes.'

'And the pair of you were discussing financing the purchase of the course?'

'Along the way, yes.'

'I'm guessing buying it would be a cheaper option than building a new resort from scratch elsewhere?' Fox enquired.

'That depends on negotiations.'

'Always assuming you intended keeping it as a golf course. I'm guessing if the membership sums didn't add up, you could always apply to rezone it and build a lot of nice executive homes . . . '

Scoular glared at Fox. 'Which of my competitors have you been talking to? Not one of them's to be trusted — and baseless gossip can lead to a libel action, Inspector.'

It was Clarke's turn to step closer to Scoular as a couple of new diners entered the restaurant. 'Seen anything of Lord Strathy recently?' She watched his jaw tighten as he turned his attention towards her.

'Ramsay?' he eventually said. 'Why do you ask?'

'He's one of your investors, isn't he? Maybe I should even say 'partner'?'

'What if he is?'

'He seems to have gone to ground.'

'Oh?'

'You've not heard from him?'

Scoular made show of looking at his watch. 'Was there anything else?'

'Just for confirmation, Salman bin Mahmoud was what we might call a business associate? He had control of the family money and some of that money was being put towards projects you were in charge of?'

'I'm a facilitator, that's all.'

'Is that a yes?'

'I've told you as much as I can. If you've not found me cooperative, it might be time for me to get my lawyers involved. Meantime, maybe you could busy yourselves elsewhere — finding whoever killed Sal would be an excellent start.'

He pushed his way back through the curtain into the dining room. Clarke and Fox had a view of the tables. They all looked full. Having waited a few seconds, Clarke crooked her index finger at Fox and pushed open the curtain. The room was L-shaped, and as they turned the corner, they saw a separate, glassed-in private area. It contained a single oval table around which sat six diners. Scoular was apologising while one waiter topped up glasses and another cleared the empty plates. Four men, all in suits and ties; one woman. Lady Isabella Meiklejohn.

Clarke pushed open the door and walked in, Fox right behind her.

'This is intolerable,' Scoular began to object. Clarke ignored him.

'I left you a message,' she told Meiklejohn.

'Did you?' Meiklejohn wore a crimson jacket over her short black dress. Her lipstick matched the jacket. She smiled what she probably thought would suffice as an apology, her eyes on her glass as she raised it to her mouth.

'We've been trying to reach your father,' Clarke told her.

'Whatever for?'

'Do you know his whereabouts?'

'I do not; nor do I especially care.' She smiled for the benefit of the other guests.

'Get a message to him,' Clarke commanded, 'Tell him to call me.' She watched as Meiklejohn made show of giving a toast with her glass. 'Better let you get back to the sales pitch then . . . ' She stared at each of the four men in turn, as if to memorise their faces.

194

Fox shifted slightly, allowing her to leave the room ahead of him. With a slight bow of the head, he followed her, catching up only when they reached the pavement. Clarke was removing a parking ticket from the windscreen of his car. She handed it to him.

'Recognise any of them?' she asked.

'No.'

'Maybe we should have brought along your man from the business pages.'

'Gut feeling, though — bankers, maybe councillors.'

Clarke nodded. 'And Issy Meiklejohn for window-dressing.'

'Nothing more?'

Clarke stared at him. 'What's your thinking, Malcolm?'

'She wouldn't be the first woman in history to mask her intelligence.'

'You reckon she's running the family firm?'

'Not so different from Salman bin Mahmoud's role — maybe that was the initial connection between them: kids with their eyes on the prize.'

Clarke couldn't help but agree; not that she was about to give Fox the gold star he seemed to be expecting. She gestured towards the parking ticket he was holding. 'Make sure you pay that. The fine doubles if you don't, and I'm not sure your body armour works where Edinburgh's wardens are concerned.'

17

Camp 1033 was still cordoned off. Rebus pulled in next to a yellow Portakabin that had been placed adjacent to the gate. As he opened the door of his Saab, a gust caught it. He thought the hinges might snap as it blew all the way open. Climbing out, it took him two goes to close it again. The door to the Portakabin was locked, no one answering his knock. The solitary uniform the other side of the cordon gave him an unwelcoming look.

'The very definition of a short straw,' Rebus told the man as he approached.

'Change of shift in the offing. Is there something I can help you with?'

'I'm related to the deceased. Wondered if DS Creasey is available.'

'He's not here.'

'I got that impression,' Rebus said, looking around.

'You the one who found the body?'

'That's me,' Rebus admitted.

'I was told I might be seeing you. Message is: bugger off and leave us to get on with it. I know you used to be on the force, so you'll appreciate the sentiment.'

'You're only doing your job, son. Fact they've stuck you out here tells me all I need to know about the esteem you're held in by your fellow officers.' Rebus turned to head back to his Saab.

'Make sure Creasey knows I need a word.'

'I'll be sure to do that, aye.' The officer cleared his throat and spat on the ground.

Rebus sat in the Saab and considered his next move. His phone pinged, signalling the arrival of a text from May Collins.

4.30 meet here x

Plenty of time before then, so he drove a little further along the road, heading towards Tongue. A hand-made sign on a post caught his eye. It pointed down a rutted track. The only word on the sign was WELCOME.

'Nice to feel wanted for a change,' Rebus said to himself, manoeuvring the car along the track. It ran between a series of hillocks, clumps of thistles the predominant vegetation. Eventually he caught sight of what looked like a farm steading. Smoke rose from the chimney of the timber-framed main house. A couple of large barns stood behind it, and there was a smattering of tired-looking caravans. A man, topless, shirt tied around his waist, was splitting logs with an axe. Rebus recognised him as Mick Sanderson and gave a wave.

He parked the Saab next to a familiar-looking Volvo and got out. He saw powder marks on the Volvo's doors, dashboard and steering wheel. Forensics had been busy — and hadn't bothered tidying up after themselves. He approached the chopping block, noting a motorbike propped against a nearby tree. A couple of young women were scattering feed to some hungry chickens, while another couple worked on the vegetable beds. Sweat glistened on Sanderson's torso.

'Saab's still working then.' He nodded towards his handiwork.

'Running better than ever,' Rebus said.

'We both know that's a lie. If you want to get back to Edinburgh, you'll let a proper garage give a diagnosis.'

'I wanted to thank you anyway.' Rebus held out a hand. Sanderson rested his axe against the woodpile and took it. 'Also wanted to offer something by way of payment.'

'No need for that.'

'If you're sure?' Rebus gave a shrug, looking around at the young workers nearby. 'How many of you are there?'

'Changes all the time. Some stay a few weeks, others longer.'

Rebus nodded, feigning interest. 'I notice my daughter's here. Maybe I'll just go say hello . . .'

Sanderson started to say something, but Rebus was already heading for the farmhouse. Before he got there, however, the door was opened by a man in his fifties, face lined, long grey hair pulled back in a ponytail. He wore grubby denims and a blue shirt that had lost almost all its colour.

'You must be John,' he said, cracking a smile that didn't quite meet his eyes. The eyes were blue and piercing, the pupils small. He hadn't shaved in a couple of days and his wrists were festooned with cotton bracelets of various designs. He leaned with one hand on the door frame, the other on his hip.

'Come inside,' he said. 'I'm Jess.'

Rebus entered a large open-plan space. There

198

was a log-burner in the fireplace, a chaotic kitchen area, futons and oversized bean-bags instead of sofas and chairs. Against one wall were piled yoga mats in a range of colours. A woman sat at a table in the kitchen area, filling jars with cooked vegetables. Rebus nodded a greeting, but she ignored him. She was only a few years younger than Jess Hawkins, her face weathered, long straw-coloured hair starting to clump. On the floor next to her sat a contented toddler, chewing a toy of some kind.

A staircase led from the centre of the room to the upper floor. It looked hand-made and not particularly safe, bearing in mind the toys and clothes that littered most of its steps.

'Just thought I'd have a word with Samantha,' Rebus said, keeping his tone conversational. Hawkins gave him a pained look.

'She's not in a mood for talking, John. Space to breathe is what she needs.'

'I'm right here,' Rebus yelled up the stairwell. 'I just want to help!'

Hawkins had placed a hand gently on his forearm, but removed it when Rebus glowered at him.

'Space to breathe,' Hawkins echoed softly. 'When the time's right, she'll come back.'

Rebus was still staring at him. 'Like she went back to Keith after her little fling with you?' He gestured towards the woman at the table. 'What did *your* partner make of that?'

'We're as free to love as we are to live,' Hawkins countered. 'Would you like some green tea? Maybe just water?'

'Keith Grant died not far from here.'

'I'm aware of that — the police have asked their questions.'

'After he found out about you and my daughter, he slept at the camp — you probably saw his car parked there. It's not like you wouldn't recognise it.'

'What point are you trying to make, John?'

'Maybe he came here.' Rebus was letting his voice rise, hoping Samantha would hear it loud and clear. 'It's what I'd do in his situation.'

'You see similarities between the two of you? Or is this you projecting?' Hawkins sounded as if he really wanted to know.

'Do you sleep with all the women here, or just a chosen few? Maybe that's why you set this place up after making and losing a fortune on the stock market. Internet's a wonderful thing, isn't it? Your story's right there for anyone to find — all the way from a council estate to the City of London, then you take one risk too many and you've gone from Moët to muesli — '

'You're hurting, John. I wish there were some way to help you . . . ' Hawkins looked almost pitying as he turned away and approached the table, standing behind the woman and touching the back of her neck. She gave a warm smile he couldn't see. Rebus took a couple of steps towards her.

'Angharad?'

She looked up at him. 'We know one another?' The accent was unmistakably English upper class. Rebus looked from her to the babbling infant, then fixed his eyes on Hawkins.

'No wonder he hates you,' he commented.

'Who?'

'Lord Strathy.'

Hawkins smiled again. 'It's not hate, John, it's simple greed.'

'You'll have known about that in your time, eh?'

'We're all looking for answers in our different ways. You were a policeman. You looked out when you should have been looking in. You've spent your whole adult life as part of the state apparatus, doing their dirty work so they could keep their own hands clean.'

'Without people doing the job I did, everything breaks down,'

'You might not have noticed, but everything *is* breaking down. And that job of yours ended up costing you your family.'

'Fuck off.'

Angharad Oates tutted without pausing in her task.

'You can't hide out here forever,' Rebus went on. 'The world doesn't stop at that welcome sign you've put up.'

'I wish I could help you,' Hawkins repeated, stretching out his arms.

'Then bring my daughter down here to talk to me.'

'She doesn't feel she has your trust.'

'She's wrong.'

'Give it time — give *her* the time she needs.'

'Does everybody fall for this quack psychology of yours? Do you even believe it yourself?'

'All that's on offer here is an alternative to the

world you seem happy to live in.'

'Anger and ill will,' Oates intoned, handing the infant a sliver of apple.

'Anger and ill will,' Hawkins echoed. 'Rising levels of greed and stupidity. You'd be a fool to look out there for answers.' He waved an arm in the direction of the world beyond the steading.

'So how come my daughter chose Keith over all this?' Rebus asked.

'I thought about it.' The voice came from the top of the stairs. Samantha was standing there, arms by her sides, tears drying on her cheeks. 'I thought about it but I couldn't.'

'Because of love,' Jess Hawkins said, nodding his understanding. Angharad Oates reached up, taking Hawkins' right hand and squeezing it.

'Samantha, can we talk?' Rebus asked. But after a moment, she shook her head and disappeared into one of the rooms. Hawkins opened his mouth to speak, but Rebus silenced him with a pointed finger. 'Any more pish about living and loving, I swear I'm going to smack you in the mouth.'

He watched as Oates's free hand curled around the paring knife in front of her, angling it towards him.

'Try it,' she said, baring her immaculate teeth.

'You might want to leave now, John,' Hawkins said as he patted her shoulder.

'Carrie needs her mum,' Rebus stated.

'I know.'

Hawkins was still nodding as Rebus walked to the door and left.

18

'They're all here,' May Collins said, coming from behind the bar to lead Rebus to the corner table. 'Took a bit more arranging than I thought.' Four people sat waiting for him. Two walking frames were parked nearby.

'This is my dad Joe,' May said.

The small, hunched man looked to be having trouble with his breathing. The hand he held out had a perceptible tremor, the skin like crepe paper. He wore glasses with thick lenses and his head was more liver spot than hair. Next to him sat a woman who could almost have been his sister.

'Helen Carter,' May said. Then, raising her voice, 'Helen's a bit deaf, despite the hearing aid. Aren't you, Helen?'

The woman clucked and nodded.

Across the table sat a man of similar vintage, taller and thinner than Joe Collins, with angular features and no apparent need of glasses.

'Stefan Novack,' May Collins said. 'Helen and Stefan both live in Tongue. Stefan was kind enough to give her a lift.'

Rebus took Novack's hand while looking at the figure seated next to him. This young man held up his hands.

'I know,' he said.

'This is Jimmy Hess,' May Collins was explaining. 'His grandad's not great today.'

203

'Your grandad being . . . ?'

'Frank Hess — Franz, actually, just like Joe is Josef.' Jimmy gestured towards May Collins' father. 'And as I always say, no, we're not related to Rudolf.'

'Not that we ever see Frank in here,' May went on.

'Not really a drinker,' Jimmy explained to Rebus. 'Not these days.'

'Get yourself seated and I'll fetch you a drink,' May Collins told Rebus, giving him a pat on the arm.

'Just sparkling water,' he said, settling himself at the head of the table.

'Very sorry for your loss,' Jimmy Hess said. He was a large man and ungainly with it. Late thirties maybe, no sign of a wedding ring. Dark hair receding rapidly at the temples.

'I appreciate you standing in for your grandfather,' Rebus said. 'But this is probably a waste of your time.'

Hess held up his hands again. It was something he obviously did a lot, probably without even being conscious of it. 'Thing is, Grandad used to talk to me all the time about the camp, and I sat in when Keith was asking his questions, so maybe I'm more useful than you think.'

Rebus nodded his understanding. 'As you all know,' he began, addressing the table, 'Keith was my daughter's partner. Someone killed him at Camp 1033, and it looks like his computer and some of his notes were taken. I've been studying what's left and I know the camp had become an obsession. I'm just wondering what he learned from talking to you.'

'I didn't catch all of that,' Helen Carter said, leaning so close to Rebus they were almost touching. 'You know I wasn't a prisoner?'

Rebus smiled. 'You worked in the dispensary. There's a bit about it in Keith's files.'

'And you *did* marry one of the internees,' Hess called across the table. 'I've still got a toy horse Helen's husband carved when he was inside.' He looked to Rebus. 'A lot of internees were let out to work the fields and take exercise.'

May Collins placed Rebus's drink in front of him.

'No nodding off now,' she warned her father, whose eyelids were drooping.

'Blame the conversation,' he barked at her, his voice still heavily accented.

'You were another of the prisoners who was able to leave the camp?' Rebus asked him.

'Of course.'

'And you were a newly promoted officer, I think — meaning a different accommodation block to the lesser ranks?'

'Correct.'

'How did you end up in Camp 1033?'

'My platoon was surrounded. We had no choice but to surrender.'

'And you, Mr Novack?'

Novack's right hand moved with slow deliberation towards the glass on the table in front of him. His fingers curled around it without making any attempt to raise it. 'Before 1033 was a British camp, it belonged to the Poles.'

'You got on the wrong side of General Sikorski? So you weren't here at the same time as Mr Collins and Mr Hess?'

'Not quite, no — though Helen was a constant throughout.' Novack looked at Helen Carter and gave a slight bow of his head.

'I only caught a little of that,' Carter said, fiddling with her hearing aid.

'Offer her a post-prandial rum, however,' Novack said quietly, 'and you will find her hearing miraculously unimpaired.'

The sly glance she gave him confirmed the prognosis.

'I returned here immediately after the war,' Novack continued for Rebus's benefit. 'I had fond memories of the place and the people — and I'd found that there wasn't much of a life waiting for me back in Poland. Camp 1033 was still operational then, of course. It only closed in 1947. Internees were used as unpaid labour — no need to send them home, as there had been no official armistice at war's end. And of course the country needed workers.'

'Is that when you were released, Mr Collins?' Rebus asked.

'Exactly so.'

'And like Mr Novack, you chose to stick around?'

A further twitch of the shoulders. 'I had fallen in love.'

Rebus turned to Jimmy Hess. 'And your grandfather?'

Hess was nodding. 'Same thing.'

'Odd, isn't it?' Helen Carter broke in. 'I don't

think many British POWs stayed in Germany after 1945.'

'You only have yourself to blame for being so accommodating,' Novack said. 'I don't mean you personally, Helen, but Scottish people in general.'

'So nothing but happy memories of the camp?' Rebus enquired.

'There was hardship,' Novack said. 'The place was freezing in winter, stifling in summer. Even after British soldiers replaced the Poles, there were incidents. It was thought someone had tried to poison the camp's delivery of bread — isn't that correct, Helen?'

'A lot of the men got food poisoning. Just one of those things.'

Rebus's eyes were on Novack. 'You don't think it was random chance?'

'People were friendly in the main, but try to imagine it — exotic foreigners arrive in your midst and are free to walk around the community, charming your womenfolk . . . '

'Leading to a certain resentment?' Rebus guessed.

'Best if Joseph tells it,' Novack stated.

'What is there to tell?' Collins barked across the table.

'A fellow internee died, Joseph.'

'Died how?' Rebus asked into the uncomfortable silence.

'Firing squad. He'd shot and killed one of the guards.' Novack's attention turned to Helen Carter. 'The guard was a friend of your sister's, wasn't he, Helen? I'm not quite remembering his name . . . '

'His name was Gareth,' she intoned in a voice that was almost a whisper, her rheumy eyes beginning to fill. 'Gareth Davies.'

'Two men, one woman.' Novack offered a shrug.

Rebus turned his attention back to Joe Collins. 'The revolver you kept on the wall behind the bar — what was that about?'

'I found it washed ashore. Probably belonged to a guard, tossed away to mark the end of the conflict.'

'You had it made safe?'

'No need — the mechanical parts had seized; it was never going to work.'

'When it went missing, what did you think?'

'It is of no consequence.'

Behind Rebus the door clattered open, a shadow looming over the table.

'What the hell are you up to?' Robin Creasey demanded. Rebus turned to face him.

'Just doing your job, DS Creasey. Someone has to.'

'A word with you outside, right now.'

Rebus gave a sigh of apology as he rose slowly from the table, following the detective out onto the pavement.

'You've been back to the camp,' Creasey stated.

'You got my message, then?'

'So what is it you feel you need to tell me?'

Rebus made show of considering the question. 'Now that I think of it, I'm not sure it's anything you should concern yourself with. Probably got enough on your plate as it is.'

'Whereas your plate should have been cleaned and put away by now.'

'Meaning?'

'Meaning why the hell are you still here?'

'My daughter's partner was murdered, in case you've forgotten.'

'And the last thing I need is you trampling over that inquiry. What the hell were you doing visiting Strathy Castle?'

'News gets around.'

'The gardener has a mate who's a copper in Thurso. Asked him to check if there's someone on the force in Edinburgh called Fox. There is, sort of, but the description didn't match. The real Fox is a couple of decades too young, for a start.'

'Doesn't mean to say it was me at the castle.'

'Except you just admitted it.'

'Stupid of me . . . ' Rebus stuffed his hands into his pockets. Both men turned as the door to the bar opened again. Stefan Novack was wrapping a scarf around his neck.

'I have another appointment,' he explained. 'Josef has fallen asleep and Helen needs to get home to take her pills. I hope we were of some use to you.'

'I'd have liked a bit more time,' Rebus said. 'Can we talk again?'

'As you wish.' Novack was holding the door open so that Helen Carter could manoeuvre her way out of The Glen with her walking frame. She didn't seem to recognise Rebus. The pair of them headed to a waiting car, Novack unlocking the doors.

'What was your little meeting about?' Creasey asked.

'Keith interviewed them, but there's precious little sign of any of that in the papers in his garage. Whoever took his laptop had to have good reason. There was also a memory stick with the audio recordings — again, missing.'

Creasey screwed up his face. 'Come on, John, we've already discussed this. Every housebreaker and mugger knows something like a computer or a mobile phone can be resold.'

'His notebooks are gone too, though. You telling me they were going to sell those?'

'So the story you're trying to foist on me is that he was murdered in cold blood because of his interest in a Second World War internment camp? That makes more sense to you than a personal grudge, a falling-out or a robbery?'

Rebus jabbed a finger towards Creasey. 'Are you pinning this on my daughter?'

'We're keeping an open mind.'

'Who else have you got? Jess Hawkins?'

'Why him especially?' Creasey sounded genuinely interested.

'Because his Jim Jones Brigadoon cult is practically next door to Camp 1033.'

'And?'

'And he or one of his minions could have decided it was the only way to deliver Samantha to the cause.'

The two men stared at one another in silence for a moment. Rebus exhaled noisily and ran his hand through his hair.

'I don't know, Robin. I really don't.'

210

'Where does Lord Strathy fit into your theories?'

Rebus shook his head. 'A favour for an ex-colleague in Edinburgh.'

'This guy Fox?'

'Not him, no. You know Strathy owns a lot of the land around here, including Camp 1033 and Hawkins' commune?'

Creasey raised an eyebrow. 'I'm not sure I did know that.'

'Keith wanted the community to buy the land the camp's on, turn it into a visitor attraction.'

'And?'

'And now his lordship seems to have dropped off everyone's radar.'

Creasey looked a bit more interested. 'Since when?'

'Good question. I'm not really sure. But my gut tells me the gardener at the castle — guy by the name of Colin Belkin — might once not have been such good friends with cops.'

'He's got a record?'

'Worth a bit of digging, I'd say.'

Creasey worked his jaw as he did some calculations. 'My team's pretty stretched as it is . . .'

'They all stuck in that Portakabin?'

'We've got the use of the police station in Tongue — just as soon as we track down whoever has the key so we can unlock it.'

'I could always lend a hand if you're short of bodies.'

'Nice try, John, but . . . well, you know damned fine what I'm going to say.'

'I should butt out, go home, keep out of your hair — something along those lines?'

'You should be focusing on Samantha and Carrie — they need you a lot more than the dead do.' Creasey studied his watch.

'Don't let me keep you.'

'I've got a thing in Inverness tonight. Need to get going.'

'Had a chance to check my prints against those found in the Volvo?'

'Yours, mine, Samantha's and Keith's. Plus a child's partials that we're guessing belong to your granddaughter.' Creasey paused. 'You know Samantha visited Hawkins' place the day Keith died? Don't bother answering — I can see the answer on your face. Does that sound to you like her fling with the man was over?'

'You're not having her, Creasey. No way I'm letting that happen.'

Creasey stared at him. 'Nothing I've said has made a blind bit of difference, has it?'

'I can assure you I've taken it on board.'

The slow shake of the head the detective gave in response told Rebus he wasn't fooled. He watched as Creasey crossed the road to his car and climbed in. The door to the bar opened and Jimmy Hess emerged.

'Best be off,' he said, shrugging himself into his fleece.

'Thank you for coming. I hope your grandfather perks up soon.'

'He's ninety-three years old. I doubt perking up is on the cards.'

'But his faculties are intact — enough for

212

Keith to have put a few questions to him?'

'The pair of them talked. Not sure my grandad was much help. His memory's not what it was, and it was such a long time ago.'

'I wouldn't mind a word with him at some point.'

'I'll see what I can do.'

'Who looks after him, if you don't mind me asking?'

'Just me. We manage for the most part.'

'Must be tough when you're at work.'

Jimmy Hess's face darkened a little. 'I packed in my job so I could be more help. Part and parcel of being a family, eh?' He looked up towards the gathering dusk. 'You never know what's round the next corner.' He slipped the hood of his fleece over his head and began to walk.

After a moment or two, Rebus headed indoors. Joe Collins was napping at the table, hands resting in his lap. Music was playing through the speakers, but only just audibly. The bar was back to regulars again. The media had moved on; ditto the ghouls. Rebus hoisted himself onto one of the bar stools.

'What'll it be?' May Collins asked.

'Coffee, strong as you can make it.'

'Bed not comfy last night?'

'Brain wouldn't switch off.'

'You sure coffee's the answer?'

'I don't know, May — what was the question again?'

She was laughing as she headed to the machine.

19

The Jenever Club hadn't quite opened for the evening, but its door was unlocked, which was why Dennis Jones was able to walk in and demand to see Morris Cafferty.

'People usually call me Big Ger,' a voice barked from the mezzanine level.

Jones took the stairs two at a time. He had a large frame and still considered himself fit. Played badminton and squash. He'd been partnered with a colleague, Gillian Bowness, for a varsity doubles competition. That had been the beginning of his trouble.

Cafferty was seated at the last banquette along. He was on his own, and was folding closed the screen of his computer as Jones approached.

'Take a seat,' he said, 'and tell me what's on your mind.'

'I think you already know.' Jones was breathing hard, powered by adrenalin.

'Does your wife know you're here?'

'All she told me was that someone had footage. Had to come from here, so I did a bit of digging. Didn't take much in the way of detective skills.'

'And now here you are, so what exactly is it I can do for you?'

'I won't let you do this to her.'

'Who?'

'Jenni.'

214

'I assume you mean Assistant Chief Constable Lyon? What did she say to you?'

'Just that she was fixing it and I wasn't to worry. But if fixing it means dealing with trash like you . . .'

'You'd rather it was all made nice and public?' Cafferty gave the beginnings of a chuckle, stopping as he saw Jones's hands forming themselves into fists. 'Don't do anything radically more stupid than you already have. Now sit down while I tell you something I haven't yet told your good lady.'

He bided his time until Jones bent to his will and slid onto the banquette.

'The footage we caught of you here is tame stuff — a smooch and a snog, a bit of powder up the nose. You should see what sometimes goes on. But I pride myself on knowing who's who. Your uni job didn't interest me, but your life partner did.' He paused. 'Which is why I had someone keep an eye on you for a week or two. That country park near your place of work — a beautiful spot and woefully under-used. Car park's often completely empty . . .' He was watching the effect his words were having. Dennis Jones began visibly to deflate. 'Bit reckless really, don't you think? Though I did admire your friend's agility. Must be all that badminton.' He paused again. 'I can't be sure what you told the missus, but pictures like that on the front page of a red-top . . . well, that's a marriage killer right there.'

He leaned forward, elbows on the table. 'This isn't about you, Dennis. I doubt Jenni's too bothered about you and your career. Hers, on the other hand . . . ' He leaned back again. 'How do you think she'd react if she knew you'd come here? I'll tell you: she'd be apoplectic, because you're in danger of royally pissing me off. One call to the media, one email attachment, and she's all over the papers. So while I can quite understand the macho posturing, it's time for you to slope off home and leave your wife to deal with the shitty nappy you've left on her pristine floor.'

He opened the computer lid again, signalling the end of the meeting.

'You've not heard the last of this,' Jones blustered, getting to his feet.

'You best hope I fucking well have,' Cafferty responded with a glare before turning his attention to his screen.

He listened to the footsteps stomping back down the staircase, then slid out from his seat and checked over the balcony. His visitor had gone. Taking out his phone, he made a call.

'Malcolm?' he said when it was answered. 'You still at your desk? Be downstairs in fifteen minutes . . .'

★ ★ ★

It was a large black Mercedes, its rear windows heavily tinted. As Fox exited Leith police station, the driver emerged, closing the door after him. Fox crossed the street. The driver wasn't very tall, but he looked as if he could handle himself, all wired nerves and attitude, wrapped in a leather bomber jacket.

'Back seat,' he stated.

Fox got in next to Cafferty. The driver stayed on the pavement, lighting a cigarette and checking his phone.

'Problem?' Fox asked, skipping the pleasantries.

'Just thought you ought to know I've had a visit from Casanova.'

'I assume you mean Dennis Jones?'

'My thinking is, he sees something's not right, the way his missus is acting, and she eventually blurts it out.'

'Telling him everything?'

'Not quite — but he's savvy enough to walk it back to me.'

'And?'

'And I don't want that happening again. Only room for three in this relationship, Malcolm — you, me and your boss.'

'It's not a relationship.'

'Can't disagree with that, insofar as I've heard hee-haw from either of you.'

'Trust me, we're working on it.'

'And?'

'And we're at the start of the jigsaw. Edges nearly finished but a lot still to fill in.'

'So show me the outline.'

Fox was shaking his head. 'Not yet.'

'Soon then?'

He half turned so he was facing Cafferty. 'Is this to do with Salman bin Mahmoud? Dirty money mixing with clean? Golf resorts and landed gentry?'

'Okay, so you've been busy,' Cafferty accepted with a slow nod. 'But I need those pieces filled in sooner rather than later.'

'Keeping you company isn't helping with that.'

'You going to tell Lyon about her stoked-up husband?'

'Looks like I might have to.'

'Guy like that, impetuous and hot-blooded . . . '

'What?'

'He might need keeping an eye on. Who's to say his straying days are behind him?' Cafferty's eyes were on Fox. 'Got to admit, though, you're a lot craftier than I gave you credit for.'

'How's that then?'

'Look on his face when I mentioned the footage of him and the coke. He didn't know I had it, which tells me his missus doesn't know — and that means you kept that detail to yourself. Didn't want her knowing more than she needed to, afraid she might take it out on you?' He wagged a finger. 'I should have known someone with the name Fox would have a bit of slyness about them. Now bugger off and get busy on Stewart Scoular. Clock's ticking, Malcolm . . . '

Fox shoved open the door and got out. The driver was grinding what was left of his cigarette underfoot. He crossed the road and re-entered the station, passing through security and climbing the stairs. There was water damage to the ceiling above him, a pail readied on the top step for the next time it rained. The station had been built early in the nineteenth century as a courthouse, before becoming the home of Leith

218

Council for a time. It was a solid stone edifice, but like many police stations of similar vintage, upkeep was prohibitive. He wondered how many more years it had.

'More than me, in all likelihood,' he said to himself, his breathing a little laboured as he reached the landing.

Clarke was at their shared desk. Most of the rest of the team had clocked off for the day or were in the process of doing so, but Siobhan Clarke was sticking around. The records from the victim's mobile phone provider had come through, six months' worth. They'd already accessed his phone so knew about the more recent calls, and had spoken to everyone he'd been in touch with on the day he died. An upmarket wine and spirits shop in central London featured, as did two private banks (one London, one Edinburgh), a local tailor specialising in tweed and sporting wear, and a Michelin rated restaurant in Leith. The banks had proved stubbornly resistant to questions about their client's financial situation. A far-from-complete set of printed statements had been brought from Salman bin Mahmoud's Edinburgh home, and showed a balance in the low five figures.

'Not being cheeky,' Christine Esson had said, 'but that doesn't seem much.'

Then again, as Graham Sutherland had pointed out, the super-rich often had other means of salting away and accessing funds. Forensic accountants were busy both at the Met in London and at Gartcosh. It hadn't been difficult for Fox to add Stewart Scoular's name to the mix, alongside Isabella Meiklejohn and Giovanni Morelli.

Nor did the deceased own either of his sports cars — both were leased. The home in Edinburgh was owned outright by the family, purchased as a long-term investment most likely, while the London penthouse was a rental costing almost exactly double what Fox earned in a month.

Fox sat alongside Clarke and picked up the two books sitting on the desk. They were hardback thrillers.

'Present from Christine,' Clarke explained. 'One for me, one for John.'

Fox opened one of the books at the title page. 'Signed and everything,' he said. 'Now if only you had some downtime . . . '

'What did Cafferty want, by the way?' Fox stared at her. 'The office has windows, Malcolm. You get a call, and quarter of an hour later you say you're heading to the gents.'

'I'd put my jacket on,' Fox realised.

'Which strictly speaking isn't needed for a call of nature. So I walk over to the window and see a big shiny car and a big shiny heavy.'

'He was just after an update.'

'You really can't be doing this.' Clarke frowned. 'Did you ask why he's so interested in Stewart Scoular?'

'He's keeping his cards close to his chest.'

'He's not the only one. There's stuff you're not telling me, and I can't honestly say I like it.'

'I told you about Special Branch,' Fox said, lowering his voice.

'That's not it, though.' She shook her head. 'One thing I sense is that you think you have the brass on your side — hence all that guff about having a certain amount of armour.'

'Leave it, Siobhan.'

'You know me better than that. What's Cafferty trading? Something too juicy for your bosses not to let him have his way?'

'I said leave it.' Fox's voice had stiffened. He took a deep breath and exhaled. 'Isn't Brillo due an evening walk?'

'I took him out at lunchtime, remember?'

'That was six hours ago.'

'How many walks do you think he needs?'

'Maybe you should check that with John.'

'Yeah? And maybe you should check with Special Branch how happy they are about you bringing a known gangster into this inquiry.'

The silence between them lengthened, Fox's jaw flexing as he clamped his teeth together. 'Any word from Rebus?' he eventually asked.

Clarke gave a sigh. 'We seem to be back to radio silence.'

'And the elusive Lord Strathy?'

'Ask as many questions as you like — I'm not forgetting that you're keeping stuff back from me and it's going to keep pissing me off until you tell me.'

'Understood. But to get back to Lord Strathy?'

'Still nothing. I got the Met to pay a visit to his various London haunts.'

'They must be loving us down there.' Fox managed a thin smile.

Clarke lifted one of the sheets of telephone

numbers. It was now fully annotated. The original bills had shown only calls and texts sent by the victim, but now they also had calls to his phone.

'Gio, Issy, Gio, Issy, Gio,' she reeled off. 'Almost two dozen chats on his last day alive.'

'I believe young people prefer it to actually being in the same room as someone.'

'Then there's Stewart Scoular, though not with nearly the same frequency.' Clarke glanced at the writing on her notepad. 'Eighteen calls in six months — nine from and nine to.'

'And nothing to indicate that a meeting was being set up at Craigentinny,' Fox stated, 'unless it was with Meiklejohn or Morelli.'

Clarke nodded. 'But we do have these,' she said, tapping another sheet. 'A dozen calls to the landline at Strathy Castle. Once a fortnight, pretty much.'

'No mobile signal up there?'

'That's my thinking.'

'Talking to Issy?'

Clarke offered a shrug. 'We'll ask her. Got to be either her on a home visit, or else her father.' She rubbed her eyes. She and Fox were now the only occupants of the MIT room. Footsteps could be heard descending the staircase as the ancillary staff finished their working day. 'How's that search on Issy going, by the way?'

'The internet is its usual glorious swamp. Wild-child stuff from her early days; PR repair jobs courtesy of a few society glossies. Apparently she spends a large chunk of her life helping charities.'

'Between university lectures and society balls? When I was at uni, there were some just like her — a whole raft of poshos we only saw once a year in the exam hall.'

'While you had a bath full of coal for a bed?'

'School of hard knocks, Malcolm.'

'I thought your parents were lecturers?'

'Way to burst my class-conflict bubble.' Clarke shook herself, trying to clear her head.

'Call it a day?' Fox suggested.

'I will if you will.'

'Thought I might stick with it a bit longer.' He tapped the computer screen. 'Plenty on here about Issy the socialite, but it's the business brain we're really interested in.'

'Meaning talking to your business contacts?'

'I hope you've noticed that none of them has leaked yet.'

'Doesn't mean to say they won't.'

'I should probably give the ACC a call too, keep her posted.'

'I'm going to assume she knows about Cafferty.'

'Assume what you like.'

'Might be easier if I just took a baton to your head until you fess up.'

'That wouldn't be very professional. But let me propose something. I do a bit more work here while you walk Brillo and have a bite to eat . . .'

'Yes?'

'Then we meet up and go see if Lady Isabella Meiklejohn is at home and receiving visitors — after all, we've yet to see where she lives.'

'Other thing is the deceased's house,' Clarke added. 'I know a crew's been through it, but I wouldn't mind a nosy.'

'And there's a set of keys somewhere around here.' Fox's gesture took in the office.

'Rendezvous at eight?'

Fox did a quick calculation in his head. 'Eight it is.'

20

Isabella Meiklejohn lived a literal stone's throw from Gio Morelli, but unlike her friends, she was making do with a second-floor flat on St Stephen Street, almost directly across from the Antiquary pub. Her voice on the intercom had been wary, switching rapidly to irritation when the two detectives identified themselves.

'Not more bloody questions,' she complained as she buzzed them in.

The tenement stairwell was on the shabby side. A bicycle was chained to the landing rail next to her door, and Clarke asked if it was hers.

'Full of surprises, aren't I?' she said with a cold smile, ushering them in. The hallway was narrow and cluttered. A mannequin acted as a coat and hat rack, while a stuffed pine marten in a glass case did duty as a table of sorts, its lid covered with unopened mail, keys and head-phones. Clarke caught a glance of the galley kitchen — obviously the maid's day off. Both bedroom doors were closed. The living room was cuboid, with just the one window. An open door gave a view into a box room, which had become a study of sorts — desk, computer, printer. Dance music played through a portable gadget that Meiklejohn silenced with a spoken com-mand.

There were some books piled by the fireplace, but not huge amounts, and no visible bookcases.

Plenty of garish art on the walls, possibly the work of friends or fellow students. Meiklejohn flounced back onto the sofa, legs tucked under her. A glass of red wine sat on the floor, next to a half-empty bottle and a full ashtray. The smell of tobacco lingered.

'Hard work cycling uphill into town,' Clarke offered, 'especially for a smoker.'

'Nothing wrong with my lungs.' Meiklejohn glanced down at her chest before giving Fox what she probably thought was a coquettish look.

'Any word from your father?'

'No.'

'And you're not beginning to worry?'

'Should I?'

Fox cleared his throat. 'The calls between you and Mr bin Mahmoud on the day he died: can you remind us what they were about?'

'Probably the usual — a bit of gossip, maybe plans for the weekend.'

'Not business, then?'

'Business?'

'When we bumped into you at that restaurant earlier, you looked to be dining with some of Stewart Scoular's investors.'

'Did I?'

'That's what I'm asking.'

Meiklejohn lifted her glass and turned her attention to Clarke. 'What do you think, Inspector?'

'At first I thought you were getting a free feed in exchange for flashing your tits at a bunch of men old enough to be your father.'

226

Meiklejohn hoisted the glass in a toast before drinking. 'And now?' she said.

'Scoular is part of a consortium that's been trying to buy a golf course in Edinburgh. Some of the same people are probably part of the scheme to build a new upmarket resort between Tongue and Naver — on land largely owned by your father.'

'Owned by the Strathy Estate,' Meiklejohn corrected her.

'Which equates to the same thing, more or less. So what we're wondering is, was your role at the lunch maybe more substantial? Do you speak for your father at such gatherings?'

Meiklejohn took her time placing the wine glass back on the floor. 'And how exactly,' she drawled, 'does any of that get you nearer to identifying Sal's killer?'

'We're just working with the pieces given to us,' Fox said. 'Seeing how they might fit into the overall picture.'

'Are you sure KerPlunk isn't a better analogy? Because when I look at you, I see two people with nothing but the straws they're yanking on.'

'You do want Mr bin Mahmoud's killer caught, Lady Isabella?' Clarke butted in.

'Of course I do.'

'And you still claim that he had no obvious enemies?'

'Envious racists apart, no.'

'No one who owed him money or he owed money to? No commercial disagreements? No spurned friends or lovers?' She gave a bit of extra weight to the final word.

'We never fucked, Inspector.'

'Why not?'

Meiklejohn met Clarke's stare. 'I don't think that's any of your business.'

'You and Gio Morelli aren't an item?'

'No.'

'Stewart Scoular?' This time the question came from Fox.

'What the hell has my love life got to do with any of this?'

'Is that a yes?'

'It's a big fat fuck you.'

'How well did your father know the victim? Well enough for Salman to phone him at Strathy Castle?'

'I wouldn't know.'

'Or was it you he was calling?'

'I spend as little time up there as humanly possible.'

'But you took Salman there, yes?'

'For a couple of parties.'

'Parties your father attended?'

'I'm not saying they didn't know one another socially, but my father spends more time in London than he does anywhere north of the border.'

'And London,' Fox interrupted, 'happens to be where Mr bin Mahmoud was studying.'

Meiklejohn gave a slow nod, as if remembering something. 'My father did arrange for him to visit the House of Lords — Sal loved that. But actually something came up, so Pops couldn't make it and he had a friend show Sal round instead.'

'I'm guessing VIP visits to the House of Lords would impress Stewart Scoular's would-be investors.'

'I still fail to see what any of this has to do with Sal's death. Now if you don't mind, I've got a seminar I need to be prepping for.'

'Tomorrow morning?' Clarke asked. 'What time?'

Meiklejohn had to think about it. 'Eleven.'

'What's the topic?'

'Poetry of the . . . ' She looked around the room for help answering.

'Not a lot of obvious textbooks here,' Clarke continued. 'I'm not sure you go to many of your classes. It's all just a bit of a lark to you — or it was, until things that were more fun came along. Things like Salman and Gio and maybe even Stewart Scoular.' She turned away from the sofa. 'We'll see ourselves out.'

'*Paradise Lost!*' Meiklejohn called to the retreating figures.

'Is that the one with the snake?' Fox asked Clarke.

'And the tree of knowledge.'

'Could do with one of those,' he muttered, pulling the door closed after them. He was a few steps down before he realised Clarke was studying the bicycle.

'Did we check the CCTV for bikes?' she asked. 'Near the scene of the crime, I mean? Isn't there a bike lane right next to the warehouse?'

'You don't think . . . ?'

'Just being thorough, Malcolm. Which is

229

maybe why we should also put some thought into Lady Issy and Stewart Scoular.'

'If they're lovers, you mean?'

'Present, past or even future.'

'What's your best guess?'

'Jury's out,' she said with a shrug. 'One thing, though — no great show of conspicuous wealth at Lady Issy's residence.' She lifted a set of keys from her pocket and gave them a shake. 'Here's hoping for better things elsewhere.'

★   ★   ★

The house on Heriot Row already felt abandoned. Clarke tapped the code into the intruder alarm to reassure it she meant no harm. Fox had found the light switches. The hall was large and had been recently modernised: white marble floor; gold trim wherever possible; statuary, presumably of Middle Eastern provenance. Clarke scooped up some mail. None of it looked interesting, so she added it to the pile on the table by the door.

'Who else has keys?' she asked.

'Deceased's lawyer,' Fox stated.

'None of his friends?'

'Not that we know of. This floor and the two above belong to the bin Mahmoud family. There's a garden flat below, owned by a guy who has a software business. He's been interviewed; says his neighbour was quiet for the most part — a few car doors slamming and engines revving after a party, but that's about it.'

'Mr Software never merited an invite?'

'No. The one substantial chat they seem to have had was when the deceased mooted buying the flat, but the owner wasn't for selling.' Fox saw Clarke glance at him. 'Not exactly grounds for murder.'

'On the other hand, I'd say Salman was probably unused to people saying no.'

'We could invite the neighbour in for a chat?'

But Clarke was shaking her head as she pushed open the door to the drawing room.

The word that sprang to mind was 'opulent': two huge plush sofas; a large wall-mounted TV with sound system; more statuary and ornaments. A vast antique carpet covered the wooden floor. The bookcases were filled with a range of oversized hardbacks, most of them histories of art and antiquity. One whole shelf, however, had been set aside for books about James Bond and Sean Connery. In front of these sat two framed photos of the actor, taken in his Bond days, both autographed.

Next door was a contemporary kitchen, nothing in its capacious double fridge but vegetarian ready meals and bottles of white wine and champagne. The separate freezer contained only a few trays of ice cubes. Fox was checking behind another door off the hall.

'WC and shower,' he said.

He followed Clarke up the curving stone staircase. The master bedroom contained a large bed and a wall-length built-in wardrobe with mirrored doors. Salman bin Mahmoud's various suits, jackets and shirts were neatly arranged, some still in the polythene wrapping from their

231

last dry-clean. Tiered drawers inside the wardrobe held underwear, belts, ties, jewellery.

'Liked his cufflinks,' Fox commented.

Condoms and a selection of over-the-counter pills sat in a bedside drawer. There was no reading matter by the bed. Clarke picked up a remote and pressed the power button. From a recessed area at the foot of the bed a flat-screen TV rose into view. When she switched the TV on, it was tuned to an Arabic news channel.

Fox went to check the en suite bathroom. 'I'm not the expert here,' he said, 'but I'm seeing nothing that could be described as ladies' toiletries.'

'So one-night stands rather than a regular girlfriend?' Clarke switched the TV off and returned to the hallway. The next door led to an office. Desk drawers gaped and the computer had been removed by the investigators. The walls were lined with framed posters from Sean Connery's run as James Bond. There were also dozens of replica Aston Martin DB5s in different sizes.

'Think I had this one,' Fox said, lifting the model to inspect it. He pressed a button and the roof sprang up along with the ejector seat, the figure in the seat landing on the floor.

Clarke was studying a map of the Middle East, which sat at eye level when she lowered herself onto the desk chair.

'Did he think of himself as an exile?' she wondered aloud. 'Below the surface trappings, I mean?'

'You're asking if he was happy or just putting

on a show?' Fox could only shrug. 'All the interviews we've done, nobody's said anything.'

'I'm not sure his circle of friends and hangers-on would be the types to pry.'

'Meaning?'

'Were they interested in him or just in what he represented — specifically moneyed exoticism? And meantime he's worried sick about his family back home?'

Fox was still mulling that over as he followed Clarke to the next room. It was another large sitting room, more comfortable than the formal one downstairs. Sofa and two chairs, home cinema system, the shelves filled with framed photographs. Most were of Salman's family — not just his mother and father, but what looked like uncles, aunts, cousins. A black-and-white photo, creased and faded, showed his grandparents or maybe even great-grandparents. But there were more recent photos too, dating to his time in the UK. Clarke had seen a few of these already — they were copies of photos printed in society magazines, the ones Fox had stored on his computer. Others showed Salman with friends and admirers at parties, including one in the VIP area of the Jenever Club. Isabella Meiklejohn and Giovanni Morelli featured in most of these. Usually Salman was hugging Isabella, but in one he had wrapped his arms around Gio from behind, both men laughing with their perfect teeth.

'How much do we know about Morelli?' Clarke asked.

'He's studying English lit, comes from a

233

well-to-do family in Rome, father an industrialist and mother a countess or suchlike.'

'Did any of them know each other before they parachuted into Edinburgh?'

'That first time we spoke to Morelli and Meiklejohn, didn't they say something about meeting at a party?'

Clarke nodded, deep in thought. 'That's how the three of them met specifically, which isn't quite the same thing. Maybe it's just my prejudice showing again, but the rich are the original networkers, aren't they? Same Caribbean beaches in summer and alpine ski resorts in winter. And when families end up there, the younger members tend to congregate. There are only so many party invitations after all . . .' Her eyes met Fox's. 'Did anyone ask them during their interviews?'

'I've not listened to the recordings; just looked at the edited highlights. Are you saying we head back to Lady Isabella's?'

'I doubt she'd let us in this time.'

'But we could insist.'

Clarke was shaking her head. 'It can wait,' she said.

One further room on this floor: a large bathroom with jacuzzi bath and a shower big enough to share. Then up a further flight of stairs to a couple of guest bedrooms, both en suite, beds made, towels and robes laid out, never to be used.

'Salman had a cleaner, right?'

'A local company. They told us he was great to work for, a complete charmer, et cetera.' Fox followed as Clarke headed back downstairs to the sitting room. 'We're not ruling out that this was just a random hate crime — wrong time, wrong place — or connected somehow to the other attacks on overseas students?'

'Come on, Malcolm, this is different. He wasn't slapped about and called a few names — he was stabbed to death in a part of town where he didn't belong.' Clarke's eyes were sweeping the room and its contents one last time.

'And the attack on Morelli — is that connected to the muggings or the murder?'

Clarke picked up one of the photos. 'Is that Stewart Scoular in the background, talking to the woman in the dress that seems both backless and mostly frontless?'

Fox peered at the print. 'Looks like,' he conceded.

She exhaled and put the photograph back. 'We should talk to him again.'

'Scoular?'

'Morelli,' she corrected. 'You're right — we need to find out if there's something in his friendship with Salman that led to both men being attacked. Let's get him down to the station tomorrow.'

'Rather than his home?'

'I think we've maybe been tugging the forelock, Malcolm. We need to start making people feel a lot less comfortable — cop shop's a pretty good place for that, wouldn't you say?'

Fox considered for a moment, then nodded his agreement.

21

'You,' Cole Burnett told Benny through lips cracked with dried blood, 'you are fucking dead, my man.'

Burnett was strapped to a rickety metal chair, the kind you'd find tossed into a skip when an office building was being refurbished. One of his eyes was swelling nicely and, stripped to his underpants by Benny, you could see where the bruises were starting to appear on his ribs and kidneys. Face pockmarked with acne; close-cropped gelled hair. It had taken longer than hoped to track him down, and then instead of getting into the car when told, the teenager had turned and fled. He was faster than Benny, and knew Moredun and Ferniehill better, heading down footpaths and across parkland, neither of which the car could deal with. After which he had become invisible. It had taken favours and a bit too much cash for Benny's liking before the neighbourhood started to whisper in his ear. Texts came and went; rumours turned out to be unfounded. But eventually Benny had prevailed.

Not that the boss was entirely happy. The club was open for the evening, meaning Benny'd had to bring Burnett to a garage workshop down a lane near Tollcross, a garage whose roller-shutter door was seldom seen open, except in the dead of night when a car might arrive requiring a change of number plates and maybe even a paint job. Place wasn't soundproofed, but the locals knew better than to pry or complain.

Burnett's clothes sat in a pile near the chair. Benny had been through them, not finding much. A bit of grass and some tablets — now safely stowed in his own pockets. Couple of hundred in cash, ditto. The bank cards he'd left, along with the condom. Couldn't take a man's last condom — maybe Burnett would get lucky later, though Benny doubted it. He finished his latest cigarette and stubbed it out against the oil-stained concrete floor. The garage was empty tonight, the inspection pit covered over. Most of the tools were kept in a series of padlocked metal lockers, which was why Benny had brought his own bag from the boot of the Merc. It sat on a workbench, directly in Burnett's line of sight.

'Gie's a smoke then,' Burnett said, not for the first time. His other greatest hits included 'Freezin' here, man' and 'You know who I am?' He was putting this last one to Benny yet again when Big Ger Cafferty arrived, giving Benny a moment's withering look as he passed him on his way to the chair. The boss was dressed in a black puffa jacket, zipped to the neck. Steel-toecapped shoes, the kind you'd wear on a construction site. Black leather driving gloves. Black baseball cap. Without bothering to remove the cap, he crouched slightly so his face was level with that of the seated figure.

'You know who *I* am?' he asked.

'You're that cunt that used to be somebody.'

Cafferty half turned to smile in Benny's

direction. 'Some baws on the boy, eh?' Then he swiped Burnett's face hard with the back of his hand. The force was enough to send the chair toppling sideways, Burnett's head connecting with the floor with a thud.

'Bastard,' the teenager spat.

Cafferty squatted next to him. 'Bastard is the right word, bawbag. But a bastard who knows all about you. Knows you think you're the dog with two pricks. Right now I could slice both of them off and leave you howling at the moon. Cockless Cole, your old comrades will call you. How does that sound?'

'Better than being an old sweaty bastard with a gut.'

'I sweat when I get excited. And to tell you the truth, I'd almost forgotten how the anticipation of GBH gets me excited.' He placed one hand around Burnett's throat and started to squeeze. Burnett tried twisting himself free to no effect, his eyes bulging as he gasped for air. Cafferty gave it a good twenty seconds before easing off. 'Got your attention yet, Cockless?'

'Untie me and try that again.' Burnett's eyes were filled with rage. Cafferty turned once more towards Benny.

'He reminds me what I was like before I learned better.' Then, to Burnett: 'Anger's all well and good, but there's such a thing as the survival instinct too — you might want to start using it.'

'Fuck is it you want?'

'We want a phone.'

'A phone? Is that all?'

238

'The phone you took from the wee Chinese girl you thumped.'

Burnett thought for a second. 'It's long gone.'

'Then you're going to get it back.'

'What do you need it for?'

'I don't — but she does. And you're going to tell her you're sorry.'

'Am I fuck.'

Slowly Cafferty rose to his full height. He placed his right foot on Burnett's left cheek and began to press down. 'Shattered jawbone takes a while to heal. Milkshakes through a straw if you're lucky.' Burnett's lips were mashed together so that Cafferty couldn't make out what he was saying. Benny, holdall in hand, had taken a couple of steps forward, just in case he was needed. 'I like you, Cole,' Cafferty continued. 'I like what I've heard about you. I think maybe we can come to an arrangement.' He paused. 'You know how things work in Dundee? Cuckooing, they call it. Find an easy target, set up a lab in their house, make the stuff quick and cheap and get it out on the street. Your hood'd be good for that — and I reckon you'll know more than a few suitable locations. Give the phone back and I'll bring you into the game. You'll be a player rather than the ballboy. How does that sound?'

He didn't ease his foot off, not straight away. But eventually he did. Burnett's nose was running with a mixture of mucus and blood, his underfed chest going in and out, breath coming in broken rasps. Cafferty gestured to Benny, who grabbed the chair and righted it, none too gently. Burnett glared at his abductor, then at Cafferty.

239

'Give me the other options.'

'They're right there in my associate's bag.' Cafferty nodded to let Benny know the holdall could now be opened and its contents made known to Cole Burnett.

★ ★ ★

Not much more than an hour later, Burnett was in his mate Les's aunt's place, swigging cheap alcohol, using it to wash down a few more pills. Nice buzz going, almost enough to distract him from memories of the garage. Les lived with his aunt. Burnett had wondered if he was even shagging her. They were related and everything and she had to be twenty years older than him, but she was still tidy. Les had always denied it, though, and whenever Burnett had tried giving her the chat, she'd told him to behave himself. She was out somewhere tonight and the usual crew were in her living room. The pizzas had been delivered. They had plenty of everything — except answers to the questions they were firing at Burnett.

'Cafferty, though, man, what was he like?'

'He give you that damage?'

'Did you let him?'

Burnett hadn't bothered wiping away the blood. He wore it to show them all who he was, what he'd survived.

'He's an old man,' he advised them through swollen lips. 'His time's well past.'

'What did he want, though?'

'He coming for us?'

'Better bring an army with him, eh?'

The can Burnett gripped in his right hand held super-strength lager. It had been out of the fridge too long and was beginning to get warmer than he liked, so he drained it. The voices around him took on the quality of chirruping insects. But there was another voice inside his head, and it was telling him to play along for now. Fetch the phone from the stash under his mum's bed. Somehow get it back to its owner. Show willing. Be nice. He even had a few cuckooing houses in mind — he was sitting in one right now. Play along. Show willing. Be nice.

For now.

For now.

But not forever . . .

22

Ron Travis had kept the café open for them. Rebus had thanked him and asked him to sit in. The two of them carried trays over to the table, where Joyce McKechnie and Edward Taylor waited. Drinks and slices of cake were doled out before Rebus took his seat.

'I've been through everything in Keith's garage,' he said, 'and done a bit of reading on the internet, so I know now that Keith thought Camp 1033 stood for all such camps, and that they showed us ourselves, good and bad. The good is that the community welcomed people like Stefan, Joe and Frank, helped them make their homes here. But on the other hand . . . '

'The poisoning?' McKechnie asked.

'I was thinking more of the shooting.'

'Ah yes,' Taylor said, 'poor Sergeant Davies. He'd been seeing one of the local women.'

'Helen Carter's sister.'

'Indeed.' Taylor turned to McKechnie. 'What was her name?'

'Chrissy. Moved south around 1950.'

'Still alive?'

'You'd have to ask Helen.'

'A detainee had certain feelings for Chrissy,' Taylor continued. 'Jealous of Sergeant Davies, he grabbed the man's own gun and shot him in the head. Went to the firing squad for it.' He studied Rebus. 'Nothing in Keith's notes?' Rebus shook his head. 'Well, you're right — it was certainly a story that intrigued him.'

'No connection to the gun behind the bar at The Glen?' Rebus asked.

'That was found much later by Joe Collins — washed up on a beach, wasn't it?' Taylor looked to McKechnie, who nodded her agreement.

'Either of you remember the name of the man who went to the firing squad?'

'Hoffman? Something like that,' Taylor offered.

Rebus realised that he knew the name. 'I saw a Hoffman mentioned on one of Keith's lists — he was quite senior in the camp, wasn't he? Deputed to make sure things ran smoothly?'

Taylor was nodding. 'Germans kept the camp regulated. Separate quarters for officers and lesser ranks.'

Rebus noticed that Joyce McKechnie was playing with her watch strap, hinting that she had somewhere else to be.

'Just a couple more things,' he said. 'I saw the calculations Keith had done. I know you wanted to turn the camp into something tourists would benefit from . . .'

'Keith approached the Scottish government, Historic Scotland . . .'

'And kept getting knocked back.'

'It was pretty dispiriting,' Taylor agreed.

'And you couldn't do it by yourselves without a lot of work and private funding. The land the camp is on is owned by Lord Strathy?'

'The Strathy Land Trust, to be precise,' McKechnie said, 'but ultimately, yes, it belongs to the Meiklejohns.'

'And did Keith have any direct dealings with the family?'

'He tried, at least once. Never any answer to his calls and letters, so he drove over there. Don't you remember him telling us, Edward? He interrupted some gathering or other — marquee on the lawn and all that. Reading between the lines, he made a bit of a scene. There were photos from the party in one of the glossies. I showed them to Keith and that's when he told me they'd manhandled him off the property.'

'Manhandled? Not by the gardener, by any chance?'

'I've no idea.'

'You don't still have that magazine, do you?'

'In a pile somewhere.'

'I'd be grateful if you could . . . '

'Effect some archaeology?' McKechnie nodded and smiled.

'You know about the golf resort?' Taylor asked Rebus.

'A little.'

'Meiklejohn was never going to sell. If he has his way, everything will be flattened, landscaped or built on.'

'Which would entail doing the same to the steading currently occupied by Jess Hawkins and his friends?'

'Ah, how much do you know about *that*?'

'I know one of his lordship's previous wives currently lives there, which gives him yet another reason to hate the place.'

'Hawkins does seem to be somewhat of a

244

marriage wrecker — '

'I did think,' Travis interrupted, leaning his elbows on the table, 'that the nights Keith slept at the camp, maybe there was an element of reconnaissance.'

Rebus stared at him. 'To what end?'

'Payback,' Travis said simply. Then, after a pause: 'One other thing — the night he died, a motorbike rumbled past here.'

'Not so unusual,' Taylor said. 'Plenty of locals use them.'

'And tourists, too,' McKechnie added.

'This was pretty late, though — I was in bed; I'm sure the sound woke me up.'

'A big bike, then?' Rebus enquired. 'Like the Kawasaki they keep out at Stalag Hawkins? Have you told the investigation?'

'I'm not sure they thought it relevant — it probably isn't.'

'And as I say,' Edward Taylor added, 'lots of folk around here use them — I've even seen your daughter on one.'

Rebus stared at him. 'Samantha?'

'Riding pillion with Hawkins at the controls. Used to ride a bike myself back in my younger days.'

'Mind you,' Ron Travis commented, 'size of some of our potholes, you could lose a bike in them if you're not careful.'

The conversation continued for a further minute or so until they realised Rebus had long ago ceased listening, his mind somewhere else entirely.

★   ★   ★

245

Samantha eventually opened the door to him, a pained look on her face.

'What do you want, Dad?'

'Are you okay?'

'What do you think?'

'And Carrie?'

'Still at Jenny's.'

'Have you told her yet?'

'Yes.' She attempted to blink back a tear. 'I'm just here getting some of our stuff; we're staying with Jenny and her mum.'

'Julie Harris — I've met her. Can I come and visit?'

'Not tonight.' She angled her head, determined that the tears would not escape. 'They took me to see him. To identify him, I mean. And they got my fingerprints. And all the time it was happening, I was thinking: this is what my dad used to do; this is how he spent his working life. No emotion, no warmth, just a job to be got on with.'

'Samantha . . .'

'What?'

'I have one question that needs answering.' She just stared at him, so he ploughed on. 'You're sure you've no inkling who sent Keith that note telling him about you and Hawkins?'

'No.'

'Do you remember the wording?' He watched her shake her head. 'I've learned a lot about Keith these past couple of days. He had a good heart and he cared about people. That's why the camp fascinated him — he saw echoes in it of

246

things that might happen again.' He watched her recover her composure as his words sank in.

'You're right about that,' she said quietly.

'But all that passion he had tells me he might well have wanted a face-to-face with Hawkins, maybe after you had that argument?'

Samantha's face darkened. 'How many times do I have to say it? Jess has nothing to do with this!'

'But is it true you sometimes went out on his motorbike?'

'Ages back — and what the hell's that got to do with anything?'

'We have to give them something, Samantha — the cops, I mean. Because if we don't, all they've got is you. Creasey knows you took Carrie to the commune that day. I'm guessing someone there told him.'

She scowled and turned away, disappearing down the hall. He wasn't sure what to do, but she was suddenly back, thrusting a piece of paper at him. He took it from her. Just the one word, all in capitals, done with a thick black marker pen: LEAVE.

He looked at her for an explanation.

'Stuck through the letter box — someone without the guts to say it to my face.' She gestured towards the note. 'They think I did it, and they're not the only ones, are they?'

'I don't think you did it, Samantha.'

'Then why are you so desperate to put someone else — anyone else — in the frame?'

Rebus reached out and took her by the wrist while he tried to find the right words, but she shrugged herself free and took a step back inside the house.

'I'm closing the door now,' she said, almost in a whisper.

'Is it the same writing as the other note?' Rebus asked.

Instead of answering, she shut the door.

He looked down and realised he was still holding the piece of paper.

★   ★   ★

After closing time again at The Glen, Rebus was perched on a stool, nursing a well-watered whisky. He'd asked May Collins if Helen's sister Chrissy was still alive.

'Died a few years back — I remember Helen heading south for the funeral.'

She was in the office now, putting the day's takings into the safe. Cameron was outside, smoking a roll-up. Rebus took out the note and unfolded it. He felt helpless and was struggling not to turn that feeling into anger.

I don't think you did it . . .

Despite everything.

He was rubbing his stinging eyes when Cameron barged back into the pub.

'Someone's just had a go at your car,' he exclaimed.

'What?' Rebus slid from the stool and strode towards the door. He followed Cameron outside. The Saab was parked kerbside about forty feet away, the closest he had been able to get to the pub at the time. As they approached the car,

Cameron walked out onto the roadway, pointing to the bodywork. He flicked his phone's torch on so Rebus could see the damage. A long, ugly line weaving its way along both rear door and front.

'You saw them?' Rebus asked, running a finger along the scratch.

'Car pulled up, driver got out. I wasn't sure what he was doing. Drove off again. Thought it odd so I came and looked.'

'What did he look like?'

'I was checking my phone,' Cameron said with a shrug.

'The car, then?'

Another shrug. 'Mid-sized. Dark colour.'

'Some eyewitness you make, son.' Rebus looked around. 'No other cars on his hit list?' He paused. 'I'm assuming it was a he?'

'Think so.'

He glanced at his phone, checking for signal. 'Go back in and get yourself a drink,' he told Cameron. 'I'll be there in a minute.'

'Sorry I didn't . . . '

'Don't worry about it.' Rebus had already started calling Creasey's number. He walked the length of the roadway, checking the other parked vehicles. No damage to any of them.

'I'm off duty,' Creasey eventually answered.

'Murder inquiries must've changed since my day.' Rebus could hear music in the background — supper-club jazz by the sound of it. 'You at home?'

'Enjoying a well-deserved rest and about to turn in for the night.'

'Did you do that check on Colin Belkin?'

'Turns out you were right.'

'He has a record?'

'Had to go back a few years, but yes — a few minor assaults and the like.'

'Did you speak to him?'

'Sent a couple of uniforms.'

'I think they maybe pissed him off.'

'How so?'

'Someone just had a go at my car. Drove off when spotted.'

'And you're stretching that all the way to Colin Belkin? How do you reckon he got to you?'

'Remember his friendly cop in Thurso, the one who checked up on Malcolm Fox? You could do worse than ask him.'

'In my acres of free time, you mean? I'll be sure to add it to the list. You think this Belkin character's going to cause you trouble?'

'I've already seen evidence of his temper. Seems to be very protective of his employer.'

'Don't do anything rash, John.'

'Perish the thought, DS Creasey.'

'And Samantha and Carrie are okay?'

'I'll let you get back to your jazz. Speak tomorrow.'

Rebus ended the call and went indoors. May Collins had taken the stool next to his. She was holding a glass with a half-inch of whisky in it. He saw that his own glass had been topped up. Cameron was the other side of the bar, his cider already half finished.

'I took the liberty,' Collins said. 'Though if you don't want it . . .'

'After you've gone to the trouble of pouring it?' Rebus lifted the whisky to his lips and took a mouthful.

'Cameron says your car got keyed.'

'Aye.'

'Any idea why?'

'Serves me right for parking in a dodgy part of town.' He paused. 'I'm assuming it's not an everyday occurrence around here?' He watched her shake her head. 'Well, anyway . . . ' He held up his glass to clink it against hers, then did the same with Cameron.

'Here's tae us,' Cameron said.

'Wha's like us?' Collins added.

'Might just leave it there,' Rebus said, unwilling to finish the toast. But the words echoed in his head anyway.

Gey few, and they're aw deid . . .

Day Four

23

Clarke and Fox were waiting in the interview room at Leith police station when Giovanni Morelli arrived. He wore the same scarf around his neck, tied in the same style. Dark blazer, pale green chinos with matching V-neck jumper (cashmere most likely), leather slip-on shoes with no socks. A pair of sunglasses had been pushed to the top of his head.

'Heading to the beach after?' Fox suggested as Morelli was ushered in. 'Or is that what you wear to classes?'

'I was brought up to dress well,' Morelli commented with a shrug. Clarke gestured for him to take the seat opposite her and Fox. She had a thick dossier in front of her, its manila cover kept closed. She had padded it with blank sheets from the photocopier to make it look more substantial, and had written Morelli's name on the front in nice big letters. Alongside it sat a selection of photographs of various parties Morelli and the victim had attended. He reached out and turned one of them towards him, the better to study it.

'He was fun to be around?' Clarke made show of guessing.

'Definitely.' Morelli leaned back in his chair, angling his right leg across his left knee and undoing his blazer's single shining button.

'We came to realise,' Clarke said, 'that though

255

we know quite a lot about you, we hadn't actually had a proper chat.' She patted her hand against the folder.

Morelli looked from one detective to the other. He hadn't shaved for a few days, but Clarke doubted it was laziness. A five o'clock shadow suited his complexion and jawline and he knew it.

'Okay,' he said, drawing the word out.

'You come from a wealthy background, grew up in Rome, yes?'

'Correct.'

'That night in Circus Lane, you told us you'd met Issy and Sal at a mutual friend's party in St Andrews . . .'

'Not quite — Issy and I were at the party. We met Sal there for the first time.'

'Meaning you already knew Issy?'

The Italian nodded. 'We were sixteen, seventeen, still at school. Our families ended up at Klosters at the same time, and we met at a party there.'

'Klosters the ski resort rather than Cloisters the Tollcross pub?' Clarke enquired, glancing towards Fox: *prejudice vindicated*, she was telling him.

'We discovered we liked similar books, music, films . . .'

'No coincidence then that you both applied to Edinburgh University?'

Another shrug. 'It has a good reputation. And of course there are no fees.' He said this with a self-deprecating smile.

'Because of EU rules,' Fox agreed. 'Which are about to end.'

'Bloody Brexit,' Morelli commented.

'Have you noticed any changes during your time in Scotland?' Fox went on.

'Changes?'

'A hardening of attitudes.'

'Racism, you mean? Not especially — it's a bigger issue in England, I think.'

'Yet you were attacked . . . ' Clarke watched Morelli give another shrug. 'So if that wasn't a race crime, what was it? You'll appreciate that you're not dissimilar to Mr bin Mahmoud — to the untrained eye, I mean, on a dark night, an under-lit street . . . '

'With your hood up,' Fox added.

'You think they mistook me for Sal?'

'Only problem with that hypothesis,' Clarke continued, 'is that you were treated leniently — much more leniently — by comparison. It could have been by way of a warning, and when Mr bin Mahmoud seemed not to have taken that warning, they upped the stakes.'

Morelli leaned forward a little. 'But who were these people? What had he done to them?'

'That's what we're attempting to ascertain, Mr Morelli.'

'He had no enemies.'

'We keep hearing that. But he was running an unsustainable lifestyle, judging by his bank account. Was he maybe borrowing? Were there drugs issues? We appreciate you were his friend — one of his very closest — and you want to protect his reputation, but if there's anything that could help us, we need to hear it sooner rather than later.'

257

Clarke sifted the photographs as she waited. Fox had clasped his hands across his chest, a benign look on his face. Morelli ran a palm along his jaw, as if to aid his thinking.

'Stewart Scoular,' he began, his voice tailing off.

'Yes?' Clarke prompted.

'There was a millionaires' playground in the Highlands, the scheme required investment. Stewart was courting Sal.' His eyes met Clarke's. 'Is that how you say it?' He waited for her nod before continuing. 'And of course you are correct, whenever there was a party, there were stimulants.'

'Sourced from where?'

'Stewart again, I think.'

'Not a man called Cafferty?'

'The one who owns the Jenever Club? I've met him a few times — he's a gangster, yes?'

'We would say so.'

'He liked me to tell him stories of the Mafia, the Camorra, the 'Ndrangheta. My parents live in a nice part of Rome, but they have security — if you have money in Italy, you never feel completely safe.'

'We've looked up your family,' Fox said. 'Your father especially. It seems he's not only a successful businessman but a hard-nosed one too. Didn't he once sack an entire workforce with no warning? There are even rumours of links to Mafia figures . . .'

'In Italy, to be successful is to be hard-nosed. And wherever money is being made, the underworld isn't far behind. My father treads carefully, I assure you.'

'Did Cafferty have any dealings with Mr bin Mahmoud?' Clarke enquired.

Morelli thought for a moment. 'Not really. We only ever saw him at the club. He might appear out of nowhere, shaking hands, offering complimentary drinks. I don't think he impressed Stewart.'

'Explain.' Clarke rested her forearms on the table.

'Stewart would be hosting potential investors. He wanted to wow them. A private club will do that, no? But Cafferty always seemed to know when they were on the premises, and he would come asking questions, seeking information — and with no subtlety.'

'What do you think was going on?'

'To my mind, Cafferty is just a hoarder — he gathers information and contacts. Much of it may never be of use to him, but he gathers it anyway. Also, I think he liked to get under Stewart's skin.'

'So why does Mr Scoular continue to frequent the club?'

Morelli gave a thin smile. 'Cafferty has a reputation. Some people find that attractive. They want to rub shoulders with dangerous people because it makes them feel a little bit dangerous and powerful, too. Do you understand?'

Both detectives nodded.

'There is one further possibility to be explored,' Morelli went on. 'You say I was the victim of a hate crime, or else I was mistaken for

Sal. But I could have been targeted precisely because I was part of his circle — another way of sending a message to him.'

'But if he had no enemies . . .'

'None that he knew of,' Morelli qualified. 'None that any of us knew of. And yet he was murdered and I was attacked.' He offered another shrug.

There was silence in the room for a few seconds until Fox broke it.

'What will you do after university, Gio?'

'I may continue my studies.'

'Here or in Rome?'

'Who knows?'

'You've been friends with Isabella for some time,' Clarke said. 'Have you ever met her father?'

'Yes.'

'Here or at Strathy Castle?'

'Here, London, up north . . . '

'Parties?'

'Of course.'

'He owns the land this millionaires' play-ground of Mr Scoular's would be built on.'

'It is a foolish location — too windy, too cold.' Morelli made show of shivering. 'The one thing this country does not do well is weather.'

'Was Salman at these parties?' Fox enquired.

'Some.'

'They were pitches for funding?'

'In a way, I suppose.'

'Your family has money — your father is an industrialist . . . '

'You're wondering if I've ever been asked to

260

contribute — the answer is yes. But I've always declined. I grew up knowing business and commerce and the people involved. None of it appeals to me. Give me books and art — *those* are what's important.'

'Nice to have the choice,' Clarke commented.

'I know I am pampered, privileged, a dilettante — I have heard it from my father's own lips.' Morelli's face fell a little at the memory.

Clarke exchanged a look with Fox. A twitch of his mouth told her he felt they were done here. She pushed back her chair, rising to her feet. Fox did the same. Morelli looked up at them.

'Finished?' he asked.

'Thank you for coming in,' Clarke said.

The two detectives escorted him from the room and watched him descend the stairs to the ground floor.

'He didn't seem particularly intimidated by our interview room,' Fox commented in an undertone.

'Might need to toughen up the decor,' Clarke agreed. 'Either that or we're just going soft in our old age.'

'Speaking of which — any word?'

'Not a peep.'

'Walkies at lunchtime, then?'

Clarke nodded resignedly and took a look at her phone. No missed calls or messages.

'Could just be his way of avoiding all the changes here,' Fox offered. 'The new flat and everything.'

'That's not it,' Clarke said. 'He's working a

case and he'll be damned if anything gets in the way of him solving it.'

'Begs the question — why have local CID not run him out of town?'

'Give them time,' Clarke said, turning and heading into the MIT office.

24

Rebus was in the kitchen, eating a bacon roll and talking with Cameron and May. Cameron had mentioned the possibility of T-Cut to get rid of the damage to the Saab.

'And you should report it,' May added. 'When all's said and done, it's a criminal act.'

'I phoned Creasey and told him,' Rebus answered. 'He's doubtless putting his best officers on it.' He dug the note from his pocket and held it up so they could both read it. 'Meantime, this was shoved through Samantha's door.'

'Christ, some people . . . ' May Collins shook her head, rising and heading to the sink.

'Why, though?' Cameron asked, still chewing.

'Because someone wants her gone,' Rebus said.

'Is that what your car's all about? A warning?'

'Maybe.' Rebus folded the note up again and pocketed it. There was the sound of a distant thump. Someone was outside the pub's front door. Collins, dish towel in hand, went to investigate, returning a few moments later, Julie Harris at her shoulder.

'What's wrong?' Rebus asked, rising to his feet.

'They've arrested Sam — taken her to Inverness.'

May Collins' eyes were on Rebus. 'Is that serious?'

'One way to find out,' he said.

Five minutes later he was in the Saab, heading south. Cloud was low, rain threatening and a couple of Dutch-registered motorhomes impeding his progress. He thought things through, knowing it made sense from the investigation's perspective. Keith had pretty obviously been killed the same night his car ended up abandoned in the lay-by. Stood to reason it had been driven there by whoever killed him, meaning he and his killer had probably been in the car when it was driven to the scene of the murder — how else had the killer got there? Someone he knew; someone he trusted.

Even if they'd recently been arguing.

Why dump the car in such a conspicuous spot, though? Because the killer panicked, once the initial shock had worn off. Panicked, stopped the car and fled the scene. Nearest house to the lay-by was Samantha's. And where was Carrie while all this was happening? Creasey and his troops would doubtless reckon her old enough to be left alone for an hour — an hour being all it would have taken, maybe even as little as forty minutes. Premeditated? That was a question they couldn't answer as yet. What mattered to them right now was coming up with a convincing suspect and pushing that suspect into confessing. Rebus couldn't know what the autopsy had thrown up, or what evidence might have been gleaned from the crime scene. Would they want all Samantha's clothes and shoes for analysis? The Volvo had already been checked and he doubted they'd found anything incriminating there — if they had, Samantha would already have been charged.

Why take Keith's laptop and notebooks? He suspected CID wouldn't worry themselves about any of that — details to be ironed out later or brushed aside.

Once past the motorhomes, he put his foot down, only to be overtaken quarter of an hour later by a parade of motorbikes with German plates. The road was relatively benign thereafter, passing places appearing with enough regularity to mean oncoming vehicles didn't slow him by much. At Lairg, he branched off the A836, keen to get onto the faster A9 as quickly as possible.

Traffic was sluggish as he neared Inverness, the rain pelting down now, the Saab's wipers just coping and no more. He began to wonder if the old car would get him back to Naver in one piece. He knew where the police HQ was and reckoned they'd have taken her there. He bypassed the centre of the city, staying on the A9 until the turn-off for the main infirmary. His destination was directly opposite it, which he supposed could come in handy from time to time. He dreaded to think how many hours he'd wasted driving out to Edinburgh's Royal Infirmary once it had relocated from the city centre to the outskirts. All to take a witness statement or try to collar an injured suspect.

Of course she's a suspect, he thought to himself as he headed into the car park. When he turned off the ignition, the Saab's engine coughed a complaint loud enough to be noticed by a small group of smokers congregated at one corner of the building. They seemed to be finishing their break, readying to head indoors. But one of them lingered and began walking in Rebus's direction.

'Didn't think we could keep you away,' Creasey said, staring up at the sky to gauge when the next heavy shower would arrive. 'But you know how these things are. This has to happen.' He gestured towards the HQ.

'Can I see her?'

'Don't think so.'

'Legal representation?'

'Everything by the book, John,' Creasey attempted to reassure him. 'And she's holding up okay.'

'She has a daughter at home . . . '

'We won't be holding her — or charging her at this point.'

'Good, because you'd look a right twat when the real killer pops up.'

The sigh Creasey gave was theatrical. Rebus decided on a change of tack.

'Didn't have you pegged for a smoker.'

'I'm not, but some on the team are, and I don't like to be left out. Some of the best ideas come when people allow themselves to switch off for a few minutes.'

Rebus nodded his agreement. He reached into his pocket and handed over the anonymous note. 'Shoved through her door sometime yesterday. Not everyone's on her side.' He paused. 'Might even be more ominous than that.'

'How do you reckon?'

'Someone might want her running, giving you

266

more reason to put her at the top of your list.'

'The killer?' Creasey studied the note again. He held it up to what light there was.

'Doubt you'll get prints, but you could try.'

'I'll hang onto it then.'

'Remember,' Rebus said, 'it was a note like this that told Keith about Samantha and Hawkins.'

'Same person?'

He gave a shrug. 'Don't suppose you've done anything about Colin Belkin yet?'

'Not yet, no.' Creasey was looking in the direction of the Saab. 'Halfway point to home, I'd guess.'

Rebus shook his head. 'Edinburgh can wait. I'm staying here until my daughter no longer needs me.'

'I thought she made that decision when she kicked you out of her house.' Creasey's eyes had hardened.

Rebus gave as good as he got, his voice deepening. 'You got nothing useful from the autopsy; there's no sign of a weapon or the items taken from Keith's satchel — no prints on the satchel either, I'm guessing. Don't let the brick wall you're slamming your head against cause you to do something rash.'

'Like charging your daughter? Your daughter Samantha with her prints on the car and the satchel?'

'She didn't do it!' Rebus snapped through half-gritted teeth.

'Then there's nothing to worry about,' Creasey said with a thin smile, turning away and heading back to work.

Rebus considered walking up to the front desk and causing a fuss, but he knew it would be futile. He heard a car door open and saw a figure he recognised emerge. It was one of the journalists who'd been hanging out at The Glen.

'Catch any of that?' he said as the journalist started to approach.

'Bits and pieces.'

'Do I know your name?'

'Lawrie Blake. Remember, I told you I'm friends with Laura Smith at the *Scotsman?* Which means I know a fair bit about you, Mr Rebus.'

'I couldn't be more thrilled about that, Lawrie.'

The young man nodded towards the Saab. 'I recall you were getting it fixed in Naver. Still doesn't sound too healthy. My brother owns a garage not far from here — he's a hellish good mechanic and I know he's sorted Saabs in his time. I could give him a call.'

'Kind of you, but I need to head back north.'

'I also know a car-hire place — not far from my brother's workshop, and with a café halfway between them.'

Rebus thought for a moment. 'I've met some silver-tongued journalists in my time,' he eventually conceded, 'but few I've taken to like you, young Lawrie.'

'I'll even buy the coffees,' Blake said, 'while we chat about Samantha and this mysterious note.'

It took Rebus only a few seconds to finish making his mind up.

'Lead the way,' he said.

Blake's brother would take a look at the Saab and let Rebus know what he thought, but it might take a day or two. The scratch would need a respray, always supposing the matching colour could be found. Rebus had said to focus on the engine, then had given the Saab a pat on its bonnet, promising he'd be back. The car-rental office had a hatchback he could have immediately, with a special low rate for a five-day hire. He had asked if it boasted a CD player, having lifted Siobhan Clarke's compilation from the Saab. The nod from the rental clerk sealed the deal.

The café was a Costa, and Laurie Blake added sandwiches to their order. Rebus offered to go halves but the reporter was adamant.

'A promise is a promise.'

They found a table by the window and tucked in.

'There are more attractive parts to Inverness,' Blake assured Rebus.

'It's not my first visit,' Rebus replied.

'The A9 murders?' Blake smiled. 'I'm pretty good at my job.'

'I'm beginning to sense that. So will you write something about the note?'

'What did it say?'

'Just the one word — 'leave'.'

'Pity we don't have the note itself.'

Rebus lifted a paper napkin. 'I could recreate it for you.'

'That might qualify as fake news.'

269

'You think your readers would mind?'

'These days, probably not.' Blake bit into his sandwich and chewed.

'If you're good at what you do, you've probably come across Lord Strathy in your travels?'

'Of course.'

'The plans for rocket launch pads and golf resorts?' Rebus watched Blake nod. 'And the wife who left him to join a commune?'

'Same commune your daughter's friendly with.'

'How much do you know about them?'

'I know their landlord wants them gone — it's been rumbling through the courts and various lawyers' offices the past couple of years. I dare say the fact his wife left him to go live with Jess Hawkins hasn't endeared Lord Strathy to the place.'

'He owns Camp 1033, too,' Rebus said, keeping his tone conversational.

'Which is why he was never going to sell to your son-in-law.'

'They weren't married.'

'So that's one thing I've learned today.' Blake paused, still chewing, and tapped a note into his phone. 'Mind if I ask you about Samantha?'

'Yes. Very much.' Blake looked ready to remonstrate, but Rebus held up a hand. 'Later we can maybe talk about that. You know the contents of Keith's satchel have gone missing, presumably taken by his killer?'

Blake nodded. 'Creasey said as much.'

'Why do you think the killer took them?'

The reporter's eyes narrowed slightly. 'What do you mean?'

'Isn't it obvious?'

'Not really.'

'When you were in the bar, did you notice the gap on the wall underneath the optics? Three nails just sitting there?'

'No.'

'Maybe that's the difference between a reporter and a detective. An old firearm used to be displayed there. Unusable as a gun these days . . . '

'But pretty good for clubbing someone?' Blake nodded his understanding.

'It was lifted around a month ago — just one more missing piece of the puzzle.' Rebus paused meaningfully. 'But it gets better. Lord Strathy seems to have gone AWOL too.'

Now the reporter's eyes widened. 'Are you sure?'

'Can't believe the Fourth Estate haven't cottoned on to it, if I'm being honest.' Rebus pretended to be interested in whatever lay beyond the window. 'If you were to publish something by day's end, you'd have an exclusive.'

Blake gave him an appraising look. 'Don't think I can't see what you're doing. You'll fight tooth and nail for your daughter.'

'I'm not bullshitting you, Lawrie. Everything I've told you can be fact-checked. All the years I was a cop, I learned that coincidences are as rare as unicorns.'

'You don't believe in unicorns?'

'I believe in Samantha. Put what I've told you

271

online or don't, it's up to you.'

'Do I name my source?'

'If you do, I'll run you over in a cheap-deal two-door rental.' Rebus drained, the last of his coffee, then realised his phone had pinged with a message. It was from Creasey.

She needs a lift back. If you can't do it, might take a while.

'I have to go,' he told Blake. He took out a pen and scrawled his number on the thin paper napkin, sliding it across the table. 'Nice doing business with you.'

* * *

Samantha looked less than thrilled to see him waiting for her as she stepped out of the building.

'All they said was that my lift was outside.'

'I happened to be passing,' Rebus said. 'But if you'd rather wait for a uniform to take you . . . '

She stepped forward and gave him the briefest of hugs, her head pressing into his shoulder, then followed him wordlessly to the car.

'You've junked the Saab?' she asked as she fastened her seat belt.

'It's just having a bit of a holiday.' He kept his eyes on the windscreen. 'How did it go in there?'

'How do you think?'

'It's a game they have to play, Samantha, that's all.'

'It's not a game to me, Dad,' she said coldly.

'Did you tell them about the fight you had the night Keith died?'

'Yes.'

'Good.' He sensed her looking at him. 'Means they might have some hard questions for Hawkins and his group.' He turned towards her. 'Think about it — where else was Keith going to go after he stormed out?'

'The camp, obviously. He felt safe there. Said it was like a second home.' She took a deep breath. 'Now can we please get going?'

They drove in silence after that, Rebus getting used to the rental car's foibles and controls, Samantha finding a radio station whose signal didn't fade for the first part of the journey. When all that was left was static, she slotted home the CD, studying the track list. 'Who did this?'

'Old colleague of mine called Siobhan.'

'She has catholic tastes — Mogwai *and* Orange Juice?' She thought for a moment. 'Keith was a big Mogwai fan.'

'He liked his music? I didn't see much evidence in the house.'

'No one needs albums these days, Dad.'

'I do.'

'We actually met at a gig in Glasgow, Keith and me. Well, the bar afterwards. Clicked straight off.'

'Was he always a history buff?'

Samantha nodded. 'For a while it was the Clearances. There were homes torched around Strathnaver, clearing the land for sheep rearing. The factor was tried for murder but let off.'

'Landowners are a bit more benign these days. You ever met Lord Strathy?'

'Just his ex-wife.'

'You and her get on okay?' Samantha gave a one-shouldered shrug. 'Night Keith died, Ron Travis heard a motorbike.'

'The guy who owns that backpacker place? Is that why you were asking me about being on the bike with Jess?'

'I'm just saying what Travis heard . . . '

'Really? That's what you're doing?' She shook her head and turned up the music, folding her arms to signal that she wasn't in the mood for any more talk. Eventually, north of Lairg and with no traffic on the road to speak of, she announced that she needed a pee. Rebus pulled over and she opened the door. He busied himself with his signal-less phone until she returned.

'Thanks,' she said. He nodded and made to start off, but she gripped his left arm, causing him to turn and make eye contact.

'I know you think I did it. It won't stop you trying to cover up for me or put someone else in the frame, but I know that's what you think.'

'Samantha . . . '

She thumped her closed fist hard against her chest. 'It's like you fired a bullet at me and it hit me right here.'

'Speaking of guns, there's an old revolver missing from The Glen . . . ' He was about to say more, but she was already flinging open the door.

'Enough!' she yelled, beginning to stride down the road ahead of the car. Rebus started the engine and followed her. He knew how thrawn, how determined she could be. He lowered the passenger-side window and drew level with her.

For a moment, he thought she might leave the roadway altogether and start tramping through the bracken.

'You need to get home to Carrie,' he said. 'Know how long that'll take on foot?'

'I'll hitch.'

'Just get in. We don't have to talk. You don't have to look at me. I'll just drive.' He pulled ahead of her and applied the brakes, watching in the wing mirror as she approached. She passed the car and went another twenty yards or so, but then came to a halt. Rebus stayed where he was, waiting. Eventually her shoulders slumped a little and she turned on her heel, getting back in and fussing with the seat belt.

'I loved him,' she said, as much to herself as to her father.

'I know that,' he replied quietly, easing his foot down on the accelerator.

'And I didn't do it.'

Rebus nodded but said nothing. Did he believe her? He wanted to. He *needed* to. He'd switched off the CD, so the only noise was the car engine. Samantha lowered her window and let the breeze have its way with her hair. Eventually Rebus found some words.

'I know I wasn't a great dad. Not much of a husband either. Sometimes I tell myself I did my best, but I know that's not true.'

'You were okay,' Samantha muttered. 'Remember the mirror in my room, when I was wee?'

'The one on the dresser — how can I forget? I had to come in every night and drape a towel over it.'

275

'Because I was convinced it led somewhere dark and scary.'

Rebus smiled at the memory. 'I wonder why I didn't just take it away.'

Samantha's eyes met his. 'Because I needed it to look into when it was light outside.'

He nodded slowly, his gaze returning to the road ahead.

'You were okay,' he heard her say. Then she reached forward to turn the CD back on.

Average White Band: 'Pick Up the Pieces'.

He hoped that was what they were doing.

25

Siobhan Clarke's call was eventually answered.

'I've got just about enough signal for a bollocking,' she heard Rebus say by way of introduction.

'Good, because I'm primed to give you one.'

'It's online already?'

'Which is why I've had Laura Smith on the phone, screaming about how come she's not the one we gave it to.'

'You put two and two together . . .'

'All investigations leak at some point, but I know what you're like.'

'What *am* I like?'

'You stir shit up for the sake of it.'

'Not strictly true — I usually only do it when I'm getting nowhere. How's Brillo?'

Clarke looked down at the floor of her living room. 'Curled up next to me.'

'You're walking him, though?'

'We're just back. So talk me through it — maybe then I'll have something I can tell Laura while I'm buying her the first of several large gins.'

'She's the press — you don't need to go kowtowing.'

'You forgetting she's helped us plenty in the past?' Clarke sat down on the chair so heavily, Brillo's head shot up. She gave him a pat of reassurance.

'A young reporter up here, he did me a couple of favours so I decided I owed him.'

'You couldn't just take him to the pub?'

'I'm not convinced he's old enough to get served. Besides, what harm does it do?'

'Ramsay Meiklejohn is a member of the House of Lords. That makes his disappearance — if that's what it is — national news, maybe even international. The London tabloids are scenting blood.'

'I'm still not seeing a downside.'

'You might when they descend on Naver. You've only had the Scottish media to deal with so far — they're pussycats by comparison. 'Anyone seen Lord Strathy?'; 'No, but while you're here, we've a murder you might be interested in — victim's partner lives just up the road.''

'Yes?'

'Christ, John, you're throwing your own daughter to the . . . ' Clarke broke off, rising to her feet again and beginning to pace. 'You think she did it?' The question was met with silence.

'No shortage of suspects,' Rebus eventually answered.

'You're not seriously adding Lord Strathy to the list?'

'Keith went to Strathy Castle, kicked up a stink.'

'Why?'

'He wanted Strathy to sell him the camp. Strathy wasn't inclined to agree.'

'I'm not seeing grounds for murder.'

278

'Wouldn't mind asking his lordship a few questions, though — and his gardener, come to that.'

'Haven't got round yet to checking him for you — sorry.'

'Never mind. I already know he has a record, along with a history of violence. He hustled Keith off the castle grounds.' There was silence on the line for a moment. Then: 'You've spoken to the daughter?'

'She seems very relaxed about things.'

'Why would that be?'

'Might be an act.' Clarke sighed and glanced down in Brillo's direction. 'John, if you're going to be much longer, it's going to have to be a kennel job.'

'Nonsense — you spend too much time in the office as it is.'

'Not as much as Malcolm.'

'You're not able to keep tabs on him as much as you'd like?'

'He's become friendly with your old sparring partner.'

Another moment's silence.

'Has he now?' Rebus eventually drawled. 'And why's that?'

'Something to do with Stewart Scoular.'

'The SNP guy? You mentioned him before.'

'Drummed out of the party and now reinvented as a land developer. He seems to feature in Strathy's plans for your POW camp.'

'Is there a connection, do you think?'

'Only if Keith was killed because of his opposition, and frankly I still think that's a stretch.' Clarke paused. 'Is it possible you're seeing things that aren't there, John? You used to say to me that the simple explanation usually turns out to be the right one.'

'The simple explanation would bring Samantha back into the picture.'

'Exactly.' Clarke paused by her window, peering down onto the night-time street below. It all looked so peaceful, so orderly. 'You never answered my question earlier.'

'Which one?'

'You know damn well.'

She listened to Rebus exhale at length and noisily. 'She's my daughter, Shiv, and she has a daughter of her own. She can't do time, guilty or not.'

'Jesus, John . . . '

'I've put away innocent people before.'

Clarke pressed her forehead to the glass. 'I don't want to hear any of this.'

'Then don't ask. You've got enough on your plate, notably Malcolm Fox. You can't let Cafferty get his claws into him — that bastard never, ever lets go.'

'What do you think's going on?'

'Cafferty would do anything to have someone on the inside at Gartcosh, the higher up the better.'

'Malcolm's hardly — '

'But he's on his way, and it seems he has the ear of the ACC. If and when she lands the top job . . . '

'A promotion for Malcolm?'

'Even without the promotion, he's still going

to look like a prize to Cafferty. I know that sounds ridiculous and I can barely believe I'm saying it, but our slow-moving, slow-thinking DI Fox gets to inhabit spaces closed to the likes of you and me.'

'The heart of any and all Major Crime investigations?'

'Anti-terrorism, money laundering, all manner of classified stuff we have no inkling of. And yes, I know it should have been you they came for — staggers me that Fox got the nod.'

'We both know why, though . . .'

'Is this where you point the finger at me? My proximity somehow contaminated you in the minds of the wankers at the Big House?'

'The thought seems to have crossed your mind,' Clarke said.

'But just think how mundane those formative years would have been without me charging into the occasional china shop.'

She was smiling, almost despite herself.

'So what now?' Rebus asked into the silence.

'How many more days do you think you'll be?'

'You know as well as I do, it's sometimes a long game.'

'Want me to post you some clothes?'

'I should have thought to buy some when I was in Inverness.'

'So how are you managing?'

'Pub landlady, I've got her late husband's cast-offs on standby.'

'A landlady, eh? You've landed on your feet.'

'Maybe and maybe not.'

'What's that supposed to mean?'

'I've got her on my list of suspects.'

'You're kidding?'

'Her and her dad . . . '

'Her dad?'

'He's in his nineties, so he's low in the charts.' Clarke couldn't help laughing. 'But he kept an old revolver in the bar and it's gone walkabout, which maybe puts the barman, Cameron, in the picture. Added to which we have Samantha's flame from the commune . . . maybe his partner, Angharad Oates, too — Lord Strathy's ex, lest we forget — if we're factoring in her jealousy of Samantha's fling with Hawkins.'

'You're incorrigible.'

'Is that what I am? How come I feel so tired, then? I could use some of Malcolm's stamina.' Clarke didn't say anything. 'You're going to go check, aren't you, see if he's still in the office?'

'Feet up with a good book,' Clarke corrected him, knowing she was lying. 'I've got the new Karin Slaughter to keep me company.'

'Not forgetting a faithful pooch.'

'Kennels, John. I'm not joking.'

'Try telling him that to his face.'

When Clarke turned from the window, it was as if Brillo had heard every word. His head was cocked, eyes moist.

'I can hear your resolve crumbling from here,' Rebus said, ending the call.

* * *

'Thought I'd find you here,' Clarke said, entering the MIT office.

'Some of us don't have Brillo to feed and walk,' Fox replied.

'Speaking of which, when did you last eat?' Clarke reached into the carrier bag she was holding and handed a fish supper to Fox. He began to unwrap it, while she went to the kettle and switched it on.

'Salt and sauce?' he asked.

'Just salt — I wasn't sure which you were. Got you these, though.' She dug sachets of ketchup and HP out of her pocket and tossed them towards him.

'You think of everything,' Fox said. His desk was strewn with paperwork, so he transported the food to Esson's obsessively tidy desk and seated himself there. While the kettle got to work, Clarke took a look at his computer.

'CCTV,' she commented. Fox nodded, tearing at the fat piece of battered haddock.

'Christ, this is good,' he said.

'Found any interesting bicycles?'

He shook his head. 'Might be something, though. I'll tell you after.'

Clarke poured two teas, sniffing the milk before adding a dollop to each stained mug. She carried both to Esson's desk. Having freed up one hand, she lifted a chip from the pile beneath the fillet.

'Any news from John?' Fox asked.

'He sends his love.'

'I'll bet he does. I saw about his daughter on the news — formally questioned but not yet charged. That must be shredding him.'

'You know John.'

283

Fox glanced up at her. 'Was it him who tipped off the reporter about Lord Strathy?'

'Who else?'

'Bloody typical.'

Clarke stared down at the carton of food. 'You're leaving most of the batter.'

'The healthy option.'

She picked up a sliver and popped it into her mouth. 'The lack of footage doesn't mean Issy and her bike weren't there. I'm guessing Craigentinny has its share of cycle paths; not much call for CCTV on those.' Fox was nodding to let her know he'd already considered this. 'Thing is, though, where's her motive?'

'Motive is for later, Siobhan. Right now, an actual suspect would be received with thanks. Want the rest of these chips?'

'You had enough?' She watched Fox pat his not-insubstantial stomach. 'In that case, I'll eat while you show me what you've got.' She lifted the cardboard carton and followed him to his desk. They sat side by side while Fox scrolled through the CCTV.

'Thing is,' he began, 'previously we'd focused on Seafield Road, and the route Salman took from the New Town. But if his destination was the golf course car park, makes sense to look at the streets in and around Craigentinny too. Sadly, the CCTV coverage there is patchy, but I noticed this car.' He clicked on a frame, freezing it. Headlights; terraced houses; an unremarkable saloon car; the driver nothing more than a smudged outline. 'No visible passenger. And travelling towards the golf course from the direction of town.'

'Okay.' Clarke knew there was more coming. She finished the final few chips while Fox found the relevant clip.

'This is Seafield Road again, just before eleven p.m. See that parked car?' He pressed a fingertip to the screen. The car was shown from behind, rear lights glowing.

'You're saying it's the same one?'

'Same shape, similar colour.'

'Where on Seafield Road is this?'

'About fifty yards from the car park where Salman died, towards the city side. Next footage we have, no car.'

'Driver stopped to take a call, then headed off again?' She watched as Fox offered a shrug. 'It's not much, Malcolm.'

'I know that. What I'm wondering is, is it worth asking the tech people to play with it and maybe get us a number plate?'

'What's your theory?'

'There's a meeting arranged at the golf club, but this driver gets there early and finds the car park locked. Drives out onto Seafield Road and parks. He or she knows an Aston when they see one, so when Salman hoves into view, they signal, maybe with a flash of the headlights. Salman pulls into the nearest secluded spot — which happens to be fifty yards behind the parked car. The other car joins him there.' He noticed that Clarke was staring at him. 'What?'

'That's properly impressive. You're wasted at Gartcosh.'

'We do detective work there too, you know.'

'But not very much of it.'

'So I hand this over to tech support in the morning?'

Clarke nodded. 'Meantime, what make of car do you reckon? Looks pretty generic.'

'Could be any one of half a dozen,' Fox agreed. His phone was vibrating. He lifted it from the desk, checking the caller's name and then answering.

'Yes?' was all he said. Then, after listening to whatever the caller was saying: 'Okay, two minutes.'

'Cafferty?' Clarke guessed as the call ended. 'Downstairs waiting?'

'I need to do this alone,' Fox said, putting his jacket on.

'No you don't.'

He gave her a look that was almost imploring. 'Siobhan, please . . . ' As he made for the door, he turned his head, checking she was staying put.

Clarke walked over to the window. Large black car as before; driver on the pavement, his phone illuminating his face. She held up her own phone, selecting camera and zooming in as far as possible. She snapped a picture of the driver, peering at it. Too grainy to be of any use in putting a name to him.

'Pity,' she said to herself.

It always helped to know your enemies.

★ ★ ★

Fox got into the back seat next to Cafferty, the armrest lowered between them.

286

'I'm trying to be patient, Malcolm,' Cafferty drawled. 'But it goes against my nature.'

Fox opened his mouth to speak, but then noticed that Cafferty's focus had shifted. He was looking at something through the window. Turning, Fox spotted Clarke crossing the road.

'She doesn't know about the tapes or the ACC,' he managed to tell Cafferty. 'Let me deal with her . . . '

The front passenger door opened and Clarke threw herself onto the seat. The driver was moving towards the car, but Cafferty slid his window down.

'It's okay, Benny,' he said.

'Does Benny have a surname?' Clarke asked.

'I assume so. Nice of you to join us, Siobhan.'

'Shouldn't you be holding court at your club?'

'I'm after a progress report, that's all. You know Malcolm's been doing a bit of work for me?'

'I know he's been looking at Stewart Scoular, yes.'

'I feel I've not been getting my money's worth — not that money has changed hands.'

'I'm here to tell you he's not been slacking.'

'Might help,' Fox added, eyes on Cafferty, 'if I knew what exactly it is you think I'm going to find.'

Rather than answer, Cafferty kept his focus on Clarke. He even leaned his head forward a little into the gap between the back seats and the front.

'So Malcolm's been holding out on you, Siobhan? Hasn't told you about the recordings of Jenni Lyon's partner playing away from home — I hope he's cooled down, by the way. He was going to fall on his sword, but that doesn't seem to have happened. My guess is, Malky had a word with Jenni and Jenni had a word with the love rat.'

'Recordings made at your club?'

'And elsewhere.' Cafferty glanced in Fox's direction and grinned. 'Didn't know that, did you, Malky boy? I'm laying all my cards on the table right here. And I want Siobhan in the loop, because it seems to me you've been unwilling to trust her.'

'You want me in the loop,' Clarke corrected him, 'because you're trying to cause a rift between me and Malcolm — and that's not going to happen.'

The grin this time was aimed at the front seat. 'She's sharp, isn't she, Malky?'

'His name is Fox — Detective Inspector Fox to the likes of you.'

'It's that sort of attitude that can turn a concerned citizen against the powers of law and order and send them to the internet or the media with their little explosive package of recordings.'

'If you want Scoular so badly,' Clarke retorted, 'go after him yourself.'

'In fact,' Fox said, pulling back his shoulders, 'maybe we should go have a word with Mr Scoular. I'm sure he'd be tickled to know of your interest in him.'

'And one other thing,' Clarke added. 'These tapes — I'm guessing you told Malcolm that releasing them would end ACC Lyon's career.

But that's hardly a result for you, is it? Far better to hang onto them in the expectation that she'll soon be Chief Constable. Think of the extra leverage you'd have on her then.' She was shaking her head slowly. 'You never planned to release them, did you? It's all just talk — *you're all just talk.*'

'That's a gamble you're willing to take?' Cafferty's eyes were on Fox now. 'Yes or no, DI Fox? Or hadn't you better check with your boss first, see what she wants you to do?'

Fox's mouth opened a fraction, but no words formed. Clarke had opened the car door and was swivelling her legs out onto the roadway. Cafferty's hand clamped around Fox's forearm.

'Think very carefully, DI Fox.' He nodded towards Clarke's back. 'This isn't your future — Gartcosh is; Jennifer Lyon is; a seat at the top table is.'

Fox shook his arm free and opened the door. '*My* future, *my* decision,' he said, climbing out.

'Absolutely.' Cafferty was laughing lightly as Fox slammed the door closed. Clarke, having given up asking Benny for his surname, was on her way back to the station's main door. Fox caught her up.

'Lyon knows all about this?' she asked in an undertone.

'Yes.'

'That's the armour you were talking about?' Fox nodded. 'In which case, he'll think he's already won.'

'How do you make that out?'

'Even if you give him nothing, he can say you did his bidding, and Lyon knew about it and sanctioned it.'

'So?'

'So the pair of you might have to go on record and deny it — in other words, lie to whoever is asking.'

'And?'

She stopped just short of the door, turning so she was face to face with him. 'He tapes everything that happens in his club, Malcolm. What makes you think he stops there?'

'The car?'

'All it takes is for him to switch on his phone's voice memo app. Plus you've been in his penthouse. Chances are everything you said there has been recorded.'

Fox couldn't help looking over his shoulder at the car. It was starting to move, but Cafferty had left the rear window open, his eyes on the two detectives as he passed.

'He's won,' Fox said quietly, statement rather than question. 'I feel a bit sick.'

'I hope it wasn't the fish,' Clarke replied, making show of pressing her hand to her stomach.

'How can you joke about this?'

She considered for a moment and then shrugged. 'Thinking he's won doesn't mean he has. It's not over yet, Malcolm.' She watched the car glide away from them into the night. 'Not nearly over . . .'

★ ★ ★

As Benny drove to the Jenever Club, Cafferty phoned Cole Burnett.

'It's your Uncle Morris, Cole. How are things at your end?'

The teenager's voice was nasal and ever-so-slightly slurred. 'It's all good, all good.'

'Got an address or two for me?'

'Aye.'

'Well, let's not say any more until we meet face to face. You know my place on the Cowgate? I'll see you there in an hour.'

'Okay.'

'Cheer up, son — future's full of good things coming your way. Just trust your Uncle Morris.' He ended the call and placed his phone on the seat next to him.

'You really think he's got the makings?' Benny asked from the driver's seat, eyes meeting Cafferty's in the rear-view mirror.

'If he hasn't, he's all yours.' Cafferty turned his head to watch the city slide past. Leith had changed — fine dining, craft beer and artisan bread — but it was still Leith. Like an old band coaxed out on the road again, smack was making a comeback. Coke had stopped being available only to the wealthy. Crack and methadone and benzos were everywhere.

Money was being made.

But the people at the top always wanted a bigger slice. If Cafferty didn't fortify his territory, others might think he was vulnerable. He'd had meetings in Glasgow and Aberdeen, just to make sure everyone knew where things stood. Not Dundee, though — because the people shipping the drugs from Manchester hadn't wanted it. Message enough to Cafferty's mind: they'd be coming for him soon. And when they came, they would take out the street dealers first, making things nice and clear to him. That was why over the past few months he'd been bringing losers like Cole Burnett aboard. Let the marauders think they were taking out his best guys, his whole army. They would reckon it an easy win.

Then they would begin to relax. And their guard would come down . . .

'Want some music or anything, boss?' Benny was asking.

'I'm fine, Benjamin, thanks. Big Ger Cafferty is absolutely tickety-boo.'

Day Five

Day Five

26

The media and the rubberneckers had returned to Naver.

Lawrie Blake looked pleased with his creation when Rebus bumped into him on the street outside The Glen. The online world had magnified his original story, engendering conspiracy theories, dusting off the racier anecdotes from Ramsay Meiklejohn's past and inventing luridly imagined versions of the anonymous threat to Samantha. Blake had his collar turned up and was wearing a large tweed cap, his phone gripped in his hand ready to record vox pops and capture photographs. Locals, however, were thin on the ground, having retreated to the relative safety of their homes. A few parents were forced to run a gauntlet of sorts as they scurried towards the school with their gawping children. Rebus was heading to the shop for a newspaper, but Blake produced one from his pocket and handed it over. Rebus unfolded it.

'Front page, eh?' he commented.

'And pages three, four and five. I've even had a call from a press agency in London offering work. How's your Saab?'

'I've not heard. Rental's running fine, though.' He watched as a car cruised past, failing to find a parking space. There was TV equipment in the back. 'You going to be talking to them?' he asked, nodding towards the vehicle.

295

'If they ask nicely. I quite fancy a move into television.' Blake's phone was pinging every few seconds with messages. 'Has your daughter received any more notes?'

'Not that I'm aware of.'

The reporter glanced at the pub. 'You're staying here rather than at hers — mind if I ask why?'

'We're not discussing Samantha, remember?'

Blake gave a thin smile. 'Can't blame a guy for trying. Laura called me late last night from Edinburgh. She was asking who gave me the story.'

'Was my name mentioned?'

'I protect my sources, Mr Rebus.'

'I'm sure she knows anyway. It's a small tank we're all swimming in.' Rebus looked around. 'No sign of your fellow journalist, the one you were in the pub with?'

'She's at Strathy Castle, I think. I'm headed there soon.'

'Don't expect the occupants to be overly chatty — and watch out for the gardener.'

'Oh?'

'Criminal record and a temper.' Rebus put a finger to his lips as he started to unlock the rental car.

'Going somewhere nice?'

'You planning on tailing me?'

'No.'

He gave the young man a hard stare. 'Good.'

He made for the coast road, heading in the direction of Tongue. He looked to his left as he passed the backpacker café. A couple of bicycles and an old-fashioned camper van were parked out front. Ron Travis would be busy inside, catering for his guests. The Portakabin was still in place at Camp 1033, along with fluttering lengths of crime-scene tape and the same bored-looking uniform as before. Rebus sounded his horn and, having attracted the officer's attention, stuck two fingers up as he passed. Checking in the rearview mirror, he saw him dig a notebook out of his high-vis jacket. Doubtless he'd be noting the car's details.

'Good luck,' Rebus muttered with a half-smile.

He took the cratered track to the steading, parking in the same spot as before. The logs had been dealt with and were neatly stacked, their top layer covered with a tarpaulin, next to which sat the motorbike. When the door to the farmhouse opened, Mick Sanderson stepped out. His eyes were on the rental car as he approached Rebus.

'Your repair got me as far as a garage in Inverness,' Rebus explained. He gestured towards the bike. 'Another of your projects?'

'It works well enough.'

'And it belongs to you?'

'Anyone who needs it can use it. You ever ridden one?' Sanderson straddled the seat and gripped the handlebars.

'Been out on it recently?'

'The day I fixed your car.'

'And before that?'

'No idea.'

297

'Who else uses it? Jess? Maybe Angharad Oates even?'

Sanderson's smile was icy. 'What's your interest?'

Rebus offered a shrug, his hands sliding into his pockets. 'Seen much of Samantha the past day or so?'

'She's been around.'

'You know she was sent a threatening note?'

Sanderson's face softened a little. He dismounted from the bike. 'News to me.' Rebus's attention had shifted to the barn. Music was wafting from it. 'Yoga class,' Sanderson explained. 'Want a cuppa?'

'If you're offering.'

Sanderson studied him. 'I don't think you're our friend — unlikely it'll ever happen — but you're a friend's father and that gets you a mug of tea.' He paused. 'But no more of your questions, okay?'

'Fair enough, son. Lead the way.'

They walked the short distance to the farmhouse door, Sanderson pushing it open and allowing Rebus to precede him inside. The kettle was on the wood-burning stove, wisps of steam escaping its spout. Oates was seated at the dining table as before, the child on her lap. She was helping him draw a castle with coloured crayons.

'Your old place?' Rebus made show of guessing. 'You must miss it.'

'What's he doing here?' Oates demanded of Sanderson.

'Tea, and then he's going.'

'That doesn't answer my question.' Her eyes

were drilling into Rebus. Rebus nodded towards the child.

'Didn't catch his name last time I was here.'

She thought about not answering, but then relented. 'Bram — short for Abraham.'

'As in Bram Stoker? Vampires and all that?'

'Jess liked the name.'

'And he usually gets his way, eh? Like an old-fashioned lord and master. Are you stuck here all the time, or do you make the occasional getaway?'

'Mr Rebus is very interested in our Kawasaki,' Sanderson explained.

'It's a hefty machine,' Rebus said. 'Just wondering if you've managed to master it?'

'This is the twenty-first century, if you hadn't noticed.'

'So you do take it out sometimes?'

'We all do.'

'Those of you who've got a licence . . .'

'We're very law-abiding up here, Mr Rebus,' Sanderson said, handing him a mug. 'Milk's in the jug, sugar in the bowl.'

Rebus placed the mug on the table and added a splash of milk. A second mug had been set in front of Oates, who accepted it without any show of thanks. Rebus took a slurp, peering over the rim of the mug to the plastic box of crayons.

'Got any felt pens in there?' he asked, shifting his focus to Oates. 'Nice thick black ones?'

She leapt to her feet, hoisting a shocked Bram to her shoulder. 'Get out!' she barked.

'You're upsetting the wee one,' Rebus chided her.

'And *you're* upsetting all of us! Now get the hell out.'

Rebus placed the mug back on the table. 'Milk's on the turn,' he said. He was halfway to the door when he paused. 'Seen anything of your ex-husband lately? People are getting a bit worried.'

Oates half turned her head towards Sanderson. 'I swear to God, Mick, if you don't kick him out, I will!'

Rebus held up both hands in a show of appeasement. 'A peaceful, welcoming place — you really are all living the dream here.' He closed the door after him and made for his car.

A few minutes later, as he passed the camp again, he prepared to sound his horn, but there was no sign of the uniform. He wasn't much further on when his phone rang. It was Samantha, so he pulled into the backpackers' parking area and answered.

'It's me,' his daughter began.

'I know — how are you doing?'

'Press are all over this note I got. They wanted to photograph it but I couldn't find it. I gave it to you, didn't I?'

'And I handed it to Creasey. Good news is, the publicity might stop whoever did it sending any more.'

'It was you that alerted the media, wasn't it?'

'Time we got them on your side, Samantha. This isn't much, but it's a start.'

'I'm not sure whether to thank you or not.' He heard her sigh. 'Are you still sleeping at the pub? Sofa's available here . . . '

'I appreciate that, but a bed suits me better and the wee bit of distance might be good for us. How's Carrie doing?'

'Devastated. She's going to get counselling, though it might mean trips to Thurso. They can't release the body yet, so no point planning anything.' Her voice began to crack. 'If they arrest me, you'll need to make the funeral arrangements.'

'Not going to happen, trust me.'

'It's hard to trust *anyone* right now.' She gave a long exhalation and seemed to pick herself up a little. Rebus saw that Ron Travis had come to the door. He lowered the driver's-side window and gave a wave. Recognising him, Travis waved back then cupped the same hand to his mouth in imitation of taking a drink. Rebus shook the offer away and turned his attention back to the conversation, making Samantha repeat what she'd just been telling him.

'Creasey delivered it all in a bag this morning — not the clothes, I suppose they're evidence, but stuff from Keith's pockets. Money and credit cards. His phone's still missing, but attached to his house keys there's a memory stick. I'd forgotten he had it.'

'What's on it?' Rebus asked quietly.

'I've not looked. Can't be important, though, or Creasey would have hung onto it.'

'True.' Rebus was watching Travis disappear back indoors. 'Will you still be at home in ten minutes or so?'

'I'm meeting Julie for a coffee. She's picking me up so I don't have to brave whatever's

301

waiting for me in the village.'

'I'm on my way,' Rebus said, working the steering wheel with one hand.

27

Samantha and Julie were already in the car when Rebus arrived. Julie waved and smiled while Samantha got out, hugging him briefly before pressing the small plastic device into his hand.

'Sorry about yesterday,' she said.

'Me too.' He watched as she ducked back into the car, no hanging around. He hoped it was because of the chill wind and the sudden needles of rain. He got back into his rental and followed the two women into Naver. The TV camera crew had just packed up, and as they manoeuvred out of their space, Rebus grabbed it. The rental car was smaller than his Saab, easier to handle. He entered The Glen. May was serving coffees and teas to a table of regulars.

'Will I be seeing you on the news tonight?' he asked her.

'Cheeky beggars wanted to film in here but I told them where to go.'

Rebus was waiting for her at the bar when she brought the empty tray back. He held up the memory stick. 'Can I use your computer again?'

'If you promise not to plant a virus.'

He promised, heading behind the bar and through the doorway into the cramped office. There was a backlog of paperwork on the large desk. On one wall was a framed photo of a younger May embracing her father outside the pub. Rebus peered at the password taped to the bottom edge of the computer screen. The hard drive was beneath the desk, and it took him some effort to lean down far enough to slot home the memory stick. Once done, he settled himself on the swivel chair. May's face appeared in the doorway.

'Get you a drink?'

'I'm fine, thanks.'

'Not hungry?'

'Not yet.' She was looking at the screen, not quite managing to disguise her curiosity. 'Whatever's on here, you'll be the first to know,' Rebus assured her.

'I'll leave you to it then.' She began humming a tune as she returned to the bar. Rebus settled down to work.

A few dozen files. Most of them seemed to be individual photographs. He clicked through all of them. The camp, the dig, the history group. Then a few of Joe Collins, followed by Helen Carter, Stefan Novack and a man Rebus guessed must be Jimmy Hess's grandad Frank. All four looked to be seated in armchairs in different living rooms. Keith had interviewed them in their own homes.

All that remained were the four audio files. Rebus managed to turn the volume up. Even so he had to angle his ear towards the small speaker on the front of the console. First up was Novack. The recording lasted just under fifty minutes. Rebus had mixed feelings as he listened to Keith's voice; he wished again that he'd known him better in life, taken the trouble to *get* to know him. On the few occasions when he had phoned the house and Keith had answered, all he'd done was ask to speak to Samantha — no how are you? How's work? How's life treating you?

Keith was a good interviewer. He started with general chat, getting Novack used to talking. And when the questions began, they were increasingly forensic until they concentrated on the suspected poisoning and the murder of Sergeant Davies. Novack, however, had little to say on either subject. It wasn't that he sounded evasive; it was simply that he didn't know much.

'Please remember, I had been released from the camp by then.'

'But you kept in touch with the friends you'd made — sent them letters. I'm guessing they wrote back with news and gossip. And then later when you returned and started your new life . . . '

'I would tell you if I could, Keith, believe me.'

The same was true of the revolver displayed in The Glen — Novack had no reason to doubt Joe Collins' story of how he'd found it.

'I think you have more details already than I do,' he told Keith at one point.

Slowly the questioning petered out and they were back to general chat.

Helen Carter was next, Keith managing only twenty or so minutes with her before she drifted off to sleep. He must have known he was against the clock, because the questioning was brisker, the preliminaries curtailed — and he kept his voice raised to combat her hearing issues. He was interested in her job at the camp dispensary, her relationship with (and eventual marriage to) an internee called Friedrich. But quickly he zeroed in on her sister Chrissy and Sergeant Gareth Davies.

'It shocked her to her core,' Helen Carter said, voice croaky. 'Took her years to recover. Poets write about the madness of love — but to kill a man? Nothing romantic about that, let me tell you.'

Had Chrissy been seeing Davies's killer behind his back?

'Hoffman? She hardly knew him — maybe smiled at him once or twice in passing. Pleasantries, you know. Thinking was, he admired her from afar but never plucked up the courage to do anything about it.'

Keith: 'Except execute Sergeant Davies.'

'Horrible thing to happen. We had military police crawling all over the place. But it was a day or two before they found Gareth's revolver hidden beneath Hoffman's mattress. He had a room of his own — didn't share with the others. Perk of being put in charge of one bit of the camp. Wasn't liked, though, not too many tears shed when the firing squad did their duty.'

'What about the revolver in The Glen? It couldn't be the one used to kill Sergeant Davies?'

'You keep asking us about that. All I can tell you is that it turned up some time after the camp had closed, and Joe's story is he found it washed ashore.'

'Why put it on display?'

'A talking point, isn't it? No more to it than

that. Your tea's getting cold, Keith, and I'm getting tired. I know you mean well, but the past is the past is the past . . . '

The next file was Joe Collins himself. Keith had hardly got started before Collins cut him off.

'It's all about this murder, isn't it? The murder and the poisoning — those are your interest rather than the camp itself?'

'I'm not sure I'd agree completely with — '

'Ach, it's the truth and you know it. The murder weapon was found hidden in Hoffman's quarters.'

'Yet he protested his innocence to the end, according to the records.'

'Which did not delay his appointment with the firing squad.'

'They executed him in the camp, didn't they?'

'At dawn. We were to remain in our bunks, the doors locked. We were all awake, though; I doubt many of us had got much sleep. He made noises as he was led out.'

'Noises?'

'Begging for mercy, I think. Then the gunshots and the terrible silence. He was buried somewhere outside the camp. I don't think there was ever a marker of any kind. The digging you are doing will not bring his bones to light.'

'That's not why we're excavating.'

'The money you want to spend on the camp, would it not be of more use to the community in other ways?'

Instead of answering, Keith had another question ready. 'The revolver you say you found — '

'The revolver I *did* find. This obsession will do you no good, Keith. You think I had something to do with the crime? Sergeant Davies's revolver was taken away by the authorities as evidence. What happened to it afterwards no one knows.'

'Tossed into the sea, perhaps?'

'What does it matter if it was?'

'From the accounts, there were no witnesses. Davies was ambushed somewhere between the village and the camp. His weapon was wrestled from him and he was shot in the head.'

'Yes?'

'I don't understand why Hoffman would hang onto the weapon.'

'Perhaps he planned to use it again.'

'It doesn't seem to have been very well hidden. He could have left it anywhere, but he took it to his room.'

'And this is what troubles you?'

'He also doesn't seem to have courted Chrissy Carter. The two hardly knew one another.'

'Whatever the story, all I can tell you is that someone threw that particular revolver away — probably at the end of the war — and it was covered over by time and tide. But both of those have a way of bringing things back again, wanted and unwanted.'

'And you put it on display because . . . ?'

'Not as a trophy, if that's what you think. Am I the one who shot Gareth Davies? I answer that in the negative with all the force I can muster.' Collins paused. 'I cannot understand why you would spend your evenings and weekends following this hobby when you have Samantha and Carrie waiting for you at home.'

'They're very patient.'

'You think so? Well, I pray you are right.'

'What do you mean?'

'Nothing, nothing — I'm just an old man who rambles sometimes . . .'

As the recording ended, Rebus stood up, stretching his limbs and his spine. He wandered through to the bar, caught sight of Lawrie Blake speaking to what he assumed were other journalists, and retreated to the kitchen. There was a note on the table — *Soup in pot* — so he reheated the broth and sat down to eat it, feeling suddenly ravenous. He cut himself a wedge of bread to go with it and poured a glass of water from the tap.

'A proper prisoner's meal, that,' May Collins said, walking into the kitchen as he was finishing.

'Didn't fancy the bar for some reason.'

She nodded her understanding. 'They're away again, though — I don't think we're feeding them enough titbits. How's it going?'

'I've just been listening to Keith talking with your father.'

'I heard from the hallway. You seemed engrossed.'

'I'm wondering how he felt about Samantha and Hawkins — he must have wondered how many people had known or suspected and hadn't told him.'

Standing behind him, May gave his shoulder a brief squeeze. 'Have you heard from Samantha?'

'She's with her pal Julie.'

'Actually she's with the police — or she was.

They turned up at Julie's door and took her away. That's what I'm hearing.'

Rebus dug out his phone. No signal.

'Try out by the caravan,' Collins advised.

Rebus unlocked the back door and went outside. The rain had stopped, the sky bright blue. The caravan was small, maybe only a two-berth, dotted with lichen, its single window in need of a good clean. Rebus made the call. Creasey answered almost immediately.

'Don't,' the detective said. 'All we're after is a better idea of how the deceased ties to Lord Strathy. We know they argued about the camp buyout and we know things got a bit heated when Keith barged into a social gathering at the castle.'

'And?'

'And Samantha's being asked what she knew about any or all of it.'

'And?'

'And I'm sure she'll tell you in the fullness of time.'

'You're stranding her in Inverness again?'

'Relax, she's a lot closer to home than that.'

'You got the door unlocked at the station in Tongue?'

'I wish you'd leave us to get on with our job, John.'

'Why didn't you say anything about the memory stick?'

'Can I remind you for the umpteenth time — you're not the detective here. In fact, you're the father of our chief suspect. We don't tend to share with anyone unless there's good reason.'

310

He paused to take a breath. 'Have you listened to it?'

'Most of it.'

'So you'll agree there's nothing there for us to get excited about? Apart from oral history buffs, I mean.'

'The killer took his laptop, notes and phone. That has to mean something. Then there's the gun . . .'

'What about it?'

'Say Keith was the one who took it. Maybe he thought with all our forensic advances there'd be evidence that could be gleaned from it.'

'So?'

'So where is it? Was it in the bag?'

'John, the person who killed Sergeant Davies went to the firing squad.'

'Someone went to the firing squad, certainly.'

There was silence on the line for a moment. 'So what are we talking about here — a fit young man overpowered and murdered by someone in their nineties? Or maybe you think a ghost did it — there are plenty on social media who do. We've had to chase half a dozen of them away from the crime scene this week.'

Rebus leaned a hand against the side of the caravan. There were cigarette butts on the ground beneath him. He crouched to pick one up. The filter was a sliver of rolled-up cardboard. Spliffs. Looked like cider wasn't Cameron's only indulgence.

'How long will you keep her?' he asked Creasey.

'Actually we're done. That's why I've got time

311

to waste with you. Her friend is fetching her. Oh, and by the way — that news leak? Strathy and the anonymous note? Don't think I'm not aware who's behind it. So thanks a bunch for that, John. Cooperation is a two-way street, remember.'

'Well, here's me cooperating then, like a good citizen. The night Keith was killed, Ron Travis heard a motorbike.'

'He mentioned it.'

'There's a bike at Hawkins' compound. Available for anyone to use. Maybe ask if someone took it out that night. Oh, and the party at Strathy Castle, the one Keith was bundled out of? I reckon our friend Colin Belkin is in the frame for that. So maybe you could ease up on an innocent woman and go check those leads out . . . ' Rebus broke off, realising he was talking to himself. He studied his phone screen. He still had a signal. Creasey had ended the call.

'Shitehawk,' he muttered. Then, after another glance towards the remains of Cameron's spliffs, he tried the door of the caravan. It was unlocked. He ducked under the lintel and took a step inside. The space was cramped and stuffy, the area around the sink cluttered with mugs and glasses. Didn't look like the two-ring stove got much use. Breakfast cereal; some milk staying cool in a basin of water. The bed had been turned back into a table. There were American comics spread across the floor. The tiny toilet cubicle looked like it doubled as a shower, a faint aroma of waste water emanating from it.

'Help you?'

Cameron was standing just outside the caravan, tobacco and cigarette papers in his hand. Rebus tried not to look like the guilty party as he backed out into the courtyard.

'Just wondering if you happened to have a revolver lying about in there,' he said.

'What use would I have for that?'

'Maybe there's a collectors' market.'

'Steal from May?' The barman was focused on constructing his cigarette. 'You think I'd do that after all the kindness she's shown me?' His eyes finally met Rebus's as he licked the edge of the paper.

'Okay, let's say you're the shining knight then, taking it to protect someone.'

Cameron reached into the back pocket of his denims and brought out a disposable lighter. He got the cigarette going and inhaled deeply, taking pleasure in releasing the stream of smoke in Rebus's direction.

'Look all you want, there's no rusty old revolver in there.'

'You knew Keith a bit — could he have taken it?'

'Pub was always busy when he was in.'

Rebus nodded slowly. 'Easier if the place was quiet, no one behind the bar. Or it happened between closing time and reopening.'

Cameron squinted through the smoke. 'That would certainly narrow things down.'

'Ever been in trouble with the law, son?'

'Because I have tattoos and a few piercings, you mean?' He gestured towards the roaches on the ground. 'Smokes a bit of dope so he has to

313

be a bad 'un.' His mouth formed a sour smile. 'Sam always said you were a bit of a dinosaur. I'm starting to see what she meant.' A final draw on the thin cigarette and it was done. He flicked it to the ground. 'Came out to tell you Joyce McKechnie left a bag for you. I've put it on the kitchen table.'

'Thanks.' The two men's eyes met again and both gave slow nods. Rebus watched Cameron head indoors, waited a few moments and then followed.

The kitchen was empty, but a mug of tea sat where his soup bowl had been. He took a mouthful before opening the carrier bag. Magazines. McKechnie had folded down the relevant corners. Gatherings at Strathy Castle; events where Lord Strathy had been a guest. One showed him cutting the ribbon on an upgraded school playground. In another, he was opening a birdwatching facility in 'the heart of the Flow Country'. To Rebus's untrained eye, the Flow Country looked like miles and miles of bugger all: flat, treeless, colourless. But Strathy looked happy enough, or at least well fed and watered. If the society occasions were anything to go by, he liked his wine. Glass of red raised in almost every shot, mouth open as if he were about to start cheering. Pink-faced, paunchy, thinning hair and a roguish sparkle in the eye.

From the dates of publication, Rebus reckoned he knew which party it was Keith had crashed. The names of the photographed guests meant little to him, but he recognised Lady Isabella Meiklejohn and Salman bin Mahmoud.

Stewart Scoular was there too, off to the right in one shot, behind someone's shoulder in another. Siobhan had mentioned an Italian friend of bin Mahmoud's and there was one name — Giovanni Morelli — that fitted the bill. Handsome face, arm around Lady Isabella's waist. Wait, though . . . here was someone else Rebus recognised. Martin Chappell, stood next to his wife Mona. Both were holding champagne glasses and smiling for the camera. Rebus had never met Chappell, but he knew who he was.

He was Chief Constable of Police Scotland.

In the photograph, Mona Chappell was sandwiched between her husband and Stewart Scoular, as if the three were old friends. Rebus took out his phone and photographed the page a few times from different angles. Stepping outside and finding a signal, he dispatched them to Siobhan Clarke. He waited a couple of minutes, wishing he still smoked. The smell from Cameron's roll-up lingered in his nostrils, the taste clung to the back of his throat. For luck, he touched the inhaler in his pocket. Hadn't needed it this whole trip. He wondered if it was the quality of the air.

'Maybe just the lack of tenement stairs,' he said to himself, heading indoors again, scooping up the mug of tea and making for the office.

He knew the final recording would be Frank Hess. But when he clicked on it, he wondered if something had gone wrong — it wasn't even half the length of the others. When he began to listen, he understood why. For the first few minutes everything was fine. Keith asked Hess about his

315

post-war years, his various jobs — mostly labouring and building work — his family. But when it came to Camp 1033, Hess grew agitated.

'I have erased it from my head — all of it.' The voice was slightly high-pitched, Germanic but with touches of Scots intonation. 'If others wish to remember, so be it. I want to be allowed to forget — that is my right, no?'

Keith: 'Yes, of course. But you must have happy memories of that time too. You were allowed out of the camp most days. I believe you worked on several farms and repaired some of the dry-stone walls, walls we can still see today. You mixed easily with the local community.'

'So what? I ask you, Keith: so what? It was long ago and everyone I knew is now dead. Why would I want to remember any of that?'

'Helen isn't dead; Stefan and Joe aren't dead.'

'As good as — and we will all be feeding the worms soon. This world is on a path to chaos. Have you not noticed? I have heard it compared to the 1930s. Everyone bitter and pointing the finger at the person they think is to blame for their misfortune. It was an ugly time then and it is an ugly time now. Please don't ask me to dig it all up again.'

'All I'm trying to do is — '

'No, Keith, no — enough. I tried to tell you many times that this is not for me. Switch it off. We are finished here.'

'There are so few of you left who remember. Just one last question about the revolver then — '

'Enough, I said!'

316

A third voice interrupted. Rebus recognised it: Jimmy Hess.

'Christ's sake, Keith, you trying to give him a heart attack?'

'We're just talking, Jimmy.'

'Maybe so, but now you're done. You okay, Grandpa?'

'I feel terrible.'

'I told you he wasn't keen,' Jimmy Hess was saying. 'Pack your stuff up — I'll see you for a drink later.'

'I didn't mean to upset you, Frank,' Keith apologised.

'If that was true, you would not have come here in the first place,' the old man barked.

'Look, I'm switching it off,' Keith said, at which point the recording ended.

Rebus knew now why Frank Hess hadn't made it to the pub that evening. Maybe he *had* been unwell, but it wasn't just that. What was that quote about the past being another country? There were things in his own past he would rather not linger on, too many skeletons for just the one closet.

'How's it all going?' May Collins asked from the doorway.

'How long have you been there?'

'Not long.' She gestured towards the empty mug. 'Need a top-up?'

Rebus shook his head. 'Frank Hess isn't the talkative sort, is he?'

'Frank's a grumpy old sod. By all accounts he was a grumpy *young* sod, too. His only daughter died in a car crash about ten years back. Her husband was in the car with her. He died too. Been to a party, drinking, not thinking it mattered — roads around here deserted and all that. Off the road and into a tree.' Collins sighed. 'Don't think that improved his general outlook on life.'

'So it's just him and Jimmy?'

Collins nodded. 'Jimmy has two sisters but they're down south. Either one of them would take Frank, but he won't budge. They come up sometimes, give Jimmy a bit of respite.'

'Families, eh?' Rebus commented, for want of anything else to say.

'I reckon we all live too long these days, that's the problem. What's that film where you only get to reach a certain age? Sci-fi thing.'

'Michael York,' Rebus said. 'I forget the title, but I seem to remember they were culled when they reached forty.'

'Bad news for both of us,' May said with a smile. 'Did you get any joy about Sam?'

'They're done and dusted with her. Few questions about Keith and Lord Strathy.'

'The land buy?' She watched as he nodded. 'Joyce told me about the magazines. You reckon Strathy's vanishing act is connected?'

'Christ knows, May.' Rebus ran a hand across his forehead. 'Maybe I'm not so different from the ghost-hunters who've been heading to the camp.'

Collins laughed. 'I heard about that. They had equipment and everything — wands attached to machines. Waving them around, waiting for a reading.'

'Pretty much what I'm doing here.' Rebus nodded towards the computer.

'You're doing more than that.' He sensed her reaching a hand out towards his shoulder again. He stood up and she lowered her arm. He crouched to remove the memory stick. By the time he'd straightened up, she was gone.

28

Siobhan Clarke had been to Gartcosh before, but not often and not for a while. An hour or so's drive from Edinburgh; probably less than half that from Glasgow. The land surrounding it still had a bleak post-industrial feel. There were no houses, hotels or shops that she could see. Instead, the place sat in splendid isolation, far away from the world it investigated. The Scottish Crime Campus had the look of a modern polytechnic, albeit one protected by a high fence and whose only entry was via a guardroom. Her warrant card had been checked; she had been photographed and a visitor pass printed out.

'Make sure it's visible at all times,' she was told.

Having passed through a set of glass double doors with an airlock, she waited for Fox to do the same. It was a short walk to the complex's main entrance. During those steps, something happened to Fox. His gait became more confident and his shoulders slackened, his face relaxing. This was a place where his abilities made sense and were recognised. Clarke wondered, had their roles been reversed, whether she'd feel the same. As they crossed the atrium, he couldn't help playing tour guide, pointing in the vague direction of the HMRC and Procurator Fiscal units. Having climbed the stairs, it was the turn of Counter-Terrorism. But

320

they were headed to the other side of the concourse and Fox's own domain, Major Crime.

Fox's staff card, swinging from a lanyard around his neck, was far from a flimsy visitor's pass and could be used to unlock at least some of the secure doors around them. He ushered Clarke inside one of these and they walked down a narrow corridor. The offices either side were identical glass boxes. His colleagues sat at computers mostly, peering at screens, sometimes speaking quietly into microphone headsets. Others were making phone calls or huddled in discussion. It all looked as exciting as an accountancy firm, the men in shirts and ties, the women wearing unshowy blouses in muted colours. There were a few waves or nods of welcome in Fox's direction as well as inquisitive looks towards Clarke. She had spoken on the phone many times to Major Crime personnel; knew some of their names from email correspondence. But she didn't recognise a single face.

Fox entered one of the rooms. Two desks, only one of which was occupied.

'Where's Robbie?' he asked.

'Getting a coffee,' the bespectacled young woman said. 'And good morning to you too, Malcolm.'

'Sorry, Sheena,' he apologised. 'This is DI Clarke.'

'Siobhan,' Clarke added with a smile.

'Post-it note for you on your desk,' Sheena told Fox. He plucked it from his computer screen and read it.

'Fraud unit,' he explained to Clarke. 'Far as

they can tell, Scoular's clean. Has dealings with offshore banks and corporations, but that's not unusual in his line of work.' He crumpled the note and flicked it into a waste-paper bin.

'Nice to meet you, Sheena,' Clarke said, following him as he made his purposeful exit.

A coffee cart sat on the far side of the concourse, a small chatty queue in front of it. There were seats nearby and Fox approached one of them.

'Hiya, Robbie.'

The man looked up. He was in his thirties, head completely shaved. When he stood, Clarke saw that he was well over six feet tall and as lean as a picked bone.

'Been away, Malcolm?' he enquired.

'But keeping busy — how about you?' Fox realised that Robbie's eyes were on Clarke, so he made the introductions.

'Either of you want a coffee?' Robbie asked, shaking Clarke's hand.

'Love one,' she said before Fox could demur. They joined the queue. Robbie had binned his finished cup.

'Where do you live, Siobhan?' he asked.

'Edinburgh. How about you?'

'Motherwell.'

'I go there for the football sometimes. You a fan?'

'As it happens. What's your team?'

'Hibs.'

'I feel your pain.' Fox was beginning to look impatient with how slowly the queue was moving. 'Malcolm's not got time for football

322

— or much else for that matter.'

'That's not true,' Fox said defensively.

'Last film you saw?' Robbie asked him. 'Last book you finished?'

'He's always like this,' Fox complained to Clarke. 'Likes nothing better than trying to wind people up.'

Robbie grinned, eyes still on Clarke. 'Know why I get away with it?'

'Because people need to keep on your good side?'

'And why's that, do you think?'

'They're always after some favour or other.'

'Always after some favour or other,' Robbie echoed, shifting his attention to Fox. 'And it has to be done asap, especially if it's Major Crime asking — does that pretty much sum it up, Malcolm?'

Fox had reached the head of the queue. Without asking Clarke, he ordered two cappuccinos. 'Robbie?' he asked.

'Same for me.'

Having paid, there was then another long wait while the barista got to work.

'Worth it, trust me,' Robbie told Clarke. 'So you get along to a game now and then?'

'Not as often as I'd like.'

He handed her a business card. 'If you fancy a drink before or after the next time our teams meet in battle . . . '

'Siobhan's partner is a DCI,' Fox said in warning.

'Can't blame a man for trying.'

'A DCI with scant interest in football,' Clarke

qualified, pocketing the card.

They took their coffees back to the seats, finding a quiet spot.

'They're supposed to be breakout areas,' Fox said, prising the lid from his coffee so it would cool more quickly. 'Theory is, different disciplines can mingle and share intelligence.'

'Whereas in reality,' Robbie said, 'nobody shares a single bloody thing they don't need to — scared they'll end up not getting the credit.'

'Not strictly accurate,' Fox muttered into his cup.

'But you're absolutely right,' Clarke told Robbie, 'in assuming we're just another in that long line of people who need a favour. Malcolm tells me there's nobody to match you at Gartcosh when it comes to CCTV.' She hoped she wasn't laying it on too thick, but he looked the type who liked having his tummy tickled. 'Tidying up images, turning blurs into identifiable faces and suchlike.'

Robbie gave a shrug that was mock-modest at best. 'I like to think I'm pretty good,' he eventually conceded.

'Which is why we've driven all the way from Edinburgh to see you.'

'The Saudi student?' he surmised. Clarke nodded slowly. 'Had to be, I suppose; pretty quiet in Edinburgh otherwise, no?'

'Drugs, gangs, muggings — pretty quiet, yes.'

'You've got Malcolm helping now, though. He'll have those cleared up in no time.'

'Unless you keep us hanging around all day,' Fox said.

'I assume it's night-time footage? Not brilliant lighting? Maybe glare from headlamps making things more difficult still?'

'That's about the size of it,' Clarke said. She hadn't taken her eyes off Robbie, hoping her look was endearing rather than desperate.

'It's a car near the crime scene,' Fox added. 'Driving down a road to start with and then parked — we *think* it's the same car.'

'Picked up on council cameras?'

'Does that make a difference?' Clarke asked.

'Speed cameras are built to read number plates. Council ones are more of a general deterrent.'

'Not as good, in other words.'

'If they've been driving around the city at night, could be they've triggered a speed camera anyway — empty streets, drivers often put the foot down without thinking. Red traffic lights are another possibility — road's clear so you whizz through and the camera clocks you.' Robbie looked at both detectives. 'You've not checked, have you?'

'No,' Fox conceded.

'I might as well do that too, then, eh?' Robbie took a sip from his cup.

'We'd be hugely grateful,' Clarke told him.

'You can pay me back by making sure my team gets maximum points from yours next season.'

'You drive a hard bargain,' Clarke said with a smile, holding out her hand to seal the deal.

* * *

325

They had almost reached the ground floor when Fox came to a stop, recognising the figure climbing the stairs towards them. Clarke knew the face too: ACC Jennifer Lyon. She was reading from a sheaf of papers while holding a conversation on her phone, a shoulder bag and briefcase making life no easier for her. But she ended the call when she saw Fox. The phone went into her bag along with the papers.

'Malcolm,' she said, managing to turn the single word into both statement and question.

'Potential progress on the bin Mahmoud case,' he explained. 'Just need Robbie not to sit on it too long.'

'I'll see to it there's no slacking,' Lyon assured him.

'This is DI Siobhan Clarke. She's helping me today.'

'From the look she just gave you, I'd say DI Clarke regards that as somewhat of an understatement.' There was a thin smile for Clarke but no free hand for any more tactile greeting. Then, to Fox: 'I need a word with you anyway, Malcolm.' And to Clarke: 'In private, DI Clarke. Maybe you could get yourself a coffee or something.'

Clarke watched them climb the remaining stairs, Fox gesturing for her to wait in the atrium. Instead of a coffee, she headed to the loos, seating herself and taking out her phone. Rebus had sent her some magazine photos. She studied them casually, then called him.

'The Chief Constable,' she said.

'I know.'

'I'd seen some photos from the party, but not that one.'

'Friends with Stewart Scoular, you think?'

'It's the first I'm hearing of it.'

'It's the party Keith crashed, making no friends and kicking up a fuss about the community buyout of Camp 1033.'

'Slow down, this is all new to me.'

'Keith wanted the Meiklejohns to sell some land to the community so they could turn Camp 1033 into a visitor attraction. He wasn't getting any joy so gatecrashed that party. Remember the gardener?'

'Colin Belkin?'

'I reckon he'd be the one who kicked Keith out. I've met Angharad Oates, by the way, out at the compound, where she looks after Jess Hawkins' young kid. There's a Kawasaki there that someone might have heard on the road the night Keith was killed.'

'Lot of threads, John. I'm guessing you're beginning to see a pattern?'

'Maybe. Meantime your pals Lady Isabella, bin Mahmoud and Morelli were at the selfsame party.'

'You don't think Keith could have had dealings with them?'

'If only I were in a position to ask them that, the ones who're not murder victims, I mean.'

'There can't be a connection . . . '

'Two killings, Siobhan.'

'Hundreds of miles apart, John.'

'But can you ask anyway?'

'I'm a bit busy.'

'You don't sound it. In fact, from the echo, I'd guess you're on the bog.'

'Must be your phone.'

'If you say so. But you will talk to Meiklejohn and Morelli?'

'I'm seeing so much of them, I might suggest a flat-share.'

'You reckon they're involved?'

'We've got some CCTV we're checking.'

'Robbie Stenhouse is your man for that.' When she didn't answer immediately, Rebus spoke again. 'You've already seen him?'

'How the hell do you know about Robbie Stenhouse?'

'Guy's a legend. Did you happen to notice any other faces in those pics I might find interesting?'

'Not really. You already know Stewart Scoular.'

'I like how he slithers his way into every other photo. If it's his consortium behind the golf resort, and the party was a way of buttering up potential investors, he'd be far from happy about Keith shouting the odds. Remember what happened at that Donald Trump place in Aberdeen?'

'I watched the documentary.'

'People like Scoular need to feel they're controlling the story. Keith definitely wasn't helping with that.'

'And yet, all the dozens of newspaper profiles and mentions in the business pages, not a single word about Keith and the rest of his group. They hardly had any media presence.'

'He didn't pose a danger, is that what you're saying?'

'I'm saying he could be safely ignored.'

'Maybe someone failed to get that message, Siobhan.' Rebus gave a long and noisy exhalation.

'Anything else to report?' she asked. 'How's Samantha?'

'Still not been charged. I think there's the hint of a thaw between us, too.'

'That's good.'

'You at Gartcosh right now?'

'Waiting for Malcolm — Jennifer Lyon needed a word with him.'

'What about?'

'I'm not sure.'

'Is this you stonewalling me?'

'Only a bit.'

'How's that dog of mine doing?'

'Not getting as much attention as he needs.'

'A feeling we all know, eh? You any closer to a result?'

'I'll have a better idea once Robbie's worked his magic'

'Good luck then — talk to you later.'

Clarke ended the call. She had a text from Graham Sutherland asking how it was going.

Leaving soon, she texted back.

As she exited the toilets, she saw there was still no sign of Fox. No visibly vacant seats either. A passing officer, white shirt and epaulettes, asked her if she needed help.

'Just waiting,' she told him with an exasperated smile. Two more minutes and she'd head back to the car; five after that and she'd be off, let Fox find his own way back to Edinburgh. But she knew she wouldn't do it.

She needed to share the news about the Chief Constable.

* * *

Fox had been abandoned by Jennifer Lyon in her office's anteroom, seated across from her secretary, who was busy at her computer. Finally she opened the door and crooked a finger. By the time he went in and closed the door, she was seated behind her desk.

'Anything to report?' she asked briskly.

'Making progress on the bin Mahmoud inquiry.'

She dismissed this with the briefest of nods. 'And Mr Scoular?'

Fox considered his response. 'If there's dirt — proper dirt, I mean — it's well hidden. The Fraud Unit have come up empty-handed. I can show Cafferty we've done the work — including surveillance — but that's about all, unless we opt to go nuclear: phone tap, computer inter-cept . . .'

'Surveillance?'

'Just me in my free time.'

'Explains why you look so bleary.' She paused. 'But it's appreciated.'

'I don't mind in the least.'

'And no one on the team has twigged what you're up to?'

Fox swallowed. 'Not as far as I'm aware.'

'Not even DI Clarke?'

'No, ma'am.' He noticed that the ACC was

staring at him with almost preternatural calmness.

'Malcolm,' she drawled, pressing the palms of her hands together, 'we need, you and I, to talk about Morris Gerald Cafferty . . . '

29

The looks on the faces of the team back in Leith ranged from expectant through hopeful to sceptical. Clarke responded with a shrug while Fox announced that the CCTV would be 'fast-tracked'.

'So we can expect to hear back in weeks rather than months?' Ronnie Ogilvie posited.

'Don't be so negative, lad,' George Gamble said, stifling a post-lunch belch. 'That's always been my job.'

There were a few tired smiles at this. Clarke had walked between the rows of desks — desks across which (Christine Esson's aside) paperwork sprawled — and negotiated her way past further heaps of paper on the floor until she reached the Murder Wall. It was dispiriting how little of note had been added to it recently. There seemed to be not quite enough oxygen in the room. They were in danger of beginning the process of going through the motions. The look on Graham Sutherland's face when he emerged from his lair told her he wasn't far off telling them to go back to square one and recheck everything they'd already checked.

'Gartcosh?' he asked.

'In train,' Clarke replied.

'Modern electric or clapped-out diesel?'

The joke was weak but merited something. She managed a twitch of the mouth. Sutherland stood next to her.

332

'A sudden bout of guilty consciences would be nice,' he stated. 'The assailant or someone who knows them. Somebody *always* knows something. In the old days, we'd be on the street hearing the gossip.'

'We could try offering a reward.'

'It's crossed my mind.'

'Another press conference? Rekindle some media enthusiasm?'

'They've all moved on to the elusive Lord Strathy.'

'According to one source, he's hanging out with Lord Lucan in a Monte Carlo casino,' Tess Leighton piped up from behind her computer.

'I can check that lead out if you like.' Christine Esson had her hand raised like a kid in a classroom.

Clarke lowered her voice before asking Sutherland if he was getting any grief from on high.

'No more than usual,' he muttered. 'Though the Saudis have slightly changed their tune. There's some trade negotiation under way and they're using our apparent incompetence as leverage. Salman has gone from *persona non grata* to revered martyr in pretty short order.'

'Expediency wins the day.'

'With us as the whipping boy.' Sutherland stared at the wall. 'None of which should distract us from the job at hand. You don't think we maybe missed something early on? Worth another look at the autopsy, the scene-of-crime report —'

'Why not the forensics too?' Clarke interrupted. 'Then we can bring everyone in for interview again and nudge the Met into sifting through their findings for the tenth time.'

'I've reached that point, have I?' Sutherland asked, looking sheepish.

'Only slightly earlier than anticipated.' This time they shared a smile.

'Guys,' Christine Esson called out, 'you're going to want to take a look at this.'

They started to gather around her desk, Clarke slowed by an incoming text on her phone. It was from Laura Smith.

Turn-up for the books!

'Well, well,' George Gamble was saying, breathing heavily after the effort of walking halfway across the room.

'Looks like Issy Meiklejohn's doorstep,' Fox was saying, eyes on the news feed playing on Esson's monitor. 'Can you turn the sound up?'

Esson was doing just that as Clarke arrived. Several cameras and microphones were being pointed towards where Issy Meiklejohn stood, her hand gripping her father's forearm in a show of support and apparent relief.

'Never knew there'd be such a fuss,' Ramsay Meiklejohn was saying, his face redder than ever, eyes darting from camera to camera, questioner to questioner.

'Who instigated this?' Sutherland was asking. 'How come we're last to know?'

'Shh!' Christine Esson said. Then, realising what she'd done: 'With respect, sir.'

'Just a few days' much-needed R&R,' Meiklejohn was explaining. 'Catching up on sleep; fresh air and exercise.'

334

'Somewhere nice, Lord Strathy?' one reporter yelled from near the back of the scrum.

'Nowhere that's getting a free advert,' Issy Meiklejohn broke in. 'I'm just glad my father is back in one piece, not that I ever had any concerns. My view is that this whole charade was an attempt by the police to divert attention from their manifest failings in finding the murderer of my friend Salman bin Mahmoud. It's their inept handling of *that* case that should be your focus now.'

Her father nodded along, pushing out his bottom lip to underline his wholehearted agreement.

Sutherland was jabbing the screen. It was live video from a local news website. 'You say you know where this is?' he asked Fox.

'Me and Siobhan were there a couple of days back.'

'Then why in God's name are you still here? Go fetch!'

'And if he's unwilling to play ball?'

'We're a murder inquiry and we have questions for him. If he won't cooperate, place him under arrest.'

Clarke's eyes were still on the screen, focused on Meiklejohn's daughter. 'Might be a two-for-one deal,' she advised.

'So be it,' Sutherland said. 'Now get moving, the pair of you!'

★ ★ ★

It was not a long drive from the police station to St Stephen Street, despite the vagaries of

335

roadworks and temporary diversions.

'Has there ever been a time when Edinburgh hasn't been a building site?' Fox said through gritted teeth. They were in his car for a change. Clarke had wound her window down a couple of inches for some fresh air.

'Are you really not going to tell me what Lyon wanted?'

'Correct.'

'But it was to do with Cafferty and the videos?'

'As the Pet Shop Boys sang, my lips are sealed.'

'That was Fun Boy Three.'

Fox's brow furrowed. 'You sure?'

'Well, if you're not going to play nice, maybe I should keep my news to myself.'

'And what news might that be?'

'John sent me some pics from a magazine spread at Strathy Castle.'

'I've seen them.'

'You've got some of them on your computer, but not these ones — one of them shows our dear Chief Constable and his wife looking very chummy next to Stewart Scoular.' She saw him staring at her. 'Eyes on the road, Malcolm.'

'When did this happen?'

'While you were meeting the ACC.'

'And you kept it to yourself because . . . ?'

'I was thinking it through. Want to hear my theory?'

'Go ahead.'

'Say the Chief Constable is one of Scoular's investors . . . '

'I'd think it's above his pay grade, no?'

'He could probably manage the odd few thousand — and Scoular would definitely want him on board.'

'Other investors would certainly be reassured,' Fox agreed.

'My guess is, Cafferty found this out.'

'How?'

'Probably because Martin Chappell has the sort of name Scoular would want to drop into a lot of his conversations.' She watched Fox nod slowly. 'And if we were to find any dirt on Scoular . . .'

'That would hasten Chappell's retirement, so as to hide any potential embarrassment to Police Scotland.'

'Putting Jennifer Lyon on the throne.'

'Makes sense,' Fox said.

'So now I've told you, will you take it to the ACC?'

'I'll have to think.'

'If you *do* go to see her, I want to be there too.'

'Duly noted. You didn't get round to telling Graham?'

'No, and I think it should stay that way, unless we start to see a connection to the murder.' Clarke's phone was buzzing. Not a number she recognised, but she answered anyway.

'DI Clarke?' the voice said. 'This is DS Creasey. I'm a member of the Keith Grant inquiry team.'

'Yes?'

'You've heard of it?'

'I'm a friend of John Rebus. He didn't give you my number?'

'Actually he did — texted it to me just now, said you'd be a useful contact. Didn't say you were friends, though.'

'What can I do for you?'

'I'll keep it quick — signal comes and goes on the A9. You've heard about Lord Strathy's reappearance?'

'Yes.' Fox gave Clarke an inquisitive look, but she ignored him.

'I'd like to talk to him before he leaves Edinburgh. Is there any way you could facilitate that?'

'Way ahead of you, DS Creasey. We have a few questions for him ourselves.'

'Can you keep him busy until I get there? Might take another couple of hours.'

'A couple? I'm guessing the speed cameras will be working overtime. Strathy will be at Leith police station for as long as we can hold him. Text me when you arrive and I'll come meet you.'

'I'm grateful.'

Clarke had another caller waiting. She hung up on Creasey and tapped the icon.

'Sounds like you're driving,' she heard Rebus say.

'Malcolm is. On our way to pick up his lordship.'

'You need to ask him about the party Keith gatecrashed — we have to know what really happened.'

'DS Creasey is on his way here as we speak.

338

He'll be the one with the questions.'

'But you'll have first dibs.'

'And all I know about the case is what you've told me. Fill me in on Creasey, though.'

'He's capable, but not exactly inspiring. There's a line he's following that he expects will lead to Samantha.'

'Not a complete idiot, though?'

'No.'

'And willing to drive a hundred and fifty miles to interview a minor player.'

'Strathy might be a lot more than that, Siobhan. As far as I can tell, he's trading on his name and the fact that he owns a castle. He's got land he wants to develop and protest groups standing in his way. He might have seen Keith and Jess Hawkins as movable obstacles. It would be a big win for Strathy if Hawkins were to be connected to Keith's murder.'

'Set up to take the fall, you mean?'

'Bear all this in mind when you're asking your questions. Just because someone looks like Billy Bunter doesn't mean they don't possess low animal cunning.' Rebus paused. 'Any further thoughts about the Chief's involvement?'

'Party line is, there's no involvement.'

'Brushing him under the carpet?'

'Hang on,' she said, turning to Fox. 'Quicker if you turn here.' He did as he was told, only to notice a bin lorry halfway along the street, blocking the route. With a growl, he hit the brakes and began reversing. 'I'll talk to you later, John,' Clarke said into her phone. 'Right now I need to apologise for my navigational skills . . . '

At St Stephen Street, the media were packing up. While Fox found a parking spot, Clarke rang Issy Meiklejohn's doorbell.

'What?' the intercom crackled.

'Detective Inspector Clarke,' she announced.

'That didn't take long.'

Clarke listened as the buzzer signalled that the door had been unlocked. She climbed to Issy's landing. The door to the flat was already open. Issy stood there like a sentry.

'Need a word with him,' Clarke said.

'He's tired.'

'Nice trick with the doorstep conference, by the way — friendly media, all hand-picked?' She peered over the taller woman's shoulder.

'Come back later,' Issy Meiklejohn demanded.

Clarke shook her head. 'My boss wants Lord Strathy at the station. Only way this ends is with your dad accompanying me there. Nice comfortable car outside, no markings, no fuss.'

'This is preposterous.'

She gave an apologetic shrug. 'Nevertheless,' she said, her voice drifting off.

'Wait here a minute,' Meiklejohn said after a moment's thought. She closed the door, leaving Clarke on the landing. Clarke gave the handle a surreptitious turn, but it was locked.

It was more like two minutes before the door opened again. Lord Strathy was dressed in an olive-green tweed suit and open-necked white shirt. He hadn't shaved, silvery bristles showing on his jowls. He looked bemused and there was a slight whiff of whisky on his breath. His daughter had donned a three-quarter-length crimson coat, covering her black polo neck and tight trousers tucked into knee-high boots. She checked she had her keys and her phone, then ushered her father out and closed the door again. Clarke composed a quick text to Fox.

Here we come.

'My father's solicitor wants to know which station she should meet us at,' Issy Meiklejohn said. 'Her name's Patricia Coleridge and she's very, *very* good . . .'

'I know her,' Clarke said. She turned her attention to Lord Strathy. 'Criminal law is her thing; interesting that's the kind of solicitor you know.'

'Patsy's father went to the same school as mine,' Issy Meiklejohn said. 'The two families have known one another ever since.'

'Why doesn't that surprise me?' Clarke said in an undertone as they headed down the stairs.

* * *

Issy Meiklejohn was left to fume on a chair in the corridor while her father was escorted into Interview Room B at Leith police station. Sutherland had given the nod for Clarke and Fox to ask the questions. He'd already had a word with Patricia Coleridge, assuring her that no charges were being levelled and her client was not being cautioned, adding the caveat that if he failed to cooperate, that situation could rapidly change.

Clarke knew that Coleridge's mind would be as sharp as her business suit. She had already unzipped her large leather notebook and unscrewed the top from her expensive-looking pen. She had a thin mane of straw-blonde hair, prominent cheekbones and piercing grey eyes. A spectacles case sat untouched next to her. There would be no recording made, everything nicely informal.

Strathy looked around the small enclosed space in apparent befuddlement.

'You don't have to answer anything,' Coleridge advised him as, after a peck on the cheek, he took the seat next to her. 'A simple 'no comment' will suffice.'

Fox had carried in some of the paperwork from the inquiry and was studying the timeline.

'I doubt I can be of much use,' Lord Strathy announced, hands held out in front of him, palms upwards.

'Where have you been the past few days?' Clarke asked, jumping straight in.

'No comment.'

'Around the time you disappeared, there were two murders. One here and one up north. Odd coincidence, you going to ground.'

'No connection, I assure you.'

'You knew we'd want to question you — afraid of what you might let slip?'

Coleridge gave a theatrical sigh as she played with her pen. 'Is crass speculation all you have to offer us, DI Clarke?'

Clarke ignored her, maintaining eye contact with Ramsay Meiklejohn. 'When was the last time you saw Salman bin Mahmoud?'

He puffed out his cheeks. 'Weeks ago.'

'How many?'

'Four or five maybe.'

'Here or up north?'

'In London. A small gathering at his home.'

'Business or pleasure?'

'A bit of both, I suppose — no such thing as a free meal these days, eh?' He turned to smile at his lawyer, who remained solemn-faced.

'Remember,' she reminded him, ''no comment' will do.'

'I've done nothing wrong, Patsy,' Meiklejohn told her.

'Yet you can't account for your whereabouts these past few days,' Fox stated.

Meiklejohn turned his attention back to the two detectives. 'I can account for them perfectly well. I merely choose not to.'

'But you weren't in hiding?'

'No.'

'And it's not that you were running scared?' Clarke added. 'I don't mean scared of us questioning you — scared of something or someone else?'

'Absolutely not.' But neither detective could miss that he shifted a little in his seat as he spoke.

His lawyer attempted to deflect attention with a query of her own. 'It might help if we knew precisely why you think Lord Strathy can help you with any of this. Salman bin Mahmoud was a business acquaintance, nothing more.'

'Business relationships can go sour, though, especially where large sums are concerned. The golf resort near Naver was projected to cost tens

343

of millions, quite a few of those making their way into your pocket, Lord Strathy. Salman bin Mahmoud was one of your investors, yes?'

'In a very minor way.'

'He owed you money?'

'On the contrary — he was preparing to top up his initial investment. His death came as a shock and a blow.'

'A financial blow, you mean?' Strathy nodded. 'What about the buyout of Craigentinny golf course — were you involved in that too?'

'Not in any monetary sense. Stewart Scoular had mentioned it, of course.'

'How well do you know Mr Scoular?'

'We do business occasionally.'

'But he's invited to your parties, the ones you host at Strathy Castle?' Clarke gestured to Fox, who removed the magazine photos from their folder, placing them on the table. A sunny, windy day; smiling faces outside a large white marquee; champagne flutes held aloft.

'There's Salman bin Mahmoud,' Clarke said, pointing. 'And there's Stewart Scoular.'

'And your own Chief Constable,' Meiklejohn countered. 'An acquaintance of mine, you know.'

'Meaning an investor?'

'Is this going anywhere?' Coleridge interrupted, checking her slim gold wristwatch.

'This was the day of the incident, wasn't it?' Clarke was asking. 'A man called Keith Grant came barging in . . .'

'Was it the same day?' Meiklejohn sounded genuinely uncertain.

'The same Keith Grant who was murdered in

344

one of the huts at Camp 1033, on land you own, just a few days after Salman bin Mahmoud met his end.'

'All of which I'm sure is very interesting,' Coleridge broke in again, 'but I think you've had quite enough of my client's time.' She closed her notebook with a flourish and began screwing the top back on her pen, having written precisely nothing.

'Two projects,' Clarke pressed on. 'Two men connected to them end up dead, and suddenly you, Lord Strathy, are nowhere to be found.'

'We're walking,' Patricia Coleridge said, nudging her client as she rose to her feet.

'An officer from Inverness is on his way here with some further questions for Lord Strathy,' Clarke told her.

'Unless you're arresting my client, Inspector, we're leaving right now.'

'If you're scared, we can protect you,' Fox announced, leaning across the table so he had Meiklejohn's attention. 'Is it Stewart Scoular — is that who you're afraid of?'

'No comment,' Meiklejohn stuttered, beginning to pull himself up to standing.

'Your daughter is in business with you, yes?' Clarke asked, her tone hardening. 'Funny she didn't mention you visiting the victim's home in London.'

'No reason she should know.' Meiklejohn had begun coughing, and as he stood up, he had to steady himself, hands gripping the back of his chair. But when he tried to move, his knees buckled, his face growing more crimson than

345

ever, wincing in pain. Coleridge had pushed open the door.

'Issy!' she called. But Issy Meiklejohn was right there, her mouth open in shock as she saw her father. Clarke was already on the phone, summoning a paramedic.

'There's a defibrillator in the building,' Fox was saying.

Lord Strathy was bent forward, hand to his chest, flanked by the two young women.

'We need an ambulance!' Issy yelped.

'I'll be all right,' he told her, his free hand patting the back of hers. 'Just need a bit of air.'

'You're going to the hospital,' she said, her tone firm. Then, to Patricia Coleridge: 'How could you let them do this, Patsy? How *could* you?'

The look Coleridge cast towards Clarke and Fox left them in no doubt that she would find a way to deflect the blame onto them if she possibly could.

Graham Sutherland had appeared in the doorway, other officers and support staff vying for a better view of the drama. When he locked eyes with Clarke, she managed nothing more than a lifting of one eyebrow. He'd told her once that he found it charming, though she rather doubted its power over him right this second.

346

30

When Creasey's text arrived, she went down-
stairs to greet him. He had parked somewhere by
Leith Links and was walking along Queen
Charlotte Street towards her.

'DI Clarke?' he guessed, waving a hand.

'How was the drive?'

'About what you'd imagine.' He was making
to pass her and enter the police station, but froze
when he saw the look on her face. 'You let him
go?'

'He was rushed to hospital. Chest pains.'

'Faking it?'

'I don't think so.'

'Shit.' He angled his head heavenwards. 'Did
he tell you anything useful?'

'Not especially.'

'The interview was taped, though?'

'Afraid not.'

He lowered his head to gaze at her. 'Really?'

'We were trying to keep it casual.'

'How far is the hospital?'

'They won't let you see him.'

'I need to try.'

'You don't want a coffee or anything first?'
Clarke watched as he shook his head. 'We'll take
my car, then. You could probably do with a break.'

'I could definitely do with a break — my hope
was, Lord Strathy might be it . . .'

Clarke texted Fox to let him know the score

347

while she led Creasey to her Vauxhall Astra. They drove in silence for the first few minutes, Creasey leaning back into the headrest.

'The A9 hasn't improved then?' she commented. 'Still, must be nice to get away from John for a bit.'

Creasey snorted. 'He's a piece of work, as they say.'

'Not many things I've not heard him called. Good detective, though; never gives a case a minute's rest.' She paused. 'You think Samantha did it?'

'Her or her lover — that would be the standard scenario.'

'So those are your chief suspects?'

'Everyone but John Rebus thinks so. He's got half a dozen conspiracy theories lined up.' He half turned in his seat so he was facing her. 'Smoke and mirrors most likely.'

'And yet here you are, DS Creasey.'

'What do you mean?'

'One of John's theories has brought you all the way to Edinburgh. He thinks you maybe lack imagination — your trip here tells me he's wrong.'

'You worked with him for a long time?'

'Felt like.'

'He doesn't seem to be relishing retirement. I know his daughter's freedom and good name are on the line, so he's desperate — but I also sense he's enjoying it, though maybe he wouldn't see it that way.'

Clarke was reminded of the case files stacked up in Rebus's new flat. She knew he was planning to break open the unsolveds. *Something to keep me warm in my old age . . .*

'I think he feels he let Samantha down,' she confided. 'Not just once, but over and over.'

'And now's his chance to atone?' Creasey chewed on this while staring at the passing parade of shops. 'I should have asked — how's your own case looking?'

'Like you, we could use a break.'

'They *are* two distinct cases?'

Clarke nodded. 'With a few linked players. Your victim wasn't making himself popular with Lord Strathy; Lord Strathy had business dealings with the bin Mahmoud family; my victim was best friends with Lord Strathy's daughter. And so far no clear motive in either case.'

'I told you I've got a motive.'

'Jealousy? A love triangle? I don't think you believe that.'

'She'd visited her ex-lover the day her partner was killed. He found out and they argued.'

'So they leave their daughter alone in the house and drive to the internment camp? Does that make sense to you?'

Instead of answering, Creasey leaned back into the headrest again and closed his eyes.

'Not too much further,' Clarke reassured him. Then: 'We're finding Lady Isabella a bit interesting. I think she has a head for business, though she hides it well. From what little I've seen of her father, he's far from CEO material.'

'He's a figurehead, you mean? His daughter tucked away behind the curtain, pulling the strings?'

'She's close to Stewart Scoular — he's the contractor who seems to sign up the investors.'

'He's also been a guest at Strathy Castle.'

Clarke glanced at him. 'Yes, he has.'

'I can do a Google photo search as well as the next person,' Creasey explained.

Clarke's attention was flitting between the windscreen and a new message on her phone.

'Want me to read it out to you?' Creasey asked.

'Just an MIT colleague, wondering how long I'll be.'

'They're missing you already?'

Clarke shook her head slowly. 'Just pissed off I'm dodging the flak.'

'You're being blamed for Strathy's collapse?'

'In my absence, almost certainly.'

'But you weren't alone in the room with him?'

'I was with another DI called Fox.'

'The one whose identity Rebus stole?'

'Yes.'

'So this Fox guy will have your back?'

A wry smile just about broke across Clarke's face as she signalled to take the exit into the grounds of the Royal Infirmary.

★ ★ ★

Having been told to wait in the A&E reception, Clarke fetched them a hot chocolate apiece.

'About as nutritious as the machine gets,' she apologised.

Creasey took an exploratory sip and winced. 'Christ, that's sweet.'

Clarke settled next to him on the row of hard plastic chairs. 'So how are you finding our capital city so far?'

He managed a weak smile, but didn't speak. A couple of minutes later, he was on his feet, pacing the waiting area. None of the patients paid him any heed, too busy with their own troubles. He didn't look sick, which probably made him a concerned friend or relative. Clarke had been to this place many times before, could even put names to some of the green-uniformed paramedics. It wasn't a particularly busy evening; on the surface, all was calm. But she knew that behind the scenes there could be trolleys filled with people waiting for beds to be freed up elsewhere in the hospital, forgotten about for the moment as some new and greater trauma took precedence. Creasey had his phone out, reading from the screen as he walked to and fro. Eventually he ran out of things to check, seating himself again and picking up the beaker of hot chocolate, studying the skin forming on its surface.

'You'll be late home,' Clarke offered. 'One thing about this job — it plays havoc with everything else. You live in Inverness?'

'Culloden.'

'Married?'

'Not yet. You?' He watched her shake her head. 'My boyfriend says maybe next year.'

'What does he do?' Clarke asked.

'He's a GP.'

'Two sets of unsociable hours to juggle.' She was rewarded with another fleeting smile. 'I've

351

been dating another cop lately; not sure that's going to work out.'

'Things mostly do, though, don't they?'

'I suppose . . . ' She broke off as Issy Meiklejohn came striding towards them from the guts of A&E. Clarke and Creasey both got to their feet.

'I'm Detective Sergeant Creasey,' Creasey said by way of introduction. But Issy Meiklejohn's ire was directed at Clarke.

'What the hell do you think you're doing here?'

'Not my idea,' Clarke offered. 'How is your father?'

'Undergoing tests as we speak.'

'I was hoping for a word,' Creasey stated. At last he had Meiklejohn's attention.

'Why?'

'I'm part of the team investigating the death of Keith Grant.'

'What on earth has that got to do with my father?'

'We're talking to everyone who knew the deceased.'

'In which case you're wasting your time.'

'Mr Grant was keen for your father to sell the land housing Camp 1033. I believe things became quite heated.'

'My father made it perfectly clear that there would be no sale. The sum proposed was a pittance in any case. End of story.'

'All the same . . . '

Meiklejohn took a step closer, her forehead inches from Creasey's. 'End. Of. Story.' Then, turning towards Clarke, 'Our solicitor is preparing a complaint with reference to your conduct.'

'Noted. And I really do hope your father's okay.'

Meiklejohn's face softened just a little, the tension leaving her jaw. 'Thank you. There's no immediate cause for alarm.' Her eyes lingered on Clarke for a further moment before she turned and walked away. She'd got as far as the reception desk when she paused, seemingly lost in thought. Then she turned once more and retraced her steps.

'A word in private, she said to Clarke, 'if you please.' She quickly ruled out both the waiting area and the outside world and headed to the women's toilet instead. Clarke gave Creasey a shrug before following.

Behind the door stood two narrow cubicles and a single hand basin. Meiklejohn seemed satisfied that neither cubicle was being used. She rested her considerable frame against the door, barring entry to anyone else.

'Can I trust you?' she demanded.

'That depends.'

'Neither of these cases concerns my father. So if I were to reveal something to you, there'd be no need for you to share it with anyone else.'

'The reason he's been lying low?'

'He's frantic, you know. He feels that any association with a criminal case will not only tarnish his good name, but might also jeopardise his future business dealings. He wasn't in hiding, not from your enquiries and not from anyone he feared.'

'I'm listening . . .'

Meiklejohn looked to the heavens — or at least the stained ceiling — for guidance. 'This goes no further?'

'Unless I judge it to be pertinent.'

'All I want is for you to stop harassing my father.'

'With respect, I don't think that's — '

'He's having an affair, all right?' Meiklejohn blurted out. 'A woman in London. She's married. Her husband doesn't know anything about it. All very clandestine.'

'Yet he confided in you?'

'He always has.' She made it sound like a burden. 'Anyway, past few days the woman's husband was overseas. It was their first chance to spend some serious time together, so that's what they did. Rented apartment, food delivered, drinks cabinet well stocked. It was only towards the end that he bothered checking the news and saw himself featured. Came to me straight away.'

'Because you're good at fixing things.' It was statement rather than question. 'The woman involved will back this up?'

'I'm not giving you her name.' Meiklejohn folded her arms.

'Tough to let this go without corroboration, Issy.'

'What if I ask her to contact you? Give me your number.'

Clarke recited it while Meiklejohn tapped it into her phone.

'I'm trusting you, Inspector. Please don't let me down.' She turned to pull open the door.

'While I've got you here . . . ' Clarke said.

'Yes?'

'Keith Grant.'

'What about him?'

'The day he gatecrashed your father's party . . . '

'Hugely embarrassing.'

'It was a pitch to potential investors?' Meiklejohn nodded. 'Was that the only time you met him?'

'I didn't meet him per se. He just came stomping across the lawn towards us shouting about that bloody camp.'

'Until ejected by Colin Belkin?'

Meiklejohn peered at her. 'You're awfully well informed.'

'I like to be.'

'My father told me afterwards who he was — I knew about the camp, of course, and the mad plans some people had for it.' She offered a shrug.

'Jess Hawkins was a bigger thorn in your father's side?'

'It's a waiting game. Next year there's a revaluation — hike the rent and the raggle-taggle gypsies will have to move on.'

'Including your ex-stepmother.'

'No great loss to either my father or me.'

'Well, it's not as if he lacks for female company.'

'That remark is beneath you, Ms Clarke.'

'Detective Inspector Clarke, actually.'

'Can I go?'

'Answer me one thing first — Lord Strathy

tells us he visited Mr bin Mahmoud in London only a few weeks prior to his death.'

'Yes?'

'So why did you lie?'

'I didn't,' Meiklejohn bristled.

'Neither he nor Salman mentioned it to you?'

'Obviously not.'

'Cooking something up between them without your knowledge?'

For a moment it looked as though Meiklejohn would give an answer, but with a cold smile she pulled open the door and made her exit. Clarke stood in front of the mirror, staring at her reflection without really seeing it. Then her phone buzzed with an incoming call: John Rebus.

'Nothing much to report,' she told him, pressing the phone to her ear. 'Strathy was lawyered up, didn't say much, then collapsed and is currently in A&E.'

'Just another day at the office, eh? Did Creasey make it down in time?'

'No. He's here with me at the Infirmary.'

'Strathy didn't give you any plausible explanation for his vanishing act?'

'He may have had his reasons — nothing to do with either case. I'm having his story checked.'

'The story being . . . ?'

'Need-to-know basis, John.'

'Precisely why I'm asking.'

'Maybe later, eh?' She paused. 'Creasey seems pretty good at what he does.'

'She said, attempting to redirect the conversation.'

356

'I can't discuss it, not at the moment.'

'Will Creasey get the chance to speak with Strathy?'

'Probably not tonight. He's undergoing tests with his daughter standing guard.' Clarke had a sudden thought and yanked open the toilet door. No sign of Creasey in the reception area. Given his chance, he had taken it. 'Got to go,' she told Rebus, ending the call. Raised voices came from behind the partition to the rear of the reception desk. Clarke had just reached it when Creasey was escorted out by two orderlies, Issy Meiklejohn bringing up the loudly angry rear.

'That's one more complaint!' she bellowed in Clarke's direction before disappearing behind the partition again. Creasey was holding up both hands in a show of surrender, so after a final glower, the orderlies followed Meiklejohn. Creasey made show of readjusting his jacket and tie.

'That wasn't exactly clever,' Clarke told him.

'Bet you'd have done the same, though.'

She couldn't disagree. 'And?'

'He was wearing an oxygen mask. Doubt I could have made anything out even if he'd been willing.'

'She *will* make that complaint, you know.'

'Maybe you could intercede, now she's your bestie.' Creasey indicated the toilet. His own phone was ringing. 'Better answer this,' he said, walking towards the exit.

'Never a dull moment, eh?' a voice piped up.

Clarke looked down at the seated figure who had spoken. A young man cradling his injured shoulder.

'Know what an ex-colleague of mine would say to that?'

'What?' he asked.

'One of Rod Stewart's finest . . . '

She was about to join Creasey outside — nothing to be gained from hanging around A&E any longer — when he burst in through the doors.

'I have to head north.' He looked distracted, eyes everywhere but on her.

'What's up?'

'Can't say.'

'Thanks for the vote of confidence.' Now his eyes did meet hers, albeit briefly. He led her outside by the forearm, checking to left and right for potential eavesdroppers.

'We may just have found the murder weapon.'

'The revolver?'

'Rebus told you?' He watched her nod. 'Looks like matted blood and human hair on the grip.'

'Found where?'

'Just off the road, edge of a field. I have to get back right now.'

'Car's this way,' she said, leading him to the Astra.

While they drove, Creasey busied himself with calls. The revolver would be taken for forensic examination. The search around the drop spot would be resumed and intensified, in case the killer had ditched anything else: bloodied clothing maybe, or the items missing from the satchel. The press would learn about it soon enough, so a press conference might be an idea, with one of Creasey's bosses made ready to read out a statement.

'Let's try to keep this under wraps, eh?' Creasey concluded. 'And job well done — make sure the team get that message. No slacking, though. If anything, we need to be busier than ever.'

'How big is the team?' Clarke asked when he'd finished.

'We're stretched,' he admitted.

'Commuting from Inverness?'

'We've put together a base at Tongue. Officers from Thurso, Wick, Ullapool, Dingwall . . . all over really. You've got it easy down here, all the resources you need.'

'Lives of pampered luxury,' Clarke commented. 'Which means I can offer you a sandwich before you leave.'

Creasey shook his head. 'I'll stop for petrol on the way, grab something then.' There was a gleam in his eye, the gleam all self-respecting detectives got when sensing a break in a difficult case. 'It was your old friend John who noticed the revolver, you know, noticed it was missing from behind the bar of The Glen.'

'Work out who took it and you've got your murderer.'

But Creasey was shaking his head. 'Most likely culprit is the victim himself. Part of his obsession with the camp. Might just have been in his satchel.'

'So how come the killer used it? If it was safely hidden in the satchel, I mean?'

'Maybe Keith got it out thinking he could scare them off, and they took it off him. Or else the killer knew it was there and wanted it.'

'A rusty old wartime revolver?'

Some of the initial excitement was leaving Creasey's face. 'Lot of work still to be done,' he agreed.

'Just as well you'll be nice and fresh in the morning then.'

'I'll manage,' he said. Clarke didn't doubt it for a moment.

At Leith Links there was the briefest of handshakes before he drove off. As his car disappeared into the distance, Clarke took out her phone and called Rebus.

Call failed.

She tried again with the same result, so composed a text instead.

Revolver located. Creasey rushing back.

Then she pressed send.

Fox must have seen her from the office window. He had come downstairs and was on the police station's doorstep.

'I hope you've got news.' he said.

She made eye contact and held it. 'Can I trust you?' she asked.

'You know you can.'

'Really, though?'

But then when it came down to it, what did she owe Issy Meiklejohn? And how far could she trust *her*?

'Okay,' she said, 'but let's grab a bite first — I'm bloody famished.'

31

Rebus was in his car, heading out towards the camp. Siobhan's text had taken its time reaching him and Creasey wasn't answering his phone. The camp and its yellow Portakabin were on his way to the police station at Tongue. At one or the other he was hoping for answers. But before he was halfway there, he began to see lights — not on the road, but behind a low dry-stone wall. A couple of officers in high-vis clothing were by the roadside, torches sweeping the ground around them, despite there being plenty of light left in the evening sky. As Rebus slowed, they waved him on. He drew to a halt and began to reverse. One of the officers was quick to approach, standing behind the car so that he had to brake. The man then came to the side window, which Rebus had already lowered.

'Keep moving, sir,' the officer commanded.

Instead of complying, Rebus undid his seat belt and got out. 'Just wanted to congratulate you,' he said. The officer was intent on blocking him from getting any closer to the search party. 'On finding the gun, I mean,' he continued. 'I was going to say well done to DS Creasey. He's not about, is he?'

'Back in the vehicle, please, sir.'

'It's a long drive from Edinburgh for him, isn't it? There and back in a day. But he'll want to see if you turn up anything else — maybe the phone or laptop . . . '

The officer was having none of it. He had stretched both arms out, forming a one-man shield. Over his shoulder Rebus could make out the small white tent they'd erected. There was a lamp shining inside it.

'Forensics still here?' he speculated. 'Late one for them.'

'Sir . . .'

'Revolver will already have gone for analysis — bit of a priority, I'd imagine. Turned up anything else?'

'I'm going to have to arrest you. And I'll make sure you're taken to a nice, far-distant police station for processing, Mr Rebus.'

Finally Rebus made eye contact. It was the officer from Camp 1033, the one he'd given the V-sign to.

'Just naturally nosy,' he explained.

'Doesn't mean you can't spend a night in the cells. Not quite as comfortable as a bed at The Glen, so why don't you turn your car around and go back there?'

'You'll let Creasey know I was asking for him?'

'You can count on it.'

Defeated, Rebus got back behind the wheel. But before moving off, he composed a text and sent it to Creasey: See *you in the pub?* Took a while for it to go — one single bar of signal. With the help of a passing place, he did a three-point turn and drove slowly towards Naver. The officer flicked the Vs as he passed.

'Fair play to you,' Rebus said as he returned

the gesture through the open driver's-side window.

★ ★ ★

He'd been seated at a corner table for over an hour, skimming one newspaper after another and even a months-old magazine about angling. Now that Lord Strathy had raised his head above the parapet, the media interest had evaporated. May had vetoed the turning-on of the TV. She'd put Rebus in charge of the music, which was why Siobhan Clarke's CD was playing.

'You know how to liven up a pub,' she'd teased him, topping up his glass of cola.

He hadn't told her about the gun. Creasey's team would want her or her dad to identify it, after which the fun and games would start. But that could wait till tomorrow — May looked exhausted, the busy days taking their toll. Even Cameron appeared to be flagging. Rebus glanced at the single security camera, fixed to a corner of the high ceiling. As May had already admitted, it was for show only, never turned on.

'But don't tell the insurance that,' she had added.

When his phone sounded, Rebus snatched at it. Creasey's voice sounded echoey, almost as if he were calling from an orbiting spaceship. Rebus walked outside and stopped on the deserted pavement.

'Was it good fortune or good policing?' he asked.

'I assume Siobhan Clarke spilled the beans,

363

right after promising to my face that I could trust her.'

'Trust has to be earned — that's why she trusts *me*. So talk me through it.'

'Pretty straightforward really. Weapon wasn't found at the scene, so stood to reason the killer took it. They were most probably in the victim's car, driving it back to Naver. They realise they've got the murder weapon sitting right there next to them, so they wind down the window and toss it.'

'And leave the window open — explains why the passenger seat was damp.'

'Maybe trying to clear their head,' Creasey said. 'It rained that night but not until two a.m. Car was most likely in the lay-by by then.'

'They must have been fairly sure the gun would have no prints on it.'

'If they were thinking straight, yes.'

'No blood on the seat, though . . . '

'Maybe the revolver was lying on the notes or the computer. And to go back to your first question, once I had my hypothesis, I decided to test it by having officers walk the length of the route from the camp to where the Volvo was abandoned, some on the road itself, checking the ditches, others in the fields either side.'

'Proper policing,' Rebus conceded. 'I bet the ones you sent out loved you for it, too.'

'They're loving me now — though my bank manager won't.'

'Beers all round, eh? Well, you'll be pleased to hear that some of them are still hard at it. What time do you think you'll be back?'

'I'm heading to Inverness.'

'Good luck finding someone in the lab this time of night.'

'Overtime's been approved and a willing body or two found.' Creasey paused. 'I just need to see it with my own eyes, John.'

'Any chance you could send me a photo?'

'So you can go shoving it in the face of everyone on your list of likely suspects? I don't think so.'

'Reckon you'll get prints? God knows how many pub regulars have handled it down the years.'

'All that's for later. I'll catch up with you sometime tomorrow. Until I do — play nice.'

'Did you get talking to Siobhan about me?'

'A little.'

'Then you probably know playing nice doesn't feature heavily on my list of qualities. Have fun at the lab, son.'

'John . . . ' Sounded to Rebus as though another warning was coming, but he'd already ended the call.

★   ★   ★

Cole Burnett lay on his bed, earbuds in, music pounding in an attempt to overwhelm his thoughts. It wasn't working, though, not tonight. His parents were out, Christ knew where. Pub, party, dogging site. He barely exchanged a word with them these days. Stuck to his bedroom, smoking his weed and dropping tabs. One of them might put their head around the door occasionally, mutter something about food being on the table. He was never hungry; he'd eat later. At dead of night he might raid the fridge or get some toast and jam on the go, if either of them had bothered to buy bread.

Tonight he had a multipack of crisps and a jar of peanut butter. Scoop the peanut butter out with a finger and suck on it. Brilliant stuff. To wash it down he had a four-pack of energy drinks, half-bottle of vodka, litre of lemonade. King of his castle, blinds open, window ajar. The posters on his walls harked back to childhood — Marvel superheroes and cartoon characters. Plus one from the *Walking Dead* TV show and one from *Narcos*. He loved *Narcos*. The doing he'd got at the hands of Cafferty and his sidekick, that would have turned out a lot differently — a *lot* differently — if he had been able to pull a gun from his waistband. He knew where to get one, too. People who knew people. Expensive, though, and up until now, while sometimes fantasising about the power that ownership would confer, he'd never felt the urgent need.

But that was changing. And he'd heard that if you rented and brought it back unused, you'd get a decent chunk of the deposit refunded. Fired, there might be a bit of money due, but not much. Traceability, he'd been told. Bullets could be matched to the pieces that had fired them.

'So here's a tip for you, Cole — if you use the thing, dig the bullet out of wherever it's ended up. Do not leave it at the scene.'

He replayed the conversation in his head as he

stared at the ceiling, hands clasped around the back of his head. He thought of Les's aunt, of her home of nine years being turned into a factory. She'd be the one going to jail when the bust came. Cafferty would remain nicely distanced from the fallout. He lived in a top-floor flat in a nice part of town. He had his club and his big car and his hangers-on. He had a lot of things Cole wanted. Yet who was he? What was he? Just another fucker who got lucky. Wasn't like he had an invisibility cloak or some Marvel-style weaponry. His only shield was his rep; the sort of hard man drunks talked pish about in old men's pubs.

Cole raised himself up from his prone position, swung his feet off the bed and onto the carpeted floor. Stopped the music. Walked to the window, pushing it as far open as it would go. He wanted to stick his head out and howl at the sky, a sky that had only just turned dark.

Instead of which, he returned to the bed. Sat on it. Looked at his phone. Gnawed on his bottom lip. Made his decision and called the number.

'Fuck is it?' the voice at the other end demanded.

'I can get you the dough,' Cole said. 'So how soon can I have it?'

'You fussed about make and model?'

'As long as it works.'

'Tomorrow then. Deets later.'

The call was ended. Cole picked up the open can of energy drink and took a slug before starting to text some mates. Time to ask a few favours . . .

Day Six

Day Six

32

Rebus, May and Cameron were in the kitchen finishing breakfast when they heard a noise at the pub's locked and bolted front door. May went to investigate, Rebus knowing full well what she'd find. Sure enough, she returned slightly flustered, trying not to show it.

'Cameron,' she announced. 'Our fingerprints are needed. Police are waiting in the bar.'

'What's going on?' Cameron asked.

'They found a gun. They think it might be the one from here.' She fetched her jacket from the coat rail. 'I've got to go with them — they need Dad's prints too.'

Cameron pushed a last corner of bread into his mouth as he rose from his chair. Rebus was up too. He followed May into the bar. The print kit had been set up on one of the tables. Robin Creasey was studying the photographs of John Lennon.

'Have you had any sleep?' Rebus asked.

'Not much.' He turned his attention to May. 'You and your father will have to come to Inverness, I'm afraid. That's where the firearm is and we need an identification.'

'Won't our fingerprints be proof enough?' May enquired.

'Would showing May a photograph suffice?' Rebus added.

'I don't think so.' But Creasey produced his

phone anyway and opened its picture gallery, holding the screen close to May's face as he used a finger to slide between shots. Rebus changed position so he could view over May's shoulder. A rusty revolver, with a piece of white muslin cloth covering a section of the grip. He knew the cloth's purpose: blood and hair beneath, not the sort of thing you wanted civilians seeing. As Creasey flipped back through the gallery, he had eyes only for May, checking her reaction. She had placed a palm to one cheek as if to aid concentration.

'Looks similar,' she eventually conceded.

'We think there are marks that will correspond to the nails on the wall.' Creasey nodded to where a photographer was busy getting close-ups of the gap below the optics while an assistant held up a simple wooden ruler as a measurement aid.

'Easier just to bring the gun here,' Rebus suggested. 'Inverness is a hellish long trip for a frail old man.'

'We'll be fine, John,' May attempted to reassure him. Then, to Cameron: 'You going to be okay on your own?'

The young barman was seated at the table while his prints were taken. 'These'll be destroyed after, won't they? Not kept on some Big Brother database?'

'Never fear,' Creasey said, which didn't seem to console Cameron in the least.

When May's turn came to sit at the table, Rebus drew Creasey to one side. 'So what's your thinking now?' he asked in an undertone.

372

Creasey gave the beginnings of a shrug. 'As ever, I'm keeping an open mind.'

'The gun was lifted from here for a reason. Maybe the same reason it was used against Keith.'

'Or it was just handy in the heat of the moment. Like I say, I'm ruling nothing out.' Creasey rolled his shoulders and gave his neck a few stretches.

'Racking up the miles,' Rebus commented. 'How long till Forensics finish with the gun?'

'I'll have a report later today. Blood and hair have gone for analysis. They're checking for fibres and prints. It dates to the 1940s. Hasn't been decommissioned but it's corroded to hell, trigger and cylinder jammed. Barrel full of gunk and no bullets in any of the chambers.'

'Serial number?'

'Just about readable. Luckily there's a guy in the lab knows someone who fancies himself an expert. If it can be traced, we'll trace it.' Creasey opened his notebook and glanced at it. 'It's a Webley .38, Mark 4, apparently. Turned them out by the crateload during the war.'

'State it's in, has it definitely spent time in the sea?'

Creasey fixed Rebus with a look. 'You're doubting Mr Collins' story?'

'Like you, I'm ruling nothing out.'

'Amount of wear and tear makes his version of events feasible. If we need to, we can probably carbon-date the sand in the cylinder.'

The scraping of chair legs against the floor caused them both to turn round. May Collins was on her feet.

'Ready when you are,' she told Creasey, all businesslike. Then, to Rebus: 'Pay's not great, but there's a shift for you here if you're willing.'

'I can manage,' Cameron argued.

'If needed, I can be here,' Rebus said. May nodded without meeting his eyes. She fastened her jacket and checked she had her phone.

'Best behaviour while Mummy's gone,' she said, pausing at the door until Creasey had opened it for her. Rebus and Cameron watched as the rest of the crew followed. Once the door was closed, Cameron bolted it again.

'Not nearly opening time yet,' he explained. 'Not that I couldn't do with a drink after all that.' He was behind the bar by now, his fingers touching the three thin nails. Then he flinched and cursed, tugging the sleeve of his jumper over his hand and rubbing at the nails and the mirrored glass behind.

'They'll call that tampering with the evidence,' Rebus chided him.

'I call it protecting the innocent,' Cameron countered. 'Do we need to get some more tea on?'

'Wouldn't go amiss. And if it's okay with you, I need time on the computer, look a few things up.'

'What sort of things?'

'Local history to start with.'

'You could always consult Keith's group.'

'Might end up at that, but meantime . . .'

Cameron nodded, whether he understood or not. 'I'll get that brew going,' he said, heading in the direction of the kitchen.

374

Having rung the bell, Rebus could sense Samantha hesitating on the other side of the door, checking through the spyhole. He heard the sound of a chain being slid open and the lock being turned.

'Can't be too careful, eh?' he offered as the door swung wide. 'Unlike the old days.'

She ushered him inside, sliding the chain back across afterwards. 'Reporter walked straight in yesterday,' she muttered.

'Which one?'

She shrugged, already slouching back towards the kitchen. It was messier than ever. Samantha's face was paler even than before, cheeks sunken, hair unwashed.

'How's Carrie?' he asked, watching his daughter slump onto one of the chairs around the breakfast table.

'Full of questions I either can't answer or don't want to. She keeps looking at photos on her iPad — holidays and birthdays and Christmas . . . ' She got up, heading for the kettle and switching it on. 'This is what we're supposed to do, isn't it? Make tea and pretend it makes everything bearable for a while?'

'Is it all right if I ask a question?'

She gave him a quick glance. 'Do you ever stop?'

'It's all I seem to be good for.'

She was concentrating all her efforts on lifting two tea bags from the box, placing them in mugs next to the kettle. It took her a moment to work out what came next. She walked to the fridge, checking the date on the milk.

'I'm not even sure what day it is,' she said to herself. Then, to her father: 'Go on then.'

'They've found the murder weapon. It's the revolver that used to sit behind the bar in The Glen.'

'They hit him with it? Why not just shoot him?' She thought for a moment. 'I think I remember it. May's dad found it on the beach.'

Rebus nodded. 'I don't suppose you ever saw it here? In Keith's bag maybe?'

She was shaking her head as she handed him his tea, having forgotten to take the tea bag out.

'And he never mentioned taking it from the pub?'

'No.' She sat down again, her own tea forgotten about, the mug still over by the kettle. Her eyes met his. 'Remember when that man abducted me, back when I was a kid? He did it to get at you. And afterwards, Mum took me to London. We couldn't live in Edinburgh any more. Is that what I'm going to have to do with Carrie? Make a new life elsewhere? I'll need to find a job, whatever happens . . .'

'I've got money. Best you have it now rather than when I'm gone.'

'Jesus, Dad.' Her head went down into her hands. 'Is one fucking death not enough to be getting on with?'

'Sorry.'

After a moment, her head lifted again. 'Why did they use the gun?'

'Maybe to make a point,' Rebus offered.

'What do you mean?'

'The camp, the revolver, the stuff still missing . . .'

'It's to do with the camp then? Not me, not Jess?'

'Creasey and his team might take a bit more persuading,' Rebus cautioned.

Samantha remembered her tea, got up to fetch it. 'I see Strathy turned up. I remember how excited Keith was the day he went to the castle. On his way to work he'd seen the vans — the marquee company and caterers. He knew what he was doing — maximum embarrassment for his lordship. He was like a kid afterwards, bouncing off the walls like someone had given him too much sugar, when all he'd really been given was a burst lip.'

'Courtesy of the gardener?'

'I told him he should report it, but he laughed it off.'

She checked the time on her phone.

'I'm seeing Julie,' she explained. 'Means running the gauntlet again.' She exhaled noisily. 'I just want to go back to being *me* — does that make any sense?'

Rebus nodded. 'Mind if I stick around?' he asked. 'Not here, but the garage?'

'You'll need to unlock it. Key's on the hall table. Put it through the letter box when you're done.'

'You'll be locking up the house?'

She gave a slow, regretful nod. 'Everything's changed,' she said.

33

After a couple of hours spent in the garage, Rebus felt the need to clear his head. He walked to the rear of the bungalow. The garden was basically just lawn, a tool shed, a swing and a folded-away whirligig clothes line. After less than a minute's battering by the wind, he changed his mind and climbed into his rental car. One bar of signal on his phone, so he called Creasey.

'You're worse than a bloody newshound,' Creasey answered. 'And there's nothing to report.'

'That's not why I'm calling.'

'In which case, I can give you two minutes.'

'I've got a fair idea who wrote the notes,' Rebus began.

'She's had another?'

'I meant the one telling Keith about Samantha's fling with Hawkins.'

'Okay, I'm listening.'

'Angharad Oates.'

'I suppose that's credible. Not sure it makes any difference to — '

'Are you forgetting the motorbike? They all get to use it. The night Keith was killed, Ron Travis heard it.'

'So to your mind, because Oates wrote a couple of anonymous letters, she then murdered Keith, making it more likely that her lover Jess Hawkins and your daughter might be thrown together again?'

'She'd know who the police would most likely point the finger at. Plus, chances are, it'd lead to Samantha getting out of Dodge.'

'John . . . '

'Okay, how about this — the day Keith barged into that party at Strathy Castle, he was hauled away by Colin Belkin, who gave him a smack in the mouth as a send-off.'

'And?'

'And these are leads you should be following.'

'I've got the lead I need right here at the lab.'

'Prints on the revolver?'

'You'll find out soon enough.' The line went dead. Rebus felt like punching something. Instead of which, he started the engine.

★   ★   ★

The cemetery lay a mile inland from Tongue, above the village and just off the road to Altnaharra. A low stone wall surrounded it, with high metal gates giving access for hearses. Rebus reckoned that at one time there'd have been a horse-drawn procession from the nearby communities. Maybe not even horses — the coffin carried aloft by family or friends. Only a handful of the gravestones looked new; most were weathered, their inscriptions faded. The grass had been mown recently, though, and fresh flowers had been added to several plots. Not an easy place to hide, and Rebus saw Helen Carter straight away. She was leaning on her walking frame, deep in thought — or more likely

379

remembrance. Rebus approached her, clearing his throat to announce his presence.

'I heard the car,' she said.

'And here was me thinking you're stone deaf.'

'I've got my hearing aid in.' She pointed to one of her ears.

Rebus took up position next to her and studied the name on the headstone.

'Anniversary of his death,' she explained.

'I know — I looked him up online. Thought he'd be in one of the war cemeteries.'

'We guessed he'd want to be here,' Carter said quietly. 'Chrissy did anyway.'

Rebus took stock of the scenery. It felt like they might be the only living things in the whole landscape — no livestock visible, no birdsong. Then he turned his attention back to Sergeant Gareth Davies's grave.

'Age twenty-nine,' he recited. 'How old was Chrissy?'

'Nineteen. Two years younger than me.'

'I heard she died a few years back.'

'She had a good life down south, and a long one.'

'You kept in touch after she left?'

'She didn't often visit — too many memories.'

'It was a terrible thing to happen.'

'And such a stupid thing, too.'

'Sergeant Davies's killer must have harboured strong feelings for her,' Rebus agreed. 'That was what it was, wasn't it — a crime of passion?'

'It's what was said at the trial.'

'You don't sound convinced.'

Helen Carter took a deep breath. 'Chrissy

wasn't the bonniest of lassies — she'd tell you that herself. But she liked the attention of men, and she found ways to make sure she got that attention.'

'She was a flirt?'

'It went a bit beyond that.' Carter almost had a glint in her eye. 'Another good reason for her to head south — our parents weren't going to stand for much more of it. They were religious, as was I, I suppose. They knew they could trust me not to get into trouble.'

'But not Chrissy?'

'No.'

'Were you dating your future husband at this time?'

Carter considered for a moment. The breeze had caught her hair. She pushed some strands back behind her ear.

'Should we go sit in the car?'

'A friend is picking me up soon.'

'Stefan Novack, by any chance?'

She smiled. 'You *are* a detective, aren't you?'

'The pair of you just seemed comfortable with one another as you were leaving the bar that day.'

'Well, maybe you're right.' She gave a slight shiver. 'I can feel this wind getting into my bones.'

Rebus put his arm out for her to take, but she waved the offer away, gripping the handles of her walker and shuffling towards the gates.

'Do you come here on Chrissy's behalf?' he asked.

'I suppose so.'

'You never did answer my question about your boyfriend . . .'

381

'Fred,' she said. 'Friedrich, actually. We were friends for a while, lovers eventually.'

'Your parents approved?'

'Not overly. There was always that element of 'sleeping with the enemy'.'

'Did they grow to like him?'

'They grew to *accept* him.' Her heady eyes drilled into Rebus's. 'Why are you asking about all this?'

'I've listened to the recording Keith made of his interview with you. You told him Chrissy didn't really know Hoffman. He wasn't part of her coterie?'

'They'd met on several occasions. The evidence pointed to him as Gareth's killer.' She offered a small shrug.

'Could there have been another reason why Sergeant Davies was targeted?'

'I can't think of one.'

'And none of her other admirers might have been jealous of him?'

'I'd imagine they were *all* jealous of him.'

'These were British guards or internees?'

'Both. As I say, Chrissy had a certain reputation and she was hell-bent on upholding it.'

'She sounds a handful. I don't suppose *you* were jealous of her, Helen?' They had reached Rebus's car. He opened the passenger-side door.

'Maybe I was — just a little.'

'But then you had Friedrich . . . '

The car door was still open, but she seemed reluctant to get in.

'As a friend, yes,' she said. 'But if I'm being

honest, I had my eye on Franz, too. A bit naughty of me, but I think I was trying to stir Friedrich into action, if you know what I mean.'

'Franz? As in Frank Hess?' Rebus watched her nod. 'Another of Chrissy's admirers?'

'Oh yes — until Gareth came along and swept her off her feet.'

'And was Joe Collins part of that group too?'

Carter wrinkled her brow in thought. 'Not that I remember. Josef was a bit gruff, a bit of a grouch. We always wondered . . . ' She broke off.

'What?' Rebus asked.

'We wondered if, given a gun, would he shoot the lot of us? I mean, we used to ask that question a lot — me and Chrissy and the other girls. They all seemed so polite and so charming, but until they surrendered, they'd been merrily slaughtering our menfolk. Plenty at Camp 1033 were still loyal Nazis. One or two even went to Nuremberg.'

'Shall we get in?' Rebus gestured towards the car's interior, but she shook her head. 'What if I told you,' he continued, his voice dropping a fraction, 'that Joe Collins' revolver had been used to kill Keith Grant?'

Her face didn't change. 'Is that what happened?'

'Yes.'

'Then I don't really know what to say.'

'Keith was bringing the past back to life, dusting off a few ugly truths some people might have wanted kept hidden.'

'You can't seriously think one of us . . . ? We're almost ready for the grave ourselves!'

'Maybe there was more than one attacker,' Rebus commented. He saw she was becoming agitated. 'Then again, it could all be a con trick — pushing the investigation one way when the truth is hiding down another track entirely.' He heard a car approaching and turned towards it. 'Looks like your ride's here. Handy that Mr Novack's still up to driving.'

'Try and stop him,' Carter said with a faint smile.

The Land Rover came to a stop next to them. Novack gave a wave through the window.

'The walker goes in the boot,' Carter told Rebus. He opened the passenger door for her, then stowed the walker while she eased herself into the car. Rebus went to the driver's-side window.

'What brings you here?' Novack asked, winding the window down.

'Paying my respects.'

Novack's look suggested that he doubted this. 'You've heard about the revolver?'

'Wasn't sure word had got out.'

'I assure you it has, along with the news that Joe and May are under arrest.'

'What?' Helen Carter froze with the seat belt half strapped across her.

'They're verifying the gun, that's all,' Rebus countered. He went around the car and closed Carter's door. Novack lowered the passenger-side window.

'Joe's gun, though,' he went on. 'Used to murder a man.'

Rebus leaned in at the window. 'Do you see

your old friend Joe as a killer, Stefan?'

'Of course he doesn't!' Carter snapped.

'Maybe his daughter, then, eh?' Rebus shook his head. 'Best not let rumours get started. You never know where they'll stop.' The window began to rise, Novack's finger on the switch as he glared at Rebus, while his passenger couldn't make eye contact at all.

You're rattled, Rebus thought. *You're both rattled.*

Rather than watch the Land Rover roll away, he marched back into the cemetery, stopping once more at Gareth Davies's resting place.

'She didn't bring anything to mark the occasion, did she?' he asked out loud. No flowers of remembrance, no card or note.

Just Helen Carter herself.

34

Siobhan Clarke's mobile rang at precisely noon. She didn't recognise the number.

'Hello?' she answered.

'I'm calling because Issy Meiklejohn more or less demanded it. I have no intention of giving you my name, so please don't ask.'

The voice was clipped, upper class, English Home Counties.

'Define 'demanded'.'

'There's rather a venomous streak to that young woman, wouldn't you say?'

'I've always found her perfectly charming.'

'Is that supposed to be funny? Anyway, you know why I'm calling?'

'You're Lord Strathy's alibi, the one I'm supposed to accept on trust — without seeing your face or having a name to put to it. You'll appreciate that's not usually how we operate on a murder inquiry. Still, I'm listening.'

As were the others in the MIT office. Clarke ignored them and walked into the hallway, closing the door after her. Fox was in the admin room next door, talking to one of the staff. Clarke descended the stairs until she was beyond his eyeline.

'He was with me for the best part of five days. I doubt we were out of one another's sight for more than half an hour in all that time.'

'This was in London?'

'Yes.'

Clarke did the calculation. Five days, which finished yesterday morning. Strathy's little romp had started only a day or so after Keith Grant died and three days after Salman bin Mahmoud's murder.

'During your time with him, did you watch the news, read a paper?'

'Not so you'd notice.'

'One of Lord Strathy's business partners had been found murdered. The man was a friend of his daughter's. He didn't mention it at any stage?'

'He did not.'

'Maybe he excused himself to make or take a phone call?'

'We promised ourselves — phones off.'

'Awkward if your husband needed to contact you.'

'Look, I've told you what I can. Ramsay was with me. We were having a good time.'

'He was relaxed, didn't seem at all worried?'

'Same old Ramsay.'

'The crime I'm investigating took place in Scotland, and our legal system demands corroboration.'

'Pity we weren't engaged in a *ménage à trois*, then, isn't it?' There was a throaty chuckle as the line went dead.

Clarke stared at the screen of her phone. 'Gotcha,' she said quietly.

Back in MIT, she crossed to Christine Esson's desk and jotted the telephone number onto a much-doodled pad.

'Analyst would have a field day with those,' she said, admiring the swirls, swooshes, lightning bolts and zigzags that kept Esson busy during every phone call she made.

'What am I doing with this?' Esson asked, tapping her pen against the line of digits.

'Finding me a name, address and anything else that can be gleaned. I'd do it myself if I possessed half your skill set.'

'And that concludes Siobhan's motivational TED talk. Thank you all for coming . . .'

Clarke was smiling as she headed for her own desk. Fox had just taken his seat and was stifling a yawn.

'Still not sleeping?' Clarke guessed, noting how bloodshot his eyes were.

'Sleep's overrated.'

'Strathy's lover just called me. Christine's going to put a name and face to her.'

'She used her own phone?'

'With any luck. What did admin want?'

'I'm using too much paper.' She stared at him. 'Seriously. All the background stuff I've been printing out and photocopying.'

'I thought we had a proper budget — how much stuff have you been churning out?'

'A fair bit.'

She looked at the piles on his side of the desk. More was stacked on the floor.

'Two copies of everything,' he confessed.

'One for home, one for here?' Clarke guessed. 'So you can keep at it even when you're not in the office?' But then she made a clucking sound. 'No, Siobhan, that's not quite it — it's so you can pass one set along to either the ACC or Cafferty, and my antennae tell me the latter is the more likely.'

'Keeping him onside,' Fox intoned quietly.

'Just stuff relating to Stewart Scoular, though? Not the bin Mahmoud case per se? Tell me he's not watching us do our job . . . '

'I'm being careful.'

'How careful?'

'As much as I can be. There's obviously a bit of crossover here and there.'

'That's great news, Malcolm. Means if we ever lift Cafferty for anything, he can brag that he's got you tucked into his breast pocket like a little silk handkerchief. I thought we'd covered this when we were walking back here from his big shiny gangster car?' She saw the look Fox was giving her. 'What is it you're hiding?'

He started shaking his head.

'Please tell me you've not gone all lone wolf and reckon you can deal with him without anyone's help?'

Having stopped shaking his head, Fox made a zipping motion with his fingers across his mouth.

'Can we have a grown-up conversation here?' Clarke insisted.

'Not quite yet.'

She was about to remonstrate further, but Christine Esson was approaching.

'Fast work,' Clarke commented.

'This isn't that,' Esson said. 'But it's kind of interesting nonetheless. Just got a message about the Chinese student who was mugged on Argyle Place. Seems her phone's been returned to her, along with an apology.'

'An apology?'

'In English and Mandarin Chinese, apparently. The student's friend, the one who helped translate for her, she got in touch just now. Says the Chinese is really ropy, wonders if the apology was fed into some online translation site.'

'What does it say exactly?'

'She sent a photo of the note.' Esson handed her phone over to Clarke. Fox slid his chair closer so he could see it too.

Really sorry for what I did to you. Promise never to do it again. And then presumably the same message in Chinese characters. Written with the same black ballpoint pen and in the same hand by the look of it. The Chinese rendition looked clumsy, mistakes scored out and corrected. The English version was in capitals, and even that looked a bit wonky. Clarke angled the phone's screen towards Esson. 'Would you say this person's hand was shaking?'

'Parkinson's?' Esson suggested.

'But in the real world?'

'Written under duress or in an emotional state,' Fox answered.

Esson took her phone back. 'Phone and note were in a Tesco bag stuffed through the victim's letter box.'

'How did the mugger know where she lives?'

Esson shrugged. 'I'm guessing maybe her phone? Probably got a tracker or something — maybe a food delivery app. People are increasingly sloppy with their personal information.'

'A mugger who grew a conscience,' Clarke pretended to marvel.

'I assume you don't think that's the case here?'

'I suppose what matters is that we can remove her from the wall. Hugely doubtful she ties to the attacks on Salman and Gio.'

'Do you want to tell the boss or shall I?' Esson asked.

'It's all yours, Christine. We've done sod all to earn the privilege.'

35

Clarke and Fox had just returned from a late lunch — soup and a roll at a café on Constitution Street — and were settling themselves at their shared desk. Clarke could see from the corner of her eye that Christine Esson had news. Sure enough, as soon as they were seated, she was on her feet and striding towards them.

'Here comes DCI Sutherland's favourite student,' Clarke teased.

'She's about to become yours too,' Esson retorted, handing over a sheet of paper. 'Name's Violetta Pakenham. Lives in Kensington. Owns a boutique there. Married, two grown kids.'

'I know that name,' Fox said, getting to work on his computer. A moment later he had what he was looking for. 'Probably George Pakenham's wife. He's one of Stewart Scoular's investors.'

'I can see why Lord Strathy would want the affair kept hush-hush,' Clarke commented. 'Piss off Pakenham and you'd mightily piss off Scoular.'

'And everyone else in the consortium,' Fox added. 'These things are built on sand, and that sand is made up of public confidence. To have one of your big names cheating with the wife of another . . .'

'Gives us a bit of leverage, if we want it,' Esson argued. 'I mean, if we think there's anything

392

about the case that Strathy's been hiding from us . . .'

'He tells or we leak?' Clarke nodded her understanding and met Fox's eyes. 'Do we think he's hiding anything?'

'I'm not sure, and I certainly don't want him sparking out on us again.' Fox busied himself on his keyboard for a moment, then angled his screen towards Clarke and Esson. The photo he'd found showed a couple at a red-carpet event. The man was in his seventies, the woman much younger.

'Just the twenty-year age gap,' Esson commented.

'What about Issy?' Fox asked Clarke. 'She's the one who put Mrs Pakenham in touch with us. She must know her dad is playing with fire.'

'Reckon she told any of her mates?'

'I'd say she's good at playing things close to her chest.'

'Or else Scoular would probably already know.'

Fox nodded. 'As Christine says, this gives us leverage. Fetch Issy in, get her to tell us *everything* she knows or suspects.'

'Okay,' Clarke said after the briefest consideration, 'let's do it.'

⋆ ⋆ ⋆

An hour later, the two uniforms who had been sent to St Stephen Street to collect Lady Isabella Meiklejohn escorted her up the stairs and into the same interview room she'd been made to wait outside while her father was being questioned the previous day. She took her time composing herself, ignoring Clarke and Fox, who sat opposite.

'Turns out I was wrong to trust you, Detective Inspector Clarke,' she intoned as she adjusted her jacket. 'I'd be an idiot not to know why I'm here.' Finally she looked up, her eyes throwing darts in Clarke's direction.

'How is Lord Strathy?' Fox asked in a voice that was almost genuinely solicitous.

'He's no longer in danger. Some lifestyle adjustments have been suggested.'

'By his doctors or by you?' Clarke enquired. Meiklejohn gave her another withering look.

'Should I be calling Patsy and inviting her to join us?'

'Depends how many other people you want knowing that your dad's sleeping with the wife of someone he's doing business with.'

Meiklejohn gave a sour smile. 'I did warn her to make sure the call couldn't be traced. Dozy bitch doesn't even have the sense.'

'George Pakenham's had ties to Stewart Scoular's business for quite some time,' Fox stated. 'The two of them seem pretty chummy.' He was sifting through the details he'd found, including a dozen or so photos taken at trade awards dinners.

'And?'

'I'd imagine you'd like it to stay that way.'

'Which entails cooperating with you?' Meiklejohn stretched out her arms. 'In what way have I *not* been cooperating?'

'Craigentinny golf course,' Clarke said, leaning forward a little. 'Late at night, a meeting arranged in the car park — why?'

'Sorry, whose meeting is this?'

'Your friend Salman. Something to do with the planned takeover? Something Salman had to see for himself?'

'I know nothing about it.'

'Stewart Scoular was heading the team. Don't tell me he never discussed it with you? Your father was in the mix too, Issy, and we think you act as his representative.'

'Which means,' Fox added, 'that you know more than you're telling.' He held a photograph in front of her face. 'Any idea whose car this is?'

'Not mine.'

'Whose, then?'

Meiklejohn scrunched up her eyes as she studied the photo. 'Are you serious? It's just a blur.'

'A blur that'll soon have a licence number. What type of car does Stewart Scoular drive?'

'He doesn't see the point.' She saw that a bit more explanation was required. 'Living in the city — plenty taxis, decent public transport.'

'So he doesn't own a car,' Clarke stated. 'What if he's invited to a party at, say, Strathy Castle?'

'He'd rent something suitable, a Merc or an Audi.'

'No lifts in Mr bin Mahmoud's Aston?'

Meiklejohn gave a snort. 'Bit cramped.'

'Roads up there would be tough on an Aston anyway — wouldn't look good when he had to hand it back,' Clarke agreed.

'Hand it back?' Meiklejohn sounded puzzled.

'It's leased — didn't you know? Same goes for the DB5 in London. The house here is owned by the Mahmoud family trust, but the London penthouse is a rental. Not what you'd call a fortune in any of the bank accounts we've found.'

'And credit cards going unpaid,' Fox added, 'in danger of maxing out.'

Clarke was studying Meiklejohn. 'This is coming as a surprise?'

'Sal was loaded.'

'Maybe at one time, but his father's situation had altered things; a lot of the money was untouchable.'

'That can't be right.' Meiklejohn was shaking her head. Clarke leaned further across the desk towards her.

'Why's that?'

'He was about to sign up to The Flow.'

'The Flow?' Fox echoed.

'That's the name Stewart gave it — actually my father's idea. The company is being incorporated this week or next.'

'The Flow is the country club project near Naver?' Clarke watched.

Meiklejohn nodded. 'It's been proving a difficult sell, the financial climate being what it is — Brexit and so forth. Stewart has some promises from America and Hong Kong, but even so . . .'

'How much did Salman intend contributing?'

'Ten or thereabouts.'

'Ten million?' Fox shared a look with Clarke:

where the hell was he going to get that kind of money?

'Father was over the moon when I told him.'

'Lord Strathy stood to turn a decent profit from the project?' Clarke asked.

'The trust did, certainly.'

'And the trust is what keeps everything afloat?'

Meiklejohn nodded again.

'So with Salman's death . . . '

She expelled some air. 'In Stewart's words: we redouble our efforts.'

'Which in your father's case meant heading off for a few days with his married lover?'

'The ways of the flesh always take precedence where my father's concerned.'

'So a major investor has just been killed and your father doesn't hold a meeting or a conference call? Doesn't consider cancelling his plans so he can comfort his daughter, who's just lost a good friend in shocking circumstances?'

'You *have* met my father? I didn't imagine things?'

'What about the murder of Keith Grant? When did he learn of that?'

'Probably at the same time he found out from the media that he was supposedly missing.'

'And what did he say to you about it?'

'Not a damned thing.'

Fox shifted a little, signalling that he had a question of his own. 'The scheme hasn't died with Mr bin Mahmoud, though?'

Meiklejohn considered this. 'I see what you're saying — someone was trying to scupper The Flow?'

'Bit drastic if they were,' Clarke cautioned.

'Or else,' Fox added, 'the meeting that night was with someone Salman thought was good for the money — a loan perhaps.'

'I keep telling you, Salman had money.'

'Paperwork says otherwise — unless you know where he might keep a chunk of it hidden?'

Meiklejohn shook her head.

'Would Stewart Scoular know?'

'I can't see Sal confiding in him.'

'Mr Morelli, then?'

Meiklejohn shrugged. 'You've got me thinking, though. Plenty competitors out there to add to cranks like Keith Grant and Jess Hawkins.' She folded her arms determinedly and made eye contact with Clarke. 'I'm sure you're wrong about Sal's finances. The ten mil was a lock. He'd promised me and there's no way he wasn't going to deliver.'

'He didn't though,' Clarke said quietly. Thinking: *someone made sure of that . . .*

★   ★   ★

They took Brillo for a walk across Leith Links. Clarke threw a ball for the dog to retrieve while Fox called Gartcosh to see if Robbie Stenhouse had made any progress. When Clarke turned towards him, Fox shook his head at her. She made a kicking motion with her right foot.

'Siobhan wants me to remind you,' Fox said into his phone, 'about that football match — tickets and drinks on her if we get a quick result.' He listened for a further few seconds, nodding to himself. 'I know you will, Robbie. That's why we all worship you as a deity.' He ended the call and gave a sniff. 'To be fair,' he explained to Clarke, 'the man is as thorough as he is scrupulous — and there's no shortage of cameras in Edinburgh for him to check. One small nugget, though . . . '

Clarke tossed the ball again. 'Any time you're ready.'

'Sticker in the rear window, he *thinks* it might say Avis.'

'A rental car?'

'In which case we're looking at someone who's either just visiting or doesn't have a car of their own.'

'Or they do, but they don't want to use it,' Clarke added. 'Issy seemed so certain Salman had funds available. Is there something we're not seeing?'

'His reputation might be enough to get him a bank loan.'

'In which case there'd have been documentation in at least one of his houses, no?'

'Cafferty used to be a loan shark, didn't he?'

'Shillings and pennies, Malcolm. I think even Cafferty might baulk at handing over ten million quid.'

'I know I would, most days.'

Clarke had taken her own phone out and was checking its news feed. There was a short piece about a weapon having been recovered in the Keith Grant murder case, a publican and her father helping police with their enquiries.

'Hope you know what you're doing, John,' she muttered.

'We could go talk to Avis,' Fox was suggesting, 'show them the photos, see if they can ID the car. We've got a rough idea when it would have been taken out and returned.'

'Did Robbie say anything about the number plate?'

'He thinks he can get most of it into a readable state, probably by tomorrow lunchtime.'

'Let's cut him some slack then.' Clarke scuffed the ball across the grass with her foot, Brillo, tongue lolling, giving chase.

'Have you thought about bringing Brillo into the office?' Fox asked. 'I doubt the team would mind.'

'Gamble's got an allergy to dogs apparently.'

'He's got an allergy to hard work, too, but you don't hear us complaining.'

Clarke managed a smile. 'I keep coming back to the money, Malcolm. If Salman was about to hand it over, The Flow was a huge step closer to becoming a reality. Who gained most from that not happening? Not Issy or her father, not Stewart Scoular.'

'People up north who didn't want it,' Fox answered. 'Only thing is, none of this would be in the public domain. It's the reason why commercial espionage has become big business.'

'Your source told you that, did he?'

'Want me to see if he knows something we don't about The Flow? Who the competition might be?'

400

Clarke gave a slow nod, so Fox got his phone out and made the call. Brillo was seated on his haunches at Clarke's feet, the ball ready and waiting. But she was busy with her own phone again, rereading the news story about the recovered weapon. There was a photo of Camp 1033 and she clicked on it, enlarging it with her fingers. Keith Grant was described as a campaigner who had been raising funds to buy the camp and bring it into the community as a 'tourism resource'.

'Can't be a connection,' Clarke muttered to herself, giving the ball another almighty kick.

But stranger things had definitely happened.

36

Rebus had taken a shift behind the bar so Cameron could have a break. Usual handful of regulars, armed with anecdotes about the revolver, May and her father. He had tried putting Cameron's mind at rest, but the memory of his fingerprints being taken lingered and the young man wasn't entirely reassured. When a barrel needed changing, Rebus went into the kitchen and saw Cameron pacing the yard outside, puffing on a joint and checking his phone. He left him to it and told the customer he'd have to pick something else.

'But I always have lager.'

'They say variety's the spice of life,' Rebus coaxed him.

'Give me a can of lager then,' the man decided.

'I knew there was a touch of the rebel in you,' Rebus said, reaching into the chiller.

Cameron was in the cellar changing the barrel when May Collins arrived back. Eyes followed her all the way from the door to the rear of the bar. She disappeared into the corridor, hanging up her jacket before returning.

'Christ,' she said, taking in the looks of her clientele, 'if this was a Western, the piano player would have stopped.'

This raised a few smiles, after which people went back to their conversations and newspapers.

'And what the hell is that?' she asked Rebus, gesturing towards the loudspeaker attached to one corner of the ceiling.

'Leonard Cohen,' he answered.

She rolled her eyes before turning to the optics and pouring a whisky. Rebus could sense her staring at the space where the revolver had sat. Eventually she turned again, slopping water into her glass before taking a swallow.

'It went well then,' Rebus said.

'They grilled my dad for over an hour, John. At his age! And then they started on me. How long's the gun been missing, who do I think could have taken it?'

'It is the same gun, then?'

'Our prints — Dad's and mine — are on it.' She watched Cameron emerge from the cellar. 'Yours too. Creasey's on his way here to have a chat with you.'

'Joe's okay, though?' Rebus asked.

'He's shattered. Slept all the way to the house.'

'You don't want to stay with him?'

'He refused the offer.' Her shoulders slumped a little. 'How has it been here?'

'Fairly quiet. I took a trip to the cemetery, bumped into Helen and Stefan.'

'Any chance we can maybe live in the here and now just for a bit?'

'You should go rest. Hate to say it, but the bar's coping without you.'

She shook her head. 'Don't want anyone whispering that I'm hiding. Bad enough I seem to be a murder suspect all of a sudden.'

'I still think Keith lifted the revolver. Killer

took it from his satchel.'

'Might have had the decency to wipe my prints off when they'd finished.' She flinched. 'Sorry, that wasn't exactly tactful.'

'Take a break, half an hour or an hour.' Rebus looked to Cameron, who backed him up with a firm nod.

'Maybe I will then . . . ' She broke off as the door opened. Two detectives walked in, one of them Creasey, another a younger woman Rebus hadn't seen before.

'Need a wee chat,' Creasey informed Cameron. 'Somewhere quiet if possible.'

'Kitchen?' Cameron suggested, eyes on his employer. She nodded.

'DC Larkin will take care of you,' Creasey said. Larkin went behind the bar, following Cameron into the corridor. Creasey's attention had already turned to Rebus. 'And I need to borrow this one, too.'

'Looks like that's my break over,' May Collins said. Then, to the bar generally: 'Everyone happy being served by a murder suspect? It's either that or time to finish up and vamoose . . . '

By the time Rebus caught up with Creasey, he was in the front seat of his Mondeo. Rebus climbed into the passenger side and closed the door. 'I told her she's not really a suspect,' he said.

'Prints on the gun handle are mostly partials, but still good enough.'

'May, her father and Cameron?'

'Plus the deceased's — though that's between us for the time being.'

'So Keith did swipe the gun?'

'He really thought it was the one used to kill the soldier, didn't he?' Rebus gave a slow nod. 'To answer your question, I doubt either Ms Collins or her father did for Keith — which doesn't mean they're not involved in some capacity.'

'What about Cameron? Any motive there?'

Creasey gave a tired smile. 'Anyone but your daughter, eh? Well, that's why I wanted to speak to you. I need to go see her and I thought it might help if you were there too.'

'Tell me her prints aren't on the gun?'

Creasey shook his head. 'But one of the partials is much smaller than the others. Almost certainly a child's.'

'Carrie?'

'Rather than take the girl's prints, I thought maybe a chat would suffice.'

Rebus reached across to his seat belt, buckling himself in. Creasey started the engine and pulled away from the kerb. Rebus called Samantha. She was at Julie's, as was Carrie. He got directions and passed them to Creasey.

'What is it he wants?' Samantha was asking. 'I've told him everything I know.'

'We'll be there in a couple of minutes. I'll explain then.'

The house was a new-looking bungalow on the hillside overlooking the village. Two cars were already parked in the driveway, so Creasey stopped next to the grass verge. Julie Harris ushered them in.

'Kettle's on,' she said.

Samantha was in the living room, Carrie and Jenny playing in Jenny's bedroom. While Creasey started explaining the visit, Rebus went into the kitchen to help with the drinks.

'Is she okay?' he asked.

'Sam or Carrie?'

'Both, I suppose.'

'There's a counsellor they're going to start seeing, maybe an hour a week for a wee while.'

The kitchen was neat and unremarkable, photos and a to-do list stuck to the refrigerator door.

'Your partner?' Rebus asked. The family were posing next to a human-sized Goofy and Donald Duck.

'Disneyland Paris, two Christmases back. I'd have binned it, but Jenny wouldn't let me.' She turned briefly to look at Rebus. 'Walked out two months later. He's good with the upkeep, I'll give him that. Sees Jenny every couple of weeks.'

'He's still local?'

'Aberdeen. New job, new life. All right for some, eh?'

'You grew up here?' She nodded. 'I've actually not met too many people who did.'

'Bright lights elsewhere.'

'The same lights some people escape by moving here?'

She handed him two mugs. 'How does he take it?'

'Whatever way we give it to him,' Rebus said, heading for the door.

Carrie was eventually summoned to the living room, Julie Harris replacing her in the bedroom.

406

The girl climbed onto her mother's knee, looking wary. It had been decided that Samantha should ask the questions. The story was quickly told, once Carrie had decided saying nothing wasn't going to get her anywhere.

'Nobody's in trouble,' Samantha attempted to assure her. 'It's just a piece of the puzzle that needs to be filled in. There was a rusty old gun in Daddy's shoulder bag, wasn't there? Did he show it to you?'

Carrie bit her lip and shook her head. 'Found it,' she said, in a voice not much above a whisper.

'And you took it out?'

'It was really heavy.'

'I'll bet it was. Did Daddy see you?'

She shook her head again.

'So you just put it back and left it where you'd found it?'

A nod.

'And never said anything to Daddy?'

Carrie turned her attention to the only stranger in the room. 'My daddy's gone to heaven,' she explained to Creasey. 'He won't come back for a long time.'

Samantha Rebus worked hard at keeping her composure.

'Where was this, Carrie?' Rebus asked quietly. 'The rusty old gun, I mean?'

'The garage.'

'The bag was on Daddy's desk?' Another nod. 'Lying open?'

'I just wanted to look. I wasn't going to take anything.'

'What else was in there? Maybe some

notebooks and a computer?'

'Those were on his desk.'

'So he'd been working? Could you see anything he'd written?'

A shake of the head. Samantha's eyes were on Creasey.

'Is that enough?' she asked.

'I think so,' he replied. 'Thank you for your help, Carrie.'

'You're welcome.' She slid from her mother's lap and skipped out of the room.

Samantha squeezed her eyes shut. 'So the gun's the one from The Glen,' she said, as if getting things straight in her mind, 'and Keith took it as part of his research, and someone hit him over the head with it. I still don't understand why.'

'We're working on it,' Creasey said with some confidence.

'I never knew he had it, swear to God. If Carrie had told me, I'd have made him get rid of it.' She opened her eyes and stared at the living room door. 'That's what I'd have done,' she said.

'Carrie's not to blame,' Rebus cautioned, but Samantha wasn't listening.

'If she'd only *said* something . . . '

'Your father's right, Ms Rebus. You shouldn't start — '

She silenced him with a glare. 'Maybe the two of you could just go away now.' She leapt from the chair and left the room.

Rebus and Creasey sat in silence for a moment, then Creasey rose slowly to his feet.

'Do you ever drink any of the cups of tea that

408

get made for you?' Rebus asked, gesturing towards the still-full mug.

'Don't really like the stuff,' Creasey admitted. 'But people do seem to enjoy making it.'

37

Siobhan Clarke was stretched along her sofa, Brillo tucked in next to her and an old episode of *Inside No. 9* on the TV, when her phone rang.

'Hello?' she answered.

'It's Robbie. Robbie Stenhouse.'

'I don't remember giving you my number, Robbie.'

'I have ways — and I wasn't sure this could wait.'

Clarke lifted herself up to sitting, swinging her feet to the floor. Brillo awoke with a start and she comforted him with a pat.

'You've got something for me?'

'It's a rental, right enough. I've run the plate and the car's based out at the Avis concession at Edinburgh airport. Give me your email and I'll send you everything I've got.'

She did so, realising that she was now patting Brillo rather more briskly than the dog would like.

'Does the offer of a Hibs-Motherwell match still stand?' Stenhouse was asking.

'Half-time pies on me. I'll check the fixture list once we've put this case to bed.'

'Speaking of which, I might call it a night. It's a tungsten-silver VW Passat.' He reeled off the registration number, Clarke jotting it down on the front page of the day's *Evening News*.

'Thanks again, Robbie,' she said, ending the

call. She chewed on the pen, lost in thought for a moment, and then called Malcolm Fox. 'It's an airport rental,' she told him. 'Robbie's emailing me the specifics.'

'Told you he was good.'

'Good enough to track down my phone number.' She broke off. 'He asked you for it, didn't he?'

'About an hour after we left Gartcosh. Not that he'd thank me for revealing his secrets.'

'Not so secret — even long-retired DIs know about him.' She paused again. 'You out somewhere?'

'Just picking up some takeaway,' Fox said, explaining the background noise Clarke could hear. 'Does the airport mean it's someone who's just arrived in town? Don't tell me it's going to be some London connection the Met hasn't bothered to mention . . .'

'Remember what Issy Meiklejohn told us, though: Stewart Scoular rents cars sometimes.'

'Added to which, she doesn't own one, so if she felt the need . . .'

'We'll know more in the morning. Rendezvous in Leith or meet at Avis?'

'Avis at nine?'

'Suits me. So what's on the menu tonight?'

'Indian. Probably waiting for me as we speak. Have you told Graham Sutherland yet?'

'He's over in Glasgow.'

'Keep him in the loop or hand him a delicious surprise?'

'Let's wait and see what we get from Avis. If it turns out to be a tourist who got lost on their way to their hotel . . . '

'Way to burst a boy's balloon, Siobhan.'

'Enjoy your curry.' Clarke ended the call and tossed the phone into the space left by Brillo, who had vacated the sofa and was watching her reproachfully from the middle of the living room floor.

'Okay, I'm sorry,' she apologised. A curry? No, but a single fish wouldn't go amiss. She rose to her feet, saw Brillo start to wag his tail in expectation.

'Got it in one,' she said. 'A single fish and a battered sausage. Maybe even a jaunt to the airport tomorrow if you're lucky.' She stepped into the hallway, Brillo bounding towards the door to the outside world.

'One thing about an airport rental,' she told the dog as she grabbed her coat and his lead, 'no shortage of CCTV out there. Meaning whoever it was, we've got them.'

* * *

'Wish I hadn't mentioned a curry,' Fox muttered to himself, rubbing his hand across his growling stomach. Hours since he'd eaten. Needed to empty his bladder too, but it was too public on the Cowgate. He had a thing in his glove box, a 'He-Wee' he thought it was called. But any of the night-time carousers wandering past could glance down and catch him in the act. So instead he shifted a little in his seat and hoped Scoular wouldn't be too much longer in the Jenever Club. No sign of Issy or Gio tonight — though they could have arrived before he did.

Fox picked his notebook up from the passenger seat. Scoular had taken a private-hire cab from his home in Stockbridge, not stopping anywhere en route. He had been inside for ninety-five minutes, during which time the street had altered in character. The pedestrians now were younger and noisier. There were music venues nearby, club nights and concerts starting. One stag party had swaggered past, tapping out a tattoo on the roof of Fox's car and turning to beam smiles at him. Soon after, a hen party had arrived at the Jenever, dressed in pink sashes over matching T-shirts printed with the bride-to-be's face. Writing on the back of each: *Sue's Booze Crew.* The doormen decided they could go in, and were rewarded with a peck on the cheek or a squeeze of the backside. A little later, a couple from the party were back out again to smoke cigarettes and chat to the doormen, who had perked up as a result.

He had the radio on — Jazz FM. Not a brilliant signal, due to the Cowgate being akin to a canyon, a narrow sunken stretch with high buildings either side. Better than nothing, though. And now he had something to think about too: an airport rental. They'd agreed nine in the morning, but Fox reckoned the Avis office would open much earlier. He might get there ahead of time, present Siobhan with a fait accompli. Not that she would thank him for it; quite the opposite. Might do it anyway, though.

The hen party women were back indoors, the night-time chill proving too much for their

413

skimpy outfits. One of the doormen had offered his overcoat, receiving yet another kiss, this time on the lips as far as Fox could tell. When the women had gone, both doormen shuffled their feet in a little dance.

Small comforts, Fox mused. You took them where you could.

And now the doors were opening again, and Stewart Scoular emerged, a woman on his arm. She wore heels and a tight black dress with a cream jacket draped over her shoulders. Fox had expected to recognise her, but it wasn't Issy Meiklejohn. He thought about trying to get a photo with his phone, but he was too far away and couldn't risk the flash. Besides, if he needed a name, Cafferty could probably provide it. A taxi was being summoned by one of the doormen, Scoular slipping him a banknote by way of a tip. Fox was reminded of a Glasgow cop he'd known who tipped everyone, from café staff to barkeepers. Always gave to beggars and *Big Issue* sellers, too.

'It's nice to be nice,' he had explained. 'And now and then, one or two might even reciprocate.' Meaning a nugget of gossip or inside gen. 'Just wish I could claim it back,' he had added with a chuckle.

Fox had only worked alongside him a few months, was having trouble summoning a name. Last time he'd seen him had been the funeral of a fellow officer. There had just been time for a brief handshake and a hello.

He watched now as the back door of the black cab closed, the same doorman doing the honours. A brief wave and the taxi moved off with its cargo. Fox followed, having jotted down the exact time of Scoular's departure from the Jenever. Result or not, if necessary they could show Cafferty that there had been no lack of effort. Always supposing the ACC's plan didn't work out. Never did any harm to have a backup.

He knew within a few minutes that they were headed to Scoular's home. He remembered the man's boast at their first meeting, about how he didn't always live there alone. As far as Fox could see, nothing was happening on the back seat — no faces converging. He followed the cab to Stockbridge, staying well back at the drop-off. As Scoular and the woman went into the house, he started moving again, catching up with the taxi a few hundred metres further on. He flashed his lights until the driver signalled and stopped. Fox pulled up behind him, walked to the driver's window and showed his warrant card.

'Thought I had a flat,' the driver said.

'Nothing like that. Wanted to ask you about the couple you just dropped off.'

'What about them?'

'Any interesting chat?'

'I wasn't listening.' The driver saw from Fox's look that he wasn't falling for it. 'Really didn't say much of anything,' he conceded. 'Busy with their phones. He made one call, overseas I think.'

'What makes you say that?'

'He asked what time it was there. They were confirming a conference call of some kind, at a time to suit everyone.' The driver shrugged. 'That was about it. Can't say he looked too happy, though.'

'No?'

'Seated next to a dolly bird like that, no way I'd be scowling.'

'Did her name get a mention? Had they just met, do you think?'

'Not a scooby.'

'Anything else?'

The man shrugged again. Fox thanked him.

'Will you put in a word next time I get a ticket?'

Fox managed a thin smile. 'Drive safely,' he said, retreating to his car.

Scoular was worried, it seemed, and unable to switch off, even on a date. Overseas: the Far East maybe, or the USA. With bin Mahmoud gone, there was a gaping financial hole that needed to be filled, meaning more hard work for Stewart Scoular. No way was he behind the killing — it was the last thing he'd needed. Didn't mean there wasn't a connection, though. Didn't mean there weren't secrets he was keeping.

Fox added the details to his little notebook. Time to go home, he reckoned, with a brief pit stop at a curry house.

He had an early start in the morning, after all.

Day Seven

38

As Fox walked towards the Avis desk, he saw a figure he recognised holding something out towards him.

Siobhan Clarke. A cardboard beaker of coffee. 'Good morning,' she said.

'You're here early,' Fox replied.

'You too.' She made show of checking her watch. 'Had the feeling you would be.'

Fox looked towards the rental desk. A businessman was being served, his wheelie case parked next to him. 'Have you . . . ?'

'That wouldn't be very comradely, would it? Buying a coffee and waiting — *that's* what colleagues do.'

'All right, you've had your fun.' He took a sip from the cup, then prised off the lid. It was a cappuccino, as far as he could tell. Clarke opened her shoulder bag and lifted out a dozen sheets of paper, held together with a paper clip.

'This is what Robbie sent me. Close-up of the cleaned-up number plate; DVLA details; a few shots of the car as it travelled through the city that night.'

'He must really like you,' Fox commented as he sifted the sheets. The businessman was wheeling his suitcase towards the exit.

'Shall we?' Clarke asked, heading to the desk, Fox at her heels.

A supervisor had to be called, the clerk

handing the phone to Clarke so she could explain. Then the supervisor spoke to the clerk and the clerk got busy on her keyboard. Fox had asked to speak to someone from the security staff, and a man had arrived, Fox telling him that he needed CCTV from the date the car was rented.

'Main concourse, Avis desk and parking bays will do for starters.'

'That's a big ask.'

'Big asks are all a murder inquiry ever has. Your cooperation at this time would be appreciated.'

The man puffed out his cheeks but headed off anyway to make a start, taking with him one of Fox's business cards.

'System's a bit slow today,' the clerk was telling Clarke.

'That's fine,' Clarke responded. Not that it was. She was holding onto her coffee cup like she might at any moment wring the life from it.

'Sure you should be having caffeine?' Fox asked.

She stopped drumming the fingers of her free hand against the counter. A couple of customers had arrived and were queuing behind the two detectives.

'Maybe I could serve them first?' the clerk requested.

'They can wait,' came the terse response from Clarke.

'Okay, here we go,' the young woman said half a minute later. A printer whirred somewhere below the counter. She slid from her stool and crouched to retrieve the sheets of paper. 'The physical paperwork will be in one of the filing cabinets, along with the credit card receipt. But meantime . . . ' She handed over the printout. Clarke sought the renter's details. Fox beat her to it, jabbing the name with his finger.

'Giovanni Morelli,' he stated, repeating it silently as if trying to make sense of what he was seeing, while Clarke continued to scour the form.

VW Passat with 1,200 miles on the clock, rented the morning Gio's good friend Salman was murdered, returned first thing the following day, fewer than thirty miles having been added to the car's total mileage.

'Ten into town,' Clarke said, 'and the same back.'

'Around five from the New Town to the murder scene,' Fox added, nodding his comprehension. He turned his attention to the clerk. 'Where is this car right now?'

The clerk tapped away at her keyboard. 'It's onsite.'

'Has anyone else rented it since Mr Morelli?'

She looked past Fox's shoulder to where the queue was growing and becoming impatient.

'Don't worry about them,' Clarke said. Then, turning towards the queue, 'A police matter. Thank you for your patience.'

The clerk got busy again on her keyboard. 'It's due to be issued to a new customer today.'

'Not going to happen,' Clarke said. She fixed Fox with a look. 'We need Forensics out here.'

'It'll have been valeted?' he checked with the

clerk. She nodded her agreement.

'Blood's not going to shift for a bit of vacuuming and polishing,' Clarke told him. She already had her phone in her hand, entering the number she needed. Fox turned back towards the clerk.

'Keys, please. And a note of whatever bay it's in.' He was finding it hard to concentrate and knew it would be the same for Siobhan. There were procedures to be followed, but all he could think about was Giovanni Morelli.

'Haj?' Clarke was saying into her phone. 'I need a crew at the airport. Avis parking lot. Car there may have been used in the bin Mahmoud homicide. DI Fox and me are here already.' She listened to whatever was being said to her and watched as the clerk handed Fox a slip of paper and a key fob. 'Yes,' she assured the scene-of-crime boss, 'we can secure the immediate area. But be as fast as you can, eh?'

'We'll let you get back to work,' Fox was informing the clerk. 'But we *will* need all the documentation you mentioned, so when you've got a free second . . . ' He saw that Clarke was already making towards the exit, having abandoned her coffee on the counter. He placed his own cup next to hers and started moving.

★ ★ ★

'Why?' she asked, as they crossed the road. They weren't quite running, but they weren't quite walking either. Fox had buttoned his jacket in an attempt to stop his tie flapping up around his

422

ears. 'I don't get it, Malcolm. I really don't.'

'Let's not get ahead of ourselves,' Fox cautioned. 'This might only prove that he was there that night.'

'You saw the photos — no sign of a passenger in the Passat. So unless Salman gave his killer a lift to the murder scene in his Aston . . . '

'Could be a third car we've just not seen yet.'

'Or Issy on her bike, eh?' Clarke shook her head. 'It fits; it's just that it doesn't make sense.'

'Morelli's the one we need to be asking.'

She looked at him, 'Reckon he's a flight risk? Parents with money and powerful friends . . . '

'Let's see if the car can offer us some clues.'

They were nearing the Avis lot now, 'Which bay?' Clarke asked.

'Forty-two, like *The Hitchhiker's Guide*.' He saw the look on Clarke's face. 'Just attempting a bit of levity.'

They walked the rest of the way in silence. There was a kiosk, and the man stationed there had obviously been alerted by the clerk in the terminal. He led them to bay 42 and left them to it.

'Tempting to take a look,' Fox said, holding up the key.

'Better not,' Clarke warned him. She was circling the car, pressing her face close to its various windows. It had definitely been through a wash, and the inside looked pristine. When her phone pinged, she checked the screen.

'Forensics?' Fox guessed.

'The DCI,' she corrected him. 'Wants to know where we are.' She made the call, lifting the phone to her ear. Fox was wishing he'd not dumped that coffee. The temperature hadn't got into double figures yet and there was no shelter to be had. Not that Siobhan Clarke seemed bothered. Her cheeks were suffused with colour, her eyes gleaming. When she met Fox's gaze, there could be no mistaking her confidence, which, if not misplaced, meant he'd soon be on his way back to his desk at Gartcosh.

He knew he shouldn't feel entirely sad about that, but he did.

39

Joseph Collins took his time opening the door of his cottage, his walking frame proving an impediment. Rebus greeted him from the path, where he was admiring the garden.

'Can't all be your own work?' he speculated.

'Mostly May these days. What the hell do you want?'

'Wondered how you were doing — can't have been easy yesterday. May's still not over it. All the rumours, and the eyes on her when her back's turned.'

Collins squared his shoulders. 'We're strong, the both of us.'

Rebus had approached the front step. 'Can I maybe come in?'

'Why?' Collins was peering at him through glasses that needed a polish to clean them of various smears and smudges. Seated in the bar, he had seemed stooped and tremulous, but his eyes were the same ones that had seen warfare and bloodshed. The young Josef Kolln was visible to Rebus, trapped deep within an aged receptacle.

'Because,' he intoned, 'your gun was used to kill an innocent man, meaning it's time you came clean. For May's sake as much as yours.'

'Go to hell.'

'I was a cop for over thirty years, Mr Collins — I've *been* to hell. What I saw in Camp 1033

425

wasn't as bad as some, but it'll still haunt me. Keith didn't deserve what happened to him, but he deserves your help.'

'Your own daughter most likely did it.' The old man was growing agitated.

'You really think that?'

'I don't know what I think.'

'I'm more interested in what you *know*. See, there was a reason that gun was put on display. You were goading someone, letting them know you knew.'

'Knew what?'

'The truth about who killed Sergeant Davies. And with Keith digging the whole story up again, no telling what might happen. He believed it was the same gun. Maybe he thought he could get it tested for DNA. That's why he lifted it from behind the bar. You always told people the truth — that you found it washed ashore. But I don't think you did much to dispel the other rumours. In fact, once they'd started, you got to like them, because they pointed the way to the real story.'

Rebus had taken another step towards Joseph Collins. He could see past him into the narrow hallway beyond. Family photos on the walls, the usual clutter of a long life.

'Stefan Novack, Helen Carter and Frank Hess — Keith interviewed all of them. Stefan drives, but he wasn't at the camp at the time Sergeant Davies was murdered — unless you know different. Helen's sister had more than her share of admirers, some of whom became her lovers. Was Helen jealous? Did she have a thing for

Sergeant Davies? Then there's Frank, who admired her but doesn't seem to have been admired back.' Rebus paused. 'And then there's you. You knew both Frank and Helen. Which means you knew her sister too. I began to wonder if the gun was your way of telling people *you'd* done it. See, planting the murder weapon in Hoffman's room means it had to be someone with access to the camp. Helen worked there; you and Frank Hess were interned there.'

'Leaving only a few hundred other potential suspects.' Collins sounded suddenly weary, shoulders starting to droop. The gnarled, liver-spotted hands were trembling as they gripped the walker. 'Tell me, Mr Rebus, which of us had the strength to cause Keith's death? You say the revolver was in his possession — we must have fought him for it, no? Wrestled it away from him? Can you picture that? Really? Can you?'

Rebus waited a moment before taking a final step. His face was now inches from Collins'.

'Time to end it, Herr Kolln — for both our daughters' sakes.'

Collins' eyes seemed to cloud over a little. He lifted one hand from the walker and rubbed it across his lips. Then, with slow deliberation, he began to back away from the doorway, hauling the walker with him.

'You're right,' he said as he retreated. 'I never told him it wasn't the same gun. He never lost his thing for the ladies, you see — it was my way of warning him off my wife . . . *both* my wives, come to that.'

427

'Who, though?'

'Go talk to Frank, Mr Rebus.' Slowly the door began to close.

'From what I know of him, that could be pretty one-sided.'

'Try anyway.'

The door clicked shut, leaving Rebus on a spotless path in a well-kept garden.

'I will then,' he said quietly, scratching a hand through his hair.

★ ★ ★

The house Frank Hess shared with his grandson Jimmy sat on a short terrace leading off the main road down towards the shore. The sun was out, the day becoming pleasantly warm. Rebus thought he could hear the semi-distant crashing of waves. It struck him he'd yet to visit the beach. Maybe soon. He had rung the bell three times before he heard a voice bawling from somewhere inside.

'What do you want?'

'Mr Hess? It's John Rebus, Samantha's father.' He had prised open the letter box and was yelling through it.

'Go away.'

'I can't do that, Mr Hess. We need to talk.' He placed his eye to the slit in the door, withdrawing rapidly as a walking stick was jabbed into the space.

'It's about the revolver and why Keith took it from the pub. He tried asking you about it. Seemed to make you angry. Mind you, judging by today, I'd say that's probably your default setting.'

'Leave us alone.'

'Is Jimmy there? Can I speak to him?' Rebus risked placing his eye to the letter box again. He could see the old man's torso, the chaotic hallway behind him. He let the flap close again and tried the door handle. The door wasn't locked, so he took a step inside. The walking stick caught him across one shoulder but did not deflect his attention from the objects he had seen from outside. He lifted the heavy leather jacket from its hook, studying it as another blow landed against his back. The old man was wheezing and spluttering. Rebus crouched down and picked up the crash helmet, in which nestled a pair of leather gloves. He turned towards Frank Hess, deflecting the latest blow with his elbow.

'Jimmy has a bike,' he stated.

'No,' Hess said, making to land another blow. Rebus dropped the jacket and snatched the end of the walking stick, holding it tight while Hess tried to wrest it away from him.

'So he just likes dressing in the gear?'

'He's a good boy. He looks after me.'

Rebus nodded. 'Unconditional love — he'll do whatever it takes to keep you contented. You guessed why Keith had lifted the gun. You knew why Joe kept it on display behind his bar. Always with an eye for the ladies — hit you hard that Chrissy had no time for you but seemed perfectly happy giving herself to anyone else.' He paused for a moment, watching as Hess's chest rose and fell, as if he was having trouble catching a breath. 'No love for Hoffman in the camp,' he ploughed on. 'No one about to complain if he went to the firing squad — easy to plant the revolver in his room and then get word to the authorities.' He paused again, studying Hess. The man was medium height, and had lost any weight he'd carried in younger years. Folds of flesh hung from his neck. His cheeks were sunken, teeth yellow. 'You've been filled with rage all your life, haven't you, Herr Hess? Not much you can do with it at your age. Jimmy, on the other hand . . .'

Hess's eyes lit up suddenly, the years seeming to fall from him, until Rebus could see the young conscript, the zealot, the unlovable admirer of the local flirt.

'My grandson has done nothing,' he spat. He looked around the hallway as if seeking something, then padded off deeper into the house.

Rebus did his own looking. No bike. There was a narrow close to one side of the house, but he hadn't seen one there either. He took out his phone: no signal. He was putting it away again when Hess emerged from the gloom, brandishing a carving knife.

'The hell are you doing, Frank?' Rebus said, hands in front of him, palms facing the oncoming figure.

'I could kill you, you know. You said so yourself — a man filled with rage.'

'Unlike Jimmy, you mean?' Rebus nodded as if in understanding, then flung out his left hand, wrapping it around Hess's wrist, twisting until

430

the knife dropped to the floor. He took a step forward, his mouth close to the old man's ear.

'You don't ride a bike, though,' he said in a quiet voice, before turning and leaving the house.

He entered the close. A couple of old bicycles, one of them dating back to childhood by the look of it. A small rear garden. More junk: rotting wooden doors; a makeshift cloche constructed from discarded window frames in which only weeds seemed to be thriving; old car tyres and hubcaps. In one corner stood a small shed, bought not too many years back judging by its condition. He yanked open the door and peered in. A rotary lawnmower gathering cobwebs; boxes of tools; garden implements hanging from nails. No motorbike. He closed the door and stalked back to his car, checking his phone for signal as he drove. When he gained a single bar, he stopped and called Creasey.

'You need a search warrant for Frank Hess's house. And you need to question the grandson.' He paused. 'Grandson and grandfather both,' he corrected himself.

'And why is that, John?' Creasey's voice was in danger of breaking up. The single bar was fluttering.

'I'll explain when I see you. Just get on it.' He ended the call and continued driving, finding a space outside The Glen. He walked in as Cameron was finishing mopping the floor.

'Careful you don't slip,' the barman warned him.

'I never slip, son, which doesn't stop me

431

falling on my arse sometimes. Question for you: does Jimmy Hess own a motorbike?'

'No.'

'You sure?'

'Positive.'

'He has all the accoutrements.'

Cameron was nodding. 'That's because he sometimes borrows Callum's.'

'And who the hell is Callum?'

'Him and his dad run Torries farm. Mad keen on bikes is Callum, though you'll mostly find him on an ATV.' He saw Rebus's blank look. 'You'd probably call it a quad bike. Handy for getting around the fields.'

'So Torries farm, how do I find it?'

Cameron started a complicated explanation, but Rebus cut him off.

'Easier if you come with me.'

'But we're opening — '

'Do what the man says.'

They turned their heads towards the voice. May Collins was standing in the doorway behind the bar, drying her hands on a cloth. Her eyes were on Rebus.

'Dad says you paid him a visit. Looks to me like you've got the scent of something, so what are you waiting for?' She made a shooing motion with her fingers.

'I'll grab my jacket,' Cameron said.

In the brief time he was gone, Collins and Rebus maintained eye contact without a word being exchanged between them. But there was a faint smile on Collins' lips as Cameron squeezed past her, shrugging his arms into his denim jacket.

'Good luck,' were her parting words as the two men left the bar.

It was a twenty-minute drive, east at first and then winding inland. The farm's main compound lay down a rutted track, Rebus taking it at speed. It was a hire car after all. At the sound of the approaching engine, a young man wearing a blue boiler suit appeared in the yard from one of the barns.

'That's Callum,' Cameron said. Rebus stopped next to a muddy quad bike and got out. Cameron and Callum were shaking hands and exchanging greetings by the time he reached them.

'I'm John Rebus, Samantha's dad,' he said by way of introduction.

'Sorry for your loss,' the young man said. He was brawny and red-cheeked, with wild hair and a no-nonsense manner. 'What brings you out here?'

'You're friends with Jimmy Hess?'

'Since school.'

'He borrows your bike sometimes?'

Callum gave a quizzical look. 'He does, aye.'

'When was the last time that happened?'

'I'd have to think.'

'Recently, though? Just over a week back?'

'Something like that.'

'Did he say why he needed it?'

'Jimmy just likes to hit the road sometimes, let off a bit of steam. His grandad's not the easiest man to live with.'

'I know I couldn't do it,' Cameron confirmed.

Rebus turned to him. 'You don't need to, though, do you? Frank Hess hardly ever visits the pub.'

'Never, actually,' Cameron corrected him. 'Says it's because he's not a man for the drink, yet if you visit the house . . . '

'What?'

'Plenty whisky bottles, and Jimmy's definitely not a fan of malts.'

Rebus focused his attention on the farmer again. 'So how long did Jimmy have the bike for?'

'Just the one day.'

'Day and night?'

'Being on a bike at night is a joy. You don't need a destination, not up here. The drive is everything.'

'If you thought about it, you could get me the exact date?' Rebus persisted.

'Yes.'

'And when he brought the bike back, how did he seem?'

Callum looked from Rebus to Cameron and back again. 'Wait a sec, this is my mate you're talking about.'

'And you're going to be talking about him a lot more, not to me but to a murder inquiry.'

Callum was shaking his head, while Cameron looked stunned. Rebus's phone was vibrating in his pocket. He lifted it out.

'You get a signal all the way out here?'

'Mast over that way.' Callum pointed towards a distant hill.

Rebus pressed the phone to his ear, turning away from both young men. 'Yes, DS Creasey, what can I do for you?'

'You know search warrants don't come ten a

penny? I need to convince my boss to convince a judge — which means you need to convince me.'

'Best done face to face — where are you now?'

'Just past Lairg, heading north.'

'Thing is, as soon as Jimmy Hess's grandad talks to him, we've got a problem. Anything that could be evidence is going to get ditched. And your way takes time, Robin.'

'John . . .'

But Rebus had already made up his mind.

*　*　*

Having dropped Cameron at the pub, he headed back to Frank Hess's house and tried the door. Locked now. He rang the bell, but there was no answer. Peered through the letter box. No sign of the crash helmet or jacket. Cursing under his breath, he stalked down the close and into the garden. There was a door to the kitchen, but it was locked too. The window was grimy, but he could see in. The carving knife lay on the worktop. The drawer it had been taken from gaped open. A frying pan on the stove and pots and dishes in the sink. Two mugs on the drop-leaf table. No sign of life.

He stepped back and stared at the upstairs windows. Both had their curtains closed. He headed to the shed and opened it, started rummaging, then decided it would be easier if he shifted the lawn-mower. He dragged it out and got to work, tossing tools behind him to make more space. Boxes of screws, nails of odd sizes, most of them rusted, hooks and pieces of wire

435

and old three-pin plugs. Plastic flowerpots, rolls of twine, cans of oil . . .

He noticed that the workbench had a drawer. It was stuck shut, so he left it. But having gone through the last box, he had nothing to show for his efforts. Sweat was causing his shirt to cling to his back. He checked that his inhaler was in his pocket, just in case. Then he looked at the drawer and decided to give it another go. This time he used a large screwdriver, wedging it into a gap. Some of the wood began to splinter, but the drawer moved out a fraction. He tried again; more movement. He gripped the sides of the drawer in both hands and —

'You're trespassing,' Jimmy Hess said. Rebus turned towards him. Hess filled the shed's doorway. 'Criminal damage, too.'

'Police are on their way, son,' Rebus said, breathing hard. 'But it's you they'll be talking to, not me.' He reached a hand through the gap in the drawer and lifted out a laptop. He sensed Keith's notebooks were in there too, at the back, harder to reach. 'Best go prepare your grandfather.'

Jimmy Hess was shaking his head. His large, round face showed no emotion. Gone was the jovial figure who had sat at the table in The Glen; gone, too, the concerned and solicitous grandson who had brought an end to Keith Grant's interview.

'I don't think so,' he told Rebus.

And then he lunged, hands around Rebus's throat, pushing him back until Rebus collided with the rear wall of the shed. He felt his airway

436

constrict, his eyes bulging and watering at the same time, blurring his vision. He had his own hands around the younger man's wrists, but couldn't budge them. He sought a pinkie, intent on bending it back until it snapped, but his strength was already ebbing. His knees buckled and he sank towards the floor, sharp corners of various objects digging into him. Changing tactics, he reached for Jimmy Hess's face, clawing at it, seeking the vulnerable eyes. But Hess just turned his head to and fro, making purchase impossible. The sea was roaring in Rebus's ears now, and the world had turned blood-red like a sunset. Hess's teeth were bared in effort. Rebus only wished he could have given his tormentor a more even fight . . . and been more help to Sammy . . .

Sam . . .

Samantha . . .

His hands fell away and his eyes fluttered once before closing.

A deep darkness lay beyond the roaring.

40

The Leith team were in high spirits, except for George Gamble, who sat with arms folded, having warned anyone who'd listen: 'Don't count your fried chickens.' His chair creaked as he leaned back in it.

Most of the team had gathered in the vicinity of the Murder Wall, perched on desks or standing expectantly while Graham Sutherland considered their next move.

'I'll talk to the Fiscal's office,' he announced, 'that's probably job one.'

'Surely job one is getting Morelli in here and interviewing him under caution,' DC Phil Yeats said. He was handing round the teas and coffees, this having become a routine he seemed to welcome. ('Detective wages for a Tea Jenny's work,' had been Ronnie Ogilvie's comment one night in the pub after Yeats had left.)

'We need to remember he's a flight risk unless we get him to surrender his passport,' Malcolm Fox added.

'In good time, Malcolm,' Sutherland said. He had taken up position in front of the wall display, facing his team. 'Car's gone to the workshop at Howdenhall. If there's trace evidence to be found, they'll find it. I'm promised news by close of day.'

'Search warrant for Morelli's home?' Esson piped up.

'As soon as I've had a word with the Fiscal. Do we have any thoughts as to motive?'

'Not exactly,' Siobhan Clarke offered, 'but there's premeditation there. I'm guessing he thought it less risky to head out of town to rent the vehicle. CCTV from the airport shows him dressed very unshowily. Malcolm and I have had dealings with him, and he's always immaculate.' The team had been handed printouts of the CCTV stills. They studied them as Clarke continued. 'Hooded sweatshirt, jeans and train-ers.'

'What's the backpack for?' Ronnie Ogilvie asked.

'How many people fly into Edinburgh with no luggage at all?' Clarke answered. 'He's trying not to stand out. But the hoodie brings me to another thing — it's what he was wearing the night he claims he was attacked.'

'Claims?'

'Remember what I said about the thought that's gone into this: if Morelli's viewed by us as a victim . . .'

'He's less likely to seem a possible suspect.' Ogilvie nodded his understanding.

'All of which is great,' Sutherland interrupted. 'But it remains speculative.'

'Pretty compelling all the same,' Fox stressed. 'Car at the murder scene; renter known to the victim; prearranged meeting. Don't forget — last call on Salman's phone was to his good pal Giovanni.'

'Which we dismissed because of who Morelli was and what had allegedly happened to him,'

439

Christine Esson added. 'When in fact he might just have faked a mugging by dunting his head against a wall.'

Sutherland was nodding thoughtfully. 'Let me talk to the Fiscal, get things moving. But in the meantime let's keep this under wraps — no leaks for a change.' He paused. 'Understood, George?'

Gamble froze, digestive biscuit halfway to his mouth. 'Don't look at me, boss.'

'Just making sure you're paying attention. And let's hear it for Siobhan and Malcolm. It's because of them that we're as far along as we are.'

Sutherland started clapping, the others joining in. The applause was the usual mix: genuine enthusiasm and relief, topped with a sprinkling of resentment that the collar belonged to someone other than the celebrant.

'Thanks, folks,' Fox said, hands clasped together.

'Don't let it go to your big baldy head,' George Gamble retorted.

As they returned to their desks and Sutherland headed into his office to make the call, Clarke saw Fox run a questioning palm over his scalp.

'He was winding you up,' she told him in an undertone.

'I know that.'

But Clarke knew that next time Fox went to the toilets, he'd he angling his head in front of the mirror in an attempt to take a really good look.

41

He awoke with a start and lashed out, but the face above him belonged to Robin Creasey.

'Bloody hell, John, thought I'd lost you there.'

Rebus's hand went to his windpipe. He sensed damage. Swallowing brought a searing heat to his throat. He tried speaking, his voice barely a whisper.

'Keith's computer was here.' He gestured towards the drawer. 'Jimmy borrowed a motorbike, the night Keith was killed. Ron Travis heard it.'

Creasey switched on his phone's torch and aimed it into the drawer. 'Something at the back,' he said.

'Keith's notebooks.'

'I'll get someone here to stand guard. And an ambulance for you.'

Rebus shook his head, the action causing immediate dizziness. He accepted Creasey's help as he made to stand. The world birled around him as he took his inhaler out, aiming it between his chattering teeth. Wasn't sure it would do any good, but he took a couple of puffs anyway. As he made his way tentatively from the shed, he saw Frank Hess standing in the kitchen doorway. The man's eyes were judging him.

'Where will he have gone?' Rebus demanded in the same strangulated whisper.

'Don't worry about that, John,' Creasey said.

441

'Let's just focus on you for the moment.'

Rebus grabbed a fistful of Creasey's jacket lapel. 'Let's not,' he said.

'Jimmy is a good boy,' Hess was intoning, more to himself than anyone else. Rebus thought he could see tears in the old man's eyes. He got Hess's attention and pointed towards Creasey.

'More you tell them, the better — for your grandson, I mean. You need to do the right thing now, Frank. Start making up for all your wrongs.'

Hess glowered at him. 'You and I are no longer young men. Keith was a young man, impatient, full of ideas. He thought he could change things.' He stabbed a finger towards Rebus. 'For how long were you a policeman? And did you change the world? Did you change *anything?*'

'I'll tell you one thing I didn't do — kill a man because I was jealous of what he had. But then you as good as killed a second time, didn't you — framing Hoffman, seeing him executed? And to stop that coming to light, you sent your grandson to kill yet again. And my guess is you were fine with that.'

'It was not planned! It was not!'

Rebus turned his head towards Creasey. 'Get the shed sealed off, dust those notebooks for prints, check if there's anything useful in the house. Warrant might be a bit easier to arrange now, wouldn't you say?'

'I'll need a statement from you too. And I still think you should go to hospital.'

'I promise I will — just as soon as you've got

hold of Jimmy Hess.'

'Don't go looking for him, John,' Creasey called out as Rebus headed on fragile legs towards the close. By way of answer, Rebus gave a little wave of one hand.

42

Interview Room B, Leith police station.

Interview Room A did exist, but it had been out of commission for months due to a leak in the ceiling that would prove costly to fix. Siobhan Clarke had checked that the AV recorder in IRB was working. Graham Sutherland sat next to her. Malcolm Fox had argued that there should be someone present from Gartcosh, to which Sutherland had answered with a one-word question: why?

Clarke could imagine Fox fuming somewhere in the building, maybe on the phone to Jennifer Lyon to register his displeasure. The warrant to search Giovanni Morelli's home having been secured, Esson and Ogilvie had been dispatched there along with half a dozen well-trained uniforms and a brace of forensic technicians. Morelli had been asked for his cooperation — and his keys — on his arrival at the station. His lawyer now sat alongside him, shuffling papers. Clarke hadn't been at all surprised when Patricia Coleridge had announced her arrival at the reception desk. She was dressed identically to her previous visit. Clarke guessed she had an array of business wear racked and ready. Same expensive notepad and matching pen, plus an iPad with a leather cover that doubled as an angled stand.

Next to her, Morelli looked a little more

nervous than before. His chair had been pushed back so he could cross one leg over the other without the table getting in the way. He wore loafers with no socks, several inches of tanned and hairless ankle showing. He had already made his protestations of innocence and now he just wanted to be elsewhere.

'Shall we get started?' Graham Sutherland said, after they had all identified themselves for the recording. He then sat back and let Clarke take over. She began by placing a sequence of photographs in front of Morelli.

'This is you, yes? At Edinburgh airport eleven days ago. Not quite as dapper as usual but quite recognisable. You're renting a car from the Avis concession. Here's a copy of the documentation you signed, and here's a record of your credit card transaction.'

'No comment.'

'Really?'

Coleridge leapt straight in. 'My client need say nothing at this point, DI Clarke.'

'I just thought it might be simpler for him to agree that the evidence shows he rented a car for one day. This car . . . '

Photos of the Passat in its Avis parking bay, and also being driven through Edinburgh's streets as the long summer dusk shaded towards night.

'I agree the quality isn't brilliant. But our expert has produced a clear enough image of the number plate.'

Coleridge studied the photos while Morelli stared at the wall nearest him. 'You're telling me these all show the same car? I'll admit the licence plate is legible in one of them, but as for the rest . . . ' She gave Clarke a hard stare. 'How many silver VW Passats do you think there are in the UK, Inspector?'

'Once we rule out the ones that don't have an Avis sticker on the rear windscreen, you mean?' Clarke pretended to guess. 'Fewer than you might think.' She produced more photos. Robbie Stenhouse had certainly earned his half-time pie and Bovril. 'Same car, 10.30 p.m., driving past Craigentinny golf course — you played there with your friend Salman, didn't you, Mr Morelli? With Stewart Scoular making up the threesome.' She gave him an opportunity to answer, an opportunity he declined. 'We think the car had tried entering the nice secluded car park, but it was locked for the night. So here's the same car on Seafield Road, 10.50 p.m., parked as if waiting for someone. Not too long after, Salman bin Mahmoud was drawing into the warehouse car park just behind where this car was parked. Soon after that, he was attacked and killed.'

'Your point being?' Coleridge asked.

But Clarke's attention was firmly fixed on Morelli, who was doing his damnedest to avoid meeting her eyes. 'What did he ever do to you, Mr Morelli? Issy will be devastated when she finds out.'

Morelli uncrossed his legs and angled his head a little. It was enough of a tell to satisfy Clarke at this stage. She got to her feet and walked around the table so she was in his eyeline. He turned his head away from her, and found that he was met by Graham Sutherland's equally piercing gaze.

'Car's being checked for DNA, Mr Morelli,' Clarke continued. 'Not yours, but Salman's. We're assuming you've disposed of the clothes you were wearing, but when you cut someone the way you cut your friend, there tends to — '

'I'm seeing no evidence here of any malfeasance or even impropriety on my client's part,' Coleridge broke in to protest. 'DCI Sutherland, you must realise that it is not the function of any police investigation to — '

'Ms Coleridge,' Sutherland interrupted in turn, 'what's required here is a credible explanation from your client as to why he would travel out to Edinburgh airport to rent a car for one day, putting fewer than thirty miles on the clock before returning it. Once he's done that, perhaps he can further elucidate his reason or reasons for driving through Craigentinny — not exactly turf I'd think he was familiar with — not half an hour before Salman bin Mahmoud arrived there to meet someone. Quite the coincidence, isn't it? As is the fact that Mr bin Mahmoud's last telephone conversation that day was with Mr Morelli. They spoke for just under five minutes, between 7.15 and 7.20 p.m. I'd be keen to know what was said, perhaps what arrangements were being made. By failing to explain himself, your client is digging himself a very deep hole. You'd serve his interests best by making him aware of that.'

He leaned back a little to let the room know he'd finished. The silence lingered. Clarke had returned to her chair. Having unscrewed the top from her pen and then screwed it back on again, Coleridge eventually turned towards Morelli. Sensing that something was needed from him, he inhaled at length and noisily before opening his mouth.

'No comment,' he said.

★ ★ ★

Despite his solicitor's protestations, they were holding onto the Italian for the twenty-four hours allowed in law. He'd been placed in a cell and given weak sugary tea in a thin plastic cup. The Fiscal Depute had convened the team for a meeting, then taken Sutherland aside for a private word.

'Nothing from the car,' Tess Leighton said as she ended the call she'd just been on, 'They're giving it another go. but I didn't sense any great confidence.'

Clarke checked the screen of her own phone. She had asked Christine Esson for regular updates from Morelli's mews house. So far all she'd had was: *Nice place!* She sent another text by way of a nudge — a single question mark — and walked over to the kettle, where Fox was dunking a herbal tea bag in a mug.

'Phil's gone to fetch milk,' he explained. 'So meantime . . .'

'You're offering me second use of your peppermint tea bag?' Clarke shook her head. 'I was hoping for more from the car.'

'Me too. But it still leaves Morelli with a lot of explaining to do.'

448

'Or else he keeps his trap shut and walks out of here tomorrow.'

'Nothing from Christine?'

'Just that he keeps a lovely house.'

'He'll have a cleaner — we need to ask them if he bagged any clothes for them to dispose of. Maybe there's a knife missing from a set in the kitchen . . . '

Clarke nodded slowly. 'Christine knows all that, Malcolm.'

'Must be something we could be doing.'

'Wee trip to the cells for a spot of waterboarding?'

'Few slaps would probably do it.'

'Back in John's day,' Clarke agreed. Then: 'Coleridge wants her client assessed as a suicide risk.'

'Why?'

'I assume the hope is that he'll be given preferential treatment.'

'I watched the recording.'

'And?'

'You were good.'

'Anything I missed?'

'When you mentioned Issy . . . '

'Ah, you noticed that.'

'You touched a nerve. Bit more of that wouldn't have gone amiss.'

Clarke nodded slowly and watched as the Fiscal Depute left Sutherland's office, heading for the stairs.

'She doesn't look overly optimistic,' Fox commented.

'They never do, until we've got a confession

and maybe a dozen eyewitnesses.'

Fox smiled over the rim of his mug. He sipped at the tea and savoured it. 'Not too bad,' he said.

'Phil's not exactly hurrying with that milk.' Clarke checked the time on her phone.

'Ask him and he'll tell you the first shop he tried had run out. I'd put money on it.'

'While in fact he's just been enjoying a saunter?' Clarke turned as Fox gestured towards the doorway. Phil Yeats was striding into the room. He hoisted a carrier bag as he approached the kettle.

'Nearest place didn't have any,' he explained.

'You keeping a crystal ball tucked away somewhere?' Clarke asked Fox, while Yeats frowned, wondering what was under discussion.

'Get a brew on then!' George Gamble roared from his desk.

'No rest, eh?' Clarke commiserated as Yeats judged whether he'd have to refill the kettle.

'What did the Fiscal say?' he asked in return.

'That you play a crucial role in this hard-working team.'

'Sod off, Siobhan. Maybe you can run the errands next time.'

'Just teasing, Phil. Honestly, what would we do without you?' She paused. 'Bring mine over to my desk, will you?'

She left the young DC to it, Fox following her back to their shared computer. A ping had alerted her to an incoming message. Once seated, she held the phone up so Fox could see it. A one-word text from Christine Esson.

Bingo!

450

43

The specks on Giovanni Morelli's tan leather loafers were minuscule. One of the scene-of-crime team had taken it upon himself to study each and every pair of shoes on the neat racks in Morelli's wardrobe. Eventually, having noted the flecks under a magnifier, he'd opted for luminol.

'Positive for blood,' Esson announced. She had taken up the same position as Sutherland earlier, the DCI himself now part of her audience, arms folded, feet apart. His jaw was rigid, telling Clarke that he was as full of nervous tension as anyone else — he just didn't want to show it. 'Shoes have gone to the lab. If it's the victim's blood, a match shouldn't take long.'

'No bin bags out the back stuffed with stained clothing?' Tess Leighton asked.

Esson shook her head. 'We finally traced his cleaner and she's walking Ronnie through the scene. She's no memory of having to dispose of anything out of the ordinary. Morelli doesn't do much cooking, so there's never a lot in the swing bin. It's Brabantia, by the way — one of their nice stainless-steel ones. Whole place looks ready to be photographed for a magazine. One thing the cleaner did say is that she *thinks* a knife might be missing from the kitchen drawer.'

'Thinks?'

'She can't swear to it.'

'That's not much use,' Leighton muttered.

'Another word with the Fiscal needed,' Fox nudged Sutherland.

'I'll be the judge of that, Malcolm.'

'Get the bastard up from the cells,' Gamble growled. 'Ask him some *proper* questions.'

'As opposed to what, George?' Clarke bristled.

'He needs intimidating, that's all I'm saying. Couple of brawny, no-nonsense Scots coppers . . . ' Gamble was looking at Fox as he spoke.

'He thinks he's in *Life on Mars*,' Tess Leighton commented with a roll of her eyes.

'Second interview can wait until we've had the lab report,' Sutherland cautioned.

'What if that doesn't happen till after we've had to let him walk?' Gamble argued.

'He'll be made to surrender his passport. Don't fret, George — he's not getting away.'

'I've known folk hightail it, passport or not, boss.'

'I think George has a point,' Clarke said in a level voice. 'I'm not sure we need the report.'

'You think he's suddenly going to get chatty with his expensive solicitor sitting right there beside him telling him 'no comment' will suffice?'

'I actually do.'

'Something up your sleeve, Siobhan?'

'Just female intuition maybe.'

Sutherland gave her a look that told her he didn't totally believe this. But he said okay anyway.

* * *

452

Prior to Giovanni Morelli being brought up from his cell, and while Sutherland was confirming that Patricia Coleridge was on her way, Clarke stepped into the corridor to make a discreet call, after which she descended the station's ornate staircase, stopping at the front desk.

'Anyone asks for me,' she told the officer there, 'send them straight up. I'll be in IRB.'

The officer nodded his understanding. As Clarke climbed the stairs again, she saw Fox waiting for her at the top.

'You're up to something,' he commented.

'I'm really not.'

'You are, though. I thought we were partners.'

'The kind who turns up at a car-rental desk half an hour early to steal some glory?'

Fox made a show of wincing. 'Brillo must be due a walk, surely.'

'Nice try, Malcolm. Though if you're offering . . .'

'I'm not.'

'Didn't think so.' She leaned in towards him until her lips were only a centimetre from his ear. 'Watch and learn, Mr Brawn.'

He was attempting a scowl as she headed back into the office.

* * *

'Here we are again,' Patricia Coleridge announced, with no obvious enthusiasm.

Clarke had once more checked the recording equipment before switching it on. Sutherland was in the same seat as before, opposite the

453

lawyer and her client.

'The cell is disgusting,' Morelli was telling Coleridge. 'The toilet — unbelievable. The sandwich they gave me — inedible!'

'Just a little longer, Gio,' Coleridge consoled him. Notebook, iPad and pen laid out, hands pressed together above them as if in prayer, eyes flitting between the two detectives opposite.

'I assume there's news of some kind?' she demanded.

'A forensic search of Mr Morelli's home has uncovered a pair of shoes with spots of blood on them,' Clarke announced. 'That blood is being analysed as we speak.'

'So it could well be my client's?'

'We both know that's not the case, though.' Clarke's attention was focused on Morelli. 'You got rid of everything else you'd been wearing, but no way you were going to part with such a lovely pair of shoes. You wore chain-store stuff when renting the car — less conspicuous that way — but for a meeting with Salman . . . well, he'd be expecting the usual sharply dressed Gio.'

'You don't have to say anything,' Coleridge reminded her client.

'Cooperation now could play in your client's favour. Once we have the blood match, we won't have much need for his assistance.'

'No comment,' Morelli said.

Clarke could sense Sutherland growing uneasy, realising how little they had to play with and wondering why Clarke had been keen to hold the interview. She wished she could reassure him, but couldn't think how.

'Can we talk about the knife that's missing from one of your drawers in the kitchen?'

'Knives get thrown away all the time,' Coleridge drawled.

'No comment,' Morelli repeated. Sutherland shifted slightly in his seat again. Clarke risked a glance in his direction.

Relax.

'When the test shows that it's Salman bin Mahmoud's blood on your shoes, Mr Morelli, what then? Reckon 'no comment' will suffice in a courtroom?'

'This is outrageous.' Coleridge tossed down the pen she'd only just picked up and fixed Sutherland with a look. 'You've dragged us in here with no new evidence, just a succession of wild theories and suppositions — is this really the way you run your major cases, DCI Sutherland?'

Sutherland looked like he was struggling to form a suitable answer, while Clarke's attention had turned to the interview room door, beyond which she could hear raised voices. Eventually Coleridge noticed them too.

'What the hell's going on?' she was asking as the door was yanked open. Issy Meiklejohn appeared, Malcolm Fox behind her, his hand grasping her forearm.

'*What the fuck did you do?*' Meiklejohn screamed at Morelli. '*You fucking murdering fucking . . .*'

Morelli was on his feet so fast that his chair tipped over and clattered to the floor. He had his hands raised as if to fend off the apparition before him. Saliva flew from Meiklejohn's mouth as she yelled, her face puce with rage, both rows of teeth visible.

'Get her out of here!' Graham Sutherland was saying to anyone who would listen,

'How did she get in?' Coleridge was demanding. 'The Fiscal needs to be told. This is appalling. Surely any possible prosecution is now — '

'I did it for you, Issy,' Morelli blurted out. 'I did it for you.'

'You murdered our friend!'

'He was lying to you to get you into his bed! There was never any money for The Flow!'

'DCI Sutherland!' Coleridge howled. 'I must protest in the strongest terms!'

'Get her out,' Sutherland repeated. Fox had his arms around Meiklejohn's waist now, pulling her backwards as best he could.

'Bastard,' Meiklejohn said, all energy spent and replaced by a low, steady sobbing.

'Issy . . . ' Morelli had taken a step towards her.

'No,' she said. 'No.' She shrugged Fox aside and disappeared from view.

'DCI Sutherland,' Coleridge was saying, attempting to regain both her composure and control of the situation. 'None of this is admissible anywhere — you must see that.'

Fox was making to close the door from outside. He gave Clarke a look and she gave him one back — a look that ended with a wink.

'If we're pausing the interview,' she said to the room at large as Morelli righted his chair and sat down, head in his hands, 'maybe I should switch off the recording?'

'Best if we take a break,' Sutherland agreed.

'Better still,' Coleridge said through gritted teeth, 'if you explain how a member of the public got past the desk downstairs — almost as if they knew where to find us.'

Clarke was affecting a look of complete innocence as she reached towards the machine and pressed the stop button.

'No, leave it on,' Morelli said. 'I want to explain.'

'That's very unwise, Gio,' Coleridge warned him.

'I want to explain,' he repeated, with a bit more iron in his voice.

Clarke turned the machine on again.

44

'He wore motorcycle gloves,' Rebus said croakily. He was in The Glen, seated at the same corner table where he had first met Jimmy Hess. Creasey sat opposite, next to May Collins. She had made Rebus a drink comprising hot water, whisky, honey and a squeeze of lemon, plus a couple of ibuprofen tablets that he'd struggled to swallow. 'Hence no prints,' he continued. 'Drove the Volvo back here, maybe thinking he'd buy himself some time that way. Walked to the camp to retrieve the bike — no one on the road that late of an evening, meaning no witnesses.'

'John did tell you it was to do with the camp,' Collins admonished Creasey. He turned his head to her.

'Are you sure you didn't know anything about it? Your dad goading Frank Hess all these years? He didn't drop a hint of any sort?'

She glared at the detective. 'Definitely not. All I knew was that there was always a bit of needle between them.'

'Why did your father never come forward?'

Rebus watched May Collins shrug. 'I think maybe he liked tormenting Frank, or it could be he just wasn't overly bothered. He'd been through a war — what was one more innocent life?'

Creasey's phone vibrated and he checked the screen, his face unreadable.

'Any sign?' Rebus wanted to know.

'He can't get far.'

Rebus was reminded of the stories about escapes from Camp 1033. The runaways would head into the wilderness but soon give up. He imagined Jimmy Hess running, the laptop under his arm. He would run, then rest, then run again, growing thirsty and hungry and cold. Eventually he would realise the futility of it, but would he be able to find his way back, or would the peatlands all look the same, lacking landmarks of any kind? Of course, he could be sticking to another course, following the coast to east or west. But patrol cars were on the hunt, hiding places in short supply and easily searched.

'Callum's farm?' he suggested.

'Two officers are there, just in case.'

'What about Frank?'

'Under lock and key in Tongue. We'll transfer him to Inverness later.'

'He's *your* catch — shouldn't you be there?'

'Soon as I'm sure you're okay.'

'I keep telling you I'm dandy.' Rebus swallowed, wincing in pain again.

'Christ, John,' Creasey said.

May Collins reached out and gave his hand a squeeze. 'At least let a doctor take a look,' she said.

Rebus was about to protest when the door to the bar rattled open and Samantha burst in. She spotted them and flopped down next to her father, giving him as much of a hug as the cramped space would allow.

'Are you all right?' she asked.

459

'Might have to skip choir practice tonight.'

'You've seen a doctor?'

'He's refusing,' May Collins said. 'Can I get you anything, Sam?'

Samantha shook her head.

'How's Carrie?' Rebus wheezed.

'She's okay, but you're not.' She turned to Creasey. 'He's got COPD, you know. Finds breathing hard enough as it is.'

'I did consider bundling him into a patrol car in handcuffs,' Creasey replied. 'Short of that, I'm not sure what I can do.'

Samantha turned back to her father again. 'You're a stubborn old goat.'

'With the bleat to match.' Rebus stroked his throat with thumb and forefinger.

'It was Jimmy, then?' she said. 'Killed Keith, tried to strangle you?'

'Jimmy,' Rebus confirmed.

Her brow wrinkled. 'Because of something that happened seventy-odd years ago?'

'Some people have long memories.'

May pointed towards the bar. 'It was that bloody revolver that started it. Wish to hell I'd taken it down when I had the chance.' She took Samantha by the wrist. 'I'm so, so sorry, Sam.'

'It was that camp,' Samantha said quietly. 'It got under Keith's skin. He couldn't let it go . . .' Her eyes flitted between the detective and the publican. 'Can I have a minute with my dad?'

They nodded and headed to the bar. Samantha took Rebus's hand in hers.

'Suppose we can plan the funeral now,' she said. 'I could do with a bit of help with that. And maybe a move south, too — if you wouldn't mind us living nearer you.'

'I reckon I could cope. You need to think it through, though, once the dust settles — Carrie's schooling and all that.' He paused. 'And I'm sorry if I ever had any doubts about you.'

'You've got a suspicious mind. Comes with the job.'

'Doesn't mean we can't go on together, though, eh?'

She smiled and wrapped her arms around him again. Over her shoulder, Rebus saw Creasey lift his phone up, checking an incoming message and then motioning to May Collins that he needed to be elsewhere. His eyes met Rebus's as he walked towards the door, and he mouthed a single word, knowing Rebus would understand.

The word was 'farm'.

45

'So when is he back?' Fox asked into his phone as he walked.

'Tomorrow or the day after. Saab's been fixed, so that's one less funeral to worry about. Though he'll have to head north again at some point.'

'John always gets his man, doesn't he?'

'Even if he barely makes it out alive. Killer damn near choked him to death. Where are you anyway?'

'Clearing my head with a walk.'

'Nowhere in the vicinity of a certain penthouse of recent acquaintance?'

'Always so suspicious.' Fox paused. 'How about you?'

'I'm at John's new place. I was just going to drop off that signed Lee Child — bit of a house-warming gift. But then I sort of started on the unpacking.'

'He won't thank you for it.'

'If it's left to him, it could take months. Anyway, I won't get it finished tonight — I'm out for dinner with Graham in a bit to celebrate.'

'What's the music?'

'One of John's — R. Dean Taylor.'

'Never heard of him. Isn't it a bit early to be celebrating? Long way still to go.'

'Taped confession, though, Malcolm.'

'That was a nice trick you pulled. Of course, it only takes Issy to tell her old pal Patsy that you

462

phoned and told her everything, then invited her to pay her respects in person . . . '

'A confession's still a confession. No duress involved.'

'He's been in love with her for a long time? Morelli and Issy, I mean.'

'Since they first met in their teens,' Clarke agreed. 'Never became physical — her choice, I'm guessing. But when Morelli found out she intended studying in Edinburgh, he signed up to the same course — which is a bit creepy if you ask me.'

'Just a bit.'

'Salman meantime was on his uppers — he'd even been borrowing from Morelli. But he couldn't help blabbing to him about the money he'd told Issy would save her father's dream project.'

'Money he didn't actually have?'

'He was heading back home anyway to either face the regime's music or save the family business. Far as he was concerned, he was having one last go at nailing Issy before he left. So Morelli lures him to Craigentinny with the promise that he has a source who wants to help with the buyout. They argue, and Morelli pulls out the knife.'

'Which he's taken because . . . ?'

'Because he's Italian and reckoned Salman might take a bit of persuading to come clean to Issy and lay off her.'

'Why didn't Morelli just tell Issy?'

'I think because a bit of his father has rubbed off on him — no compassion, no empathy.'

463

'Ready to take the nuclear option.' Fox found himself nodding his agreement as he stepped out of a cyclist's path.

'Anyway,' Clarke was saying, 'I don't buy his version, not entirely. He chose Craigentinny because closer to home would have been too risky. Explains the fake mugging, too. Rather than an argument gone nuclear, this is about as calmly premeditated as any murder I've worked. So yes, I feel like celebrating. And meantime you're out on a *walk*?'

'I don't drink and I don't smoke — what else am I going to do, to paraphrase Culture Club?'

'Adam and the Ants,' she corrected him. 'Well, be careful out there, Malcolm — city's liable to bite you when you least expect it. I better start finishing up here — need to go home and get changed. See you tomorrow?' Fox stayed silent. 'Oh, you're heading back to Gartcosh?'

'Any reason for me not to?'

'So this is us saying goodbye?'

'You almost sound sorry to see me go. Far cry from when you first set eyes on me.'

'Happy travels, DI Fox. Come see us again sometime.'

'Bye, Siobhan.' He ended the call and slipped the phone back into his pocket. He was heading into Quartermile from Lauriston Place, having parked on a single yellow line. This time of the evening, he wasn't going to get a ticket. (The one from outside the restaurant on Hanover Street was still in his glove box.) Quartermile was quiet, a few drinkers in the bar he passed, about half the tables filled in the Malaysian restaurant next door. Food-delivery drivers were coming and going while students hauled bags from the Sainsbury's supermarket back to their digs.

Fox approached the tall glass box that Cafferty called home and pressed the intercom. He was buzzed in immediately, but stood in the vestibule a moment, gathering his thoughts before summoning the lift. He'd phoned and confirmed that Cafferty was able to see him. Cafferty had asked the reason of course, and all Fox had said was 'Scoular'.

'Good news, I hope, Malky.'

Well, that depended on your viewpoint.

Cafferty was waiting at the penthouse door for him, dressed in an open-necked white shirt and jogging bottoms, his feet bare. He padded back into the open-plan living area and snatched up a glass half filled with red wine.

'Can I tempt you, Malcolm?'

'Not a cat in hell's chance.'

Cafferty sat down in his favourite chair and waited, unsurprised when Fox stayed standing.

'About Scoular,' Fox began.

'Yes?'

'We've dug and dug again, and there's nothing there.'

'Is that right?' The apparent good humour vanished from Cafferty's face.

'Doesn't matter, though, does it? What matters to you is getting me and especially my boss working on your behalf. Because once you've done that — and you've got it on tape — you reckon you own us. Isn't that the truth?' Cafferty opened his mouth to answer, but Fox wasn't finished. 'But it's not the *whole* truth — the whole truth would have to include your raging jealousy of the man.'

'Oh aye?'

Fox started counting on his fingers. 'He's younger than you, a lot better-looking than you. Rubs shoulders with the great and the good rather than the scumbags you're stuck with on a daily basis. You see him with his friends at your club and you know there's a wall between you and them that you can't seem to scale, and Christ knows you've tried. Call it a class thing, or just snobbery — they look down on you when you know they should be looking up. And meantime Scoular sells his wee bits and pieces of coke to his pals, keeps them sweet, fixes people up with each other — a real mover and shaker. And yes, there's probably dodgy money in the mix somewhere, yet he remains completely non-stick. That's why he got to you, and that's why you started us digging. And here I am telling you there's sweet FA to show for it. He's still Stewart Scoular, property developer and darling of the society pages, and you're still you.'

He broke off. 'I might grab a glass of water.' As he walked over to the sink and lifted a clean glass from the draining board, he heard Cafferty clapping his hands slowly.

'Wee speech over and done with?' Cafferty asked once he'd finished the round of mock applause. 'Feel better for getting all that off your chest? If so, drink your drink and get your fat arse out of here. I've got calls to make and some

466

juicy wee bits of video to send out into the world.'

Fox took his time draining the glass, placing it in the sink after. He checked the time on his wristwatch.

'Somewhere else you need to be, Malcolm?'

Fox shook his head. 'Something you need to see.' He had activated his phone and was tapping in keystrokes. 'It's being streamed on the *Scotsman* website. They got the exclusive, but it'll be everywhere tomorrow. Your eyesight up to a screen this size?'

Cafferty had risen slowly to his feet. Fox turned the volume all the way up and held the phone away from him. Dennis Jones was seated on a sofa, his wife Jennifer Lyon next to him. The interview had already started, but they were getting to the meat of it. Jones and Lyon held hands, as had been arranged. The questions had been vetted. The interviewer was Laura Smith. While not exactly the tamest inquisitor, she had been warned about what gaining an exclusive meant.

'So I want to apologise publicly and profoundly to my wife especially,' Jones was saying, 'but also to everyone else involved in this sorry episode — a mess entirely of my own making. I can only hope that Jenni will be able to forgive me. I know I will work tirelessly to regain some level of trust. I've certainly never stopped loving her and I never shall. I will, of course, be resigning with immediate effect from my university post, and will be seeking counsel- ling . . .'

467

Fox watched Cafferty as Cafferty watched the scene play out. 'The ACC thinks she can ride out the storm,' he explained while Laura Smith asked one of her prepared questions. 'She's assembled a team of PR people and lawyers, so do what you like with those tapes. Story's already been broken, and my boss is controlling it. All *you've* done is make yourself a target. Every agency based at the Scottish Crime Campus is going to move your name to the top of their wanted list.' He shifted his attention to the window overlooking the Meadows. 'Enjoy the uninterrupted view while you can.'

He switched off the live feed and pocketed the phone, walked to the door in silence and let himself out. Waiting for the lift, he half expected Cafferty to emerge, ready to vent. But the lift came and Fox stepped into it, turning to face the doors as they closed. He pressed G for ground floor. Halfway down, he released the breath he'd been holding. He would give Jennifer Lyon an hour before calling her, let her know it had gone to plan. *Her* plan, outlined to him that day in Gartcosh. It had taken time to persuade her husband, but then the only other option offered to him had been divorce.

'Bloody waste of all that surveillance, though,' Fox muttered to himself. Still, the ACC owed him now, and she would not be allowed to forget.

The lift doors slid open again and he stepped out. One more door separated him from the clear fresh air of the world outside. Through the glass, he could see a hooded figure waiting just the other side.

Food delivery? No, the figure wasn't carrying anything. Tenant? Just possibly. But Fox was starting to think otherwise: one of Cafferty's collection of scumbags. A junior-level dealer most likely. He pulled open the door. Beneath the hood, the pockmarked face was hesitant.

'You going in or what?' Fox demanded to know.

Another moment before the decision was made. Then: 'Aye, thanks.' Hands stuffed deep inside the hoodie's pockets, the youth started to move past Fox, who was still holding the door open for him.

'I'm assuming you know the way — P for penthouse.'

'I know the way, aye. Cheers. Really helpful.'

'Don't expect him to be in the best of moods, mind,' Fox said as he exited the building. It was still light outside. This time of the year, it was hard to imagine the many long dark nights that would arrive all too soon . . .

Acknowledgements

This book was begun long before the COVID outbreak of 2020, but edited while the lockdown was in force. I am so grateful to my wife Miranda for putting up with me throughout, as well as for being my first reader and most telling reviewer. I'd also like to thank the staff of Forward Vision in Edinburgh for their dedication in looking after not only our son Kit but all the other young adults in their care.

Those who know the area around Tongue will realise that I have taken several liberties. There is no village of Naver, nor does Camp 1033 exist, though other camps mentioned are real, as are some of the incidents recounted.

I'm grateful to Edinburgh Central Library for pointing me in the direction of several valuable resources, most notably *Camp 165* by Valerie Campbell and *British Concentration Camps: A Brief History from 1900–1975* by Simon Webb. On one of my visits to the north coast I also happened across *Tongue and Farr* by Jim A. Johnston, which helped me explore the history of that beautiful region of Scotland.

All errors and inaccuracies are mine.

Here's to all the songs and all their singers, in times of darkness and times of light.

I. R.

We do hope that you have enjoyed reading this large print book.

Did you know that all of our titles are available for purchase?

We publish a wide range of high quality large print books including:
Romances, Mysteries, Classics
General Fiction
Non Fiction and Westerns

Special interest titles available in large print are:
The Little Oxford Dictionary
Music Book
Song Book
Hymn Book
Service Book

Also available from us courtesy of Oxford University Press:
Young Readers' Dictionary
(large print edition)
Young Readers' Thesaurus
(large print edition)

For further information or a free brochure, please contact us at:
Ulverscroft Large Print Books Ltd.,
The Green, Bradgate Road, Anstey,
Leicester, LE7 7FU, England.
Tel: (00 44) 0116 236 4325
Fax: (00 44) 0116 234 0205

IN A HOUSE OF LIES

Ian Rankin

A missing private investigator is found, locked in a car hidden deep in the woods. Worse still - both for his family and the police — is that his body was in an area that had already been searched. Detective Inspector Siobhan Clarke is part of a new inquiry, combing through the mistakes of the original case. There were always suspicions over how the investigation was handled, and now — after a decade without answers — it's time for the truth. Every officer involved must be questioned, and it seems everyone on the case has something to hide, and everything to lose. But there is one man who knows where the trail may lead — and that it could be the end of him: John Rebus.